Eve's Curse

- Book 2 in the Abomination Series -

By Felicity Thorne

Enjoy!

The Abomination Series:
Eve's Monsters
Eve's Curse
Eve's Sins
Eve's Revelations

Check out the accompanying Spotify playlist:

The Abomination Series by Felicity Thorne

https://open.spotify.com/playlist/6rVzdKXwm0lk5Bsz1G3SqZ?si=
HgeRqP-KSnyqk7RcltflDg&pi=9X79qnTQQeS8F

"If I cannot inspire love, I will cause fear."

-Mary Shelley, *Frankenstein*

"Tell me every terrible thing you ever did, and let me love you anyway."

-Edgar Allen Poe

1
You're the Worst

She was a monster.

What did that even mean? And what had just happened with Dagon? That wasn't a casual romp in the sack - some kind of switch in her had been flipped. One minute, she feared him, and the next she was dominating him. Taunting him. Tempting him. Using him. She'd received more from him than simple carnal pleasure, but what was *it*, exactly? Power? Energy? Had he given it, or had she taken it? Was she stronger, or was he weaker? Or both? She *felt* stronger.

She had so many questions. How many could he even answer? Who else could she go to for answers? Everyone else assumed that she couldn't be a monster because she was a blood healer.

Everyone but Zephlyn.

Zephlyn knew something. Or suspected something. He was likely her best bet, other than Dagon. If she tried to get help from anyone else, there would be questions about how she'd gotten her information in the first place. Questions she didn't want to answer.

Or...*or*...she could put it under her hat and pretend everything was fine. She *could* do that. Right? Nothing was really *stopping* her from doing that, was it? Just a few days ago, she had no idea that the possibility that she could be a monster even existed. She could just go back to that. Besides, Dagon could be *lying*, couldn't he, just to keep her coming back to him? That was absolutely something he would do.

She wasn't a monster. Dagon was a liar. And Zephlyn never said she was a monster either, not definitively. He just said she was weird, and couldn't be a monster *unless*...

She wasn't a monster. She was Evrys Alarie, the girl with the rare Panacea Blood, which meant she couldn't be a monster.

Momentarily deluding herself into believing that nothing was wrong, Eve went to the bathroom. She grabbed a bandage for her cut, but when she pulled her shorts down to apply it, there was no wound to apply it to. Just a hint of a red line and two faint crescent marks from Dagon's teeth. That was the fastest she'd ever healed.

Luc had told her that the more she healed people, the faster she would heal, and she had given a lot of blood today.

After she used the toilet and washed her hands, she reached for the towel hanging on the wall. When she tried to yank it from the metal ring, the entire unit ripped from the wall.

"What the..." She stood there, holding the towel, the ring hanger lying on the countertop. The screws were still affixed through it, and there were two gaping holes in the wall where she'd ripped them out, anchors and all. She hadn't even pulled that hard, had she?

She pushed it to the corner of the counter. She'd have to fix it tomorrow. These things happen.

She went out to the kitchen for a midnight snack to settle her nerves. Her cupboards were growing bare, but she had enough cereal left for one bowl. As she reached in the fridge for the milk, she grabbed a bottle of unopened juice to move it out of the way, but stopped as she lifted it. It felt light.

Too light.

She pulled it from the fridge and looked at it. Did someone drink it all and put it back empty? She squeezed the container slightly, and immediately regretted it. The plastic crumpled and cracked, and juice splashed everywhere.

"Fuck!" She rushed the container to the sink as it continued to spill its contents. "What the fuck?! Cheap-ass plastic..." she complained, rinsing the juice from her hands.

She wiped up the juice all over the floor and countertops. As she stood over the sink, wringing juice out of the kitchen rag and rinsing it out, she glanced over at the juice bottle in the other well of the sink, and a silly thought flitted through her head. She held her hand out toward the bottle and imagined she could move it with an invisible force, like Dagon had done to her.

The crushed bottle rattled in the sink.

Eve dropped the rag in the sink and leapt back, fear coursing through her veins with icy prickles. Had Dagon done something to her? Or was this just some weird side-effect of sleeping with him, like her sudden power over him in bed? She was beginning to feel like a stranger in her own body.

She slowly returned to the sink and stared down at the crumpled jug. She held her hand out again, but this time, she clenched her fist and imagined she was Force-choking the juice bottle.

It crinkled. Only a little, but it crinkled. Her heart was in her throat.

"Holy shit. I'm a Jedi," she whispered.

But she didn't want to be a Jedi. She wanted to be Eve. This new power scared the hell out of her.

She grabbed the jug and threw it in the trash can, then rinsed out the rag in the sink and finished wiping down the counter and floor. She needed sleep. In the morning, maybe everything would be back to normal. If not, she could tackle this new problem with a fresh perspective and possibly go talk with Zephlyn when he returned.

…But did she trust Zephlyn with this? She barely knew the guy.

Eve climbed back into bed and cocooned herself in the covers. She buried her face in her pillow, inhaling the comforting scent of Bo that somehow managed to survive her and Dagon's horizontal antics. She could still smell sex and Dagon in her bedding, too, but she focused on Bo's warm flannel scent.

And thought of Luc.

Her insides warmed when she pictured him. Her belly tingled when she imagined being wrapped up in his big arms. She'd been aware of a dull, hollow ache behind her sternum since he left, and now that she knew he would be home soon, it had turned to a knot.

She hated how she longed for him.

Eve growled in frustration and rubbed her sternum. Why did emotions have to be so physical? The longer she tried to fall asleep, the more she tossed and turned. It was futile.

She climbed out of bed and went to her apartment door. She peeked her head out into the hallway. All was quiet. She quietly closed the door behind her and slipped down the hallway to the apartment two doors down. Eve knocked softly on the door.

She heard the latch flip and the knob turned.

"Evie," Bo greeted her with a questioning expression on his maskless face. He was shirtless, wearing only plaid boxers. His hair was tousled, and he had a pillow line on the side of his face. Her heart melted a little.

"I can't sleep," she confessed pathetically.

He scratched his head and stepped aside so she could enter his apartment. When she was inside and he'd closed the door, he asked, "Something you wanted to talk about?"

"No."

He stared at her uncomprehendingly.

"I don't want to sleep alone," she clarified.

"Ah. Ok," he replied simply. He gestured toward the bedroom, which was in the same location in his apartment as it was in hers.

As she followed him through the living room and past the kitchen in the dark, she wondered why his apartment had such an empty feeling. Their footsteps even echoed strangely. It was the exact same setup as hers, but it wasn't filled like hers.

"Why is your apartment so empty?"

"We don't normally spend much time here. And it's just me. I don't need a lot."

When she walked into his room, however, she saw a huge bookshelf that spanned an entire wall from floor to ceiling. The shelves were overflowing, but it didn't look like they were filled with normal books.

"Are those *all* manga?!" she gaped.

"Yeah, yeah, I have a problem, I know. Get in bed." He held the covers back and gestured for her to get in.

"Okie *doki-doki*," she punned, then giggled uncontrollably at her own joke as she climbed under the covers. She was already feeling more at ease.

"You're the worst," he complained as he slid into bed next to her.

She plopped her head onto his chest and threw her arm and leg over him. "Shut up, you love me," she chirped flippantly.

He grunted indifferently.

Curled up next to his solid, warm body, Eve melted into him with a contented sigh. Ah, that was the stuff.

Eve awoke in the morning as Bo was working to extract himself from the tangle of her limbs. She purposely gripped harder.

"Nooo," she grumbled.

"God, you're like a fucking octopus," he griped as he lifted her arm from his torso, only to have her snake her wrist free from his grip and cling to him again.

"I'm a kraken," she corrected.

"Whatever. Release me, kraken. I need to shower and go get coffee."

"Just make some," Eve suggested.

"It is made. At the coffee shop. I just need to go get it."

Eve groaned cantankerously and released Bo from her tentacles. She looked over at the clock after he climbed out of bed. It was only a little after 5AM. No wonder she was still so tired.

She rolled over and sat on the edge of the bed, dangling her legs over the side as she ran her hand through her messy pink locks. She watched Bo standing in front of his closet in his boxers, sorting through it for the typical tactical cargo pants and plain t-shirt or long-sleeved shirt he tended to favor.

With most of his body exposed to her, she was again struck by just how many scars he had. He was covered in them.

"Why are you so much more scarred up than everyone else?" Eve inquired.

"I've had a lot of injuries," he replied obtusely.

"Well, duh. I know why Luc isn't scarred like that, but Zeke and Eoduun aren't, either."

"By the time they're my age, they will be," Bo pointed out.

"And what age is that, exactly?" Eve wondered.

"Thirty-four," he answered. "I'm four years older than Luc." He then added, "And Zeke has more scars than you've probably noticed. Those binding tattoos hide a lot."

"Binding tattoos?" Eve echoed.

Bo turned and looked at her with his clothes draped over his arm. "Yeah. All that tribal-looking shit is Luc's handiwork. It's what keeps Dagon from completely obliterating Zeke as his vessel, like keeping a nuclear reactor encased in steel and concrete." He started toward the door, then looked back at her. "Are you going to hang out for a bit?"

Eve shook her head. "I'll scurry on back to my apartment," she said, making her fingers look like a running spider.

"I'll stop by when I get back," Bo said over his shoulder as he went into the bathroom. As he closed the door behind him, Eve's eye shifted to the bookshelf full of manga on the far wall. There were hundreds of them. She pushed to her feet and crossed the room. She selected a book at random and pulled it from the shelf, making note of where she took it from.

An austere man with dark hair and bright blue eyes looked contemptuously up from the cover, while a cute, pink-haired girl hung from his neck and grinned cheerfully with one oddly sharp tooth, holding a two-fingered peace-sign sideways over one eye while the other eye was squinted into a wink. Two little devil horns poked up through her hair.

She flipped it open, and immediately realized that these were not just comics. Definitely NSFW, and completely uncensored. Explicit. Smut. But it was kind of hot.

"Dirty boy, Bo," she said under her breath.

She wondered if they were all like that, but just as she was returning that one to the shelf, Bo opened the bathroom door and yelled out, "Stay out of my manga!"

"I think you mean *porn*," she called back.

"Evie!"

She grinned to herself. She may have to talk him into letting her borrow one. She could totally get into that.

On her way out of the apartment, she knocked on the bathroom door. "I'm heading out. See you in a while, Daddy. Doki-doki!"

She heard an exasperated sigh on the other side of the door, and it brought her deep satisfaction.

As Eve stepped out of Bo's apartment, she glanced up and saw Eoduun coming out of his apartment. Their eyes met, and they both froze.

Shit, this looks scandalous.

Eoduun gave her a once-over, and Eve knew that it was obvious she'd just climbed out of bed.

"Morning," she said cordially. "You're up early."

"I'm always up early. But you aren't."

She laughed uneasily. "Yeah, no, not usually."

"Is Bo up?" he asked.

"Uh, yeah. But he's in the shower. So…"

"Did you tell him about our brain swap?"

"No, I didn't want to piss him off. But I did tell Luc. He wants to explore it more," Eve said.

"Is Luc back yet?"

"I haven't heard from him yet." Shit. She left her phone in her apartment all night.

"So, uh, is this something I need to, like, pretend I didn't see?" Eoduun asked, pointing between Eve and Bo's apartment door.

"It's not like that," Eve insisted.

Eoduun nodded and raised a dubious brow. "Ok."

"It isn't!"

"I said ok!" He definitely didn't believe her.

She probably wouldn't either, if she were him.

Eve returned to her apartment and hopped in the shower. She wasn't sure why she was so defensive about being caught leaving Bo's apartment. It wasn't her honor or reputation she was afraid of being tarnished. Oddly enough, it was Bo's. Just because she was enjoying some sexual freedom didn't mean that he wanted to be part of it. In fact, he seemed to want to avoid it. She didn't want Eoduun or anyone else to think that Bo was just another casual fuck.

Bo was special. He wasn't the casual fuck kind, and she would fight to the death anyone who dared question his honor.

She giggled in amusement to herself as she rinsed the shampoo from her hair. She was imagining herself in a suit of armor, jousting Eoduun on horseback to defend Bo's honor. Bo was, of course, in a pretty white gown, cheering her on from the stands. She was sure she would earn his favor. Maybe he would give her his embroidered kerchief.

Yeah, she was fucking weird.

2

What Are You Hiding, Evie?

Eve was scrambling her last few eggs in the kitchen when Bo walked through her door. The reason it was her last few was because she'd accidentally crushed the first few trying to crack them, much like she'd ripped the towel ring off her wall last night. Thankfully, though, the effects she'd experienced after being with Dagon seemed to be waning. She couldn't Force-choke an egg. She'd tried. It made her wonder if the incidents from last night were just a fluke, and the bottle had just been shifting and popping on its own from being crushed earlier. She'd seen plenty of crushed bottles snap and pop on their own in the garbage can.

"*Ohayou,*" Bo called.

"You already saw me this morning," she replied, dumping the eggs into the hot pan on the stove.

"And it's still a good morning, despite that," he teased, sliding onto his barstool at the kitchen island. He pushed her coffee cup across the counter toward her.

She gave him a wry smile and reached for the cup with one hand while she stirred the eggs in the pan with the other. She raised the cup and said, "*Arigatou.*" Her last two pieces of bread popped up from the toaster. "Did you eat yet?" she asked Bo.

"Why, are you offering me breakfast?"

"Maybe. If you butter my toast for me."

"Luc would have a field day with that one," Bo mused.

"He has a field day with everything. Butter the toast."

When the eggs were done, Eve divided them between two plates and slid one to Bo.

"You gave me more," he noticed, visually comparing the plates.

"You're a growing boy."

"Take some back. I don't need that much."

She pulled her plate away from him so he couldn't put any of his eggs on it. "No. Eat what I gave you. Don't complain. There are starving children, Bo. Think of the children."

"What if I hate them?"

"The children?!" Eve gasped.

"No!" Bo laughed. "The eggs. What if I hate the eggs?" he challenged with a raised eyebrow.

"You're not allowed to hate the eggs. Why, do you hate the eggs?" she fretted.

"I haven't tried them yet. I was just asking."

"Shut up. Eat."

Eve watched him pull his mask down and take a bite of his breakfast. No one hated her scrambled eggs. It was one of the few things she was confident she cooked well. But now she worried that he wouldn't like them.

"Wow, these are awful. You shouldn't eat them. You should probably just give yours to me," Bo said with his mouth full.

"Well, if you don't like them, I guess *I'll* eat them," Eve replied, reaching for his plate.

He threw his arm around his plate defensively. "Oh, no, no, that's ok. I'll suffer through. There are starving children. I must think of the children."

Eve heard her door swing open, and Zeke and Eoduun walked into the apartment.

"I smell breakfast," Zeke said.

"Sorry, not enough to go around," Eve apologized.

"It's terrible. You wouldn't want it anyway," Bo jested, taking another bite.

The boys walked into the kitchen and started opening cupboards. "We're going to starve to death if you don't go to the store soon, Eve," Zeke complained. He reached over and took Eve's toast from her plate.

"Hey!"

He took a bite and returned it. "It was just a bite!" he cried defensively. She saw him eyeing up her last bite of scrambled egg on the end of her fork. She sighed, then held it out for him. He grinned sweetly and ate it.

"What the hell is that?" Bo asked, pointing to Zeke's neck.

Eve's eyes widened as her eyes fell to the bruise Bo was pointing at. That was her. That was where she bit Dagon last night. Why didn't it heal? Was it because it happened *after* she gave him blood?

"I don't know. I woke up with it," Zeke replied casually. "I must've been sleepwalking again and ran into something."

Bo's interest piqued. "Do you sleepwalk often?"

"Kind of, yeah."

"You've never done it out on the road," Bo pointed out.

"Huh. Yeah, it does seem to happen more often at home. But it did happen at the suite. I walked in on Eve in the bathroom."

Bo gave Eve a curious sideways glance. "He did?"

"I wasn't on the toilet or anything," she said.

"Was it *Zeke*?"

Eve felt a rush of panic under his keen gaze. Bo was a walking lie detector, and she was a bad liar. *Keep it cool. Keep it cool. Keep it cool.*

Before she answered, Zeke said, "Of course it was me. I remember waking up in the bathroom."

"I mean before you woke up," Bo clarified. He pinned Eve with an inquisitive stare.

She didn't want to lie right to Bo's face. But what should she do? What could she do? Dagon was right there, listening. He'd promised retribution if she told his secret. But either she hesitated too long in her response, or Bo saw the deceit brewing.

"What are you hiding, Evie?" he prodded, narrowing his eyes.

She frowned. "Hey, how did I end up on trial, here?" she shot back defensively. She'd been gaslighted so many times in the past that she may have picked up a few things. When you're about to get caught lying, turn the tables.

She wasn't proud of it, but she didn't know what else to do. She couldn't reveal the truth. Not just yet.

Before the conversation could go any deeper, though, Bo looked over at the apartment door, then back at Eve. He was waiting expectantly for something.

"What?" she asked curiously.

Moments later, she heard someone step through the door and say, "Ah, I see the zoo is open early this morning."

Luc.

Luc.

Her heart summersaulted in her chest as his tall frame sauntered around the corner into the kitchen, his hands casually in his pockets, his platinum white hair slicked back on one side and falling into his face on the other. He pulled one hand from the pocket of his black slacks, slipped off his round sunglasses, and hung them in the unbuttoned collar of his dark gray, pinstriped oxford shirt. He fixed her with that dazzling aquamarine gaze and flashed a warm smile at her, and everyone else faded into the background while her insides erupted in butterflies.

It took every drop of willpower she possessed to stop herself from clambering over the counter and leaping into his arms like a flying squirrel. She wanted those arms around her. His lips on hers. His body against hers. *No. Stay in your seat. Stay in your seat. Stay in your seat.*

Luc's eyes focused only on her, as if no one else was in the room. "Hello, love," he said sweetly. He opened his arms to her invitingly. "Did you miss me?"

Her body moved without conferring with her head first. Her feet carried her right into his trap, like a moth to a flame. Her arms flung around him and her face pressed into his chest, and she completely forgot that her whole team was sitting or standing around, watching her cling to him, wagging her tail shamelessly for him. But for just a moment, she didn't give two fucks.

His arms enclosed around her, and he kissed the top of her head. She was surrounded by that familiar scent that she only now realized she'd been missing. Bourbon vanilla and smoky cedar. Money. Power. Desire.

"You smell expensive," she mused. She'd told him that the first time they met.

"Oh, I come cheap," he replied without missing a beat. He remembered.

"All right, Rico Suave," Bo interrupted. "Did you find anything at the mansion? Do we have orders today?"

"Business, business, business…why is there never any time for fun around here anymore?" Luc complained. "I just got back. Give me a minute to get settled in."

"Talk while you settle," Bo said impatiently.

Luc sighed, and Eve pushed away from him, reluctantly, returning to her seat to collect her and Bo's plates to put them in the dishwasher.

Luc stuck his hands back in his pockets and told them the highlights of what was discovered. "Zephlyn was able to get a vision from touching the teleportation sigil, but it was scrambled and didn't make a whole lot of sense. He saw shackles in a basement, vast, rocky cliffs and mountains covered in greenery, Dagon running with Lilith's grimoire, and an army of monsters. But it doesn't help us in any real meaningful way. Not yet.

"Big news, though, came in this morning from the Vatican. They have a source who was able to figure out just a tidbit of the speeches the shifters gave at the clubs. It was the same message in both, and it sounds like it may be a call to arms. Something like 'rise up for Dagon.' So, Ruth's goal was not to keep me running around; her goal was to get the message out publicly. We need to keep that from happening, because we don't know what else is in that message. But first," Luc pointed at Zeke as he slipped his sunglasses back on, "I need to have a word with our red-eyed Aquaman. Would you be so kind as to call on him for me, Z?"

Zeke barely finished a nod before a scowl spread across his face and his eyes shifted to an angry red. Dagon growled, "Stop calling me Aquaman, you insolent giraffe."

"So...what's up?" Luc asked conversationally, his tone falsely endearing as though he were speaking to a child. "How are we feeling about everything we just heard?"

"I have nothing to do with that pathetic sorceress. Those creatures will surely be disappointed when they discover they're being duped."

"But are they? You make it difficult to trust you at any level. Maybe if you gave us something, helped out in some meaningful way, it would ease our minds."

"I'm not here to ease your minds. I couldn't give a fuck less about you."

"Tell us what the shifters message was."

"I've already offered that, and my demands were ignored," Dagon replied.

"Make a reasonable offer, and maybe we'll reconsider," Luc countered, crossing his arms and tilting his head.

"Ok. How about one day a week of freedom and I tell you whatever you want to know. Even the secret about Eve." Dagon glanced over at her and winked wickedly, rubbing the bruise on his neck where she'd bitten him the night before.

Eve's blood ran cold. Her face flushed with fire. Was he about to catapult her under the bus?! Panic rose in her chest and tingled through her nerves as Luc, Bo, and Eoduun all turned their eyes to her. A cold sweat broke out across her skin.

She blurted an obnoxious, nervous laugh. "Aha, whaa?!" She pinned Dagon with an indignant stare. "Excuse me? A secret about *me*?!" she challenged. *Play it cool. Don't be over the top. Fuck, why is lying so hard?!*

"Why would you know any kinds of secrets about Eve?" Bo snarled.

"Are you jealous?" Dagon made a fake pout. "Just wait until you hear everything I have to tell. You'll be positively *green* with jealous rage."

"Evie, if you have something to tell us, now is the time," Bo urged.

"I don't know what he's talking about." Not a lie. She didn't know *which* secret he was intending to reveal. "But I can't say I'm not a little curious myself." And fucking terrified.

Dagon crossed his arms casually. "I'll tell you what. I'll give you a morsel, just to whet your appetite. Because once you hear this, you'll *need* to know more."

Eve's heart was thumping so loudly in her ears, she was afraid she wouldn't hear what he had to reveal. She focused fixedly on his lips so as not to miss a single syllable, and she saw them stretch into a devious smile.

"Look at you all on the edges of your seats."

"Spill it, Dagon," Eoduun hissed.

"Patience, Eodie. The more you goad me, the more I'm going to draw this out."

"Or I can just put you back," Luc said, drawing his index and middle finger toward Dagon's forehead.

Dagon lifted his chin defiantly. "Do it, and you get nothing."

"We can't believe anything you say anyway." Luc brought his fingers closer to Dagon's forehead, as though he were really going to send him below again.

"Eve has the Blood of Lilith," Dagon blurted.

Luc's fingers froze, half an inch from Dagon's head. "What did you just say?"

3
A Kick in the Balls Is a Kick in the Balls

"You heard me, giraffe," Dagon sneered.

Eve felt the weight of everyone's attention on her, but she looked only at Dagon. "What the hell makes you say *that*?!" she demanded.

"How do you think I can tell monsters from everyone else? They all have the Blood of Lilith. I can see it." Then, to Luc, he said, "Now, about my fee. I have so much more to spill for the right price."

"We'll talk later," Luc said abruptly, then touched his fingers to Dagon's forehead, bringing Zeke back instantly.

"Ow, goddamn it!" Zeke hissed, pressing his palms against his forehead and doubling over.

Eve wished she could read the inscrutable expression on Luc's face behind his sunglasses as he turned to her. Then again, maybe not. She wished she *couldn't* read the expression on Bo's. His eyes regarded her with something she could only interpret as disillusionment.

"He's probably lying, right?" she asked, her voice barely above a whisper.

"I'm going to take you to see Mira," Luc said calmly. "We'll run some tests."

"I don't want to go see Mira," Eve protested fearfully. She didn't want to know. Right now, she could doubt. She had that option. She didn't want Mira to take away that possibility. Sure, she might find out definitively that she was fine, but it could go the other way, too. It was better not to know. It was better to cling to the doubt.

"The tests don't usually hurt," Zeke comforted her, misunderstanding her apprehension.

"I don't need tests. I'm not a monster. I would know if I was a monster. I'm not. I can't be, right? I'm a blood healer. You told me that yourself," Eve pointed an accusatory finger at Luc. "You said it was impossible!"

"Maybe I was wrong," Luc conceded calmly.

Hot tears burned in her eyes. "I'm not a monster," she choked out.

"No one is calling you a monster, Evie," Bo said softly. "I'm half werewolf, remember? I have the Blood of Lilith, too."

"And you hate it. And you hate Dizzy. And you'll hate me, too."

His brows drew together in a pained expression. "Evie..."

"Love, take a breath," Luc interrupted, starting to walk toward her. "We can figure this all out."

She was panicking. This was her nightmare. They'd taken her into their world, given her companionship, let her get comfortable, made her feel safe and content...loved, even.

And now it was over. They would reject her, cast her out. Just as she knew would happen, the rug would be pulled out from under her.

Just as it always had, just as it always would.

Jump out before it crashes and burns you to bits, Eve.

"I have to go."

24

Eve evaded Bo and Luc by going around the other side of the kitchen island, but it brought her right past Zeke and Eoduun. She tried to brush past them quickly, but Zeke caught her around the waist.

"Whoa, whoa, what's the matter?" Zeke inquired, baffled by her distress.

She twisted in his arms and shoved his chest, and his eyes widened in shock as he slammed back into the fridge. Her surge of strength from last night had either returned or not dissipated as much as she thought it had.

"Sorry!" she apologized as she backed toward the door.

As she looked at all the shocked expressions on those faces she adored, she was bothered by how much this reminded her of Zeke's last memory of his family.

Would this be her last memory of her Knighco family?

Luc suddenly appeared in front of her as she backed away. "Where are you going?" he asked in a soft, placating tone. He didn't reach out for her, but he followed her movements.

"I don't know." She turned her back to him and slipped her shoes on at the door. She heard her team approaching behind Luc. She didn't want to look at them. She was afraid to see their expressions again.

"I will go with you. You aren't safe on your own," Luc said.

"You saw what I just did. I'll be fine on my own."

"What was that, by the way? That's new," Luc asked curiously. Coolly. Too casually. Was he secretly freaking the fuck out on the inside, like she was?

"I don't know. Ask Dagon. He seems to have all your answers."

"*Our* answers, love. And, no, Dagon isn't our only resource. I'm sure Mira can help us figure this out."

As Eve walked out the door, Luc followed. Out of the corner of her eye, she saw him gesture for the rest of her team to stay behind.

"I want to be left alone, Luc," she said. She needed to plan her escape, and she couldn't do it with him up her ass.

"Where are we going?" he wondered, ignoring her request.

"*I* am going somewhere you aren't."

"You can't run from me, Eve."

Eve's step faltered. Was that a threat? "I'm not running. I just need some space."

"I think I'm finally starting to figure you out, you know that?" Luc mused as he walked along behind her with his hands casually in his pockets. "It wasn't easy at first, because your actions sometimes defy logic. You sabotage your own opportunities for happiness. Why? Why would anyone do that? Because you see happiness as vulnerability. You kick yourself in the balls before someone else does. But you want to know a secret? It doesn't hurt any less. A kick in the balls is a kick in the balls. Doing it yourself doesn't make you less vulnerable. It only ensures that you get kicked in the balls."

"I don't have balls, Luc," she argued as she walked out of the apartment complex.

"Don't be obtuse." He finally reached out and caught Eve by the arm. "And quit walking away from me."

"Then quit following me." She twisted her arm from his grasp. "I need time to think. Alone."

"We need to go see Mira and get some answers. Thinking about it isn't going to solve anything right now. We need action."

Eve gave an exasperated sigh. "You know what? Fine. Give me some time alone, just a little walk to the training grounds, and then I'll go with you to see Mira when I get back. Ok? Deal?" She needed time to decide if she was even coming back.

It was as though he saw the desire to flee in her eyes. He took her face in his big hands and looked at her over the top of his sunglasses, gracing her with a beautiful but tormented gaze.

"If you run, I *will* find you. This is where you belong."

"That's not your decision to make."

"You already made that decision yourself when you accepted your apartment and your team. I'm simply enforcing it because I believe it to be the right one." Luc gave her an earnest smile and added, "The fact that I can't exist without you might play a little part, but purely secondary, I assure you."

"When you say things like that, it makes me trust you even less, not more."

"Keep kicking yourself in the balls. Just hurry back, love."

Luc watched her walk away towards the training grounds. She wondered if he was going to spy on her, teleporting from one place to another to follow her. She hoped not, but she couldn't discount the prospect. She kept her head on a swivel.

As she approached the training grounds, she could see Mendal, Zephlyn, and Dizzy out running drills. Of all the people she didn't want to run into right now, Zephlyn was right at the top of that list. She detoured off toward the tall grass outside of the training grounds. It was still within the compound walls, but the grass came up to her belly and she could seclude herself there for a while. She plopped down in the middle of the grass and looked up at the golden rays of the sunrise coloring the sky, hoping there weren't any ticks crawling into her hair.

She'd overreacted. She'd convinced herself over and over again that if she was a monster, they wouldn't want her anymore. So, when the other shoe dropped, she hadn't bothered to stop and listen to what they actually had to say, or to see their reactions uncolored by her own preconceptions…or misconceptions. She responded to what she'd expected, not to what she'd been presented.

Luc had been surprisingly calm about it. He was ready to tackle the issue, face it head on, and get answers. And what did she do? She threw the baby out with the bathwater. She was prepared to run away from everything she wanted, *needed*, because she was terrified of being rejected. Unworthy. Found wanting.

But she was unworthy. She was a liar. A deceiver. She took advantage of their kindness. She enjoyed their bodies however she pleased and gave them nothing of value in return. She'd given them no reason to accept her in the first place, so what reason did they have to keep her if she was faulty? Because she was. Blood healer or no, she was fundamentally fucked up.

She *was* a monster, and the Blood of Lilith had nothing to do with it.

Speaking of fucked up, what the hell was Dagon's deal? Why had he done that? She didn't think he was a particularly honorable guy, but this was low, even for him. Using her so carelessly just to get some free time? What else was he planning to tell them? Would he spill everything, just to get what he wanted, with no regard for what would happen to her? She was an idiot for putting herself in such a position that his betrayal could cause her harm. She never should've gotten involved with him in the first place. She'd known that. But she'd played his game anyway, and she lost.

That's what losers do.

She heard grass rustling, and footsteps drawing closer. She lay still, listening. Maybe they would just pass by. But who would even be way over here? Had Zephlyn seen her? She wasn't in the mood to see anyone yet.

Whoever it was, they were coming straight for her. They knew she was there. The grass rustled near her head, and Luc's face leaned into her line of view as she stared up at the sky.

"Come with me. I want to show you something." He held his hand down to her.

"I'm not ready to go back yet."

"You don't have to. Come on." He sounded impatient. Rather unlike him. Something inside her told her to get away from him right then, but…it was Luc. She shrugged it off.

She sat up and looked at him. "Did you change your clothes?"

He looked down at his dark blue t-shirt and blue jeans. "Uh, yeah. I changed."

"I don't think I've ever seen you in blue jeans."

"Huh. Well, now you have."

He was being cold. What was up with him?

"Are you ok?" she inquired.

"Fit as a fiddle. Now get up. I don't want you to miss it."

She rose to her feet and dusted off her leggings. She'd dressed in her athleticwear in anticipation of training today, but that was unlikely to happen now.

Luc grabbed her hand and began to drag her deeper into the grass. She hurried along behind him, trying to keep up. "Luc, chill, my legs are like half the length of yours. What's so important?"

"You'll see."

Something wasn't right. Her instincts were screaming at her. *Run. Run. RUN.*

Why had he changed his clothes into something so uncharacteristically casual? Why was he acting so strangely? What could he possibly have to show her that he couldn't just tell her?

Was this a trap? Had they conspired against her while she was out lying in the grass?

She tried to pull her hand from his, but he held on to her tightly.

"Luc, you're hurting me."

He completely disregarded her. "It's just up ahead. Look."

Her eyes searched the space ahead, but all she saw was the fence that ran along the border of the compound's perimeter.

"Why are we all the way over here?" she asked apprehensively. Something wasn't right. *RUN.*

"You don't see it? Right there." He pointed at the ground near the fence.

As they approached, she saw it. It was a large, flat rock, and carved into its surface, a sigil smeared with dried blood.

"How did that get there?" she gasped. "Is it one of Ruth's?!"

He pulled her closer to it, until they were standing right next to it, looking down at it. She felt a sudden, sharp poke in her trapezius from a hypodermic needle, and his arm swept under her legs, scooping her up off her feet.

Her stomach dropped. She should've listened to her gut. Too late now.

4

You Might as Well Get Comfy

Eve entered a freefall and her stomach fluttered with panic, like she'd just crested over into the big drop at the beginning of a rollercoaster ride. Then it ended just as it was beginning, with a jarring halt. Her head was spinning, her stomach twisted up in knots.

She tried to squirm, but found herself immobilized in bizzarro Luc's arms. Her arms and legs felt like they were filled with lead, and the only thing she could move was her head and eyes. He must have given her some kind of tranquilizer.

She assessed her surroundings. She was in a spacious bedroom, designed in a modern farmhouse style. Lots of shiplap, chalk white, and distressed wood. There was a couch along one wall, a large white dresser, and a four-poster bed. The canopy and gossamer white drapes on the bed matched the drapes in the large windows of the room.

A beautiful, long-legged woman sashayed into the room, throwing her long, platinum blonde hair over her shoulder. Ruthlys.

"Take her to the basement, Varghrir," she said, rubbing her heavily-jeweled hands together in anticipation. "I'm ready to start cooking."

"I want to play with her," he said, his voice suddenly not Luc's. It was gruff and gravelly.

"Forget it," Ruth said as she walked out of the room.

Eve felt her captor's body shifting and transforming around her. The arms and chest expanded and hardened, and she rose another two feet from the ground. If Luc was six-five, this guy had to have been almost nine feet tall. He was an absolute oak tree, and she was no more than a kite caught in his branches.

No disgusting flakes came off him when he changed, so he must not be a regular shifter. Not to mention, his clothes had changed with him - he hadn't needed to change outfits like the one at the club had. He had gone from jeans and a t-shirt to oddly historic-looking black trousers and a flowing black shirt with a plunging neckline. It looked like something she imagined an old vampire would wear. She looked up at his face, and the white locks had been replaced by a thick mane of jet-black hair hanging loosely around cold, icy blue eyes with pin-prick pupils. The wide, sharp jawline, straight nose, and symmetrical features should have been attractive, but he repulsed her. He was monstrous. Pure evil smiled down at her, sending a shiver of fear down her spine.

There was nothing exciting in this fear. It wasn't like when Dagon grinned at her and bullied her. Dagon had rules he had to follow. He was muzzled, in a way. This was the difference between feeding the lion through the fence and being thrown into the enclosure.

And this lion was hungry.

"They'll kill you if you touch me," Eve whispered tremulously. Her threat was less than effective.

Varghrir's eyes glinted maliciously. "You think so? Your hunter friends? You don't even know who I am. *They* don't know who I am. Or where we are. Or that we even have you. They'll just think you ran away." His deep, bassy voice reminded her of Andre the giant. Except he made Andre look like an average-sized guy.

She frowned questioningly at him.

"How did we know that?" he inferred from her look. "We know everything that goes on in that apartment." He lowered his voice and added, "I must say, you're very limber. I kinda want to see how far you bend before you *snap*."

Eve's heart was pumping ice. "How? How can you see in my apartment?!"

"What, you think a little warding and shielding is going to stop us? You guys are so worried about sorcery and specialties that you completely overlook the simplest tools. Do you know how many spy cameras you can order online with a stolen credit card? A lot. But we only needed a few."

How the fuck would they get cameras into the compound?! Before she could ask, however, Ruthlys shouted impatiently from the other room.

"Vargh! Today!"

Eve saw a flash of rage pass through Varghrir's icy eyes, and his bicep twitched. He growled and tossed Eve unceremoniously over his shoulder, wrapping one massive arm around the back of her knees, allowing her head and arms to dangle over his back.

"Maybe I'll disembowel you *today*," he grumbled under his breath.

Eve couldn't be sure if he was talking to her or to Ruth, but she got the distinct feeling it was meant for Ruth.

Eve took in as much about her surroundings as she could as she was carried through an open, comfortable living room with huge windows looking out over a gorgeous mountain view.

Wait.

"...vast, rocky cliffs and mountains covered in greenery..."

This was it. That's exactly what she saw as they passed by the window. Zephlyn's vision was coming to fruition.

They went through a chef's dream of a kitchen on their way to the basement, and Eve took note of where the knife block was and the fact that there was a door to the outside from the kitchen.

Varghrir began to shrink as they moved through the kitchen, and by the time she heard a door creak open, he was not much taller than Luc. But he still had double the muscle. She was wondering why he would shrink down again, but she got her answer as she was carried down a dark stairwell that his previous size would not have passed through.

Varghrir brought her into a jail-like cell tucked into the corner of the surprisingly cozy basement and dropped her roughly onto a hard camp cot.

"Shackled?" he questioned irritably.

"Obviously," Ruth called back condescendingly. "Her tranq is going to wear off three times faster than a normal person."

Varghrir exhaled loudly, then hoisted Eve up with one arm. He pushed her up against the cold, off-white enamel-painted cinderblock wall and shoved one trunk of a thigh between her limp legs to hold her upright. He pressed his forearm across her chest to keep her from slumping over as he guided her wrists into the double shackles over her head. Once the cold steel was fastened around her wrists, he released her upper body and got to work on shackling her ankles.

The moment she was fully encumbered by shackles and chains, Varghrir let the shackles hold her up, removing his thigh from between her legs. But not before rubbing it obscenely against her mound through her leggings.

She met his eyes levelly, a sudden protective blanket of calm, detached coldness enshrouding her like fallen snow. "Gross," she said icily. She was going into survival mode. There was no room for emotions in survival.

He narrowed his eyes and curled his lip. "I look forward to breaking you."

"I think you're in for a surprise," Eve retorted. "If I can break a god, I can break a...whatever the fuck kind of pissant critter you are."

Varghrir lunged at her, stopping inches from her face. She stared up into the depths of those icebergs as unflinchingly as she could manage.

"I'm no *critter*," he seethed, barely containing his rage. His well-proportioned, technically handsome face contorted into a menacing scowl. "I'm a fucking Jötunn, and you *will* show me some fucking respect!"

"Simmer down, Vargh," Ruth said as she approached the jail cell.

"And *you*," he turned on Ruth, pointing a giant finger in her face, "better fucking watch yourself. I *will* find a way to break this binding spell of subservience, and you will rue the day you ever decided to raise me as your *plaything*."

Ruth smiled in his face and patted his cheek. He raised his hand to intercept her wrist, but some invisible force blocked him from touching her. It only pissed him off more.

Ruth puckered her lips and laid a childish kiss on his scowling mouth. "You're adorable. Now, apologize."

"I'm sorry," he hissed.

"You love me."

"I love you." Varghrir's neck tensed with fury, his eye twitching as he spat the words at her.

"That's my boy," she praised, giving him another little peck on the lips.

Eve could feel the mobility returning to her limbs as she watched the scene before her, and she slid her feet into a standing position to take the pressure of her full body weight off of her shackled wrists.

Ruth glanced over at her. "Wow, is it wearing off already? Jesus." She waved a hand at Varghrir. "Go get me a chair. I want to indulge in a little girl talk."

"Whatever, bitch," he growled, then stalked angrily away to fetch a chair. When he returned and placed it in front of Ruth, he gave a deep, sarcastic bow. "Anything else, you bossy whore?"

"Watch your tongue, or I'll find a better use for it," Ruth warned in a singsong cadence.

"How is that different from any other day?" Varghrir said in irritation.

Ruth sat in her chair and looked up at him. "Because that's not what I'm talking about. I was just noticing how dirty my shoes were looking. Maybe they could use a little spit-shine." She looked down at her nails. "But for now, you can go keep an eye on the apartment and let me know if anything interesting happens."

"As you wish," Varghrir grumbled.

He left the cell and wandered over to a plush couch tucked along the wall in the basement, and as he plopped his enormous frame down onto it, he picked up a remote and turned on the television on the wall across from it.

Images sprang upon the screen of her apartment, in full color. Her bathroom, her bedroom, her kitchen, her living room.

"Empty," he called back.

"I wonder if they've realized you ran away yet," Ruth said to Eve.

"They won't let me go so easily."

"They'll have to. They won't find you here. We're shielded from Levi; Zephlyn can't read you or your future; and Babhdán's nose won't be able to track you through a portal. You might as well get comfy. This is your new home."

Eve knitted her brows. "What makes you say Zephlyn can't read my future?"

"I have my sources."

"Is Dagon working with you?" Eve accused.

Ruth smiled smugly. "What, did you think he was on your side?"

"Not really. But I can't see a reason for him to be on yours, either. He would never willingly become anyone's slave."

"No, he'll fight it tooth and nail. But, as you can see," she gestured toward Varghrir, "I've grown a lot more powerful since I tried to bind Dagon the first time."

"What the hell is that guy, anyway? I've never heard of a Jötunn," Eve asked.

"Oh, that's just one of many names. You've definitely heard of the Jötnar. Giants. Nephilim. Titans. Take your pick. He was sealed away like Dagon, but I raised him. I didn't even need a vessel for him. I can pull Dagon from that adorable jock, too, and let him take his preferred form. I've learned *so many* tricks from Lilith's grimoire." Ruth leaned in closer to Eve. "And secrets."

Eve glanced past the iron bars of her cell at Varghrir lounging on the couch. "He's huge, sure, but a Titan? That's his natural form, not some monster you cooked up? I thought Titans were like skyscrapers."

"That's a pure, unadulterated Jötunn right there. History and mythology exaggerate sometimes, but you have to admit, he *is* a very big boy." Ruth raised a conspiratorial eyebrow at Eve and added, "And in case you wondered, it applies in every department."

Eve grimaced. "Not interested."

Ruth scoffed. "Good. Because I'm not one to share what's mine. I was just bragging."

"But I could take him if I *was* interested," Eve said defiantly.

Ruth's calm demeanor faltered at Eve's sudden threat, and it made Eve smile. She was in no position to be smiling, but the surprised look on Ruth's face amused her.

"In fact, I think he's already keen," Eve sprinkled salt.

"He's not genuinely interested in you, skank. He's just bullying you."

"You're right. That's probably all it is. I'm sure you have nothing to worry about." Eve looked over at Varghrir on the couch. He was engrossed in a show about Vikings, mumbling things to himself about what they were getting wrong in their depictions. Eve had just been talking shit, of course, but now that she thought about it, she wondered if she really *could* use him. It made her skin crawl, but desperate times, and all.

He could be her ticket out of here.

Ruth crossed her arms haughtily. "Don't get cocky. Just because you have my brothers and the bi-curious duo wrapped around your finger doesn't mean you have any special powers of seduction. They've just gotten addicted to the blood. And Varghrir knows better than to fall for that."

"Dagon was more than happy to fall for it."

Ruth smirked. "And look where that landed you. Who really fell for what, hm?"

Dammit. Point Ruth.

"I do have a question, though," Ruth continued. "What is up with you and Babhdán? I've been watching you for a couple of days, and I've seen him climb into bed with you, heard the sob stories you told each other, and then…you just sleep? What the fuck is that?"

Had she completely missed the conversations about Bo sleeping with her to keep Dagon from her dreams? Maybe the audio didn't come through well or something. Or maybe Ruth had an angle.

"So what?" Eve replied. "Luc was gone, and I don't like to sleep alone."

"Is Babhdán not good enough for you or something?" Ruth challenged.

"What?" Eve was confused. Where was this coming from? "That's neither here nor there."

"So, what, you like the flashy rich brother, and you'll let the cute boytoys tag team you in the middle of dinner, and of course Dagon's power is irresistible, but what about Babhdán? Are you just stringing him along because you can?"

"Hold on, are you mad because I'm *not* fucking your brother?" Eve laughed incredulously.

"Why are you treating him differently? You think he doesn't see it? Do you know nothing about him? He picks up on *everything*."

"You've been watching me for a couple of days, so that makes you an expert on my relationship with Bo? Pfft," Eve scoffed.

"You must make him feel like the odd man out. That's the cruelest thing you can do to him."

Holy shit. Was this genuine concern for big bro's feelings? "Says the bitch who threw him across a damn highway," Eve retorted. "And not that it's any of your goddamn business, but I treat Bo differently because our relationship *is* different. But, if anything, it's because I'm closer with him than any of the others, not the other way around. I care about Bo. So fuck yourself right up the ass with *your* bullshit concern for him. If you cared so much for him, maybe you shouldn't have ruined his eye and let Dagon kill his girlfriend."

"Girlfriend?" Ruth laughed. "Nuns can't be girlfriends. You know what that blood healer bitch was putting him through, don't you? I know he told you the story."

"They loved each other."

"No, he loved *her*. She loved her *God,* and, even though she knew she didn't love him the way he deserved to be loved, she kept him dangling like a yo-yo. Babhdán needs someone who will love him fully and completely, because that's the only way *he* knows how to love. He's just gotten used to accepting whatever scraps he's thrown, and it's fucking sad. So I don't feel even the least bit bad about the bitch dying. Dagon did him a favor, even if he'll never see it that way." Ruth pointed an accusatory finger at Eve and added, "And you were just starting him on the same fucking path. If you can't give him everything, you shouldn't give him anything at all."

Guilt settled in Eve's chest. "Bo doesn't love me like *that*," she countered.

"The fuck he doesn't. They all do. It's disgusting." Ruth slapped her jeaned thighs and stood up. She called to Varghrir, "This isn't fun anymore. Time to bleed this bitch."

5

Dominate Him. Control Him. Own Him. Kill Him.

Panic surged through Eve like a shock from an electrical outlet. She couldn't let them bleed her. If Ruth got her blood, who knew what kind of spells she could unlock, what kind of havoc she could wreak, and who she could hurt. Eve needed to keep her talking.

"Wait, before that, I have one question," Eve implored.

Ruth rested her hands on her hips and canted her head impatiently. "What?"

"Why Dagon?"

"What do you mean *why Dagon*?"

"Why do you want him so badly that you would go to all this trouble just to chain him to you and have him hate you the way Varghrir clearly does? What is your endgame?"

"Like I'd tell you that."

"Are you the reason he betrayed me?"

Ruth laughed derisively. "Oh, sweetie. I know we keep throwing the word 'betrayal' around, but in order to betray, some sense of loyalty must first be involved. Did you honestly think he bore any fealty toward you? You're a means to an end. With you, I can free him from his frat boy meat puppet. You can't think you actually mean something to him. And even if you did, you can't possibly be so deluded to believe you mean more to him than his own freedom."

Was he the one who put cameras up in her apartment? Was he secretly meeting with Ruth when he had nightly free-reign of Zeke's body? Had Dagon made a deal for his freedom in exchange for Eve? How long had it been going on? Was Eve's arrival at Knighco what spurred Ruth's reemergence?

But when Ruth had popped up, she didn't seem to know that Eve was a blood healer yet. Wouldn't Dagon have told her as soon as he knew? And why would Dagon have jumped in front of Ruth's attack? Was it orchestrated, to make Eve trust Dagon's intentions?

She remembered the way Dagon had manipulated her body without even touching her last night. If he could use a form of telekinesis, why didn't he use that to stop the stakes from striking? Why did he use Zeke's body? For blood? Was it so she would be forced to give him blood to heal him?

Everything always circled back to Eve's Panacea Blood.

Ruth stared hard at Eve. "I can't believe you even need to ask 'why Dagon?' You've been with him. You've felt his power. That's like asking North Korea why they want nukes."

Eve shook her head. "But *why*? Why do you need nukes?"

"You're the kind of person who looks at a jewelry store and says, 'Look at all those pretty gems. I can't afford them, but I'm sure they'll look nice on someone else who can.' I'm the type of person who looks at a jewelry store and says, 'Look at all those pretty gems. I can't afford them, but I deserve them. Who do I have to go through to get them?'"

"So, what are you after? Money? Power?"

Ruth sneered. "Bitch, I want it all. The whole world will bow to me." She gave Eve a contemptuous once-over and said, "And I won't have to sleep my way to the top. I can use my *brain* and my *skills* to get what I want."

Eve mirrored the sneer. "Except that won't get you the one thing you *really* want, will it? It won't get you love. You have to actually spellbind men into loyalty and love. That must be a lot of work." Eve tilted her head. "See, I wouldn't know. I just can't keep them away from me." She stepped forward as far as her shackles would allow. "Even your brothers love me more than they love you."

Ruth scoffed and rolled her eyes.

Eve went on, lowering her tone, "And not only do they love me, they are devoted. They will come for me not because they *have* to, but because they *choose* to. Can you say the same for Jolly Green?"

"I don't need some illusion of love. I need absolute obedience. Trust me, my power supersedes yours any day of the week."

Eve gave Ruth a measured look. "You know, you could stop all of this and come back to them. They would find a way to forgive you. You could make amends."

Ruth looked down at her fingernails. "How naïve. Babhdán must be rubbing off on you."

"I mean it."

"Enough. Shut up," Ruth snapped. Eve had struck a nerve.

Varghrir brought Ruthlys a caddy with empty vials and the medical equipment needed for drawing blood samples.

"You know, my blood doesn't work like that," Eve pointed out, still trying to delay. "Once it goes into those vials, it'll be no different from regular blood."

"I don't need it for healing," Ruth responded simply.

Shit.

"So, what, are you just going to bleed me dry?"

"You don't slaughter the goose that lays the golden eggs after it lays one egg. No, I know exactly how much I can take at a time without killing you. Like I said, better get comfy. You're my new bestie."

"I'd hate to boot Varghrir from that coveted position."

Varghrir snatched up her shackled arm and held it out toward Ruth with a painfully firm grip.

"Damn, easy, big boy," Eve complained.

"I saw you with Dagon last night on the cameras. You like it rough," Varghrir rejoined.

"Just a couple of peeping perverts, aren't you?" Eve looked between Varghrir and Ruth, then hissed between her teeth when Ruth jammed a needle into the vein in the bend of her elbow. "Sadistic perverts."

As Eve watched her blood fill vial after vial, she was starting to feel lightheaded.

"You know, that blood might not even work for your spells," Eve pointed out. "You must've heard over the cameras that I'm some kind of monster, right?"

"If it's true, that makes it even more valuable. I read about the potential for a blood healer monster in the grimoire – the crossing of two uncrossable lines: the Blood of Eve and the Blood of Lilith. The Abomination. What I wouldn't give to know who the hell your father was. He must've been something ancient and powerful, because I've investigated your mother's family, and they are truly unremarkable." Ruth regarded Eve suspiciously. "Are you adopted or something?"

"Nope. Just a bastard, like Bo." Eve's eyelids began to droop. They felt so damn heavy. "So, what is this Abomination you read about in the grimoire?"

"There is no real name for it. It's only referred to as the Abomination. But you must be closely descended from Cain *and* from Lilith. As in, blood diluted no more than two or three generations."

"Cain?" Eve's words were beginning to slur.

Ruth pulled the needle from Eve's arm and stuck a bandage over the insertion wound. "Cain is the tainted blood of Eve. He's the only possibility for a successful cross with anything of Lilith's."

Eve heard nothing else as she descended into peaceful darkness.

"Why the hell did you run?" Dagon's angry voice burst through the blackness, and Eve opened her eyes. She was no longer in her cell, but back at her apartment. She was sitting on the floor with her back against the wall, and she was still shackled. Dagon was leaning his shoulder against the bedroom door frame with his arms crossed, pinning her with a red-eyed scowl.

"Am I dreaming?" Eve inquired. "How are you here? Is Zeke asleep? Did something happen to him?!"

"No, he's fully awake. You summoned me. Now, where the fuck are you?!"

"How the hell did I do that?"

Dagon pushed away from the door frame and took two angry steps forward. "Forget the how, *where the fuck did you go?!* Everyone is losing their goddamn shit. You need to come back, right now."

"I would if I could, dickhead! Ruth and her giant shapeshifting sidekick tricked me and kidnapped me."

Dagon's face fell, his fury gone in an instant. Then, it roared back. "What?! Where have they taken you?! Are you ok?"

Eve shook her head and laughed. "Do you care? Aren't you the one who made all of this happen?"

"It's not my fault you're so goddamn insecure about what you are! It would've come out eventually, and at least this way I could use it to negotiate time with you out in the daylight instead of all this slinking around at night bullshit!"

"I'm not talking about you betraying me to my team. I'm talking about you betraying me to Ruth. Putting cameras up in my apartment. Acting like you were trying to protect me just to build rapport with me. Making plans with the enemy and feeding her information while we chased our tails."

"What the fuck are you talking about?" Dagon seemed genuinely perplexed. "Why would I join up with *Ruth*?"

She promised you freedom from your vessel. That was what she almost said, but stopped herself. If he truly wasn't on Ruth's side, and Ruth was just trying to pit Eve and her team against Dagon and weave discontent, then he didn't know that such a possibility was even on the table. And if she told him now, she may very well end up inadvertently bringing Dagon to Ruth's side. He wanted freedom more than anything, perhaps enough to allow himself to be bound to Ruth temporarily, assuming he would be able to find a way out of it later.

She needed to play this right.

"You're going to deny it? Then why does Ruth have cameras up in my apartment?"

"I don't know. This is news to me." Dagon began pacing. "Listen, we need to get you out of there, princess. Where did she take you? Did she get any of your blood yet?"

"I don't know where I am, but she bled me until I passed out. She's probably already off cooking up new monsters as we speak...dream. Whatever."

Dagon growled. "That fucking bitch. Bo should've let me kill her when we had the chance." He crouched down in front of her, resting his elbows on his flared-out knees. "Tell me everything you can remember."

Eve recounted her experience from the moment Varghrir approached her looking like Luc, the mountains she saw out the window that fit Zephlyn's vision, who Varghrir was, Ruth insinuating that Dagon had betrayed them, and Ruth taking vial after vial of blood.

Dagon stood up and started pacing again. "A Jötunn. You can use him." He stopped and crouched in front of Eve again. "Listen. You're going to need to seduce him and take his power. Jötunn are brutally strong, and some of them can shapeshift – obviously he can – and some can use psychic tricks, making people see things that aren't there. From what you told me of your situation, that should be enough to get you free. Once you're free, we can figure out where you are."

"Wait, wait, wait…*take his power*? Is that what I did to you yesterday? Is that why I kept getting weird bursts of strength and Jedi powers?"

"You should be able to pull it off with Vladimir," Dagon replied, purposely misnaming the giant.

"What the fuck does that mean? Is that just something I can *do* now?"

"I'll explain more later. Just know that you can do it." He smirked at her. "How fortunate that we fucked last night."

"…You knew this was going to happen, didn't you?"

His smirk flipped upside down. "No, I didn't fucking know. Stop accusing me of being Ruth's fucking pawn. It's insulting."

"Maybe you aren't a pawn. Maybe you're orchestrating all of it," Eve suggested suspiciously. "And how did you even know I could do that sort of thing?"

"I didn't know, not at first. But I suspected, and the longer I observed you and tested the waters, the clearer it became that you were, indeed, a special breed. A long-awaited treasure worthy of a god." His smirk returned.

"I hope you aren't referring to yourself."

"You are mine. You always have been. You always will be. You were made for me."

"Fuck off. I belong to no one."

Dagon chuckled. "Cute. Now, you have work to do, and so do I. Make me proud, princess."

Eve opened her eyes and realized she was still shackled to the wall in the cell. She looked around and saw that Ruth had left the room, but Varghrir was still planted on the couch, his enormous arms outstretched across the entire length of the backrest. She couldn't have been out for more than a few minutes.

"Vargh...Varghrir," she called out with feigned hoarseness.

His head snapped up and he turned her direction. "Shit, I was supposed to put you on the bed," he grumbled. He pushed up from the couch with a grunt and lumbered toward the cell. The door had been left wide open.

So, he was careless. Good to know.

"Can I have a glass of water?" she begged as he stood in the doorway of the cell, looking down at her with his piercing whitish-blue eyes. Thankfully, he was still in his smaller form. Not to say he wasn't fucking huge, but at least he wasn't Robert Wadlow huge right now. She put on her most innocent face. "Please?"

"You'll get food and drink when Ruth tells me to bring you food and drink."

Eve pretended to stumble to support herself on her feet. "What if I gave you something in return? I'm really fucking thirsty."

Varghrir's grumpy countenance turned lecherously sinister. He looked down at her body. "I'm listening."

"Get me a drink...I give you a drink. Have you ever had Panacea Blood?"

"What the fuck would I want to drink blood for? I'm not a stupid vampire, and I don't need healing," he chided. "I had something else in mind. As in, I get you a drink, and then you suck a little cream from me." He adjusted the growing bulge in his pants obscenely.

He wasn't going to make this easy. His vulgarity did nothing to arouse her. If anything, it further repulsed her.

She tried to push down the disgust. "If you've been watching my apartment, then you've seen how much everyone wants my blood. It isn't a vampiric thing. It's like pure sex on your tongue. But you have to drink it directly from me."

"Is that right?" He was intrigued. "I thought you guys all just had some freaky fetish."

"Get me some water, and you can try it."

46

He chuckled low in his throat through a tight sneer as he came closer to Eve. "Fuck the water. How about I just take it?"

He withdrew a knife from his trousers and held it to the swell of her breast peeking above the collar of her shirt.

Too easy.

He poked the tip into her flesh, watching as the blood quickly rose to the surface and spilled out onto her skin and the knife blade. He lifted the knife to his tongue and licked the blood from it. After a moment, he gave her an unimpressed look.

"It's just blood."

"I told you, you have to take it directly from my body. Lick me. Suck me. That's the only way it works."

He seemed dubious, but he bent down, way down, and ran his tongue over the blood on her breast.

Shit. Eve felt a slight simmer, but it was faint. Shit. Shit. This was Ruger and Cassie all over again. How the hell was she going to get it up for him, so to speak? He disgusted her.

He groaned deeply in his throat and sucked harder at her breast. When he finally lifted his head and looked down at her, his eyes were filled with an icy fire. "Shit, I just about came in my pants."

So, even though she didn't feel it, he still did? Shit. She was hoping that giving him blood would put her in the right frame of mind to want to bed him. Dominate him. Control him. Own him. Kill him.

Kill him?

He began to unfasten his pants.

"Wait! My wrists are uncomfortable. Can you take off my hand shackles? Didn't you say you were supposed to move me to the bed?"

"I don't take off the shackles for that. I just unhook the slack from the wall so you can move around more."

"Can you do that, please? I'll make it worth your while, I swear," she said seductively.

It's amazing what the promise of sexual gratification can earn you. Varghrir reached up and unhooked the chain from the wall, letting it clatter loudly to the white-painted concrete floor.

"There, *comfortable?*" he asked sarcastically.

"Much more, yes, thank you." Eve smiled sweetly. She shuffled over to the bed and sat down on it, the chain dragging noisily behind her. Before Varghrir had a chance to move, she reached out and grabbed his hand, bringing one of his thick digits to her mouth. She swirled her tongue over the pad of his finger, then took it into her mouth and sucked it erotically, looking up at his angular face shadowed beneath loose black locks. Her eyes told her he was handsome, but her mind disliked him at such a fundamental level that it was hard to make herself believe it. She needed to circumvent that part of her and finish the task at hand.

She asked, "So, you can shapeshift? Can you shift into anyone?"

"I can shift into any*thing*. Why, you want me to fuck you as a centaur or something? Because I can do that."

Oh, god, no. "Actually, I was wondering if you could shift into a more familiar form for me. Trust me, you'll enjoy it more if I'm comfortable and at ease. It makes my blood more potent."

Without a word, his body began to shrink, and his hair shifted from black to white. Within just a few moments, bizzarro Luc was standing in front of her.

No, no, anything but that. Don't taint Luc.

"No, not him. I want you to look like Dagon." She wasn't worried about tainting any memories or feelings she had for Dagon.

"Dagon as the real Dagon, or Dagon in his boy vessel?" bizzarro Luc asked in Varghrir's gravelly voice.

Eve hated the way *boy vessel* sounded, but she supposed to something as old as Varghrir, Zeke was but a boy.

But, wait…

"Say again? You know what the real Dagon looked like?!"

"Of course. He was a big deal for a long time. That's like me asking if you know what Donald Trump looks like."

Eve had seen the statues and depictions of Dagon online and in the books from the bunker library. Most of the time, he was shown with a fish tail instead of legs.

She ventured hesitantly, "Is it true that he was, like, a merman?"

Varghrir stared at her like she'd just said the dumbest thing he'd ever heard. "No."

"But he has gills. I've seen them."

"Yeah, he has gills, and he can breathe under water. But he wasn't a merman or a fish god. He didn't have anything to do with fish. That all started because his name was like the Hebrew word for 'fish,' and, like you've noticed, he has gills. But he also has wings." He leveled an expectant look at her. "So, you want the real Dagon?"

Eve's curiosity got the best of her. "Yeah, I think I could be into that. Give me the real Dagon."

6

At Least She Didn't Eat Him

Eve didn't have a chance to be nervous about her request. Varghrir shifted quickly, and Eve found herself staring up into vermilion eyes she knew all too well set in a handsome face that was completely foreign to her.

Dagon had thick, black hair that brushed his shoulders, a few stray strands hanging over his face. His skin tone was a shade or two deeper, tawnier, than Zeke's sandy complexion. His jaw was covered with a luxuriously thick black beard, cleanly trimmed, and it matched the shapely black eyebrows and dark eyelashes around his red eyes. And behind his ears, Eve saw his familiar gill slits.

Then there were the wings. *Wings.* Two enormous, black, leathery wings arched gracefully up from behind his back. They were tipped with a single, black, claw-like appendage at their apex, and hung in a relaxed, slightly open position.

Damn. Dagon was fucking hot.

"I figured you wouldn't mind if I modernized his look a little," Varghrir said in Dagon's smooth, deep voice. "Do you want the wings, or should I tuck them away?"

Eve stood up and looked his body over. Varghrir didn't change the look of his clothes from what he was already wearing, but Dagon's body filled out the outfit differently than Varghrir had. He had big, bulky muscles like Zeke, and he was at least as tall as Luc, if not a little taller.

Maybe he wasn't as massive as the giant, but he was a big fucking boy, in his own right.

She could work with this, but she was afraid of what problems those beautifully menacing wings could pose to her plan. They looked powerful. Dangerous.

"Let's put away the wings for now," she requested. "Maybe I'll have you take them out later."

As fake Dagon folded his wings in, making them somehow disappear, she looked into those familiar red eyes, rousing memories of how she'd had her way with Dagon last night. A welcome surge of arousal flooded her core. Yes. She was ready to take him down now. *Dominate. Control. Own. Kill.*

...Kill. Why did she keep thinking that? Was she really going to kill him?

Did she have a choice?

She lifted her shackled hands and twisted Varghrir's shirt in her fists. As interested as she was in seeing what Dagon's body looked like, she didn't want to draw this out. This seduction wasn't for fun. If it were, she would've had him keep the wings out. She easily pulled him close to her, and she wasn't sure if he had allowed her to, or if she was still in possession of a little of Dagon's superstrength.

She rose to her tip-toes and whispered in his ear, "I want you to drink from my inner thigh." She wasn't fully certain *how* to steal Varghrir's powers as Dagon had suggested, but something told her that if she started with blood and reveled in her own pleasure, she'd have no problem making it happen.

Varghrir turned her around and shoved her chest against the wall and, to her chagrin, hooked the chain of her wrist shackles high on the wall, forcing her hands up above her head.

Shit. This is not how she planned this. But she would still dominate him. Somehow.

He tugged her leggings and underwear down to her calves, and she felt a sharp blade slice across the inside of her thigh, near the crease of her glutes. She inhaled sharply when his bearded mouth began to suck and lick at that sensitive spot so close to her center. Desire swelled and spread from her core like wildfire.

When the sound of Dagon's voice sensually moaning against her thigh graced her ears, it made her juices flow and her sex throb. She spread her legs a little wider, inviting Varghrir to venture into her erogenous zone. She felt the thick whiskers of his beard brush between her thighs, and his tongue dipped into her folds, his face buried between her thighs and ass cheeks. Her knees weakened as she bit her lip and moaned, and she clung to the chain on her wrist shackles for support.

He withdrew his tongue far too soon, and Eve growled in frustration. She scowled at him over her shoulder, feeling a strange, boiling rage building inside of her as though it were nested inside of an impending orgasm. Pleasure and rage in the same agitated bottle, just waiting for someone to pop the cork.

While Dagon…Varghrir…unfastened his pants, Eve took the opportunity to flip around, crossing one arm over the other so she could face him with her back against the wall.

"Hurry up and fuck me," she commanded. She needed to slake this violent, animalistic hunger between her thighs. It was driving her mad.

Varghrir shoved his pants down just far enough to release his aching manhood. When he pressed himself between her legs, she lifted her thigh to his hip, stretching the leggings around her ankles to the fabric's limits until they ripped in half, and she used her leg to pull him into her. She urged his pace as he filled her with his length, and as she rolled her hips, chasing that ragegasm, she felt that same rush of adrenaline that she'd felt with Dagon. A surge of energy that only served to fuel her fire.

"Harder," she demanded, wrapping her other leg around his waist to better control him. She rocked her hips and pulled him in with her legs, riding him harder and faster until the cork exploded from that bottle in her core.

She gasped and keened through a burst of wild ecstasy and violent fury. She had an uncontrollable impulse to crush Varghrir between her thighs as she crested the wave, coming down from the pleasure into the depths of pure, violent intent.

Dominate, Control. Own. Kill.

Kill.

She clenched her thighs tightly around him and yanked on the shackles above her head. The chain broke from the hook like it was made of cheap plaster.

"What the…!" were Varghrir's last words before Eve twisted the chain from her shackles around his neck, crushing his windpipe. She swung her body around, using the momentum of her movement to flip him onto the ground. She scrambled onto his back and continued to tighten the chain around his throat while she crushed his ribs with her suddenly preternaturally powerful thighs. He reached back and clawed at her face, catching her hair in his fist and yanking on it painfully. How was he not tearing it out? His other elbow jabbed up and struck her in the ribs. With the force he was capable of, her ribs should've shattered. But they didn't. His struggling was useless against her. She already knew she was more powerful than him now, in every way possible. She'd taken something from him that was more than just his specialties or powers – something intangible, but significant. She'd taken away his power *over her*. His strength was useless against her.

But she liked his struggle. It made this all the more exhilarating.

With one last strangled gargle, the chain tore gruesomely through Varghrir's neck, severing his handsome Dagon head from his shoulders. Varghrir was no more.

Now that it was done, Eve was racked with guilt and a deep sense of horror. She'd never killed anyone before. How the fuck had she just crushed a Jötunn – a *titan*? And why had she *liked* it?! What was with all that rage and desire for violence that had seized and compelled her in her aroused state? Was this something she was going to experience every time she had sex or gave blood from now on?

Fucking hell. She *was* a fucking monster.

She boxed up her worries and pushed them to the back of her mind. She had more pressing matters to attend to. She stood up and looked down at Varghrir, who had already shifted back to his original, humungous shape. She studied him, trying to memorize his form. If Dagon was right, she should have his powers.

Well, here goes nothing.

She imagined that she was changing into Varghrir. Her skin began to tingle and crawl like it was full of spiders, and her insides twisted and bulged as though she was having a sudden bout of bad gas. She looked down at her hands, and they were growing. The ground was getting further away, and her body was expanding. The shackles crumbled as her wrists and ankles outgrew them. She stopped the growth when she was at his more manageable size. She didn't need to be almost nine-feet tall.

She stole Varghrir's pants, since she'd torn hers in half, then, with surprising ease, she folded and arranged Varghrir's enormous, 800lb-plus body – and severed head – on the cot in the holding cell and covered him with the thin, prison-grade blanket provided. She wasn't sure how she knew this, but she was certain that she now had the power to create illusions. She imagined the scene she wanted, and instantly, she saw herself lying in bed, seemingly asleep, the shackles and chains intact.

She walked out of the cell and shut it behind her. All she had to do was walk up those stairs into the kitchen and go out the kitchen door. Then she could run. She was home free, she thought, as she ascended the stairs.

And maybe find a different pair of pants to take with her.

The door at the top of the stairs suddenly opened, and Ruthlys appeared. She was surprised to see Varghrir. "Oh! I was just coming down to tell you to turn the volume down on your stupid show. It sounded like someone was being murdered down there." She began to descend the stairs toward Eve.

Eve never checked to see if her voice would match Varghrir's, so she did her best to imitate his low, gravelly bass. "My apologies." She sounded just like him.

Ruth stopped her descent and looked at Eve suspiciously. "Well, we're being awfully polite all of a sudden."

"Fine. Fuck you, I guess, if that's what you prefer," Eve replied snidely. Varghrir had been crude and vulgar, so that was how she needed to behave.

"Ah, there he is." She patted Eve on the cheek. "Later, for sure."

Oh, no. No. Nope. Not doing that.

Ruth stood in front of Eve, and it was strange to be looking *down* at the tall woman, especially since she was on the step above Eve. Varghrir's height was dizzying.

Ruth shooed her hand at Eve. "Go on, back down the stairs. We need to check on our guest."

"She's sleeping," Eve supplied.

Ruth pushed on Eve's chest. "Come on, move."

Eve reluctantly turned and walked back down into the basement, Ruth following on her heels. Eve looked over at the cell, and she still saw herself lying in the bed. She hoped to hell that Ruth saw the same thing she did.

"She's been out a long time," Ruth remarked as she approached the cell. "I didn't take too much blood, I'm sure of it."

Eve grabbed Ruth's arm, stopping her from reaching up to unlock the door. "Let's let her sleep a little longer. She can't give us trouble if she's passed out."

Ruth looked down at the giant hand on her arm, then up into Eve's eyes. "Why are you touching me?"

Eve released Ruth as though she had suddenly burned her hand. "Sorry."

"You *can't* touch me unless I *let* you touch me. So how the fuck did you just touch me?!"

Fuck. Shit. Panic swelled in Eve's massive chest, and before she could come up with a coherent response, she sucker punched Ruth straight in the nose. Ruth's head snapped back and whacked into the bars on the holding cell with a resounding ring, and she crumpled to the floor.

Holy shit, she just killed Ruth. She killed Bo and Luc's little sister. The sad little girl with the pigtails who didn't inherit the eyes.

Eve dashed up the stairs. In a panicked rush, she returned to the white bedroom with the gossamer drapes and snatched a pair of sweatpants from the closet, then fled from the house. She ran out to the dirt road at the edge of the expansive grounds. She turned and looked at the majestic mountains in the distance. She needed to get home, but where the hell was she? If she had her phone, she could check her GPS, but it was back home sitting on the counter in her apartment.

She shrank back down to her normal size and changed into Ruth's stolen sweatpants. They were a little snug around the hips, but they were infinitely better than Varghrir's giant trousers. As she walked along the quiet, peaceful dirt road, admiring the gorgeous countryside, she was plagued by thoughts of what she'd done and what she was. She had *wanted* to kill Varghrir. *Craved* it, even. Was it normal to feel that way when having sex with someone you can't stand? She'd never experienced it before, and she'd slept with plenty of boyfriends she hated. But in those cases, she didn't enjoy it. There was no pleasure in that hatred.

And with Varghrir, it wasn't hatred. She didn't know him well enough or care about him enough to *hate* him. She greatly disliked him. Feared him. Was disgusted by him. Repulsed by him. But hate was a stronger emotion than what she felt for him.

The strangest part? She'd thoroughly enjoyed the experience when it was happening. It was animalistic and primitive, and deeply, deeply satisfying. She'd relished in both the pleasure and the rage. They had worked in tandem to elevate each other, growing and building upon the other, like two waves merging to create a greater amplitude.

But what drove her to want to kill him so badly? What exactly had Dagon unleashed within her? She'd literally rent Varghrir's head from his shoulders like it was nothing. Like it was *fun*.

Ruthie had a titan and his head popped off.

What if she felt that way the next time she slept with Luc? Or Zeke? What if she wanted to kill them? Nothing on God's green earth could've stopped her from killing Varghrir. Nothing short of complete incapacitation, anyway, as there wasn't a shred of hesitation or conscience involved. No voice of reason. No angel on her shoulder telling her that maybe she shouldn't. Just pure instinct.

Like a praying mantis or a black widow.

Yeesh. At least she didn't eat him.

As Eve treaded the seemingly endless dirt road, she saw a sight off in the distance that was familiar. It was a castle on a small island with a long, beautiful bridge connecting it to the mainland. She knew this castle. She'd done a painting of it once. What the hell was it called? She couldn't remember. But she remembered what country it was in.

She was in fucking *Scotland*.

Great. How the hell was this sassenach going to get home? Even if she got to a phone, she didn't actually know anyone's phone number by heart. It was all in her phone. She needed to get a hold of Dagon again and hope to hell he felt like helping her again.

She stepped off the road and lay in a thick patch of grass. She needed to try to sleep. *Dagon, I need you. Please come to me when I fall asleep,* she begged internally.

"Holy shit, are you praying to me?" Dagon's voice broke through her thoughts.

"What the fuck?!" Eve shouted out loud. "Is that you?!"

"It's me. And you aren't asleep?" Dagon laughed in her head. *"Well, this is new. I haven't heard a prayer in ages."*

"I wasn't praying, I was just thinking about you!"

"I like where this is going."

"Help me! I'm in fucking Scotland! Have Luc send the jet or something!"

"Did you escape? Where in Scotland? And you only need to think your response. No need to be ranting and raving aloud."

Eve replied silently that she had escaped, but she didn't go into detail. Instead, she described the castle she was looking at, trying to relay her position relative to it. Dagon didn't reply for so long that she thought she'd lost her connection to him.

Finally, he came back with, *"Luc is looking up the location. He'll come to you."* He then asked in a mildly concerned tone, *"Are you all right? You feel like you're in the middle of an existential crisis. Or is this how you always feel in here? It's so…angsty."*

"I just tore the head from a Jötunn, so, yeah, bit of a crisis," she replied sourly. *"You made me into something I don't even recognize. Something I don't want to be."*

"But look how powerful you are. And I hate to break it to you, but I didn't make you into this. I just plugged you into the charger and powered you on. The rest is all you, princess."

Luc suddenly appeared in front of Eve, and Dagon's voice disappeared.

7

Tell Me What You've Done

Eve's breath caught in her throat.

Luc.

She wanted to throw her arms around him and hide her face in his chest and let him fix everything. But he couldn't fix it. And neither could she.

Instead, she let the relief she felt at his presence wash over her before the reality of her situation could corrupt it. She pressed her forehead against his chest and gingerly slid her arms around his waist, afraid of crushing him with the titanic strength she'd stolen from Varghrir. His arms encircled her, squeezing her to him.

"You have no idea how glad I am to see you," she said, her voice muffled against his shirt.

"You have no idea how much I love hearing that," he crooned.

Eve's relief was short-lived as she realized she was going to have to tell him about everything she'd done and what she was. She would rather bite off her own tongue.

But it had to be done.

"Where is Ruth? Where were they keeping you?" Luc wanted to know.

Eve inhaled a shaky breath. "The house is back that way," she said, pointing. "But, as for Ruth and the Jötunn…they didn't make it."

Luc's big hands clasped Eve's shoulders as he pushed her back so he could look her in the face. His brows puckered above his sunglasses.

"Cryptic. Explain."

"I killed them."

Luc was floored. "You…killed them. You *killed* them?" He repeated the words as though it would be easier to believe with repetition. "*You* killed them?"

Eve scowled at him. "Yeah, *I* killed them. Frankly, your disbelief is a little insulting," she grumbled, crossing her arms.

"Take me to the house," Luc commanded.

"It's a long walk. You should probably just teleport there yourself."

"I just crossed from Nebraska to Scotland. I'm running a little low on warping juice at the moment."

Eve sighed. "I just walked all the way here. My feet are getting sore."

Luc stepped in front of her and crouched down onto his knee, his back to her. "Hop on," he instructed.

Eve climbed onto his broad back and threw her arms over his chest, wrapping her legs around him and crossing her ankles over his stomach. She froze as she remembered the murderous intent that had consumed her thoughts when she was hanging from Varghrir like this earlier today.

Luc hooked his arms under her legs and stood up. He winced. "Damn, what's with the vice-grip thighs? Relax, love."

"...This is how I killed Varghrir," Eve remarked.

Luc was given pause. "Say what now? You piggybacked someone to death?"

"The Jötunn. I crushed him between my legs and tore his head off with my shackle chains."

"Goddamn," Luc marveled, a mix of both pride and shock in his tone. He walked on a few paces before he asked, "Um, Eve, my love...not that I'm doubting you, but *how* did you manage that? Jötunn are essentially proto-gods. They are incredibly powerful."

"Didn't Dagon tell you anything?" Eve was hoping he would've shared everything with Luc that he'd shared with her about her powers.

Luc told her that Dagon had only relayed how she'd been kidnapped, some of her blood had been taken, and that she had a plan to escape. Dagon had made it sound as though he didn't know the details of the plan. And then when she'd been able to reach out to Dagon just now, all he'd relayed to Luc was the information about her location.

"That asshole. He was the one who came up with the plan in the first place!"

"And what *was* that plan? How did he know you could kill a goddamn titan?"

Eve took a deep breath and steeled herself. "I've learned a few things today, but there are still a lot of things I don't know. Apparently, if I am what Dagon says I am, I'm some kind of Abomination. Ruth told me she read about it in the grimoire – a close descendant of both Cain and Lilith. She said if I am the Abomination, it must be on my father's side, because my mother's family tree isn't anything special."

"She's not wrong. Your mother's side is as average as they come, according to Mira. Nothing of note in the lineage."

"She asked if I was adopted. I'm not, right?"

"Not as far as I'm aware."

"I don't look anything like my mom. She always told me it was because I looked like my father. She said he died when she was pregnant for me, but that's all she would ever say about him. She wouldn't even tell me his name."

"Huh. You *don't* look like anyone in your family," Luc remarked thoughtfully. "Not from what I've seen in your files, anyway."

"My files? That's not creepy at all."

"You're skirting the original question, though, Eve. Is there a reason you don't want to tell me about killing the Jötunn?"

Eve rested her chin on Luc's shoulder. "You're going to think differently of me when I tell you."

"There's nothing we can't work through, love. Just tell me."

"I stole his power and used it to kill him."

Luc swallowed hard. "How?"

"I don't want to tell you how," she said shamefully.

"Why?"

"Because I'm not proud of it, ok? Let's just say I had to get close to him."

Luc's tone hardened. "You had to seduce him," he guessed.

Eve let her silence confirm his conjecture.

Luc was silent for a long time. His pace had accelerated, and Eve could feel the tension in his muscles as he carried her on his back. He was fuming. Finally, he asked evenly, "And this was Dagon's plan? How did he know how to make that work?"

God, she didn't want to tell him this part. Guilt ripped through her guts and filled her with mud. "Because it worked with him."

Luc stopped. He asked icily, "What the fuck does that mean?"

Eve tried to wriggle free from Luc's back, but he tightened his grip on her legs.

"Where the fuck are you going?" he growled.

"Let me down."

"You still don't trust me."

"I don't trust your anger. Let me down."

Luc released her, and she slid down his back. When he turned to face her, she took two steps away from him.

"Tell me what you've done," Luc said in a measured tone, crossing his arms.

Bile rose in Eve's throat. She felt like vomiting. This is why she hated lying and keeping secrets. They always come to light, and it's never a gentle process. They rip and tear their way out, leaving a gaping hole and festering fissures - damage that would leave an ugly, irreparable scar on the relationship. The bigger the lie, the greater the damage.

It was time to rip it out before it could get any bigger.

"It all started with Zephlyn, actually. When I went to him to learn about clairvoyancy, he made a few cryptic comments about me being strange, and how he was getting lilim vibes from me. He made me uneasy. So, when Dagon was still visiting me in dreams, I asked him about it, because I know he can see monsters behind human faces. He made a deal with me that if I gave him some blood, he would tell me if I was a monster.

"He came to my room last night, using Zeke's body while Zeke was asleep. I let him drink my blood, and then…well…you know what it can lead to. But, something felt different that time. I wanted to dominate him. I felt powerful, energized. And that was when I discovered that I was suddenly stronger than Dagon. He was powerless against me. He couldn't use his strength or telekinesis against me. He was completely at my mercy.

"And afterward, all he would tell me was that I *was* a monster, and that I was something he'd never seen before. Something 'both ancient and new,' as he put it. I was in denial, though, even after I accidentally broke the towel ring in my bathroom and crushed a full bottle of juice from the fridge. And then when I Darth Vader Force-choked the juice jug, I convinced myself that it was a fluke.

"Then, today, when I passed out after Ruth drew vials of my blood, Dagon came to me in my sleep, saying that I summoned him. He told me he'd essentially awakened my power last night. Charged me up. And he suggested I use that power to take down Varghrir. So…I did. But it was much worse this time."

When Eve didn't continue, Luc echoed, "Worse?" He still stood with his arms crossed, unmoving, unflinching, the expression on his face blank and unchanging. Inscrutable.

"I *wanted* to kill Varghrir, with every fiber of my being. I felt *compelled* to. I didn't just want to dominate him. It wasn't just that I knew I had to kill him and did it to save myself. I killed him because I *wanted* to."

"And Ruth?"

"Ruth was an accident." Eve told Luc about shapeshifting into Varghrir and the unfortunate run-in with Ruth.

"Hm," was Luc's only reply. He turned and began to walk up the road again.

Eve followed along behind him, staring at his back. She'd let him down. It was like a knife in her gut.

"I'm sorry," she apologized. He barely spared her a glance. If there was one thing she hated more than an outburst of anger, it was the silent treatment. It was somehow more hurtful than a punch in the face, especially when she knew she deserved it.

She wanted to touch him, but she was afraid to. He might strike her. He might shove her. But, worst of all, he might pull away from her. She reached her hand out tentatively toward his, but she lost her nerve. She instead lifted it to her chest and rubbed her aching sternum.

It wasn't until they were almost back to the house that Luc finally broke his silence. While still walking ahead of her, he said, "You apologized, but what are you sorry for?"

She hesitated. Was he really asking that? "All of it," she replied.

"No, specifically. What *specifically* were you apologizing for?" His pace had slowed.

"I'm sorry for what I did with Dagon, and for hiding it. For hiding what I knew and suspected about what I am. For being a bitchface this morning. For being shitty to you. I'm always shitty to you." Eve crossed her arms self-consciously. "For killing your sister. Do I need to go on?"

The ice in Luc's voice finally began to crack. "I'm sorry I've made you feel like you still can't trust me. So much of this could've been avoided if only you'd trusted me enough to tell me what was going on. I would have gladly helped you find the answers to your questions if only you'd come to me. We could've run tests. We could've dug deeper into the lore. We could've utilized Vatican resources. What were you so afraid of that you thought you had to hide it from me? How is it that you could trust *Dagon* more than me?"

Eve looked at her feet through blurry tears. *Left, right, left, right, left, right...* This all could've been avoided if she'd just been a person of integrity instead of a deceitful shitbag.

"I didn't *trust* Dagon," she corrected quietly. "I was just less afraid of what *he* would think of me if I was a monster. I figured he would be more accepting of it, but even if he wasn't, his opinion didn't matter as much to me."

"You kept all of this from me because you were afraid I wouldn't *accept* you?" Luc finally stopped and turned to face her. He snatched his sunglasses from his face and pinned her with an outraged stare. "Is that really who you think I am?"

"It isn't about who you are. It's about who I am. And after today, I'm more convinced than ever that my fears aren't unfounded." Eve averted her eyes. "I *am* a fucking monster, Luc. I felt it. There's something dark and terrifying inside of me."

Luc studied her while she avoided his gaze. "Eve."

"What?" She looked at his feet.

"I know my size fourteens are rather impressive, but please. My eyes are up here, love." His jesting tone caught her by surprise, and she glanced up at him. He graced her with a sad but earnest smile. "There's nothing we can't work through," he repeated. "I can be very forgiving when I choose to be. But no more secrets. You need to be honest and forthcoming with me if we're going to figure out how to fix this."

"What if it's something that can't be fixed?"

"We'll figure something out." Luc held his hand out to her. "But I fucking mean it: no more secrets, Eve. Deal?"

"No more secrets. I swear." Eve accepted his hand, and Luc brought it up to his lips and kissed the back of her hand.

She felt as though she'd just been cleansed of all her sins, and the sun was once again shining on her face. But deep down, she knew she was unworthy of his forgiveness.

Luc held her hand and they began toward the house again. "Quick aside," he said casually, "if anything were to happen and you went all Carrie on us, do you feel like a silver knife dipped in lamb's blood would do the trick? Or are we talking more of a wooden stake to the heart situation?"

Eve looked up at him in horror.

"Oh, relax, I'm kidding," he laughed easily.

"That's not funny!" Eve fumed.

Luc gave her an amused side eye. "Come on, it was a little funny. No need to rip my head off."

Eve gasped in disgust at him. "Are you fucking kidding me?" She tried to yank her hand from his, but he squeezed harder.

"That was the last one, I swear. Now calm down. We need to go collect my little sister's body, burn a Jötunn, and locate Lilith's grimoire. Lots to do before the car arrives to take us to the airport." He pulled his phone from his pocket and looked down at it. "The jet is on its way now."

Sometimes she forgot what a psychopath he could be.

Luc and Eve quietly entered the house. Eve hadn't seen or heard anyone else while she was there, but it was better to be prepared for anything. Eve pointed Luc to the basement, and they slowly descended the stairs.

"What the fuck?" Luc whispered, looking at the holding cell. Eve looked past him, and saw herself lying on the cot. The illusion she'd cast was still active.

"Oh, that was me. Hold on." Eve imagined the illusion dissipating, and there lay the monstrous Jötunn on a broken cot. It must have collapsed under his weight.

Luc turned and looked at Eve with an insulted expression. "You mean to tell me that you still had these powers and you couldn't morph into a horse and giddyup us both here in a quarter of the time it took us to walk it?"

"I'm not morphing into a horse!"

"Well not now, obviously! But good grief. So unimaginative!"

"Wait." Eve grabbed Luc's sleeve. Her blood ran cold when she saw the empty floor in front of the holding cell. "Ruth. She's gone!"

8

She Wanted to Tattoo Her Name on His Forehead

Eve pointed at the floor where Ruth had been. "She was right there when I left!"

"So...not dead. Or undead... Which begs the question, where the hell *is* she?" Luc whispered suspiciously, looking around quickly.

They searched the house, but Ruth was gone. And so was the grimoire, and the vials of Eve's blood. Yet again, she had slipped through their fingers.

They returned to the basement to dispose of Varghrir's body. Luc looked down at the monstrous, decapitated corpse. "We're going to have to do this in chunks."

"I can probably still lift him," Eve offered.

Luc pointed at the body and raised a brow at her in disbelief. "Him?!"

"Who do you think put him there? He was on the floor when I killed him." Eve grabbed Varghrir's leg and tugged at it, dragging him across the floor of the cell with ease.

"Well, fuck me," Luc gaped.

"I think it's only temporary, though, so we should probably get moving. He already feels a little heavier to me than he did when I moved him earlier," Eve said. She picked up Varghrir's head by the hair and handed it to Luc. "You can carry this."

He grabbed it and dangled the enormous gourd in front of his face, marveling at the sheer size of it. "Careful, Eve. You're giving me a big head."

"Of all the head jokes you could've made, you went with something clean? That's weird."

"Can't make heads or tails of it?"

"Maybe I spoke too soon. It's coming, isn't it?"

"That's what she said." Luc snickered adolescently at his own joke, then used the head to gesture toward the stairs. "Enough jokes. Grab the headless Norseman and let's head out."

Sometimes he was debonair, and sometimes he was…this. There was no in-between with him.

As Eve maneuvered Varghrir's body out of the cell, Luc noticed the television on the wall. It was no longer playing Viking shows, but was once again showing Eve's apartment.

"Dagon told me you said something about cameras in your apartment. Did she say how long she's been watching you? Or who put them up?"

"She said it's been a couple of days. She didn't explicitly tell me who, but she did imply that Dagon had something to do with it. He denies it, of course."

"That doesn't make sense. Why would Dagon want to help her if she wants to enslave him?"

"I think she promised him bodily autonomy. She claims she can now pull Dagon from Zeke and he won't need a vessel. He can have his own body back," Eve revealed.

Luc halted and put his fist to his hip, Varghrir's head dangling and bumping off of Luc's leg. His other hand rubbed his chin. "He would find that tempting. But why would he help you escape and help us find you?"

"Maybe he's playing both sides," Eve suggested.

"A double agent," Luc supplied.

"Or maybe we have it all wrong."

"A frame job..."

"Or maybe this *is* part of Ruth's plan, and he's just playing his part."

"A mole..."

"Stop doing that, or I'm going to make you drag this mountain up the stairs," Eve said.

Luc looked her straight in the face and whispered, "An ultimatum..." Before Eve could respond in irritation, Luc went on to say, "Dagon has always been on the Do Not Trust list, but this doesn't feel like his brand of deceit. He doesn't follow orders. The only reason he half-assed helps us is because we have Zeke to suppress and somewhat control him, and also because Dagon and I have come to an understanding...in that he understands I will destroy him if he breaks contract. And even then, it took us months to get him to the table to negotiate. How would Ruth get to him and make a deal like this without us knowing? Was he dreamwalking in her head, too?"

Eve began to drag Varghrir up the stairs. "Don't forget, he was able to communicate with me telepathically today when I wasn't asleep. He made it sound like it was because I prayed to him or something. What if Ruth was praying to him, and it forged the same kind of connection?"

"*Did* you pray to him?"

"Not what I would've called it, but I was trying to reach out to him." Eve grunted as she got Varghrir wedged in the doorway at the top of the stairs.

"Huh." Luc raised his free hand and altered the space around Varghrir so he could pass through, then said, "Still, something doesn't taste right. You know what seems more likely? Dagon using us and Ruth against each other as pawns in his own master plan. One that benefits only him."

Luc was right. That did sound like the most likely scenario.

They took Varghrir around the back of the house, and Eve dropped him in an old garden plot. Luc tossed the giant's head onto the body and then pulled an unfamiliar phone out of his pocket.

"With any luck, this can get us some answers and help point us in the right direction," he said, indicating the device.

"Whose is that?"

"Ruth's, I'm assuming. Maybe the giant's. I found it when we were searching the house."

"What if she left that purposely, knowing we would take it?" Eve postulated.

"Possible, but I don't see any hexes on it. Even if she did plan for us to take it, what is she going to get from that? She already knows where the compound is; she already has cameras inside your apartment and who knows where else; and she already has a mole. At least with this, we may be able to get some information about her and whether her mole is Dagon or someone else. Celeste will be able to discern if there's any tomfoolery or intentional misdirection involved in the data."

"*Tomfoolery*. Listen to you."

"Might not want to listen to this, though," Luc advised as he held his hand out toward Varghrir. "Cover your ears, love," Luc instructed. "And maybe take a few steps back."

When she was clear, with her ears covered, lightning streaked from Luc's hand and struck Varghrir's corpse. Eve had to close her eyes to the bright flashes. He continued the thunderous assault until the giant was completely fried, burned to ash.

Luc stuck his hands in his pockets and inhaled deeply. "Woo! Smell that ozone. I haven't let loose like that in a while. That was refreshing." He sauntered up to Eve and draped his arm around her shoulder. "Is there any greater bonding experience than disposing of a body together?"

"You got me there."

He booped her nose with his finger. "I knew there was a cute little psychopath in there." A satisfied smile spread across his face as he looked at the ash pile in the overgrown garden. "This was nice. We should do it again sometime." He then rubbed his hands together. "Now, let's check you for hexes."

His eyes scanned every inch of her skin, lifting her shirt and lowering her sweatpants as he circled her. He was enjoying it entirely too much, and her flesh was growing hot under his gaze.

Before Luc could turn his inspection into anything more, however, a car came rambling up the dirt road. Eve and Luc went back around the house and met it out front.

On the way to the airport, Luc was glued to his phone.

"What are you doing?" Eve asked.

"Working."

"Knighco work or empire work?"

Luc looked up from his phone. "Empire work?"

"The family business."

He chuckled. "Fagerberg Enterprises. But no. I'm doing Eve business. We need to get as much information as we can on whatever an Abomination is. Sister Fiona should be able to help point us in the right direction on that. If it's truly what Ruth says it is, the Blood of Eve and the Blood of Lilith, the Vatican should have sources on it. And I'm having Mira prepare the lab for some tests. There are some things I want to check."

"Like what?"

Luc waved his hand dismissively, then extended his arm across the back of the seat behind her back. "Just let me worry about all that." He pulled her closer to his side.

Tucked safely under his arm like that, confidence and competence radiating from him, Eve found it tempting to believe that he could fix everything. That was what he did – he was a problem solver.

When Eve and Luc stepped off the jet at the airport near the compound, the team was there waiting for them.

Zeke rushed to Eve, but before he reached her, Luc intercepted him, clamping his large hand down over Zeke's forehead and stopping him in his tracks. Luc murmured an incantation in a language Eve didn't understand, perhaps Latin, and Zeke's eyes briefly flashed an incandescent blue. When Luc removed his hand, Zeke blinked and shook his head. Dagon had been sealed away.

"What was that for? He was helping!" Zeke griped.

"He can't be trusted," Luc replied gruffly.

"If it weren't for him, we wouldn't be bringing her home right now!"

"He could be the reason she was taken in the first place. He can't be trusted," Luc repeated.

Zeke glowered at Luc, then turned his attention to Eve. His face brightened, and he smiled so warmly at her that it could've melted ice. He threw his arms around her and lifted her off the ground.

"I'm not letting you out of my sight again," Zeke pledged. "You scared the shit out of me."

She felt a pat on the top of her head when Zeke released her from his embrace. "Glad you're safe," Eoduun said reservedly.

Eve glanced around, seeking out Bo. He was a little off from everyone else, standing stoically with his hands in his pockets. When he saw Eve looking at him, the corners of his heterochrome eyes crinkled in a hidden smile. Eve broke away from Zeke and Eoduun to go to Bo.

She didn't run to him, but she may have walked a little faster than usual. She didn't slow as she approached, either. She just crashed straight into his chest and threw her arms around him, sending him backward a few steps. He chuckled warmly and hugged her tightly, cradling her head against his chest with his hand.

"I'm sorry," he whispered. "That shouldn't have happened on my watch. I won't let you down again," he promised.

Eve mumbled against his chest, "I thought I was only under your watch when Luc isn't home."

"You're always under my watch."

"Every breath I take, every move I make?" she teased.

"Better fucking believe it."

"It wasn't your fault, Bo. I should've seen through that Jötunn's deception. It wasn't even a good mimic, looking back on it. He acted nothing like Luc. My spidey-senses were tingling, and I ignored them. That was on me."

Luc appeared next to Eve. He began to guide her away from Bo's embrace. "We all fumbled this time. It won't happen again." He sheltered her under his arm and walked her away from the team and toward the car waiting nearby. He opened the passenger door for her and held her hand as she lowered herself into the seat. Bo, Zeke, and Eoduun followed along and climbed into the car with her.

"I'm going to jump back to the compound and make sure Mira has the lab ready," Luc told her. Then, to Bo, he instructed, "Bring her to the lab when you get back. We've got work to do."

The ride home was full of questions from Zeke and Eoduun in the back seat, but Bo was silent. Eve left out a lot of details, but she did reveal that she was discovering new powers, and was able to take out the Jötunn in order to escape. They didn't need to know the specifics just yet. Especially Bo. She would've done just about anything to delay him finding out just how much of a monster she was.

She told them why she and Luc were so wary of Dagon, without revealing the part where she'd fucked him. She told them that Ruth had implied that he was somehow assisting or supporting her efforts, and that he may have been the one to put the cameras up in Eve's apartment.

Zeke was dubious of the accusations, but he conceded that it was, even if remotely, not *completely* outside the realm of possibilities.

When they arrived at the compound garage, Bo sent Zeke and Eoduun to fetch the bug sweeper from the tactical department and remove all the cameras from Eve's apartment while he brought Eve to the lab for tests.

Eve walked into the lab with Bo, and she found Mira with her hand in Luc's hair.

Instant rage.

"Stop touching him," Eve blurted unexpectedly. She hadn't meant to say it out loud.

Mira turned and smirked at Eve, then finished fixing Luc's hair. "You brought him back in such a disheveled state, Miss Alarie," she chastised. "It sounds like you made quite a mess for him."

Fury burned in Eve's chest and throat and flushed her cheeks and ears. She wanted to snap every finger on Mira's hand for touching him. And Luc. She wanted to rip his hair out for allowing it.

"Nonsense," Luc said to Mira, but his eyes were on Eve. He smiled at Eve. "I think the experience brought us closer together, don't you, love?" He gestured her over to him.

She gladly crossed the room and stood between him and Mira. She quickly surveyed the tall, svelte woman. Skinny arms. Narrow waist. Toned, long, thin legs. Breakable.

I could take her.

Eve started imagining how she would attack Mira if she ever had to fight her. Legs first; that would be Mira's weak spot. Look at those frail little knees. One swift roundhouse, or a powerful side kick, then, when she went down, a good stomp for good measure. Break her kneecaps.

"Eve?" Luc's voice cut into her thoughts.

She snapped back to attention. "Hm?"

"Open your mouth," Mira instructed impatiently. She was holding a long cotton swab. Eve opened her mouth, and as Mira was about to swab the inside of her cheek, she paused. "Your mouth is clean, right? No, uh, *other* kinds of DNA in here, right?"

Eve's nostrils flared, and she fought the urge to spit right in her face. "Should be clean as a fucking whistle, doc. I didn't eat the Jötunn I murdered today."

Mira raised an eyebrow at her, then swabbed her mouth. "Now, go sit down. I need to take blood."

When Mira jabbed the needle into Eve's arm, Eve got the distinct feeling that she missed the vein the first three times on purpose.

"Ah, there it is," Mira sing-songed when she finally got blood. "You need to drink more water and take better care of yourself. You're quite dehydrated."

"I'll be sure to take that under advisement, doc."

"Please don't call me 'doc.' I'm not your doctor," Mira said in annoyance.

"Huh. You don't say."

Mira looked at Luc for backup, but Luc only smiled and shrugged. If Eve wasn't mistaken, Luc was enjoying the hissing and claws. And probably more so knowing it was all over him.

Eve shouldn't care. She should just let Mira have him. But she did care, and she wouldn't. She wanted to tattoo her name on his forehead.

Jesus, had her jealousy gotten *worse*?

"This will do for now," Mira said. "I may need some other samples later, but this is a start. Oh, one more thing." She reached out and plucked a single hair from Eve's head.

"Ouch!"

Mira smirked. "Ok, now we're done. Off you pop." She waved her hand dismissively at Eve.

As Eve started toward the door where Bo was waiting for her with an amused expression in his eyes, she turned to look at Luc. "Aren't you coming?"

Mira answered for him. "Oh, no, I need him for a bit longer. You just go on ahead without him. I promise I'll take good care of him and send him back to you when I'm finished."

Eve glared at Luc, but he only smiled and shrugged. Then he held his hand upright and flipped it back and forth like Beyonce in the "Single Ladies" dance.

"If you liked it then you should have put a ring on it…"

She narrowed her eyes at him, then left in a jealous huff, Bo trailing along behind her, exhaling a deep sigh as he shoved his hands in his pockets.

9

Eve et Alia

"Are you ever going to just give him the satisfaction?" Bo asked as they traversed the grounds toward the apartment complex.

"I'm not putting a goddamn ring on it."

Bo chuckled. "He doesn't need a ring. He just needs you."

"I don't know. I feel like I've gotten to a point now where admitting I like him means admitting defeat."

"It's obvious you like him. You've already lost."

"No, I lose when he's certain he's caught me."

"Hasn't he, though?" Bo perceived.

"Not yet."

"*Yet*? So, you do expect him to."

"Dammit, Bo, stop that."

He held his hands up defensively. "Hey, I just call it like I see it."

"It's complicated. Especially now. I just...don't know."

When they approached Eve's apartment, they could hear Zeke and Eoduun inside talking about the lack of food in the cupboards and fridge. She stepped through the door and kicked her shoes off, and Bo followed suit. She walked into the kitchen and found Zeke standing on the counter, scanning something that looked like a studfinder along the top of the cupboards. There was a black bag sitting in the middle of the kitchen island.

"Do you know how many of these we should expect to find?" Eoduun asked Eve, taking a tiny black device out of the bag and holding it up.

"I don't know for sure, but from what I saw, there was one in the kitchen, bedroom, bathroom, and living room."

"We still haven't found the kitchen one, but we got the other three, then."

Eve summoned up the image of the spy camera footage she saw in Ruth's basement, trying to figure out where the camera was pointing from. It had to be somewhere between belly and chest height, and it was between the fridge and stove.

She lifted the wire cooking utensil holder, and there was the tiny camera, affixed to the bottom, peeking out from underneath it.

"Got it," she announced, throwing it in the bag on the counter.

Zeke jumped down off the counter. "Did you know your towel holder in the bathroom fell off the wall?" he asked her. "And you're *really* out of food."

"Thanks. I'm aware," Eve said with a heavy sigh.

"Do you want us to run to the store for you?" Zeke offered.

"How about you boys do that," Bo suggested, "and I'll fix the towel hanger. Evie, you go relax for a bit."

"Roger that. We got you, li'l mama," Zeke said as he walked by Eve and squeezed her shoulders. Eoduun ruffled her hair as he followed Zeke past her, then turned his head back to give her a little grin, winking one of his onyx eyes at her.

After the boys left, Eve flopped onto the couch and laid her head back on the armrest. She listened to Bo reinstalling her towel hanger in the bathroom using the tools he found in the cupboard next to the stacked washer and dryer unit near the entryway. She'd never had friends like this. She wasn't used to people taking care of her. She wasn't used to people being good to her.

She didn't deserve it. She didn't deserve them. She didn't understand why they cared so much about her. She had no right to their kindness.

Bo came out of the bathroom and sat on the other end of the couch by her feet. She pointed her toe so she could poke his leg with it. He stretched his arm across the back of the couch and looked down at her.

"Thanks," she said.

"Eh, it was nothing," he replied, patting Eve's shin.

She sat up and flipped positions on the couch, lying on her back with her head on Bo's leg. She looked up at him, then reached up and tugged his mask down so she could see his handsome face. He lifted one corner of his mouth in a crooked grin.

"You look tired," she noticed.

"I'm flattered," he replied sarcastically.

"I'm not saying you look like shit," she laughed. "I just mean you look like you've had a long day."

"We all have, haven't we?"

"Luc doesn't look any worse for the wear."

"You didn't see him when we realized you were gone. I'm not sure which was worse – when he thought you willingly ran from us, from *him*, or when Dagon told Zeke that you had been kidnapped by Ruth and a Jötunn."

Eve was consumed by guilt. "I was going to run. At least, I was thinking about it, before I was taken."

"But we don't have to worry about that now, right? You realize that we don't care *what* you are, don't you?"

"You might care when we find out more about what I am," Eve countered.

"Evie, I don't care if you're the fucking devil incarnate. You're *our* devil, and you belong with us. Don't you dare try to leave us."

"Well, I don't think I'm the *devil*," she mused.

"Sometimes I wonder." When she narrowed her eyes at him, he gave her a wry smile, and it drew a smile from her own lips. She liked the way he smiled, and the way his big canines showed. She so rarely got to see his beautifully-shaped lips and gleaming teeth, and the way his nostrils flared when he grinned.

"I like when you have your mask down," she said softly, gazing up at him.

"I don't."

Eve pouted, reaching up to lift it back over his face, but he intercepted her hand and pushed it away.

"But if you like it, it's fine. I don't mind it as much around you."

"Good. Because your face is one of my favorite things, and it makes me feel special when I get to see it." Eve sat up, intending to rise from the couch to go take a quick shower, but when she turned to look at Bo, she saw the deep blush coloring his cheeks and ears. She hadn't meant to embarrass him. She would normally pick on him for blushing, but she didn't this time. She didn't want to discourage him from being maskless around her.

Besides, it was cute.

In the shower, Eve scrubbed between her legs as though cleaning herself well enough would cleanse the memory of her encounter with Varghrir from her mind. She wanted to cleanse that sin from her soiled soul. She wanted to cleave off that part of herself and cast it into a raging fire.

She thought about Dagon as she washed her hair. She understood why Luc had sealed him away for now, but she wanted to talk to him. She didn't trust him, but he was the only other entity on the entire planet that she wasn't afraid to talk to about what she'd done, and how she'd felt when she'd done it. She'd told Luc because she had to, but she wanted to discuss it in depth with someone without feeling ashamed of it. She didn't know how to work through this on her own, or if she even could.

But she needed to. She couldn't spend the rest of her life terrified of sex.

When she stepped out of the bathroom, the enticing scent of fresh pizza tickled her nostrils, and she saw a large pizza box sitting on the kitchen counter. Cassie, Ruger, and Remi were all lounging in the living room with Bo. Bo had returned his mask to its usual position over his face.

Cassie jumped up and sashayed over to Eve, throwing her strong arms around her and squeezing the daylights out of her. "I am so glad you're home safe, hon," Cassie said. "We wanted to thank you for saving Ruger yesterday, and for fixing up my leg, too, but then with everything that happened today on top of it, we thought you deserved pizza and beer, at the very least."

"Oh, hell yeah," Eve replied appreciatively. "Thanks!"

As Eve went to the kitchen to serve herself a slice and get a beer from the fridge, she heard Zeke's voice from the hallway. "Do I smell pizza? Somebody has pizza."

The boys walked into the apartment accompanied by the sound of rustling plastic grocery bags.

"You know, Luc really needs to rethink his compound design," Eoduun complained. "It is such a pain in the ass to haul groceries all the way from the garage to the apartments."

"Dude, just drop the bags off at the front door, then go park the car," Ruger suggested from the couch.

"*We* have the pizza!" Zeke exclaimed when he spied the pizza box on the counter. He rushed to the kitchen, deposited his grocery bags on the floor, and opened the box.

Cassie cleared her throat. "Ahem, *Eve* has the pizza," she corrected him.

Zeke looked at Cassie, then gave Eve pleading puppy dog eyes. If she hesitated any longer, she was afraid he would drool.

"Go ahead," Eve consented.

"Sweet, thanks!"

Eoduun brought his grocery bags into the kitchen and plopped them on the counter by the fridge. "Hey, me too, right?"

"Yes, you too," she sighed.

Zeke began putting groceries away with one hand while he ate a slice of pizza with the other. Eoduun simply grabbed a slice and left the kitchen without putting away any of his groceries. When Cassie saw Eve starting to put away groceries with Zeke, she stepped in.

"You go eat. I'll finish this."

Eve took her pizza and snuck under Zeke's arm to snag a beer from the fridge, then went out to the living room. Bo and Ruger sat on either side of the couch, and Remi was in the recliner. And Eoduun, unsurprisingly, was sitting on the floor with his back pressed against the front of the couch in the empty space between Bo and Ruger. He had the remote in his hand, browsing Netflix. Eve climbed over the back of the couch, trying not to spill her beer, and flopped onto the empty cushion behind Eoduun. She crisscrossed her legs.

While Ruger and Remi carried on their conversation with Bo, Eoduun reclined back and rested his head on Eve's legs, his dark locks spilling over her calves. He looked up at her. "What do you want to watch?"

"I wanted to watch you put your groceries away."

"Uh, *your* groceries."

"Who is going to eat them all? Who's been eating them all? Not just me."

"…Touché," he conceded. "So, what do you want to watch?" he repeated, unfazed, staring up at her with a blank affect.

"It doesn't matter. Whatever."

Eoduun turned on some murder documentary, and after he shoved the last bite of his pizza in his mouth, he reached back and grabbed Eve's legs. He uncrossed them and pulled them down around him, so that her thighs were under his armpits and her ankles were crossed over his stomach. He folded his hands together over the top of her shins, holding her in place. Her toes were dangling dangerously close to his crotch.

"Play with my hair," he demanded.

"Don't tell me what to fucking do," Eve complained as she raked her fingers into his long, silky strands.

From her peripheral vision, Eve saw Bo giving Eoduun a narrowed, sideways glance.

Ruger had taken notice as well. "Why the hell are you sitting on the floor, dude?" he asked.

"We don't allow him on the furniture," Eve jested.

"I'm comfortable," Eoduun replied simply, his eyes closed as Eve's fingers brushed over his scalp.

"Wait until you're my age, kid," Ruger said, scratching his stubbly chin. "As soon as you hit thirty-five, your back will remember every minute of that floor sitting."

Cassie came out of the kitchen and dropped onto Ruger's lap. "It wasn't floor sitting that fucked up your back," she said. "Being thrown around and beat up by monsters probably had more to do with it."

"You shut your mouth. I've never been beat up by a monster. Ever. Didn't happen." He glanced at Eve, who had an eyebrow raised at him, and amended, "*Bit*. Ok? I did get *bit*. Thank you for fixing me up, by the way. But I was not beat up. Totally different."

Remi chimed in, "Remember that time you got thrown through a plate glass window for hustling some dudes in a game of pool? That might've had something to do with your aching back, too. Just maybe."

Cassie added, "Or what about the time you fell off the top of your car when you were drunk and trying to be 'king of the world'?"

"Or the time you tried to steal that dirt bike from that vamp nest we cleared in Ohio, and you promptly wiped out and flew into a tree like a ragdoll?"

"Uh, excuse me," Ruger argued, "I think you mean I Evel Knievel'd the *hell* out of a sweet ass jump, but failed to stick the landing. Admit it, it was glorious. Totally worth it."

"You broke five ribs, broke your arm and your hand, cracked your eye socket, dislocated your shoulder, and needed like a bajillion stitches," Cassie reproached him.

"Worth it," Ruger repeated. "And you guys are only proving my point. My back was fucked up by poor life choices, not by monsters. Like I said, I don't get beaten up by monsters."

Luc's voice suddenly spoke from the open doorway. "Why is it that every time I come to see Eve, I find Eve *et alia*?"

Everyone turned to look at him as he sauntered into the apartment.

"Eve Italian?" Zeke asked around a big mouthful of pizza as he came out of the kitchen. He walked into the living room and looked around for a place to sit.

"No, Z, not 'Italian,'" Luc replied, but didn't explain further. Luc stood behind the couch and leaned over Eve, his hands gripping the back of the couch on either side of her shoulders. Eve leaned back to look up at him, and he bent down and planted a kiss on her slightly parted lips.

From her angle beneath him, she could see his eyes from underneath his sunglasses as he stood back up. He was casting a stern look at Eoduun, seated so comfortably between Eve's legs while her fingers combed through his hair.

Zeke saw Cassie perched on Ruger's lap, so he popped over to Bo and climbed onto his lap, knowing full-well that he wouldn't be welcome.

"What the fuck, Z," Bo protested.

"Come on, Daddy, everybody else is doing it," Zeke whined jokingly, throwing his arms around Bo's neck.

"For fuck's sake," Bo grumbled, shoving Zeke off his lap. Zeke exaggeratedly rolled to floor and cried out dramatically.

"Ow, rude!" he complained, then just lay on the floor where he'd fallen. He looked imploringly over at Remi, who was seated alone in the recliner.

"Fuck off, dude," was Remi's answer.

"Aw," Zeke pouted.

Eve giggled at his idiotic antics.

Bo stood up. "Well, I'm going to head to my own apartment for the night." He clapped Luc on the shoulder. "Settle in, little brother. Enjoy," he said sarcastically.

"Goodnight, Bo," Eve called to him.

"Night, Evie."

Luc took over Bo's seat next to Eve, and she perceived a distinct aura of prickliness emanating from him. He fixed his gaze on her legs around Eoduun and her hands in his hair as though staring hard enough at him would make Eoduun disappear.

"Eve, we need some girl time one of these days," Cassie suggested from Ruger's lap. "Just you and me, without all this testosterone hovering around us."

"I, too, would like to have a girls' night, Eve," Luc said. "It's been forever since we've painted our nails and dished about boys. You could spend the night and we could have a pillow fight in our panties."

Cassie snorted at Luc. "Why can I actually picture you doing that?" she laughed.

"He probably *has* done that," Zeke said from the floor.

Luc bumped his sunglasses down his nose so he could look at Eve with earnest aquamarine eyes. "I may need to borrow a pair of your panties for the pillow fight. All of mine are in the wash."

She removed one hand from Eoduun's hair so she could shove Luc's shoulder playfully. He caught her hand in his and interlaced his fingers in hers, holding it captive. He kissed the back of her hand and then held it against his thigh, refusing to let her return her fingers to Eoduun's hair.

"Why don't you come sit in my lap so Zeke doesn't have to lay on the floor," Luc suggested to Eve. Zeke sat up, but before he could say a word, Luc held a finger up at him. "No."

"Why does no one want me in their lap?" Zeke pouted jokingly.

Eve began to untangle her legs from around Eoduun. He squeezed her legs tighter with his arms, but she pulled free anyway. He grumbled in protest, but said nothing.

As Eve sat curled in Luc's lap, she could feel irritation practically seeping from his pores. He was doing a good job of hiding it and engaging with everyone affably enough, but the longer they hung around, the tenser he got.

When she got up to go put the leftover pizza in the fridge, Luc followed her into the kitchen. He helped her briefly, and as she was closing the fridge, he snatched her. He leaned back against the kitchen counter, out of sight of the living room, and pulled Eve to him, his legs caging her in on either side, his arms like a steel trap around her waist.

"When am I going to have you to myself?" he wondered. "I have something I'd like to discuss with you, privately."

Eve reached up and slid his sunglasses from his face so she could see his eyes. They gazed back at her ravenously, lingering on her lips, dipping down to her neck and chest, then back to her eyes.

"Is it sex? It's sex, isn't it?" she asked knowingly.

"It's sex."

"I thought it was sex." Thinking about being with Luc again filled her belly with a lustful heat, but she was apprehensive. What if she lost control and wanted to hurt him?

"But there is something else I want to talk about, too. A few things, actually," he said ominously.

"Like what?"

"Like *us*. We need to talk about *us*, love. It's time."

10

We're Not Feeling Murdery Yet, Right?

Eve's heart leapt up and lodged itself firmly in her throat. She dropped her eyes to his chest. "I don't know if now is the best time for this," she said apprehensively.

"It needs to be now. I'm done waiting, love. I don't even know why you're making me wait at this point. You love me. I love you. We go well together. There's no reason for you to keep pretending this thing isn't happening."

"I don't know, Luc."

"Don't turn me down," he commanded firmly.

"Excuse me?"

"You have no reason to turn me down. I'm quite certain that you're in love with me."

"How can you say that with such confidence?"

"Am I wrong?"

Eve sputtered, looking for a way to argue without lying, but coming up with nothing.

"I'm not wrong," Luc answered his own question. "It's your love I require, Eve. I have never been more sure of anything in my life. I love you, and I need you. I've known it from the first day I laid eyes on you." He bent down and kissed Eve tenderly, then looked into her eyes. "I'm staking my claim. No more games, no more hedging, no more dipping a toe in the pool. I'm pulling you into the deep end with me."

"You make it sound like I don't have a choice."

"You've already decided you want to keep me. You just need a little push." He leaned in again, and she inhaled his scent as his lips brushed against her ear. His voice was low and simmering. "Tell me I'm wrong."

She loved him. There was no denying it. Even if he scared the hell out of her, she was terrified to let him slip through her fingers. She would be destroyed if he broke her heart, but what good did it do her to keep prolonging her inevitable fall? Hell, she'd already fallen. She couldn't resist, even if she was playing with fire. She needed to just jump in and pray that he would catch her.

…But what if he didn't catch her?

And what about Zeke and Eoduun? And Bo? The entire team dynamic would change if she accepted Luc's proposal. She had strong feelings for Zeke. Shit, she even had feelings for Eoduun. How was she supposed to just cast them aside now?

As quickly as she had begun to find her resolve, it was gone again. She wanted to be sure of Luc, but she wasn't ready to go all in. She wasn't ready to lose what she had with Zeke and Eoduun. She just wasn't ready to put all of her eggs in Luc's basket.

"So, what, you want to be my boyfriend or something?" Eve asked.

"I've been your boyfriend this whole time. I just want you to officially acknowledge that you're my girlfriend."

"You're just a little bit arrogant and egotistical, you know that?" Eve said with an amused tone.

"It's been brought to my attention once or twice." He cupped her face in his hand. "Are you going to acknowledge it? That you're my girlfriend?"

Eve gazed into those hypnotic blue eyes. She didn't want to see disappointment in them. She wished he had his sunglasses on right now.

"I can't."

Luc sighed and leaned his head back in resignation. It almost seemed as though he was expecting that answer. "Can I ask why?"

"I'm not ready."

"Elaborate," he requested.

Eve chewed her lip and avoided his gaze. "I'm not prepared to lose what I have right now. I'm not ready for things to change."

"You don't want to be tied to just me," he surmised. "You have feelings for Zeke."

Eve didn't respond.

"That doesn't mean you can't be my girlfriend."

Eve met his steady gaze. "Elaborate," she said.

"If you're not ready to commit to just me, so be it. I know I'm gone a lot. I know you like Zeke, and you seem to be warming up to Eoduun. But I need something. I'm not asking you to be exclusive with me. I simply want…priority."

"You want to be the Ruger to my Cassie," she murmured.

"I'm not asking you to marry me. If you hate it, you can back out at any time." When Eve still hesitated, he said, "Just think on it. But for tonight, I want you to myself." He didn't leave room for argument.

Cassie yelled from the living room, interrupting the conversation. "Well, hon, I think we're going to split! Thanks for letting us hang out!"

Eve broke free from Luc's arms and stepped out of the kitchen to see Team Flannel off. Cassie hugged her on her way out, vowing that they were definitely going to have a girls' night soon. Eve hoped they would.

After Team Flannel left, Luc suggested to Zeke and Eoduun that they might want to let Eve get some rest, and they took their cue to leave, somewhat begrudgingly. They knew what Luc really wanted, and it wasn't for Eve to rest.

Luc closed and locked the door behind the boys, then turned to Eve. "Finally," he sighed, giving her a suggestive smile.

"Luc, wait," she protested as he stalked toward her.

"I've been waiting for *days*, love," he complained as he approached her. He scooped her up, and she wrapped her legs around his waist and locked her arms around his neck.

"There's something we need to talk about before we do anything," she disclosed timidly.

"What's on your mind?"

"A lot. But mostly, I'm afraid of hurting you."

"Why would you hurt me?" Luc puzzled.

"Because of what happened with Varghrir."

"The Jötunn?"

Eve nodded. "What if I get that overpowering urge to hurt you?" Then she added in a whisper, "To kill you?"

"Yeah, that wouldn't be ideal."

"Maybe we should wait to find out more about what's wrong with me before we have sex again," Eve proposed.

Luc gazed at her contemplatively. "Do you love me, Eve?"

She felt her cheeks burn under his searching gaze, but she didn't respond.

He didn't require an answer. "You won't kill me."

"You can't know that."

"I do know it," he asserted. He carried her toward her bedroom. "But just to be safe, we'll take it slow, ok? And if you feel any kind of homicidal itch, just tell me, and we'll stop. Simple enough."

"But what if I take your powers?"

"Take them. What's mine is yours, love," Luc said in a sugary tone.

"You don't mean that."

"I wouldn't say it if I didn't."

"You'd have to be insane to give me that kind of power."

Luc carried her to her bed and laid her down on it. He supported himself on his hands and knees above her, looking down at her. "Are you under some delusion that I'm sane? I've never claimed to be anything so boring."

Luc devoured any further protests, crushing his lips over hers, tying up her tongue with his. His large palms pressed against hers, his long fingers intertwining with hers and holding her hands down against the mattress. He lowered his hips between her legs, and Eve felt his impressive bulge grinding against her core. She squeezed her thighs around him.

"Easy, love," he whispered against her lips. "Don't crush me just yet."

She let her legs fall slack to the mattress, his gentle reminder scaring her.

"No, it's ok," he assured her. He freed one of his hands from hers so he could slide it down her thigh, encouraging her to return her legs to his hips. "I only meant to let off a little. Don't be afraid. You're not going to hurt me, remember? I'm already under your spell. You don't need to dominate and crush me."

Eve raised her free hand to Luc's handsome face, running her palm along his sharp jawline. She looked up into his beautiful eyes. Instead of an urge to dominate, control, and own him, she simply felt her heart swell.

She slid her hand around to the nape of his neck and pulled his mouth back down to hers, moaning desperately against his lips. The warm ache in her chest was spreading to her throat and welling up in her eyes. She undulated her body beneath him, rolling her pelvis against his bulge. A fire was spreading through her body that thirsted urgently for his touch.

Luc answered her pleading motions with a hungry groan and a slow, hard thrust of his hips against hers. He moved his kisses to her jawline, then gently nipped and sucked at her neck while his hand slipped between their bodies and plunged under the waistband of her shorts and panties. She mewled when his fingers stroked her drenched petals, then pushed inside of her. She clenched her walls around his long, thick fingers, reveling in the sensation of having him inside of her, even if it was only his hand. He cupped his palm over her mound and rocked it against her as he fucked her with his fingers.

When Luc freed her other hand, she took the opportunity to pull at the buttons on his shirt, but her fingers fumbled clumsily with them. "Take it off, Luc," she panted, shamelessly grinding against his hand.

Luc raised himself up and looked down at her, supporting his weight on one hand while he continued his ministrations between her legs with the other. "You take it off. And don't worry – buttons can be sewn back on," he replied with a sultry smile.

Eve didn't hesitate. Buttons flew as she tore his shirt open, revealing his hard, defined pectorals and abs. She spread her fingers over his chest and lightly squeezed the firm flesh. She allowed her hands to wander slowly down his ribs and abs, feeling the delicious ridges of his hipbones and obliques. Her fingers followed the tapering edge of his obliques to the waistband of his slacks. She tugged at his belt, then the button and fly. Finally, she plunged her hand into his pants and wrapped her fingers around his hard shaft, drawing a deep, sensual groan from him. The soft, velvety skin was stretched so taught around his engorged erection that it hardly moved with her hand as she stroked him.

"You must've really missed me," she mused, her voice low and raspy with desire.

Luc quickened his pace with his hand between her legs, and she bit her lip and whimpered over the building pressure in her core.

"You're one to talk," he replied. "I know you didn't want to admit it, but it's fairly obvious you missed me, too."

She released her grip on him and moved to push down her shorts. He pulled his hand from between her legs and helped her out of her clothes. She lay naked beneath him, taking in the view as he shrugged out of his shirt. He had muscles and ridges and dips and bumps in all the right places, and as she ran her hands over his body, she couldn't help but think he looked like he'd been sculpted by Michelangelo. Corny, but true.

As soon as he had pushed his pants down, unleashing the monster in his boxers, Eve pulled him down to her and rolled them both over, landing him on his back. She needed his flesh in her mouth.

He looked up at her desirously, but there was a hint of anxiety in his eyes. As Eve dipped her head down to suck and lick at his thick neck, running her tongue over the contours of his throat, Luc's voice vibrated against her mouth.

"We're not feeling murdery yet, right?" he inquired.

She reached down and curled her fingers around his cock while she sucked on his neck. "You're safe," she murmured against his skin. She kissed her way down his chest, stroking him as she grew closer to her target.

She settled her body between his legs and looked up at him as her lips trailed over the hollow between his thigh and pelvis. He had his hands folded behind his head, propped up on the pillow, gazing in eager anticipation down at her. When she dragged her soft, wet tongue over his testicles, he bit his lower lip and moaned. She sucked and licked them briefly while she jerked him, then ran her tongue from the base of his shaft all the way to the tip. She took him into her mouth.

Luc jerked his hips forward, his hand suddenly raking into her hair. "Fuck, Eve," he praised, his voice strained.

His response to her was like gasoline on a flame. She devoured him hungrily, taking him as deep as she could, then backing off to run her tongue over the sensitive tip. She continued enthusiastically, drinking in every gasp, sigh, pant, and moan she drew from him, until she brought him right to the precipice.

"Stop, you're going to make me come," he moaned, his hand clenching the hair at her scalp.

She ignored him and kept going.

"Eve," he panted, then groaned loudly. He thrust his hips as he expanded and swelled in her mouth, spilling his drink onto her tongue and down the back of her throat.

Eve let some of it run from her tongue down his shaft, and she swallowed the rest. She sat up and wiped her mouth on the back of her hand, then climbed back up and lay on top of him, chest to chest.

"Goddamn, love," he mumbled, looking up at her with a lazy smile. "I want to be mad because now I need a minute before I can fuck you, but how the hell can I be mad after that?"

Eve rested her chin in her hand and grinned coquettishly down at Luc. "Well, whatever shall we do while we wait?"

Luc chuckled low in his throat and rolled her onto her back. He gazed ravenously at her naked body beneath him and licked his lips. "Oh, I know exactly what we'll do."

He hooked his hands behind Eve's knees and flipped her legs up, giving him unimpeded access to her core. His tongue dipped into her soaking need. She'd been hanging on the verge ever since he'd fucked her with his fingers, so his hot tongue lapping and wiggling over that sensitive bundle of nerves was like a hammer coming down, igniting the blast that flung her into wild, euphoric oblivion.

She keened and moaned as she bunched the sheets in her fists and rocked her hips against Luc's mouth. He moaned against her spasming core, reaching one hand down to stroke himself. He lifted his head, his hand still on his cock, and looked down at her with wild, predatory eyes.

Eve saw the wind had returned to his sails, his mast throbbing, swollen to full capacity once again. He brought one of her legs up against his chest, resting her calf on his shoulder, and he pressed her other thigh down into the mattress, opening her to him as he plunged his thick cock into her slick sheath.

He leaned forward, taking full advantage of Eve's flexibility, and dominated her mouth with his while he sank deep inside of her. Eve wrapped one arm around his neck and buried her other hand into his hair, holding him tightly to her. She moaned against his lips and gyrated her hips, intoxicated by the way he filled her.

She was still riding the tailwind of the first orgasm as Luc worked to arouse another. As it began to build, the pleasant ache intensifying with every slow, deep pump, Eve felt a sweet ache swelling in her chest as well. She clung to Luc and kissed him deeply, wanting nothing more than to devour him. Not crush him, not dominate him, not own him. Devour him, so she could keep him inside of her forever.

As she teetered on the edge of ecstasy, she moved her lips to his ear and whispered the words she'd been absolutely terrified to say.

"I love you, Luc."

Her confession was immediately followed by her gasping moans as she came even harder than she had the first time.

Luc was right behind her, pounding into her hard and deep, spilling into her with a heavy, panting groan. His breath was hot and heavy in her ear as he came down, and it sent decadent shivers down her spine as she rode out the last little waves of her pleasure.

Luc let Eve's leg slip down from his shoulder, and he propped himself up on his elbow. Eve still had her arm around his neck, clinging to him, not ready to relinquish him just yet.

His eyes were full of warm adoration as he gazed down at her. "You have no idea how badly I've been needing to hear you say that," Luc confessed. He snaked his arms around her and squeezed her body against his, his face buried in her hair. "I love you more than I've ever loved anything, Eve." Then, as an afterthought, he added, "Oh, and thanks for not killing me."

Eve stroked his hair, holding him tightly as endorphins flooded her system. How had she fallen so hard? When did it happen? It felt like she'd always been madly in love with him. She'd been fighting it for so long, but he was like quicksand. The more she struggled against him, the deeper she sank. There was no escaping him.

He turned his face toward her, his body still lying on top of hers. "How do you feel?" he asked, gazing at her softly.

Like I want you to stay right here forever. "Fine. No murderous urges."

"Can you bend space with your eyes?"

She shook her head, already knowing that this encounter hadn't been anything like it was with Dagon or Varghrir. "I didn't take anything from you. It was just sex."

Luc winced. "*Just* sex? Wow, you know how to make a man feel special, love." He looked like she'd truly hurt his feelings. It wasn't a face she was used to seeing on him. Vulnerable.

"That's not how I meant it," she apologized, caressing his cheek. "I just meant it didn't feel like I stole anything from you. It just felt...uncorrupted. The way it's supposed to feel."

"How does it feel when it's corrupted?" he wondered.

"Violent. Rageful. Like I'm being dosed with adrenaline and transforming from Dr. Jekyll to Mr. Hyde." Eve was contemplative for a moment. "I wonder if whatever Dagon did to awaken these powers has worn off."

Luc's eyes darkened and the energy in the room shifted. Eve's ears felt like they were going to pop under the pressure. Luc said evenly, "That's the last thing I want to be thinking about right now. Dagon *awakening* you."

"It'll never happen again. I don't even want that kind of power," Eve assured him.

"Those powers may have saved your life. At the very least, they bought you your freedom. But there must be another way for you to gain access to them, because I *will not* share you with *him*," Luc seethed. "Dagon is off-limits."

Eve couldn't help but feel a little indignant. "Don't insinuate that I *want* Dagon. And don't even think about trying to put down rules about *sharing* me," she snapped.

Luc rolled off of her and lay on his side, facing her. "I'm not insinuating that you *want* Dagon, and this has nothing to do with jealousy. We both know I have reason to be concerned. I'm afraid you underestimate how dangerous he is, and I'm letting you know that I'm not comfortable with you having relations with him," Luc replied cooly. "I will do whatever I must to keep you happy, but I won't go so far as to let you put yourself in danger."

"You would do anything for love, but you won't do that?" she said sarcastically.

"Precisely, Meat Loaf. I know I have Bo keeping you safe when I'm gone, but I can't help but worry about you. You're like a danger magnet."

"You could always just take me with you when you go," Eve pointed out.

"I wish I could be that selfish. No, you're needed here. You've already saved lives with your blood, and you will continue to do so. You'd be wasting your time and talents following me around. Not to mention, you'd be spending half your time on the jet, bored, playing catch up, since I can't physically take another person with me when I jump. Or you'd be sitting alone in a hotel room waiting for me to get out of meetings, or watching me sit all night staring at my laptop or hunched over a stack of contracts, blueprints, bureaucratic red tape, and whatever else my father doesn't want to deal with."

"Well, damn. You make it sound like such fun. Too bad I didn't steal your powers so I could just jump with you," Eve chuckled.

Luc was thoughtful. "When you steal someone's powers, do they lose their ability to use them?"

"I think they lose their ability to use them against *me*, but I don't think they lose them outright. I think I just gain the ability to use them."

"Huh. So, in theory, it is possible that we could jump together someday. That would be fucking stellar."

"I think you're forgetting that Bo *also* has the same power you have, and even *he* can't do what you can with it. I doubt I would be able to master it. Plus, it's temporary. My Jötunn powers have already pretty much faded."

"Hm."

Luc lay silent for a long time, and Eve realized that he'd fallen asleep. She untangled herself from his heavy arms, covered him up with her blankets, and slipped into some pajamas before heading to the bathroom. She was tired, but she had too much on her mind to sleep. She went out and shut off the lights in the apartment, then padded into the kitchen in the dark and opened the fridge. She looked at some of the things the boys had stocked in her fridge. Bologna. Pickles. Beer. Cheese. Energy drinks. Lunchmeat. Coffee creamer? She didn't even use creamer in her coffee.

Bo knew that. Apparently the boys didn't.

As Eve retrieved a slice of cold pizza and sat at the kitchen island to eat it in the dark, she reflected on her relationship with Luc.

Why did he love her? Why did he want her to love him so badly? It made no sense. Maybe she wasn't terrible to look at, but she was essentially hot garbage as a person. Honestly, why did *any* of them care about her? She still wasn't fully convinced that this wasn't some cruel joke that was snowballing straight toward a devastating punchline.

What she wouldn't give to dive into Luc's head and see exactly what he was thinking.

…Holy shit, she could do that. She *could* do that! Potentially. Hell, she'd done it with Eoduun, and Luc said he could work with her to help develop her mind meld skills. If she got into his head, she would finally know what his fucking obsession was all about. She would finally know what he *really* thought of her, without question.

She stopped chewing the last bite of pizza in her mouth. What if she found things in his head that she *didn't* want to see? Specifically, his memories of fucking Mira. How he felt when he was plowing into her.

Her jealousy raged at the thought, and she felt an overwhelming urge to go and wake him up and claim him again.

As though on cue, Luc yelled groggily from the bedroom. "Hey! Where the hell did you go?"

She heard him shuffling around in the bedroom for a moment, and then he appeared in the doorway in his boxers. He ran his fingers through his messy, platinum hair as he made his way to the kitchen. Eve admired his long, toned legs and shapely calves. That narrow waist and those sharp hipbone ridges. Those chiseled abs and round, firm pecs. Those broad shoulders and strong arms. That thick, sinewy neck. That finely crafted face and those delicious full lips, curled into a sleepy smile.

And those transfixing eyes, holding her gaze.

The whole goddamn platinum membership package.

She wasn't this lucky. She was never this lucky. She'd thought it before, and she thought it again now: Girls like her don't get men like him, and this is why she doesn't trust his feelings for her. Something is terribly wrong here.

11

Against My Better Judgement

He stepped up to her, and she looked up at him from the barstool at the kitchen island. He cupped her face in his hands and planted a sweet kiss on her forehead.

"Refueling for round two?" he asked as he turned and opened the fridge. He withdrew one of the energy drinks the boys had left in there and started reading the label with a grimace on his face.

"Funny you should ask," she responded. "I was just thinking about coming in there and taking advantage of you in your comatose state, but you woke up and thwarted my plans."

He chuckled and tossed the unopened energy drink into the garbage can under the sink, then grabbed a glass and filled it with water from the tap.

"Why did you throw that drink away?!" Eve protested.

"'Drink' is being generous. Gross. You shouldn't drink that shit."

"I didn't plan to, but Zeke and Eoduun bought that, and they probably would've drank it."

"Then I saved them the trouble. Seriously. No one should drink that shit."

"You're making me want to dig it out of the trash and drink it."

Luc lowered the water glass from his lips and stared at her, an intrigued expression on his face. "Is that so? Because I said you shouldn't?"

"Because you had no right to throw it away and tell me what I should or shouldn't be putting into my body," Eve retorted.

He set the water glass down and crossed his arms, leaning back against the counter like he was settling in for a good bicker. "Well, I think I have a *little* right to *suggest* to you what you shouldn't be putting into your body. And I have some great suggestions for what you *should* be putting into your body."

She squinted at him. "Are you trying to turn this into something dirty?"

"*Me? Never.*"

Eve rolled her eyes and stood up. She walked around the kitchen island and used her hip to nudge him out of the way of the sink so she could wash the pizza grease from her hands. "Don't throw anything else away, got it? This is my space. My things. My rules."

"Queen of the castle, hm?"

"Fucking right," she confirmed as she dried her hands. She turned around and leaned over the kitchen island to reach for the napkin she'd left wadded up, intending to grab it and throw it away.

Before Eve reached it, however, she felt Luc's body behind her. He placed his palms on the counter on either side of her, looming over her back. His triceps and forearms flexed as he leaned forward slightly, his body hovering mere millimeters from hers, the heat from him seeping through her pajamas to her skin. His lips brushed her ear as he challenged in a low, seductive voice, "Does that make me your king?"

Eve's insides exploded with butterflies, and burning desire zinged from her chest to her toes. Her knees were jelly.

He leaned his hips into her, and she felt him growing hard against her ass. He slowly snaked one hand up the front of her shirt, splaying his huge hand over her firm belly and pulling her back against him. It never ceased to surprise her at how small she felt in those hands. He slid his hand further up, stopping momentarily to fondle her breasts, then continued up until his hand poked out from the collar of her shirt, and he wrapped his fingers around her throat and jaw. He held her firmly against him, turning her head to the side so he could devour a hungry kiss from her lips.

He smiled against her lips. "It's good to be king," he mumbled. He removed his hand from her shirt and turned her around to face him. He looked down at her with a lustful expression. He lifted her butt up onto the kitchen island, and she wrapped her legs around his hips.

Then she paused, looking down at the counter. "Wait, not here." She scooted over about a foot, guiding Luc along with her with her legs.

"What was wrong with where we were?"

"That's Bo's spot. You can't fuck me in Bo's spot," she informed him.

An unmistakable flash of white-hot jealousy crossed Luc's face. Eve saw it. But as soon as it appeared, it was gone.

He arched a brow at her. "I'll fuck you wherever I want to fuck you," he growled. He gripped her hair and pulled her mouth to his, dominating her tongue rapaciously.

She squeezed her thighs around him and rolled her pelvis forward against the enormous bulge jutting from his boxers. She hooked her arms around his neck and tugged him down with her as she leaned back onto the counter.

"You're jealous of Bo's spot?" Eve prodded him when his lips moved down to her neck.

"Whatever. He can have his spot at your table as long as I get you," he grumbled against her throat. He nipped her tender skin and Eve hissed through her teeth. His soft tongue quickly soothed the bite, and she knew by the way it felt that he hadn't bitten hard enough to draw blood.

"Why does it bother you?" She couldn't leave it alone. It was such a weird thing to be jealous of.

Luc whispered, "Please stop talking about my brother when I'm trying to fuck you." He pulled away from her and tugged her pajama shorts off of her. He lowered his boxers and rubbed the head of his hard cock against her slit. "Focus on me," he commanded as he slid into her.

Eve closed her eyes and arched her back as he filled her. God, she loved the way he felt inside her, like he was made just for her. She felt his hand grasp her jaw, and she opened her eyes and looked up at his handsome face.

"I said focus on me, love. Don't close your eyes. Stay with me," he implored.

"There's nowhere else I'd rather be," she assured him. She reached up and caressed the side of his face, gently rubbing her thumb around the shell of his ear. She ran her hand down the side of his neck, feeling every muscle tense and release as he thrust into her slowly, deeply. She let her eyes wander down his body so she could watch his obliques flex and press against her thighs as he buried himself into her. Her hands followed her gaze, and she dug her fingers into his hips to help guide his pace.

Damn, he looked good fucking her.

He leaned down and overtook her mouth again, kissing her possessively. His hand covered her breast, gently massaging it, then lightly pinched the bud of her nipple. She moaned into his mouth.

"I don't care if they all have a seat at the table. As long as they know it's *my fucking table*," Luc murmured against her lips.

Eve gathered that she was the "table," but she was too focused on the pleasure mounting in her core to reprimand him for comparing her to furniture.

"Oh, fuck, Luc, just like that," she moaned as he hit just the right spot with just the right pace and pressure. He was loving her slowly, hard and deep, the friction of his pelvis rubbing against her clit pleasurably as she gyrated her hips. She kept a tight grip on his hips to make sure he kept it up exactly how she wanted it.

Her moans started as she felt the oncoming wave, building in crescendo with her swelling pleasure, until she was panting and keening, clinging to him for dear life as she unraveled for him. Again.

He moaned in her ear as she came, his cock swelling inside of her, but he didn't spill just yet. "Mmm, god, Eve. I fucking love it when you come," he crooned.

As she was catching her breath, Luc grabbed her leg and guided her over onto her belly on the counter in a bent-over position with her toes barely grazing the floor. He entered her from behind and hoisted her thighs up around his hips, holding her to him like a wheel-barrow with her feet off the ground. She wrapped her legs around him, her calves pressing against his firm ass and the back of his thighs as he rammed into her, chasing his own release.

He gripped her hips and fucked her hard, taking all the abuse of the hard countertop on his own knuckles instead of her hipbones. She turned her head to look at him behind her. His eyes were focused intently on where the two of them were joined, watching himself slam into her. When he caught her looking at him, he bit his lip, holding her gaze as he expanded inside of her. His brows cinched and he gasped and groaned, coming with hard, brutal thrusts. Even though she'd already come, watching him orgasm made her insides tremble and tingle.

He rested his hands on the counter on either side of her, then dropped down to his elbows. "Goddamn," he panted, satisfied. He brushed Eve's hair aside and kissed the side of her neck. He reached over her shoulder and traced his fingers along her jawline as he whispered into her ear, "I don't know if you are aware of this, but you've completely ruined me, Evrys Alarie."

She turned her head to look back at him. She didn't believe it for a minute, but, looking into those gorgeous aqua orbs staring back so affectionately at her, she desperately wanted to.

"Don't call me that. I hate my full name," she complained, twisting beneath him to escape. His seemingly heartfelt confessions always aroused her suspicions and made her want to change the subject, to back away slowly and put some large obstacle between them.

She picked her shorts and underwear up off the floor and stepped into them as Luc pulled his boxers back up. She started to walk away to go after the wadded-up napkin she'd been reaching for when all of this started.

"No, not this time. You don't get to do this anymore," he said firmly. He reached out and halted her escape, pulling her against him and trapping her in his embrace. "You don't get to wiggle your way out of the pillow talk and avoid the 'I love you's.' I've earned it. I need to hear it, and so do you." He leaned back slightly and looked down at her, and she up at him. "I love you, Eve," he said sweetly.

She gazed up into his beautiful face, his hair dangling messily around his eyes. Like snowflakes drifting over ice.

Embarrassingly, her eyes moistened and her throat thickened. She cleared her throat and dropped her gaze to his lips. She swallowed hard, then flicked her eyes back up to meet his. "You'd better fucking mean it," she whispered.

He sighed heavily and squeezed her to him. "Have you ever known me to say something I don't mean?"

She wrapped her arms around his naked torso and pressed her cheek against his chest. Luc always meant what he said, but Eve never said what she meant. But he was right. He'd earned it. And if he needed to hear it, she needed to say it.

After all, she *did* mean it. As much as she'd tried to deny it, she did.

"I love you, too," she sighed. "Against my better judgement."

Luc chuckled. "You try so hard not to, but resistance is futile. I'm just that goddamn lovable. I'm glad you've finally accepted your fate."

"Do you ever *not* get what you want?" Eve wondered.

Luc hummed. "You've given me a run for my money."

"I wonder what that's like, getting everything you want."

"No need to wonder. Tell me what you want, I'll make it happen. Whatever you want, I want."

Eve tightened her arms around him. Whatever spell he'd cast over her, it had seeped into every pore and penetrated to her very soul. She was doomed.

12
Evil Doesn't Worry About Being Evil

Eve awoke in her bedroom a few hours later to Luc climbing out of bed. She glanced at the clock. 5AM. What the hell was with these Fagerberg boys and their inability to sleep in?

Luc walked around the bed, the light from his phone screen illuminating his face. He was pensive.

"What's up?" Eve asked groggily.

"I'll be right back." Luc quickly got dressed in his clothes from yesterday, put on his sunglasses, and disappeared.

Luc's troubled tone made Eve uneasy, and she couldn't fall back to sleep. While she awaited his return, she took a quick shower and got dressed for the day.

It would be almost another hour before Bo showed up with her coffee. Or would he? With Luc home, would Bo still make his usual morning delivery? She wasn't sure she could start her day if she didn't hear him call *"Ohayou"* from the entryway. It was their ritual.

She decided to finally break in the coffee maker on the counter, and while she waited for it to perc, she wiped down the kitchen island. Luc's voice startled her as she was finishing up.

"Cleaning up the evidence?" he asked.

She jerked her head in the direction of his voice. He was changed into a fresh outfit, business casual, per usual. He had two coffee cups in his hand. He walked into the kitchen and slid one cup across the cleaned countertop toward her.

"I got you a cappuccino. I hope French Vanilla is ok," he said.

"Oh, thanks," she replied. She reached for the cup and held it in her hand, but she didn't take a sip. She liked cappuccino, but not first thing in the morning. It was always too blazing hot to drink. She glanced over at the coffee pot on the counter, just finishing brewing, and wondered if it would be rude to pour herself a cup of black coffee. Probably.

"So where did you have to run off to at the ass crack of dawn?" she inquired, sitting in her usual spot at the kitchen island.

Luc sighed. "Well...I had to call Sister Fiona. She sent me an email this morning."

"Is everything ok?"

"Uh...it will be." He came to Eve and kissed her on top of the head. "Nothing for you to worry about."

Eve frowned up at him. A knot was twisting in her chest. "What's going on?"

Luc looked momentarily conflicted, like he wasn't sure he wanted to tell her, and the knot tightened. "We've been summoned. To Rome. Sister Fiona has concerns about what they've interpreted as 'the Abomination' in some of the texts in the Vatican archives. I'm sure it's an overreaction. It often is."

"What do you mean 'we've been summoned'? Who is we? And what kind of concerns do they have?"

"She indicated that she wanted you and me both to go, but I'm going alone, just in case they…overreact. Mira went behind my back and sent them some of her preliminary findings from your bloodwork, and it's just…it's a lot of unknowns at this point. Unknowns make the whole institution nervous."

Eve's stomach was in her feet. "That makes *me* nervous," she fretted. "What the fuck do they think I am?!"

"Uh…" Luc chuckled cynically. "Evil?"

"What the fuck?!" Eve jumped up from her seat.

Luc wrapped her in his arms, refusing to relent against her squirms. "It will be ok, love, I promise. I will meet with them. I know you aren't evil, and Sister Fiona trusts and listens to me. I just need to calm them down. Once their fears are assuaged, all will be well again."

"How are you going to convince them that I'm not evil? Even I'm not so sure of that anymore…" The memory of decapitating Varghrir with her shackle chains flashed through her mind's eye.

"You aren't evil. Evil doesn't worry about being evil."

"Not true. There are serial killers who are afraid of their own horrific urges, afraid that they are evil. And plenty of people would argue that they *are* evil."

Luc released Eve from his embrace so he could cup her face in his hands. He stooped down and kissed her forehead, then looked into her eyes from over top his sunglasses. "You aren't evil, love. And they can't possibly make that determination from some ancient texts and inconclusive lab results. They don't know you. I do." Luc stood up straight again, then sighed heavily. "But there is something else we need to talk about. Since I'll be leaving today, it's rather pressing."

"'But wait, there's more!'" Eve quoted cynically. "There goes the other shoe."

"No, just listen to what I have to say before you freak out, ok? Here, sit down." Luc guided her back to her barstool. He sat down in Bo's seat. He ran his hand through his hair and inhaled deeply, then exhaled loudly.

"I stopped by Zeke's apartment this morning to have a little chat with Dagon."

"I thought he was sealed," Eve interrupted.

"He is, but I can bypass it to communicate with him. Zeke was still asleep, so he has no idea yet. Anyway, I had some questions for him after reading Sister Fiona's email. He still wasn't particularly helpful, but he did confirm that whatever Lilithian power he awakened in you, it's still there. It isn't something that fades or goes away. It's hungry, and it will need to feed. And it's something you'll need to learn to control if you want to utilize it properly."

"It's *hungry*?! Learn to *utilize* it?! Jesus, you sound like Dexter talking about his 'dark passenger.' I don't want that power, Luc. I don't want to learn how to use it. It scares the hell out of me!"

"Do you want to control it, or do you want it to control you?" Luc reasoned. "Eve, no other specialty I've ever heard of can steal the powers of someone else. It may take a bit of experimenting and training to figure it out, but I'm confident you can learn how to control it."

"Specialty? More like a curse, Luc. No. I don't want to experiment. You want me to have sex for training? That's kind of fucked up."

Luc sighed. "Do you have a better method? And it's not just for training. Like I said, whatever has been awakened inside of you, whatever this urge is, it needs to be fed."

"With sex," Eve supplied.

"With sex," Luc confirmed. "Lilith's power, the kind of power you're harboring, is, at its core, singularly sexual in nature. You won't be able to deny that part of you now that her blood is no longer dormant in your veins."

"And if I don't indulge?"

He shrugged. "We don't know, but there's a possibility you could become unhinged. Dangerous. Feral. Honestly, I'd rather it never get to that point."

"But what if I hurt someone while training?"

"You didn't hurt Dagon when you stole his powers, did you?"

"I wanted to."

"I don't think you're going to hurt us."

"Us?"

"Me and Zeke. And Eoduun, too, I guess, if things between you and him are the way they seem."

"You didn't mention Bo," she remarked.

"No, I didn't."

"Why?"

"Should I have? Are you just dying to *experiment* with my brother?"

"No," Eve said defensively. "It's just that he leads a lot of my training."

"Not this training." Luc pinned her with a suspicious stare before saying, "This isn't his brand of biscuits. He doesn't share. He is possessive. If you start fucking him, even just for training, he will need you to be his, and it will eat him alive if you aren't. If I'm being honest, I worry he already has an unhealthy attachment and possessiveness toward you, especially after I made him sleep with you to protect you from Dagon."

If Eve was being honest, she also had an unhealthy attachment to Bo, and Luc's revelation did nothing to dissuade it. In the back of her mind, she wondered what a "possessive Bo" would look like, and something inside of her stirred.

Something that yearned to see that side of him.

13

Does It Matter If You're a Little Monstrous?

There was a light knock on the door, then Bo walked in. "*Ohayou,*" he called out. He sounded cheerful, but not as cheerful as usual. How much had he heard?

Regardless, his voice comforted Eve, and when he walked into the kitchen holding two cups of coffee, she smiled at him. "Ah, Daddy delivered," she teased, holding her hands out for the coffee. When he handed it to her, she said, "*Arigatou,*" and took a sip.

Black. Strong. Hot, but cool enough to sip without burning her lip. Perfect.

Bo eyed the cappuccino next to her that she'd forgotten about. "I've been beaten to the punch?"

Shit. Eve grabbed the cappuccino and took a sip of that, as well. She didn't want Luc to feel badly. "It's just a double-fisted drink kind of morning," she said.

It was only then that she noticed the irritated expression on Luc's face. Even hiding behind his sunglasses, she could see the barely contained jealousy.

'I don't do jealousy' my ass.

Bo rested his forearms on the counter and looked at Luc. "You need to get Evie some more barstools," he remarked.

Luc smiled hollowly. "Ah, yes, I'm in your spot, aren't I, *Daddy*?" he said tauntingly. He made no move to stand.

Fuck. Eve reached out and rested her hand on Luc's forearm. "Stop. It's a joke. Zeke and Eoduun say it, too."

"But he only likes it when you say it," Luc replied, his eyes still on Bo. "If he had a tail, it'd be wagging."

Eve's anger swelled instantly. She wanted to slap Luc, but she thought better of it. Instead, she grabbed his jaw roughly and yanked his face toward hers. His eyebrows shot up in surprise.

"*Stop it*," she seethed. "If you want to be an asshole to someone, be an asshole to me, because I'm the one who's actually pissing you off. Not him."

Air puffed angrily from Luc's flared nostrils, and he had a tense stare-down with her. If he'd raised his hand or moved suddenly, she knew she would've flinched, but she fronted as hard as she could. His expression began to soften. "My apologies," Luc said to Eve. He took her hand from his jaw and kissed the back of her fingers. "You aren't pissing me off. It's just not been my favorite morning, and by rights, it should've been." When Eve frowned in confusion, he explained, "Because you've finally confessed your love for me."

Did she see Bo's eye flash yellow just now? Eve glanced over at him, but she was greeted by aqua-blue and charcoal. Maybe she'd imagined it.

Luc continued, "And instead, I wake up to a whole can of worms dumped in my lap. You can hardly blame a guy for being on edge."

"I'm not blaming you for being on edge," Eve replied. "But that was something else. You can't talk about *sharing* me and then act like that over something so trivial."

"You and I have different interpretations of 'trivial.'"

Bo took an uncomfortable step back from the kitchen and scratched the back of his head. "Yeah, I think I'm going to come back later."

"No. Go fetch Eoduun and Z," Luc commanded. "We need to have a team meeting. A very awkward, uncomfortable one. It'll be a riot."

"As you wish, your highness," Bo said reproachfully as he turned and left.

"What the fuck, Luc," Eve confronted him as soon as Bo was out the door. "You want me to carry on with Z and Eoduun, yet you lose your damn mind over a joke with Bo?"

"It isn't the *joke*. It's the *bond*."

Eve scrunched her nose. "Uh, what?"

"I'm not worried about casual sex with Zeke and Eoduun. I mean, around here, that kind of thing is par for the course. It's not your body I'm possessive of. But Bo walks in and your face lights up and you two have this…thing. This weird domestic synchronicity. I felt like I'd just faded into the background and you didn't even see me anymore."

Eve looked at the cappuccino in one hand and the black coffee in the other, spinning them slowly on the countertop in front of her. "No one person can give us everything we need," she said. "I love what I have with you, don't get me wrong. But Bo gives me something you can't. Cassie gives me something you can't. Zeke does. Eoduun does. Hell, even Ruger and Remi do." She turned and looked at Luc. "I'm sure you get things from your relationships with other people that you can't get from me. Things you need. And that's ok. That's just how it is, and how it should be. I can enjoy the things I get from other people, the bonds I share with them, just as you should enjoy your bonds with other people."

Luc propped his elbow on the counter and rested his chin on his fist. "So, are you insinuating that I'm not the total package?" A small grin tugged at the corner of his lips.

"Oh, fuck off," Eve chuckled, then leaned over and kissed his smile. "You know what I'm trying to say."

"Just as long as you make sure to always do a thorough job of convincing me that I'm your favorite." Luc raked his fingers into her hair, holding her for another kiss.

"When it suits me," Eve answered in a playfully dismissive way.

As he kissed her again, more deeply this time, she wondered just how they were going to navigate this next phase. Everything had changed, yet nothing had.

Bo walked in. "They'll be here in a few minutes," he announced, then went straight to the recliner and sat staring at his phone, sipping his pumpkin spice latte.

Luc had definitely soured Bo's mood this morning. He was brooding.

Zeke and Eoduun walked in through the open door, and Zeke paused on his way to the kitchen as soon as he saw Luc sitting at the kitchen island. He looked from Luc to Bo, then back to Luc.

"That's so weird," Zeke commented.

"What's weird?" Luc wondered.

"I'm not used to seeing someone else in Bo's spot. Just threw me off for a second."

The air crackled, and the hairs rose on the back of Eve's arms. She gripped Luc's arm and leaned close to his ear.

"Stand down. Enough," she warned Luc quietly as she stood up.

"Did I say something wrong?" Zeke asked, perplexed, as he looked down at the raised hairs on his own arms.

"It's just been a morning, that's all," Eve said ominously as she headed out to the living room. Normally, the team would converge in the kitchen, but with all this sudden contention around *Bo's spot*, Eve felt the living room was probably a better choice. She walked by Zeke and Eoduun and gestured for them to come sit in the living room.

She walked past Bo on her way to the couch, and as she went by, she nudged his shoulder. "Quit watching porn," she razzed.

"If you insist," he responded nonchalantly, but his cheeks tinged pink. He stuck his phone in his pocket.

Zeke and Eoduun both sat on the couch with Eve, and Eve was a little surprised. Eoduun must've realized that this meeting wasn't the kind you lounge around on the floor for.

Luc stood in the middle of the living room, arms crossed, his expression unusually flat. He explained the circumstances around Eve's condition as they understood it so far, and about being summoned to the Vatican. Then came the awkward part. He explained Eve's need to explore her new powers and her need to keep the beast sated.

"Me. I'll do it," Zeke blurted, hand in the air, before Luc had even finished talking.

"What about Dagon, though?" Eoduun pointed out to Zeke. "I should do it."

Bo just stared down at the disposable cup in his hand, his face inscrutable. When he glanced up at Eve, she saw that his scarred eye was blazing yellow. She furrowed her brow at him and gestured at her own eye questioningly.

He slapped his hand over the betraying orb, and when Luc looked over at him, he acted like he was rubbing his eye. When he opened it again, it was back to its normal dark gray color.

"Eoduun and I can both do it," Zeke suggested.

Luc turned to Eve. "Are you agreeable, love?"

She shrugged, still feeling awkward about this whole conversation. "Fine with me."

"Do I really need to be here for this?" Bo asked, somewhat irritably. "I don't see how this has anything to do with me."

"It's your team, Bo," Luc answered evenly. "You're the one I've entrusted with Eve's safety when I'm gone. You're always with her. Seems like you should be in the loop about this, doesn't it?"

"I keep her safe. I don't need to have any part of this to accomplish that," Bo said curtly. Even with his mask up, staring down at his phone (which he'd pulled back out of his pocket), she could tell there was a black cloud over him. Something was eating at him. Was it Luc's bullshit attitude this morning? Was it unease over having to be present for this incredibly uncomfortable discussion? Was he feeling like Luc had supplanted the position he'd grown comfortable in in Eve's life?

Or was she arrogantly putting too much weight on it? Bo's life didn't revolve around her. Well, it did to an extent, but his feelings didn't revolve around her. For all she knew, he was dour because the smutty manga he was trying to read wouldn't load properly.

Eve's attention returned to the conversation at hand when Luc turned to look at the clock on the wall behind him and said, "I need to call a meeting with everyone before they all head out for training."

"To talk about *this*?!" Zeke panicked.

"No, you potato. This is between us, and only us," Luc reproached. "No, we have Knighco business to discuss. I need to announce that I'm going to start sending teams out again. I've held everyone here as long as I can, but everyone's growing restless. Hunters can't sit still for too long or they start gnawing on their own limbs. Plus, Celeste said she found something on Ruth's phone, so I'm anxious to hear what she has to share."

Luc sent Team Alpha out to gather the other teams in the war room, while he stayed behind to confer with Eve.

"Do you feel comfortable with everything?" Luc asked her.

"I guess. But you were too hard on Bo today," Eve criticized.

"He's a big boy. He'll get over it," Luc dismissed.

"Just be nice, ok?"

"I'm always nice."

Eve scoffed, then dropped the issue. "So, what did Mira find that made the Vatican so anxious? You never really told me."

Luc rubbed the side of his neck. "You have strange biomarkers in your DNA samples that shouldn't be there. Biomarkers of Lilith that weren't there when you were first brought in. Mira doesn't know what they mean. Your genetic profile is not what we expected. It's as if your mother is not your mother. You don't match with your family at all."

Eve had been punched in the gut. Her family wasn't her family? She'd essentially written them off after what they'd put her through, but this still felt a lot like betrayal. Like her whole life had been a lie.

"Is it possible that whatever Dagon did to me changed my DNA?"

"Not like this."

Eve's eyes were welling up with tears. Who the fuck was she?

"If it makes you feel any better, love, I don't think your mother knows it, either."

She scoffed. "How the fuck would she not know?"

"Because she did give birth to a baby girl on November 1st. But, according to your genetic profile...it wasn't you."

Eve felt weak. "Then who am I? Where's the baby she gave birth to? Am I some kind of Changeling or something?!"

"Well, you're not a Fae. But Sister Fiona does think you may have been intentionally switched."

"And the other baby?"

Luc just stared back at her without answering.

"Jesus Christ." Eve raked her hands through her pink hair. "How can you just dump all this on me like that?"

"You asked, love. I thought you wanted to know."

"I thought I did, too, but I didn't know it was going to be *this*." She looked up at Luc through blurry tears. "Who am I?"

Luc sat next to her and gathered her up into his arms. He cradled her head against his chest. "You're you. Just as you always have been. The amazing, inspiring, enigmatic Eve."

The selfish, deceitful, duplicitous Eve.

"So who are my real parents, then?" she mumbled, not entirely sure she wanted to know.

"Sister Fiona didn't tell me. I don't know if they even know yet."

"Luc...what if I really am this monster? This Abomination? I feel like we're all kind of leaning toward accepting it as truth at this point...so what does it mean? For us? For my place at Knighco?"

119

"Does it matter if you're a little monstrous? Aren't we all?" he replied simply. "We've all stared into the abyss. It's part of all of us." He kissed the top of her head. "If anything, it only cements your place here. Queen of the castle."

14

'Property of Lucius Fagerberg'

Eve sat at the corner seat at the conference table in the war room, with Luc to her right at the head of the table and Bo to her left. She could feel Zeke stealing glances at her from the other side of Bo, but she didn't return them. She was too self-absorbed in her own identity crisis to be wondering what Zeke was thinking about.

When the other teams had all gathered, Eve looked around the table. Luc was right. This was a restless crew. Nail biting. Fidgeting. Knee bouncing. Hair twirling. Skin picking. Lip chewing. No one was sitting still, save for Mira, who sat across from Eve, her arms crossed, a bored expression on her annoyingly pretty face.

"Good news, everyone," Luc said, clapping his hands together. "You get to resume hunting."

There was a mix of happy and confused sounds around the table.

"Fuck yeah," Mendal cheered. "I'm *dying* to kill something!"

"Finally, I can go to bars I haven't been kicked out of yet!" Ruger said.

"Hell yeah, I can't wait to stretch my legs!" Kai said, rocking his chair back and stretching his arms over his head as though he was getting ready to go for a run right then.

"Wait, did we take out Ruth?" Ramil asked cautiously. "Aren't we still under threat?"

"We'll keep a team or two here on standby, just in case," Luc replied, "but for now, I don't think it's beneficial for us all to sit on our hands, waiting. There are still monsters out there hurting people and multiplying. And now that we have a better idea of Ruth's motives," Luc glanced unconsciously at Eve, "I think this is a safe move."

"She took Eve from inside compound borders," Zephlyn piped up. "She got in without us being any the wiser. Do we know how? Do we care? What are we doing about that?"

"Levi is monitoring the grounds regularly now. She used a portal and a shapeshifter. We won't be caught with our pants down again, don't worry."

"I am worried, Luc," Zephlyn said. "I had the vision again this morning with the army of monsters and Dagon running with the grimoire, but this time, there was another element. I saw who was leading the army, and it wasn't just Ruth. She had someone, or *something*, at her side. Not Dagon, but something just as ancient and powerful."

Before Luc could respond, Celeste blurted, "Apep."

All eyes turned to Celeste. Her freckled face stretched into the kind of grin unique to nerds about to talk about something nerdy.

"Apep," she repeated. "The Egyptian serpent god of darkness and chaos. He was the one in Egyptian mythology who fought to stop Ra on his nightly journey through the underworld. In other words, he tried to keep the sun from rising every morning. He is no joke."

"What makes you think it's Apep?" Luc inquired.

"Because Ruth's phone is chock-full of Apep lore and mythology. If there is a piece of info regarding Apep on the internet, she's read it. There were a few others smattered here and there, but, by and large, Apep is her new obsession."

"Well, whoever the hell he is, we need to stop her from summoning him," Zephlyn said. "I can't even describe the feeling I got from him. Just pure evil. Compared to him, Dagon is nothing more than a temperamental housecat."

"Spectacular," Luc said flatly. He pushed his sunglasses up his nose and crossed his arms. He sighed heavily. "Celeste, send me a report on Ruth's phone – short and dirty. Roy, I want a rundown on Apep's powers and how to kill him – whatever you can find in the lore. Remi, send me some cases so I can assign teams. Mira, stay after the meeting because I need to have a word with you. Everyone else, train. I'll text you your assignments when I decide who to send out.

"I'll be gone for the next day or two, meeting with Sister Fiona in Rome, so if anyone has any issues and can't get a hold of me directly, Bo's your man. All right? Great. Go," Luc said with a dismissive wave of his hand.

He didn't share anything with the group about Eve's status. She'd wondered if he would. She stood up and began to follow Bo toward the door.

"Eve," Luc called. "Wait for me in the hallway. I'll only be a minute or two." He then turned his attention to Mira.

Eve wondered what he wanted with Mira. Was he confronting her about sending her results to the Vatican before consulting him? She leaned her back against the wall outside the door, and Bo stopped and did the same next to her. He shoved his hands in his pockets.

"Are we good?" he asked.

She jerked her head in his direction. "What? Of course. Why wouldn't we be?"

He shrugged. "Just wanted to make sure."

She reached over and hooked her arm through his, resting her temple against his shoulder. "I'm sorry Luc was being such an asshole this morning. He's having feelings."

"Hm." Bo was silent for a bit, then he asked, "And how are you feeling about all of this?"

"Which part of 'this'? The training? Being an Abomination? *The Abomination*? Oh, and you haven't even heard the best part, where I found out that my mother isn't really my mother. So, that's fun, too. Been an eventful morning for all of us, I guess."

"Fuck," Bo sympathized.

"Fuck indeed," Eve agreed. "I don't know how to feel. I don't know if I *am* feeling right now. I'm just kind of...numb."

"The numbness won't last. Just know, if you need me, I'm here."

She knew he was. He always was. And while she knew that Zeke and Eoduun would be there if she needed them, too, there was something different about the comfort she got from Bo. Something...deeper.

"Well, your prince awaits," Bo said as he unhooked her arm from his and took a step away from her. Moments later, Mira exited the conference room. She nodded to Bo as she walked past, but acted like Eve wasn't even there. Luc wasn't far behind her.

"Thanks for waiting," he said to Eve. Then, to Bo, "I've got it from here."

"When are you leaving?" Bo inquired.

"Anxious to have your spot back?" Luc retorted.

"Maybe."

Luc paused. "Careful, brother," he threatened calmly.

Bo's eyes crinkled in a fake smile. He slapped Luc's shoulder. "Come see me before you go," Bo told him, then turned and walked away.

Luc touched his finger to Eve's chin and turned her head away from Bo's receding back toward himself. "See? He's fine," Luc assured her.

Eve suddenly felt foolish, because she realized that Bo didn't need her to stand up for him. He didn't need her to defend him from Luc. He could do that all by himself. All she was doing by inserting herself in the middle of their little altercations was exacerbating the issue. Neither of them needed her input on their interactions. They were big boys, even if they didn't always act like it. Who was she to try to mediate, like she knew better? She needed to just butt out and let them work it out themselves.

Fucking idiot.

"I am going to have to leave soon," Luc said. "I was hoping we could get a little more time together beforehand, but I'm needed in about twelve different places right now. I'm sorry about all of this."

"I understand." She did, but it didn't mean she didn't feel the disappointment of losing him again so soon after having him back.

"I have a request. It may seem rather intrusive, but I have only the best intentions."

"You know what the road to hell is paved with, right?" she countered suspiciously.

"I only want to put a small marker on you so I can jump straight to you if I ever need to. If I'd placed one on you before Ruth took you, I would've been able to get to you immediately. But I get that it's a big ask. I know it feels a lot like keeping tabs, but I swear that it's only for emergency purposes. I just want to keep you safe."

"Oh. Yeah, that's fine, I guess," Eve said. She thought it was going to be a far more outlandish request with that work up. "As long as it doesn't say something ridiculous like 'Property of Lucius Fagerberg.'"

Luc laughed, relieved. "No, it'll just be a small sigil on any place of your choosing," he said, gesturing to her body. "It'll be like a little tattoo."

Eve tilted her head and arched an eyebrow. "Like a brand?"

Luc smirked. "I'd rather not think of it that way. ...Unless you're into that."

Eve held her hand out to him. "Will it fit on the inside of my wrist?"

"Yes." He took her hand in his, then raised the inside of her wrist to his lips, kissing it softly. "And I can remove it at any time if you change your mind." He closed his large fingers around her wrist, and she felt an acute heat from the palm of his hand. It burned for a split second, then it was gone.

He opened his hand, and she saw a dime-sized circle on her inner wrist. It was filled with tiny, intricate lines and geometric shapes, but as she brought it closer to her face, she could see that all the lines were made up of miniscule lettering. It was actually kind of neat to look at.

He raised his hand to show her an identical mark on the inside of his wrist. "There. Now we're connected, always and everywhere."

"Matching tattoos already?" she joked.

"Fucking lame, right?" He grinned. He leaned down and kissed her tenderly, brushing his hand over her jawline. "As much as I hate to leave, I need to go make my rounds. On foot. Because Rome is a ridiculous jump and I need all my reserves." He sighed heavily.

Eve accompanied him to the gym where her team was training alongside Ramil and Veris. Luc took Bo into another room to talk, and while he was gone, Eve began wrapping up her hands to train on the heavy bag. She paused, staring at the little mark on her wrist, then covered it in the wrap.

What an odd feeling that little mark elicited. Luc could find her anywhere now. If she decided to run again...she couldn't. She had no such designs anymore, but who knew what the future would bring? She trusted Luc enough to allow him that connection with her, but at the same time, it was difficult to ignore that little voice in the back of her mind that wanted to remind her about what her exes would've done with that kind of connection. She'd had a hard enough time getting away from those men she thought she loved and trusted. If they could've just branded her and then popped up wherever she went? She'd probably be dead by now.

Maybe she'd made a mistake. She loved Luc, but she was still wary. She didn't doubt that he was infatuated with her...for now. But was it truly *love* that he swore he felt? She couldn't say. As far as she could tell, *love* was new to him. So how could he be certain? How could she trust his feelings?

How could she trust hers? They'd done less than a stellar job of steering her in the right direction up to this point. In fact, she was pretty sure they actively steered her into trees just for kicks. An involuntary masochist.

She began to beat the ever-loving hell out of the heavy bag in front of her. Oh, to fight again. She missed fighting. She missed painting, too, as she hadn't touched a brush since she'd been here, but not as much as fighting. Art had begun to feel more like work than inspired expression before she was essentially kidnapped by Luc.

But fighting...fighting was where it was at. Sometimes she felt like the only reason she painted was because she was good at it, and people liked it. She felt like it was more socially acceptable as a woman to be an artist, but telling people that she was an MMA fighter brought mixed reactions, especially from men. They never accepted it the same way as if she told them she was an artist. "You're an artist? That's cool. What do you paint?" versus "A fighter? Heh heh, so are you going to put me in a chokehold if I try to kiss you? Do you have all of your teeth? Should I be scared? Hahaha." There was always a level of mockery.

And the men who looked like Luc? The men of wealth and taste? They would date an artist, sure. No biggie. But they wanted nothing to do with a fighter. She wasn't *presentable*. She might as well be feral.

But the flow of fighting, even in practice, satisfied something deep in her soul. The fluidity of movement punctuated by sudden crashes of power and resistance felt like a beautiful, violent dance. She loved the feeling of her body moving, rolling and slipping, surging and kicking, striking and feinting, the power flowing through her body and exploding into every point of contact. It was like sex. It felt primal and true. It was art of movement and power. Painting with blood and sweat.

It was *unladylike*.

Fuck that shit.

The family here at Knighco, they respected her skillset. They appreciated it about her rather than merely accepting it as a personality flaw. They treated her just like they treated each other. She was one of them, not something lesser or something to be mocked.

Well, until they all find out that she's some kind of monster that even the Vatican is afraid of. Then who knows how they'll treat her?

"Would you like a sparring partner?" a deep, polite voice inquired from behind her. She turned around and looked up at Ramil's oddly copper-green eyes. They made him look severe, especially when contrasted with his dark hair and beard. The courteous smile on his face softened some of the severity, but didn't erase it.

She didn't know Ramil well. She only knew what Zeke had told her – that he was incredibly powerful, almost as powerful as Luc, and that, before joining Knighco, he fought against them. But Zeke had sworn that he was a nice guy. It was hard to tell from looking at him. He was quite handsome, but in an overtly dangerous way.

"I heard you were an MMA fighter in your civilian life. I will try not to disappoint you," Ramil added when Eve just stared at him without responding to his question.

She cleared her throat. "Uh, yeah, I was. And I suppose I could use a partner."

She began to assess him while he wrapped up his hands and donned the sparring gear. He had a major reach advantage on her. And height. She was probably going to struggle to land anything unless she could take him to the ground.

As they began, it was clear to Eve that Ramil was taking it easy on her. He was holding back. Indoor sparring rules at the compound prohibited specialty use, but she doubted that he was this poor of a fighter without his telekinesis.

"Ramil," Eve said.

"Yes?"

"You're disappointing me," she taunted. The jab gave her just enough of an opening to burst within his reach and tangle up his legs, dragging him to the ground.

He genuinely struggled on the ground against her. She was small and squirrelly and could slip out of just about anything, and nimble and powerful enough to contort him into several different submissions he would surely tap out of.

And then, as their bodies struggled against each other, writhing around on the ground together, she felt a familiar, creeping desire tingling from her teeth to her belly.

She wanted to bite him. Hurt him. Dominate him. Her heart raced, adrenaline and arousal surging through her. He felt like a threat, and it was thrilling. She needed to crush him between her thighs. Hear him cry out. Beg. Plead. Grovel.

The sound of his agony was beautiful.

15
You're Kind of Terrifying

A strong arm suddenly hooked around her stomach, yanking her away from her prey.

...*Prey*? Opponent. Sparring partner. Ramil.

"Evie!" Bo cried as he dragged her away. He swung around, putting himself between her and Ramil. He faced Ramil. "What did you do?!" he accused him fiercely.

Luc was now at her side, flanking Bo, looking more intrigued than upset. "What the fuck just happened?" Luc asked slowly.

Ramil was dazed. Veris rushed to his side as he lifted himself into an upright seated position on the sparring mats and removed his protective headgear. He winced as Veris helped him to his feet. "Jesus, a second longer and I might have had some broken ribs," he said. "Didn't you feel me tap out?" he asked Eve. He didn't sound angry. He seemed more surprised than anything.

"I'm sorry," Eve apologized. "I completely zoned out. I didn't feel anything." She felt horrible. "Do you need healing?" she offered.

"No, he's fine," Bo interjected abruptly. He looked down at Eve. "Did he do something to warrant that?"

"I disappointed her," Ramil said with a laugh, then winced again.

He thought it was a miscommunication. Inattention to cues. An error. He didn't know what was going through her head as she tried to squeeze the life out of him with her powerful thighs. He didn't know she harbored any kind of deadly intent.

And he didn't know how much it had aroused her to try to kill him, how wet she was, even now. No one knew. And they never would, because she was never going to tell anyone, not even Luc.

There was something evil within her. A voracious bloodlust.

Luc turned his back to Ramil and Veris and bent down to Eve's ear. "Is everything all right, love?" he whispered.

She nodded. It wasn't, but she nodded anyway. "It was an accident. We were just sparring. Maybe I'm still holding on to some of that Jötunn strength."

Luc seemed skeptical, but he didn't voice it. He straightened and addressed the whole team. "Maybe you guys should go to the training grounds today. Eve, don't kill anyone, please," Luc teased, but there was a hint of sincerity in his tone. He kissed her cheek, then whispered, "You can control it. You didn't hurt me last night, right? I know you won't hurt Zeke or Eoduun."

So he did suspect the true nature of her accident with Ramil.

"I won't hurt anyone else. I promise."

Luc cupped her face in his hands and kissed her forehead. "I'll call you tonight, love."

As Eve watched him walk away and disappear out the door, she felt the emptiness hollow her chest. She missed him already. Was this something she was going to get used to? Or was he going to take a scoop of her insides with him every time he left?

Her eyes stung and her vision blurred through the moisture collecting. *Really?* She blinked and cleared her throat. This wasn't a reason to cry. What a fucking child.

She turned and caught Bo's eyes. Sympathy. Goddammit. He didn't miss a damn thing, did he?

She approached Ramil and Veris as her team gathered their things for outdoor training. She could feel Bo watching her keenly. She suspected that he thought Ramil had done something to her to spark her wrath.

"I'm so sorry, Ramil," she apologized. "I really didn't feel the tap out. I guess I was just in the zone."

"I'll live," he replied amiably. He fixed her with those unusual eyes. "I thought maybe you were paying me back for pulling my punches. I didn't do it to insult you. I underestimated you, and I apologize. I'll know better next time."

"Next time? I don't think Bo will have any of that," she said, only half-kidding.

"Bo?" Ramil furrowed his dark brows. "But...pardon my presumptuousness, but don't you mean Luc?"

"No, I mean Bo." She and Ramil both glanced over at Bo, and while he wasn't looking directly at them, she could tell they had Bo's attention.

"Let's go, Evie," Bo called to her, still not looking in their direction.

Ramil held his hand out to Eve, and she took it and shook it firmly. He said, "Well, *if* there is a next time, I will give you more. I'd hate to disappoint you a second time." He smiled at her, and, was she mistaken, or was there a little something behind that smile? Something a little more heated than just *friendly*? And did his fingers linger just a fraction of a second too long as their handshake ended?

No. Ridiculous. She couldn't honestly think yet *another* Knighco hunter was into her. Who the fuck did she think she was?

She felt Bo at her back. "We're burning daylight," he said. His hand pressed between her shoulder blades as he guided her away. "Ramil. Veris." He regarded the two with a nod.

When she joined Zeke and Eoduun on their way out the door, she noticed that they both seemed to be mildly bristling as well. What had everyone's hackles raised? Were they still on edge from her mishap?

On their way to the training grounds, Zeke blurted from Eve's left side, "So what the fuck was all that? Did Ramil try to grope you or something? Did he say something to you?"

"What? No! It was just an accident. I didn't mean to squeeze him that hard," Eve explained.

Eoduun chimed in from her right side, "Eve, he cried out, and you just squeezed harder. It didn't look like an accident."

"I didn't mean to hurt him like that. I didn't. Ok?"

"I don't care that you hurt him," Zeke said. "I just want to know what he did. I saw the way he smiled at you."

"The way he smiled at me?" Eve echoed. Maybe it wasn't just her being ridiculous.

"That was a 'fuck me' smile if I've ever seen one," Zeke said. Eoduun nodded in agreement.

Maybe that was what triggered Eve's violent, sexual urge. Maybe on a subconscious level, she perceived his desire, and maybe she felt threatened by it in that situation. Maybe it didn't have to be just sex, but a perceived sexual-like situation or struggle that triggered it. She didn't know Ramil that well, and sparring with him made her nervous. Even though she felt like she was gaining the upper hand and knew she wasn't in any real danger, there was an element of discomfort there. Maybe her response was some kind of fucked-up self-defense mechanism.

"Whatever kind of smile he gave me, he didn't do anything to me," she assured them. "And Z, weren't you the one who told me he was the nicest guy I'd ever meet? You guys are both acting like he did something wrong, when I was the one who fucked up and hurt *him*."

"He wouldn't have smiled at you like that if Luc had still been in the room," Eoduun said. "*That's* what he did wrong."

Bo finally spoke up from behind them. "Ramil is not a threat."

Zeke scoffed. "Says the guy who was first to jump down his throat."

In exasperation, Eve cried, "Stop it! Bo's right. Ramil is one of us. He's not a threat. Just be glad he was so forgiving about what I did."

"Forgiving? He probably got off on it," Eoduun grumbled.

"Enough," Bo said firmly.

At the training grounds, Bo paired up Zeke and Eoduun for sparring, leaving Eve for himself. She had sparred with Bo a few times, but she was usually paired with Zeke or Eoduun if they were available. It was unusual for him to *choose* to spar with her.

She quickly understood why he wanted her.

As he blocked her strikes, he began his interrogation, "You're hiding something."

"I'm not," she lied.

He caught her legs with a sneaky swipe and took her to the ground. He was on top of her instantly, sitting on her stomach. She couldn't beat Bo, and it drove her nuts. He never moved how she expected him to, and it was like he knew what she was going to do before she did. He repeatedly told her that she telegraphs her moves, but despite her best efforts to feint and hide her intentions, he always saw through her like she was flashing a neon sign.

She tried to buck him, but he only doubled down. "Tell me what really happened with Ramil. *Something* wasn't right about that."

She hooked her legs up around his torso and finally forced him off of her. As she tried to roll back away from him, he caught her leg and dragged her back to him. Fuck.

"I've never seen you behave like that with anyone else," he continued, barely out of breath. She was already huffing and puffing, and it pissed her off. She wrapped her legs around him, trapping him in her guard. He lunged forward and grabbed her by the wrists, slamming them onto the ground over her head. His face was close to hers. "Why did you do that to him? There is a reason. I know you, Evie. You don't zone out."

She returned his steady gaze. "Let it go, Bo," she warned.

"Tell me," he demanded.

She clenched her thighs around his hips and bucked, lifting his weight from her wrists. She slid her hands to one side, throwing Bo off balance, and she rolled them over.

But, dammit, Bo kept the momentum going and ended up on top of her again. He pinned one of her thighs to the ground with his knee, while her other leg remained hooked around his hip. She grunted in frustration as her hands were captured again. He crossed them and pressed them against her chest, using his weight on top of her to hold her down.

"I can do this all day, Evie. And I will. Fucking talk to me."

"I don't want to," she panted.

"You're not going anywhere until you do."

The fuck she wasn't. She knew how to rattle him. She looked down at his body pressed against hers. "Did you learn this position from one of your porn books?"

"Oh, this is much too tame for that. You'd know if I was showing you something from my books," he replied coolly.

Her eyes widened as she looked up into his mismatched gaze. His charcoal eye shifted to that wolfish gold-yellow, contrasting strangely with the aquamarine blue. A dark desire lurked behind that gaze, stirring a maelstrom of forbidden cravings in her belly.

Show me something, she begged internally. She knew it was wrong, but she only thought it. She'd never say it.

He arched an eyebrow, the yellow, scarred eye returning to dark gray. "You thought you'd make me lose my focus? I'm a dog with a bone, Evie. You'll give in *long* before I do."

Eve's body went limp as she submitted. That had backfired spectacularly. "I don't want you to look at me differently," she whispered.

"That will never happen."

She glanced over at Zeke and Eoduun, and found that they were barely sparring. Their attention was drawn to Eve and Bo.

"We have an audience," she told Bo.

"They can't hear you from over there."

"If I tell you a little now, can I tell you the rest later? In private?"

"Depends on what you tell me now."

Eve steeled herself. "I wanted to kill Ramil."

Bo's eyes shot wide open. "Why?"

"I don't know, but it has something to do with whatever kind of monster I am. Something in the particular brand of Lilith's blood I seem to have. I've been getting violent urges when I'm in close, intimate contact." When Bo's grip loosened on her wrists, she added, "I think it's only when I feel threatened, though. I didn't want to kill Luc last night, and I don't want to kill you right now. I don't seem to have issues being close with people I trust."

"You felt threatened by Ramil?" Bo released her hands and removed his knee from her thigh. He sat back on one knee, the other knee raised, resting his elbow on it.

She sat up and crossed her shins. "Not outright, but maybe subconsciously. I was nervous about sparring against him. He's intimidating. At the very least, I don't know him well enough to *trust* him."

He glanced over at Zeke and Eoduun. "You don't want to kill *them*, right? Does Luc know about this?"

"He knows. Well, sort of. We're still figuring it out. To be honest, the Ramil incident came as a surprise. But I don't think Z and Eoduun are in any danger."

"You don't *think*?"

"They're not in danger," she amended. She was *pretty* sure, anyway. She'd already proven with Luc that she wasn't just a mindless killing machine.

"Is there more?"

Eve hesitated. She didn't want to tell him about the awakening with Dagon. He didn't need to know that.

"There's more, isn't there?" he surmised.

"That was how I killed the Jötunn. And I stole his powers."

"Jesus, Evie," Bo marveled. He leaned toward her and whispered, "And with Ramil? Did you acquire any powers from him?"

Eve shook her head. "No, I think it needs to be a lot more... intimate...for that."

"Oh." Bo leaned back again.

"Yeah."

"You're kind of terrifying, Evie," Bo confessed.

A sharp arrow tore through Eve's heart. She turned away from him so he wouldn't see her injured expression. "This is exactly why I didn't want to tell you," she said. "I knew you'd look at me differently."

"I don't mean it like that," Bo assuaged. "I say it with the utmost respect and companionship. I say it about Luc all the time. So do you."

It was true. She had said that about Luc. But she'd never imagined in a million years such a sentiment would apply to herself.

Bo continued, "I'm not saying *I'm* terrified of you."

She turned to face him again and saw the sincerity in his eyes. "You don't hate the monster inside me?"

"I could never hate any part of you," he replied. The corners of his eyes crinkled in a smile hidden behind his mask.

The arrow melted away, and she was whole again.

Bo rose to his feet, then held his hand out to Eve. She took it, and he helped her up. "I know you aren't going to want to hear this, but I think you should have a talk with Zeke and Eoduun, and tell them what really happened with Ramil. They need to know just how dangerous this new 'training' might be. Luc didn't divulge even half of this information this morning."

"What if they decide they don't want to risk it? What then?"

Bo looked at her meaningfully. "You have nothing to worry about."

At lunch, Bo purposely left Eve alone with Zeke and Eoduun at her apartment. She knew he was giving her an opportunity to tell them about what really happened with Ramil, and how truly dangerous she could be.

So, she did. She told them exactly what she told Bo.

Zeke, in typical fashion, focused entirely on the wrong points. "Does that mean you're attracted to Ramil?!"

"That's...that's not...is that what you got from this?" Eve asked, perplexed. "How about we stick to the important point, ok? I don't think either of you have anything to worry about, but...we'll want to be careful. And, of course, if you aren't comfortable with the arrangement anymore—"

"I'm comfortable," Zeke blurted. "You can't scare me away that easily." He smiled sweetly at Eve from the other side of the kitchen island. She was sitting in her usual spot, and Zeke and Eoduun were standing on the other side. Bo's spot next to her was left open.

Eoduun's expression was harder to read, but he nodded. "I'm still in. I like a little rough play, but if you actually try to kill me, I'm pumping the brakes."

Zeke opened the fridge. "Where did the energy drink I had in here go?" After a moment of searching, he turned to Eve.

She pointed to the garbage under the sink. "Luc threw it away."

"For real? What the fuck?" He rounded the kitchen island and pulled the trash bin from the lower cupboard.

"What are you doing?" she exclaimed as he reached into the bin.

He withdrew the unopened can and looked it over. "It's still good," he said. He ran it under the tap and rinsed it off.

"Bruh, don't drink that," Eoduun implored.

Zeke dried it with a paper towel, then popped the tab. "Why? There's nothing wrong with it. It was sealed."

"It was in the *trash*," Eoduun argued.

"And I washed it. Good as new." Zeke took a big drink. "Delicious."

"At least he rinsed it, I guess," Eve sighed.

And just like that, everything was business as usual. She didn't give her teammates enough credit. She was constantly afraid that they would reject her and cast her out and turn on her, but they never did. They accepted her, even now. She didn't deserve them.

16

Just Don't Kill Anybody, And We'll Be Golden

Later that afternoon, after a long day of training, Eve came out of the shower to find Zeke and Eoduun lounging in her living room. Because of course they were.

"Why is everyone always in my apartment?" she asked.

"You never come to any of our apartments. Except for B—" Eoduun cut himself short. He looked over at Eve, unsure whether he was breaching some code of secrecy or not.

"Bo's? I've been there once. I went to Zeke's once, too. But...you're right. I don't venture out much. I guess I've just assumed that if you're not here, you have other plans or want to be left alone."

"See? We have to come to you," Zeke said. "So deal with it."

She hadn't ever given it much thought until now. She did make them come to her. But it wasn't because she meant for it to be that way. She just didn't want to bother anyone when they didn't want to be bothered.

Eoduun stood up from his position lying on the floor in the middle of the living room and walked into the kitchen. "What are we doing for dinner?" he asked.

Eve paused. "I don't know. I think there's still some pizza left over from yesterday."

"Nope," Zeke said from the living room. "Not anymore. Sorry."

Eve sighed. "You guys were the ones who did the shopping. What kind of dinner foods did you get?"

They looked at each other blankly from across the apartment. "Uh…"

"I got chicken nuggets for you," Zeke offered. "We could eat those."

"I don't want chicken nuggets," Eoduun complained.

"Well, I'm not cooking," Eve declared. "You boys figure it out."

Zeke got up from the couch and joined Eoduun in the kitchen, and they both stared into the fridge, then moved on to the freezer, arguing the whole time. Eve ignored them and flopped onto the couch. Why did they all have to eat together anyway? She would've been fine with just a couple of boiled eggs, a can of tuna, and a few carrot sticks. Dinner didn't need to be an ordeal for one person.

She wondered what Luc would make for dinner if he was there right then, and thinking of him made her chest tight. Heavy. She checked her phone. No texts or missed calls. Should she text him? She didn't want to bother him if he was busy. And he would've texted or called if he wasn't busy. So, he must be busy. She laid the phone face-down on the coffee table.

She closed her eyes and imagined his scent. The feel of his arms around her. His lips on hers. His fingers caressing her skin. His striking aquamarine eyes gazing into her soul like he wanted nothing more in the world than *her*.

Her chest clenched around her heart like a fist. He was so far away from her. She wanted to touch him so badly, but right now he was in Rome dealing with the problem that she caused. No. That wasn't correct. The problem that she *is*. That was more accurate. She was the problem. For him, for Knighco, for everyone.

And he was trying to fix it.

When was he going to realize that she wasn't worth it? How much straw could she keep piling on before he broke? Before he gave up on her? He had to be nearing his limit.

"Grilled cheese?" Zeke called out to her.

"Are you making it?"

"Eoduun will."

"As long as I don't have to make it, I'll eat whatever," she said.

She joined the boys in the kitchen and sat at the kitchen island while they made dinner. It was amusing the way they bickered and joked and teased. She wondered if Eoduun and Zeke had ever talked about that kiss Eoduun stole from him that evening that they had shared her right there in that kitchen. Zeke hadn't seemed particularly bothered by it, but she didn't see him showing any sexual interest in Eoduun, either. She knew Eoduun was still desperately in love with Zeke, but he seemed to have made room on his dance card for her now, too. She wondered if he actually wanted to sleep with *her*, or if he only wanted to share her with Zeke so he could have both at once. She wasn't jealous of any attention they paid each other. They could kiss all they wanted in front of her, or more, even, and she wouldn't be bothered by it. But she knew if they showed such attention to anyone outside of their team, that would be a different story. It would be hard for her to swallow that pill.

After eating, Eve cleaned up the mess since the boys had done the cooking. It was only fair. As she was washing up the pans, she heard her phone ring in the living room.

"It's the Sexiest Man Alive," Zeke called out to her. "I'm going to go ahead and assume that's Luc," he said as he brought her the phone.

"He put it in there like that, not me," she clarified, then answered the call.

Luc's voice flowed through the little phone speaker like milk and honey. "Hello, love."

She smiled. "Hey."

"Miss me yet?"

"Possibly."

"I want to come home," he confessed. Then, in surprise, he said, "I don't think I've ever said that."

"Then come home. Apparate your ass back here."

"I wish I could. I have another meeting first thing in the morning with Sister Fiona and some stuffy clerics, and I can't make that jump twice in such a short amount of time. It's already almost midnight here."

"You said 'another' meeting. How did the first one go?"

"I got a lot of information to sort through. It's been keeping me busy tonight."

"Is it as bad as you feared?"

"Eh, there's nothing I can't fix. Let me worry about the Vatican. You worry about you, love. I trust everything got smoothed out with Ramil?"

"Yeah, everything is fine," she said. "Except I ended up having to tell the team about my little...issue. Bo wouldn't leave it alone after the Ramil incident. He knew I was hiding something."

Luc sighed. "He always fucking knows."

"I know! What the hell?"

"So fucking annoying." After a short pause, Luc asked, "Is he there now?"

"No, just the guys."

"Both of them?"

"Generally the case," Eve pointed out.

"Zeke can't stay the night. After what Dagon did to you when he was asleep, it makes me nervous. I know he's sealed at the moment, but I don't fully trust that the seals can hold him for long."

"No one is staying the night." Eve lowered her voice. "Luc, what do I do if this doesn't work? I mean, what do I do if I try to hurt Zeke or Eoduun?"

"You won't."

"But what if I do? How do I train to control my powers if I try to hurt my partners?"

Luc was quiet a long time. When he finally answered, his voice was low. "I think you know."

Eve frowned. "If I did, I wouldn't't've asked."

"Bo."

Eve froze in place. "What do you mean 'Bo'?"

"I mean, you train with Bo. Bo is your backup plan." His voice had an edge to it.

"...But I thought you said—"

"I know what I said. And that's why he's only a backup. But I don't think it will come to that."

"Does he know this?" Eve asked hesitantly.

"I doubt he'll need much convincing."

"And what makes you think I wouldn't try to hurt him if I try to hurt Z and Eoduun?"

"Because you didn't hurt me. That's how I know you won't hurt *him*." Luc's usual cheeky demeanor had completely drowned at that point. He sounded downright dejected. Even though she had more questions, she didn't ask them.

"I'm sure I won't hurt anyone," she said optimistically. "I think Ramil was a fluke." She told Luc about her theory that maybe it was a self-defense response.

"Hm. It's possible, I suppose. I still have a lot of information to go through tonight, but I'll let you know what I find out from the texts. Just don't kill anybody, and we'll be golden, all right? Oh, and don't forget to add water to that dream catcher concoction under your bed. Don't let it dry up."

"Oh, shit."

"You forgot about it already, didn't you?"

"Well, to be fair, it hasn't exactly been the first thing on my mind the past couple of days."

"Fill it up, please," Luc commanded. "I don't need anything else to worry about."

The sharpness to his tone reminded her that all of his current stress was from her. She was a problem. *The* problem.

"Luc?"

"Yes, love?"

"Why are you doing this?"

"I'm going to need you to be a tad more specific."

"Why are you going to these lengths to protect me? What's in it for you? You're clearly stressed the hell out, doing things you don't want to do."

"Love, I would kill the pope for you. There is nothing I wouldn't do to protect you. What's in it for me? You, of course."

Kind of like climbing Everest just for a hotel pillow mint.

She looked down at the little mark on the inside of her wrist. His life would be so much easier if she wasn't in it. The urge to run flitted through her mind once more, and she wondered if he would still be able to find her if she carved that tattoo from her skin.

No, that would just cause him more grief.

Before they ended their call, she told him she loved him, and admitted that she missed him. "Hurry back to me," she beseeched.

She finished cleaning the kitchen and joined the boys in the living room. Zeke was lying on his side on the couch, and Eoduun was lying on his belly on the floor, a couch pillow under his head. They were watching *Bridgerton*.

Eve climbed over the back of the couch and sat down in front of Zeke's stomach, leaning back against him. She started to slide her cold, bare feet up the back of Eoduun's shirt.

"Hey! No!" he protested, sitting up to escape her icy toes.

She cackled in wicked delight.

He leaned his back against the couch in front of her with an irritated grumble, but then he reached back and pulled her legs around his body, tucking her thighs under his arms.

"Why the hell are you guys watching *Bridgerton*?"

"Have you seen it?" Zeke asked.

"No. Isn't it like a Jane Austen-style girly show?"

"It's more like fancy porn," he said.

Eve was dubious for about three seconds, until the next scene popped onto the screen, and she saw exactly what Zeke meant. "Oh! Ok…not what I was expecting."

She felt Eoduun's fingers tracing tiny circles slowly up the inside of her calf.

Oh.

Zeke sat up behind her and straddled his thighs around her, his feet coming down on either side of Eoduun. His broad, hard chest pressed into her back as his fingers brushed her hair away from her neck. His lips touched the erogenous zone just under her ear.

Ooh.

Zeke's low voice trickled into her ear, "We thought it might be good background noise." His fingers slid up the front of her neck and clasped over her jaw, gently turning her head around toward him. His lips crushed against hers, and he sighed into her mouth. His other hand was at her stomach, his fingers teasing at the hem on her shirt briefly before sneaking beneath the fabric. He slipped his warm hand up under her bra and cupped her breast.

She broke her kiss with Zeke when she felt her shorts and underwear being pulled down over her thighs. She looked down at Eoduun, who was meeting her gaze with dark, devious eyes. He gripped under her knees and pulled her toward the edge of the couch, then lifted them and pushed them open just enough to hook her legs over top of Zeke's knees.

"Perfect," Eoduun praised, his gaze dropping to her petals opened wide for him. His head dipped between her legs, and his hot tongue touched her a little farther south than she was expecting. She gasped at the foreign, but insanely pleasurable sensation as his tongue played around her second hole. When he finally moved up her slit and his mouth descended upon the apex of her sex, she was already primed and sensitive.

She threw her head back onto Zeke's shoulder and chewed her lip as her hips rolled, grinding herself against Eoduun's mouth. Zeke's hand ran down the back of her arm, his fingers sliding over the back of her hand and intertwining with hers. He then guided her hand to Eoduun's head, and he and she both raked their intertwined fingers into Eoduun's hair. She gripped Zeke's fingers and Eoduun's hair as she reached her other hand up and buried it in Zeke's hair. She pulled his lips to hers, and as his tongue plundered her mouth, she reveled in the sensation of Eoduun's tongue plundering between her legs, both of their hands and bodies touching her skin, and Zeke's rock-hard erection pressing against her back from under his jeans.

Being with the two of them was unlike anything she'd ever experienced, and she was luxuriating in the moment. Her pleasure was rising slowly, steadily, and powerfully, like an impending tsunami rolling toward the shore. She braced herself for the impact.

She moaned against Zeke's tongue, then tore her mouth away and gasped and panted as the wave of ecstasy crashed again and again and again, her core pulsing and hips jerking, her body writhing between the two of them.

She could've easily called it quits after that, but Zeke and Eoduun were just getting started.

"Eve, sit on Z's dick," Eoduun commanded, "but face me, not him. Reverse cowgirl. And take off your shirt."

Eve wasn't used to being ordered around, but it struck something primal inside of her, and she kind of liked it.

No violent urges yet.

Zeke undid his pants and pushed them down to his knees, and Eoduun pulled them the rest of the way off of him. Zeke took his eager, throbbing manhood in his hand and guided it up to Eve's slit as she straddled him on her knees, facing away from him with her hands grasping his knees for support. She felt the heat of his cock notch between her legs, and she lowered her slick sheath down around him, clenching him with her walls. He flexed his hips forward as she inched him deeper and deeper within her.

"Oh, fuck, I've missed you," he groaned when he was fully buried inside of her.

"Fuck him, Eve," Eoduun commanded. Eve rolled her hips, falling into pace with Zeke's thrusts, feeling him swelling and throbbing inside of her already. He was barely clinging to control. Eoduun sat back on the coffee table with his hand in his pants, stroking himself slowly, watching Eve slide up and down on Zeke's stiff cock.

Eve felt Zeke inside of her, his hands on her body, but her eyes were on Eoduun. When their eyes locked, he sauntered over to them, standing over her. He tilted her head up with his finger under her chin and leaned down, devouring her kiss aggressively. He was such an angry kisser, like he wanted to rape her mouth with his tongue. His fingers squeezed her jaw, and he bit her lower lip. She whimpered and tried to pull away, but he raked his hand into her hair and held her firmly.

"I won't make you bleed. No marks," he mumbled against her lips, then continued his plundering.

Her heart raced. He made her feel strangely. She trusted him, but there was also a sense of danger with him. He wanted control, and he took it. He didn't ask for it. He wasn't going to seriously hurt her, but he might push past her comfort zone.

Yet still, she had no violent urges tingling in her mind.

With Zeke involved, she didn't worry. But she wondered what Eoduun would be like if he had her alone. He was a rough lover. But fuck, he was a skilled one.

He finally let her up for air as his lips trailed down her neck. He bit her at the base of her neck and shoulder, but he let up just before there was any threat of bruising or welting. He wanted to bite harder.

She could tell. And then he bit again, and she cried out. He hummed appreciatively.

"Lean back," Eoduun instructed, pushing Eve back against Zeke's chest. "Z, grab under her knees and open her up."

Zeke slipped his hands under her knees and lifted them to the sides, shifting her weight from her legs so that she was lying back against him. She raised one hand up and gripped the back of his neck to help support herself.

Eoduun looked down at them, her legs opened wide again, and he feasted on the view of Zeke thrusting into her, stretching her, filling her.

And then he dropped to his knees and gripped Eve's thighs.

Eve watched in disbelief as he leaned down and ran his tongue from Zeke's balls, up the base of his shaft, to Eve's clit. Zeke groaned as he slowed his pace, fucking Eve slow and deep as Eoduun licked them both where they were joined. Eve's fingers dug into the back of Zeke's neck as she panted and mewled, feeling herself winding up for another wild release.

"Fuuuck," Zeke growled in Eve's ear as she felt him swell inside of her. His hips jerked up into her as he began to spill over, and Eoduun latched down and sucked her sensitive bundle of nerves.

She wasn't a screamer. At least, she didn't think she was. Until now.

The pure ecstasy that washed over her threatened to drown her. It was so powerful, it almost hurt.

Eoduun lifted her up just enough for Zeke's spent appendage to slide out of her, and, before her orgasm had run its course, Eoduun was inside of her while Zeke held her legs open for him. Eoduun rutted on her roughly, drawing out the final waves of her pleasure and wringing every last drop from her. He gripped her hair and dominated her mouth as he plunged into her and spasmed, a deep moan rumbling in his throat and his teeth sinking into Eve's tongue as he finished.

17
Girls' Night

Eoduun pulled his pants back up over his hips and dropped onto the couch next to her and Zeke, breathing heavily.

Eve rolled off of Zeke, her naked body squeezing between Zeke and Eoduun. She glanced over at Zeke. He was already hard again.

Zeke saw her looking, and he raised an enticing eyebrow at her.

"No," she answered. "I'm *spent*. Fuck. Holy fuck."

"Holy fuck is right," Zeke agreed.

"Holy fucking fuck," Eoduun added.

"That certainly illustrates the diversity of the word," Zeke quipped as he leaned forward and snatched his pants up off the floor. He grabbed Eve's clothes while he was at it and handed them to her.

"Are you seriously quoting *Boondock Saints* right after sex?" Eve complained as she started getting dressed.

"It's never a wrong time to quote *Boondock Saints,*" Eoduun defended. He then looked at Eve inquisitively. "So…do you feel any different? Did you gain anything from us?"

Eve shook her head. "I don't think so."

"Guess we'll just have to keep trying," Zeke said cheerfully. He slid his pants on and zipped them up. "As soon as my legs are operational again, I'm making chicken nuggets." He turned to Eve and Eoduun. "Any takers?"

"You just ate three grilled cheese sandwiches and finished off the rest of my pizza in the fridge, and now you're going for nuggets, too?" Eve grimaced.

"How dare you fat shame me," he feigned offense.

Eve laughed. "I'm not fat shaming you, you ass."

"How dare you, Eve. This is a safe space," Eoduun teased.

"This is *my* space!" she exclaimed.

"You're not being very inclusive," Zeke complained as he stood up.

"Oh my god." She clapped her hands over her face.

There was a knock at the door. Eve did a quick clothing check to make sure everyone was dressed, then started to get up to unlock the door.

Except as soon as she turned and looked, she saw that it wasn't locked. She pursed her lips.

"Come in," she called.

The door opened, and Cassie strutted in, singing, "We're goin' out tonight, feelin' all right…"

Zeke joined in from the kitchen, "Gonna let it all hang oooouuuut."

"Get it, Z!" Cassie cheered. Then she looked at Eve. "Damn, what's got him feeling like a woman?"

"Chicken nuggets, I guess?"

Eve noticed that Cassie was alone. "Where are the boys?" she asked.

"They're not invited. Team Flannel is leaving on a hunting trip tomorrow, so tonight is girls' night, and you and I are going to get fucking sloppy!"

Eve desperately wanted to partake, but she was hesitant. "Oh, I don't know if that's allowed," she said.

Cassie's eyes widened. "*Allowed*? Honey, you're *allowed* to do whatever the hell you want! Who isn't going to *allow* you come out with me?"

"I don't mean it like that. It's just, after what happened with Ruth...I'm kind of a target. At the very least, I need to let Bo know where I'm going."

"I'm not supposed to go out without a chaperone either," Zeke said from the kitchen. "But it should be fine if Cass is with you. I went out with Eoduun, remember?"

That was true. They went grocery shopping while Bo was with Eve.

"See?" Cassie said. "It'll be fine. And Remi is going to be our DD, so we're covered!" Cassie gave Eve a once-over. "Oh, hon, go get changed. And brush your hair." She turned Eve toward her bedroom door. "Chop chop!"

"What should I change into? Where are we going?"

"The Gutter, of course! I don't get to go with Ruger since he's been temporarily banned, so I've been missing out."

"Aw! I want to go!" Zeke whined. "That's not fair, last time we went, I had my night cut short and had to burn a body. I want a do-over."

Eve recalled what had happened last time with the shapeshifter. The Gutter made her nervous now.

"I don't care if you feel like a woman, Z. You're not invited," Cassie informed him. She turned to Eve. "Eve, go get dressed."

As Eve went back to her room to put on a dress, she could hear the conversation continuing in the other room.

"But what if someone hits on Eve?" Zeke nagged. "I didn't know you were going clubbing. I thought you were going out to the bar."

"What difference does it make?"

"I'm also uncomfortable with this," Eoduun said from the couch. "Zeke and I are going."

"What? No," Cassie scoffed. "You two are acting like a couple of jealous boyfriends."

Eve didn't hear anything from the other room. It went quiet. Or were they whispering? Eve quickly shimmied into the red dress she had considered wearing last time she went to The Gutter. She grabbed a pair of simple heels, leaving the Louboutins for a time when Luc could accompany her, and rushed out of the bedroom to see why things had gone silent on the other side of the door.

When she emerged, Cassie gave her a devious look and gave her a sly grin.

"We didn't say anything!" Zeke declared around a mouthful of chicken nuggets.

"About what?"

"You took my advice," Cassie said, still grinning. "You're trying it."

"Trying what?"

"Poly." She gave a sideways glance to Zeke, then Eoduun, then fixed Eve with a mischievous expression.

"Oh."

Cassie paused. "Or is it more of a 'when the cat's away' kind of thing?"

"No! It's not like that," Eve contested. "Luc knows. I'm not *cheating*."

"This isn't anyone's business but ours, Eve," Eoduun said flatly as he passed by them to go to the kitchen.

On the television, sensual sounds from yet another sex scene filled the air.

How fucking awkward.

Eve made a quick trip to the bathroom, and when she came out, Zeke and Eoduun were heading toward the door.

"I'll see you boys later," she called to them.

"Oh, you'll probably run into us at the club," Eoduun replied.

Cassie sighed. "Whatever, I can't stop you two from going. But you aren't allowed to hang out with us. It's *girls'* night, got it?"

Eve had barely left the apartment complex when she felt her phone vibrate in her wrist clutch. She pulled it out and looked at the text. It was Bo.

Where did you go?

She replied, *How did you know I went anywhere?*

Bo: *Your scent faded.*

Eve felt an odd shiver through her center. Sometimes she forgot about his super senses. She wondered what else he could detect. He probably heard her fucking Zeke and Eoduun earlier.

Her cheeks burned thinking about him listening to her sex cries. She wondered how she felt about hearing them, if he did.

Another text came in.

Where are you, Evie

She texted back, *I'm going out for a little bit with Cassie. Girls' night. But I think Z and Eoduun are showing up later.*

Where

Eve: *I'll be back. Relax, Daddy*

Bo: *Don't Daddy me. Where*

Eve: *Just The Gutter. For a little bit. No biggie.*

There were no more replies from Bo. Was he satisfied? She somehow doubted it.

At the club, Eve wondered if she should text Luc to let him know she was going out. She pulled her phone out, but Cassie quickly shut her down.

"No," Cassie said firmly, yelling over the music, and pushed Eve's phone down. "Don't worry about the texts, calls, whatever. Enjoy your freedom for a bit."

Eve put her phone away again. Luc was probably busy or in bed right now anyway. It was late in Rome.

Eve and Cassie headed to the bar and ordered a drink. Eve ordered a sex on the beach. Dammit, Bo was rubbing off on her.

Come to think of it, she couldn't remember what Luc had ordered. Probably Scotch on the rocks or a martini or a manhattan. But it bothered her just a little to realize that she knew Bo's drink order, but not Luc's. She knew how Bo liked his coffee, too. How did Luc drink his? He'd brought her a cappuccino, but what did *he* have? She knew what Bo read in his free time. What did Luc read? Did he read, or was it always business? Luc didn't seem to have a lot of free time for reading.

Whatever precious free time he had, he spent with her. For a man as busy as Luc, that was a statement in itself. And he cooked for her. The jerk could cook. Maybe she didn't know all of the little quirks about him that she knew about Bo, but she recognized his love language. He just wanted to be with her. To take care of her. Love her, and to be loved by her.

And suddenly she was racked with guilt over how much she'd enjoyed being with Eoduun and Zeke earlier. While it was an arrangement Luc endorsed, facilitated even, there was a part of her that felt like she wasn't supposed to like it quite so much.

"Earth to Eve," Cassie snapped her fingers in front of Eve's face. Eve shifted in her seat at the small table they'd sat at.

"Shit, sorry. What?"

"Seriously, you need to quit worrying about the guys."

"I'm not. Well, I am, but not about girls' night."

"Spill," Cassie said as she sipped her drink.

"I'm still trying to figure out this whole 'poly' business. It feels so unfair to them. I have feelings for Z and Eoduun, but they're not the kind of feelings I have for Bo."

Cassie stared at her blankly. "Bo?"

"Luc! Oh my god, *Luc*. I meant to say Luc, not Bo. Jesus."

"Is Bo part of the arrangement?"

Eve shook her head. "No. Well…no."

"You sound disappointed about that."

"I'm not. It's just…complicated."

"I'd say. I want some sexy details. I can't help but notice that Z and Eoduun are always at your apartment *together*. Does that mean…they do *everything* together?"

"You mean *me*? Do they do *me* together?" Eve chuckled.

Cassie hiked a brow. "Well?"

"Possibly."

"Oh, you lucky slut," Cassie gushed. "I've always wanted that, but Ruger and Remi won't even get naked in the same room."

"Well, they're brothers, so I imagine that would make it a little more awkward."

"It's not like they'd actually have to touch each other, though."

"But it's a lot more fun if they do," Eve divulged, taking a sip of her drink.

Cassie was wildly intrigued. "Oh fuck, Zeke and Eoduun? Well, I suppose, Eoduun, but I didn't realize Zeke was into that, too."

"I don't know if he would be if I wasn't part of it, but he seems quite ok with it in a, um, *team* setting."

"Damn, Eve. I want that! Two at once. What about Luc? Think you'll ever get him in on it?"

"I don't want Luc in on that, honestly. Zeke and Eoduun just *work* like that, and I think anyone else included would be weird. And with Luc, I like to have him all to myself. When I have Luc, I only need Luc."

"Aw, well that's kind of sweet," Cassie said with a little grin. "And what about Bo? You said he's not part of the arrangement, but you two totally vibe. I've seen it. You've slept with him, haven't you?"

"No, I never slept with Bo."

"Really? Shame." Cassie was thoughtful. "I always wondered what Bo would be like in bed."

A sharp splinter of jealousy stabbed through Eve's chest.

Cassie continued, "He's got that *alpha* thing going on. Whenever shit goes down, he always takes charge, even when Luc is there. Well, you've seen it. You were there at the convention center when

Ruth attacked. I bet he's like that in bed, too. I feel like if you were with Bo, you would *belong* to Bo. Is that terrible of me to be turned on by that?"

Eve's heart was racing. She wanted Cassie to stop talking about Bo like that, but it was true. She felt the same way about him. But she didn't want Cassie looking at him like that. *Thinking* about him like that. She had Ruger and Remi. She needed to stay in her lane.

"Eve? Did I say something wrong?" Cassie wondered.

"What? No. But there are a lot of sides to Bo. He can be a little overprotective, maybe, but he's kind and thoughtful, too. And easily embarrassed. And reliable. And comforting. And he's annoyingly observant. Like, seriously, I can't hide a damn thing from him. It's like he's got some kind of sixth sense."

Cassie gave Eve a knowing smile. "Ah, so that's what you meant by 'it's complicated.' You're into him."

"No, I meant that it's complicated between him and Luc. Bo and I are close, but it's different with him."

"Maybe it's because you haven't slept with him. You should just sleep with him and get him out of your system, because whatever this is you've got building up over him is going to come to a head one way or another."

"I can't sleep with Bo." If she did...she didn't want to step over that uncrossable line. If she did, there would be no turning back. Bo was special. He belonged on the little pedestal she'd placed him on, never to be taken down and played with. And taking Bo down would mean having to put Luc back, and she couldn't do that either.

"Well, someone should. Such a waste."

Eve was bristling at that last comment when the three strange men approached her and Cassie's table.

18

You Can Take Me Home, Daddy

"Hello, ladies," one of the men said saccharinely, leaning his elbows on the table. He was short, slightly overweight, tan, with a $200 haircut. He reeked of entitlement and trust funds.

The second man leaned over the table and reached his hand across to Eve, seeking a handshake. He was taller and thinner than the first man, and there was something dangerous about his dark eyes. They were soulless. Dead. "Hi, I'm Steve. This is my friend Chad," he said, pointing to the smarmy, entitled douche. "And this is my other friend, Mike." He pointed to an average sized, average-looking man standing next to him. The only noteworthy thing about Mike was the fact that he was sweating bullets and looked like he was so nervous he could puke.

Eve didn't like how much Steve was leaning over their table and all up in their space, waving his hands around so much. Something wasn't right.

Don't Think It, Don't Say It, churned in her brain, but she immediately thought it: *What if these guys are monsters? Human monsters? What if I got raped tonight by these pieces of shit? What if I'm murdered?*

No. She scoffed at herself. Who was going to rape her? She could kill all three of these men with the knife strapped to her thigh that she smuggled into the club. She was a hunter. She was a fighter. She knew more ways to take out these men than she could count on her fingers.

These men weren't a threat to her or Cassie. Women like them weren't victims. But these guys were bad news.

"I didn't see you ladies come in with any boyfriends," Steve noted.

"That's because it's girls' night, fellas," Cassie said. "And you aren't girls. Sorry."

"Oh, come on, we can be one of the girls. Just let us hang for a while."

"No," Eve said firmly, looking at her nails with a bored expression on her face. "I'm not into men."

"That's all right. I love a challenge. I bet I could change your mind," Steve pressed, leaning closer to Eve. "At least let me buy you a drink."

"I have one, thanks," Eve said.

"You don't seem to be drinking it. Do you want a different one?"

To prove him wrong, Eve raised the glass to her lips, but suddenly there was a hand on the top of her drink, stopping the motion. She looked down. She knew that rough, scarred hand.

"Don't drink that," Bo warned from behind her.

Oh, fuck. That was why Steve was waving his hands all over, reaching over the table and their drinks. He'd roofied their drinks.

And a drugged hunter with a knife isn't any more dangerous than a wet rag.

A pit opened in her stomach. She felt hollow and sick.

"Why don't you shitbags step outside with me for a minute?" Bo seethed.

"What the fuck is wrong with your eyes, man?" Mike asked fearfully as he stared at Bo.

Eve didn't even need to look to know he wasn't just talking about his mismatched eyes. She could hear it in Bo's voice. He'd shifted to his wolf eye.

He was acting calmly, but there was violent rage simmering beneath the surface. He was going to kill them. All three of them.

She knew all of this, and she hadn't even turned to look at him yet.

"The three of us against you, Crazy Eyes?" Steve laughed. "Fine. Ladies, wait for us. We'll be right back."

Eve's eyes met Cassie's as the men all left the table. From her round eyes and oddly blank affect, Eve could tell that Cassie was just as shaken as she was.

Eve's brain couldn't stop thinking about all the ways tonight could have gone wrong, and every single one of them made the bile rise in her throat. While the drug would've worn off faster on her than most women, it still would've incapacitated her for a time. She should've learned her lesson when she was kidnapped. She needed to quit disregarding her intuition. Just because she was strong, it didn't mean she was invulnerable.

"Should we...assist?" Eve wondered.

Cassie ignored Eve's question. "I can't believe I didn't see it. I should've known better. I should've *seen* what they were doing."

"I didn't see it either."

"I don't feel like partying anymore," Cassie confessed.

"I don't either. But that's probably why we should. If I go home now, I'm just going to make myself sick thinking about what could've happened. I might as well drink away the feelings."

Cassie set her jaw. "You know what? You're right. We can't let those fucking sickos ruin girls' night."

Cassie and Eve made their way to the bar for fresh drinks, and this time, Eve made a conscious effort the keep her hand over her drink as she took it back to the table.

"There's our knight in shining armor," Cassie said, looking past Eve.

"Let's go," Bo said as he came up behind Eve and stood at her side, his hand gripping the back of her seat.

"I'm not leaving. I still have a lot of drinking to do," she informed him.

"Evie."

"Bo." She looked at him and noticed that his eye still hadn't gone back to normal. Then she looked down at his black dress slacks and black Oxford shirt with the sleeves rolled up his forearms. It matched his black gaiter, and almost looked like one seamless unit. He looked dark and dangerous.

Eve asked, "Where are Zeke and Eoduun? They were threatening to show up."

"I told them to stay home. You and Zeke in public together are too tempting of a target."

"You should get a drink, Bo," Cassie urged him. "I have Remi on the hook to DD."

"Actually, Remi and Ruger are on their way to collect the bodies from behind the club and dispose of them. They expect to bring you home with them," Bo told Cassie.

Cassie groaned. "You know, *we* didn't do anything wrong. Why are we being punished for it?"

"You aren't being punished. You're being cared for."

Cassie paused. "Whatever. It's still not fair."

Eve took a long pull from her new drink and leaned closer to Bo. "You killed them?" She knew he did, but she asked anyway.

"It's what I do. I kill monsters."

"But they were human, weren't they?"

"Up for debate." Bo sighed and grabbed Eve's glass from her hand and, lowering his mask just for a moment, took a drink. "Sex on the beach," he noticed. His eye had finally shifted back to the color of charcoal.

"Jealous?"

"Hurry up and finish that. I'm taking you home."

"You can get one, too. I'll even go get it for you. When the bartender saw my ID, he said my drinks were on the house." Then Eve thought about Luc. "Are you going to tell Luc about tonight?" she asked Bo.

"He needs to know. I just killed three men on club property."

"Great. Yet another thing to add to the list of problems I've caused for him."

"You didn't cause this," Cassie said. "Those fuckers did. And Bo's the one who killed them on club property, not you."

"This isn't on you, Evie."

"It's like trouble just follows me like a shadow," she said.

"Well…I guess it's a good thing I do, too," Bo replied.

"Fucking creeper," she teased.

"It's my job."

"Would you have come tonight if it wasn't your job?" Eve wondered.

Bo looked out at the dance floor. "Doesn't matter, because it is, and I did."

"You want to dance, Bo?" Cassie asked.

Bo's eyes snapped back to the table. "God, no."

"Oh, come on."

"I don't dance."

"Everybody can dance," Cassie said. "You just move your body, kind of like making love. And you can do that, can't you, Bo?" she asked suggestively.

"I didn't say I *can't* dance. I said I *don't* dance."

A grin spread across Cassie's face. "Well, now I'm intrigued." She hopped out of her seat and reached for Bo's hand.

Eve's hand shot out and snatched his hand away before Cassie could grab it.

How dare she. Bo was *hers*.

…No, he wasn't.

"I'll dance with you, Cassie," Eve offered, trying to save face.

Cassie gave Eve a knowing look. "Or maybe *you* should dance with *Bo*."

"That's not a good idea," Bo said in a low voice.

Eve looked at him. "Why? Embarrassed about your old school moves?" she teased.

"My fucking knee is killing me. One of those bastards kicked me, hard. I'd probably look more like something from 'Thriller'."

"Oh, shit. Sorry. You want me to heal you?" Eve offered.

Bo's eye flashed yellow again. "I'll be fine." He turned his head away from her. "I just want to go home."

Eve sighed. She looped her arm through his and leaned her upper body against him. "Fine." She downed the rest of her drink and slid off her seat, still clinging to his arm. "You can take me home, Daddy."

"We're in public, Evie. Can you not?"

"I absolutely must," she grinned up at him.

Bo pulled his phone from his pocket and looked at it. "Come on. You too, Cass. Ruger and Remi will be here shortly."

Eve rode home with Bo, and by the time they arrived back at the compound, Ruger's old black muscle car was already parked in the garage.

"Did they already dispose of the bodies?" Eve wondered.

"Ruger wouldn't leave bodies in his trunk."

"How the hell did they do it that fast?"

"Ruger drives everywhere like he's got a fire to put out, that's how."

Eve noticed Bo's altered gait as they made their way to the apartment complex.

"You should let me heal you. You may have torn something."

"No."

Eve expelled an exasperated sigh. "Babhdán Fagerberg. Goddammit. You need to quit being such a stubborn bitch."

Bo raised his eyebrows at her. "*I'm* the stubborn bitch?"

"Yes. You. I'm not stubborn."

Bo chuckled. "No, not at *all*."

When they got to the stairs, Eve helped him climb them. "This is fucking ridiculous. It's obviously only getting worse," Eve said.

"I'll take some ibuprofen. I'll be fine. I just need to ice it and relax for a bit."

"Or you could just let me heal you."

"Stop it."

Bo left her at her apartment, insisting he didn't need any help to his own door.

Once inside, she felt the emptiness of the apartment acutely. Why didn't she enjoy being alone anymore? She used to crave it. Require it. Regular time alone had been a necessity for her. But the longer she was here, surrounded by people she cared about and enjoyed spending time with, the less she liked an empty apartment.

The knock on her door startled her. "Eve?" It was Zeke.

"It's open."

"What happened tonight?" he wanted to know. Worry creased his forehead. "Remi and Ruger said they had bodies to collect at The Gutter. They said you and Cassie had a little trouble."

"Oh. That." She gave him the short and dirty version of events. "We're fine, and the world has three fewer rapists or traffickers or whatever kind of monsters those guys were."

Zeke closed the gap between them and scooped her into his hard, bulky arms. He squeezed her against him. "I shouldn't have let you go. I should've kept you safe, here with me."

"It's fine. I'm fine," Eve said, her voice muffled against his arm. He loosened his embrace, and she added, less muffled, "Just think, if Cassie and I hadn't gone out tonight, those guys probably would've targeted innocent women who didn't have anyone there to step in. Us going out saved someone from that fate."

"But if Bo hadn't been there, or hadn't arrived in time…" Zeke fretted.

"No point in dwelling on that," Eve said. She pushed away from Zeke slightly so she could look up at his face.

Oh, poor, sweet Zeke. He gazed at her pitifully, his pinched brows and wide, fearful eyes striking a crack in her heart. She cupped his handsome face in her hands.

He said miserably, "Every time I let you out of my sight, someone tries to take you."

"But I keep coming back, don't I? Don't worry. I'm like herpes."

Zeke laughed, his features finally brightening. There he was. Her sunshine. His smile made her smile.

Before he returned to his own apartment, he asked her what she wanted to do about tomorrow if Luc didn't come home. "Today was great," he said. "Amazing, really…but I was kind of hoping I could have you to myself sometimes, too. I mean, if you're cool with that."

"I'm cool with it," Eve assured him.

"But we should probably talk to Eoduun. He may want the same thing sometimes, too," Zeke pointed out.

Probably not, but maybe. He did suggest that he should train with her instead of Zeke when Luc first broached the subject, but that may have been to keep Zeke and her from getting too close without him.

When Eve climbed into bed that night, she lay awake a long time, thinking about all the mistakes she'd made, and wondering if some of the choices she'd made lately belonged in the mistake pile. Had it been the right move to have confessed to Luc how she felt about him, and agreed to make him her priority? She loved him desperately. She was wild about him. But was she any good for him? No. He was so much better off without her, even if he didn't see it yet. She only dragged him down. But she'd already pulled the trigger on that, so what could she do now? She couldn't let him go. Her selfish heart wouldn't let her do that, and she knew he wouldn't, either.

And what about Zeke and Eoduun? The mind-blowing threesome they'd had today *felt* so much like cheating, even if it wasn't.

And Zeke...he loved her in a way she couldn't love him. She'd wanted him to be the one, but he wasn't. She did love him, but it paled in comparison to the magnitude of her feelings for Luc. Nothing about this arrangement and training was fair to Zeke's feelings.

And Eoduun. He loved Zeke, but he felt something for Eve, too. Maybe it was purely a physical attraction when it came to her, but he was strangely jealous or needy when she didn't expect him to be. Eoduun was a bit of a mystery to her. And holy hell, was he a dirty boy, and Eve kind of loved it. But what if he did want time alone with her? He was rough. She could tell he wanted to be even rougher, but he was holding back. Would he hold back if they were alone?

And then there was Bo.

Bo.

Eve suddenly felt the mattress shift and the blankets lift as someone climbed into bed behind her. She rolled over.

"Zeke, you're not supposed to spend the night."

"He isn't."

Eve's adrenaline surged when Dagon's low, taunting voice hit her ears. His vermilion eyes captured hers, and he draped a heavy arm over her midsection as he sidled up next to her.

"You can't be here," she whispered, frozen. "You're sealed away."

"Am I?" He traced a finger across her forehead, brushing loose strands of hair from her face. "Yet, here I am." He grinned mischievously.

Eve swallowed hard. "Get the fuck out of here."

"I think I'll stay." He slid over top of Eve and settled his hips between her thighs, his muscular, tattooed torso looming over her.

His arms came down like thick, immovable pillars on either side of her, caging her beneath him. "I've missed you, princess."

"I could kill you if you try it," she warned.

"But you wouldn't kill Zeke, and to kill me, you'd have to kill him. Face it, princess. You're helpless against me."

"You wouldn't."

He slid his fingers into her hair and gripped tightly as he leaned down, his lips brushing her ear. "Wouldn't I?" he threatened, the wicked smile audible in his tone. He thrust his hips against her, his hard-on pressing against her mound through their clothes.

Her hips jerked in response, and a gush of wetness dampened her underwear.

"You want me, don't you?" he asked knowingly.

She didn't want to want him. Why did her body always respond to him so readily, so willingly?

"I want you to leave," she said weakly.

Dagon chuckled low in her ear. "You always put up such a frigid front, but you're aching for me." His hand ran up the back of her upper thigh to her ass, and his fingers found their way up her shorts. He stroked her over her damp underwear, and he hummed. "Oh, princess, you're fucking wet."

Eve hated the tendrils of heat weaving through her core. She hated that she couldn't get her mouth to tell him to stop. All it wanted to do was taste him. Bite him. Suck him. Devour him.

What the fuck was wrong with her?

Luc's handsome face sprang into her mind. She couldn't just do whatever she wanted anymore. She had his feelings to consider.

"I don't care what my body tells you. I can't do this with you. I won't do it with you."

Dagon was unfazed. "Are you afraid of what you'll do with your new powers?"

"I'm afraid of what Luc will do to you, and subsequently Zeke, if you touch me. And, yeah, I am afraid of those powers. I don't want them. Fuck you for pushing them on me," she hissed.

Dagon laughed. "I'm just helping you achieve your full potential. You have godlike powers, princess. Embrace them. You don't have to follow the same rules everyone else does. You're special."

"I don't want to be special. I don't want godlike powers. You've fucking ruined me."

Dagon curled his finger under the thin strip of fabric on her underwear and teased her folds. Her hips jerked in response, and she dug her fingers into his forearm.

"I've *awakened* you," he corrected. "All great power comes at a cost. But you still don't seem to understand just how great your power is. Can't you see it? You can destroy *any man*, god and human alike. We'll make a formidable couple."

"We'll never be a couple," Eve hissed.

"You belong with me," Dagon asserted. He slid two thick fingers into Eve's center, and she swallowed the sound that tried to escape her throat. She pulled at his forearm, but he didn't budge. "None of these mere mortals are worthy of you," he continued. "Lucius wants to control your power. Zeke can't handle it. Eoduun wants to subdue it. And Bo...Bo wishes you didn't have it at all. He hates your monstrous side." Dagon continued his ministrations, rubbing his thumb against her clit as he thrust his fingers into her rhythmically. She tried to fight the urge to buck her pelvis against his hand. "But I want all of you. Every monstrous part. Give me all of you, and I'll give you the world," he promised. "You need me. I won't hold you back like they do. You'll be free with me. No rules, no reigns, no reason to be ashamed of what you are. I love the monster you've become."

"The monster *you made me*," she argued. Eve's thighs clenched around Dagon's obliques as his fingers worked to draw out the orgasm she was fighting so hard to suppress.

"Embrace it," he whispered in her ear. His fingers pulled painfully at the roots of her hair as he tilted her head to the side, running his tongue over the pulse point along her throat. "This blood isn't just Panacea Blood anymore," he murmured against her skin. "Ichor flows through these veins now. The blood of the gods."

Eve's eyes shot open, and she was alone in her bed.

19
Tell Me to Stop

Eve's chest heaved. She sat up and looked around her dark bedroom, but it was empty. She scrambled from her bed and turned on the light. She dropped to her knees in front of her bed and dragged the bowl out from under the bed that contained the dream catcher spell.

It was dry.

Shit.

So, was that really Dagon? Or was it all her own imagination? He was supposed to be sealed, so he shouldn't have been able to get into her head. But…what the hell was ichor? What did it mean that her blood wasn't just Panacea Blood anymore? She doubted that was all her own imagination.

Could it have really been Dagon?

Fuck.

She picked up her phone and stared at her messages. Bo and Luc were at the top of her recent conversations. How many hours ahead was Rome from Nebraska again? Her brain was still too fuddled to do the math. Luc might still be sleeping.

She clicked Bo's conversation instead.

You up?

She changed her dampened underwear and put clean shorts on while she waited for Bo to reply.

After ten minutes with no reply, she assumed he didn't notice the text. Should she just knock on his door again? Or...

"Hey! Bo! Check your phone!" she called out.

A moment later, her phone chimed. It was Bo.

What

She wasn't sure if that was troubling or comforting.

Can I come sleep with you?

Another moment passed, then:

Let yourself in

She hurried down the hall to his apartment in her bare feet, hoping no one would see her. She wasn't doing anything wrong, but she knew what it would look like if someone saw her slipping into Bo's apartment in the middle of the night.

She entered his flat and shut the door quietly behind her. She headed toward his bedroom in the darkness. Then her toe rammed into something and tripped her up.

"Fuck!" she whisper-yelled as she stumbled. "What the fuck?!" She turned on her phone flashlight.

It was Bo's goddamn boot.

She kicked it and sent it tumbling toward the door where it *should* have been.

"Are you ransacking my apartment?" Bo called from his room. His voice was clear, unimpeded by the mask he usually wore.

Eve stormed to his bedroom door. "Who leaves their boots in the middle of the fucking floor?!"

"Sorry, I don't normally have midnight visitors I need to clean up for."

Eve used her phone light to navigate to the side of the bed, making sure to get a good look at him with his mask off in the light, then placed it on the nightstand next to Bo's phone. He grunted as she climbed over him, then she slid under the covers and tucked herself up against his side. She threw her leg over his, plopped her head onto his bare chest, her face nestled near his neck, and snaked her hand over his abdomen.

"Ah, that's the stuff," she purred with a long, contented exhale.

"So, what's got you all worked up tonight?" he wanted to know.

She told him about having a dream with Dagon, what he said about the ichor, and about finding the dream catcher had dried up. "I thought it was probably a good idea to snuggle up with my Faradaddy cage tonight, just to be safe."

"Faradaddy? Really?" he said, unamused.

"You love it."

Bo was quiet for a bit, then he murmured, "Ichor, hm?"

"That's what he said. Do you know what it is? I should've googled it."

"It's the blood of the gods in Greek mythology. It's supposed to be what makes gods immortal and godly, but it's also supposed to be toxic to humans."

Eve felt a jolt of dread. "Wait, so if it's true, then…I wouldn't be a blood healer anymore. I'd be the absolute fucking opposite. No. No, I don't want that!"

Bo turned his head and rested his cheek against her temple. "Don't panic just yet. A lot of lore is exaggerated and metaphorical. As far as I know, ichor *is* only a myth." Bo reached down and grabbed Eve's hand, bringing the inside of her wrist to his face. He inhaled deeply. "You still smell pretty fucking good to me," he assured her. "Nothing toxic." Then he paused, looking at her wrist. "What the fuck is that?"

"What?" she fretted.

"Did Luc mark you?"

"Oh, the tattoo. Yeah. I'm a waypoint now."

Bo held her wrist close to his face a few moments longer, and he slowly ran his thumb over the mark on her wrist. Eve wondered what was going through his head. Was he thinking about the mark? Was he still smelling her blood? Was he wondering if it really was ichor?

He finally released her hand and asked, "So I take it everything went fine with Zeke and Eoduun today?"

"Huh? Oh. Yeah. I, uh, I didn't hurt anybody, but I didn't gain any of their powers, either." She quickly changed the subject. "Speaking of hurt, how is your knee? I'd offer again to heal you, but now I'm afraid I might poison you. Just know that I would if I could," she said.

"I took enough ibuprofen to dull it, but it still hurts like a bitch. And, again, don't panic just yet about the whole ichor thing."

As Eve lay there next to Bo, she suddenly remembered that she *had* given her blood to someone since sleeping with Dagon.

"It didn't kill Varghrir," Eve realized. Varghrir drank from her, didn't he? She'd used it to help seduce him. And it didn't kill him. She did.

"Hm?"

"The Jötunn. He drank from me, but *I* killed him, not the blood."

"Well, there, see? You're fine."

"But...what if killing Varghrir was like some kind of rite of passage or something, and *that* was what triggered my blood to become ichor?" Eve worried.

"You're overthinking it, Evie," Bo sighed.

"What if Eoduun had drawn blood, and I accidentally killed him?" she murmured to herself.

She felt Bo stiffen next to her. "Why would Eoduun have drawn blood?" he asked in a mildly angry tone.

"He's a bit of a biter."

"Hm." Bo grunted disapprovingly.

"He didn't leave any marks. But I imagine if I didn't heal the way I do, he probably would have."

"I don't like that."

"I did."

Eve noticed that Bo seemed to be breathing heavier than he had been a moment ago. Was he mad?

She added, "But I'll have to make sure he doesn't do it anymore until Mira can test my blood."

"There's nothing wrong with your blood. She tested it already. If it was toxic, Luc would've been notified immediately."

"There is something wrong with it though. That's why Luc is in Rome. Mira sent her results to Sister Fiona."

"I talked to Luc about that. It isn't toxins they're talking about. Your blood has changed, but it's not like that."

"There really is a monster inside of me," Eve whispered dismally.

Bo grumbled in frustration. "You're not a fucking monster. You want me to prove it to you?" He grabbed her arm again.

"Bo, no!"

But it was too late. She felt his sharp canines sink into her flesh, right over top of Luc's mark.

An explosion of ecstasy rocked her core, and she cried out lewdly. "Bo...," she panted as he sucked and licked at her wrist. The pleasure raging through her body was borderline orgasmic, like a drawn-out state of the moment right before a climax pulses.

He moaned, and she felt him growing hard against her leg. His fingers tightened around her hand as he drank, and the arm he had up behind his head now came down around her and trapped her against him. He reached around her body and gripped her upper thigh, holding her leg against his pelvis as he grinded his erection against her inner thigh.

"Oh, god...I want you so fucking bad," he growled against her wrist. He licked her arm one last time as his puncture marks began to heal over, then he dropped her arm. He reached across and raked his hand into her hair as he rolled on top of her, using his muscular thighs to spread hers. His other hand slid up under her ass and held her firmly against the throbbing erection straining against the fabric of his boxers.

"Fuck, I can't stop," he panted, almost apologetically, as his mouth dominated hers.

She didn't want him to stop. She was supposed to want him to stop, but she felt like a dam had burst. It was too late.

She buried her fingers in the hair at the nape of his neck and met his tongue with enthusiasm. His tongue was soft yet demanding. She licked at his sharp fang-like canines, and he groaned into her mouth. He pulled away.

"Tell me to stop," he begged. "If you don't…" He looked down at her with fire and ice in his eyes. His wolf eye was blazing.

She gazed back up at him, mesmerized by his wild desire, unable to utter a word. She loved the way he looked right now. She wanted to bottle it and drink it daily.

He thrust his hips against her, and his fingers tightened in her hair. He dropped his lips to her ear and pleaded, "Say it. Tell me you don't want me."

She whispered, "I can't."

He groaned. His lips ghosted over her neck. "Goddamn it." His hand roamed from her ass up her side and up under her shirt. He cupped her breast and pinched her nipple between his fingers. "Just once…" He murmured. "Just one time…" He was clearly having an internal battle with himself, like he was trying to convince himself that it was ok.

Part of him didn't want this. Part of him knew better. And, if Eve was honest with herself, part of her knew better, too. Bo wasn't *technically* off-limits, but, for all intents and purposes, he was. This was no emergency.

As much as she wanted him, she knew it wasn't just his body she wanted. It wasn't just sex she wanted. This wasn't the same as Zeke and Eoduun.

Bo was special.

And she was too close to crossing that uncrossable line.

"Bo. Stop." She loathed the words.

He froze, his hand on her breast, his lips on her neck, his hips between her legs. He slowly withdrew his hand from her shirt, reaching up and caressing the side of her neck. "I'm sorry," he whispered against her skin.

Even though she told him to stop, he didn't move away from her immediately. He lifted himself up onto his hands, looking down at her with his body still between her thighs. His scarred eye was still wolfish, and his expression was still hungry.

Was he…was he going to stop?

"Bo…"

"Don't say my name," he commanded in a low tone.

"…Why?"

"Because I like it."

"Are you going to stop?" she ventured timidly.

"Yes. Just…just give me a minute. Don't move. Don't struggle."

Again, she asked, "…Why?"

"Because there's a monster inside of me, too."

20
I'll Bring the Gasoline if You Bring the Matches

Eve's breath caught in her throat. *Unleash it. Show me. Devour me.*

His fists balled in the sheets, and she felt his manhood throb against her core, even through their clothes. He made an impatient hum deep in his throat. "You're not making this any easier when you look at me like that," he growled.

"Like what?"

"Like you want me." He closed his eyes and exhaled a long, shaky breath. Finally, he pushed away and sat back on his ankles. Eve could see that he was still rock-hard.

"I'm sorry," he apologized again. "I, um…" He looked down at his raging erection. "I'm going to need you to just not touch me for a minute." He moved over and sat on the edge of the bed. "I understand if you want to leave."

Eve sat up. "Just go take care of that. I'll wait."

"I'm not doing that."

"What, afraid to touch yourself with me here?" She scooted up behind him and rested her chin on his shoulder. Her core was still throbbing with need. The effects of the blood healing were still surging through her. "Or were you hoping for a helping hand?"

"How can you joke like that after what I just did?"

"Just go in the bathroom and masturbate. Everybody does it. I have no illusions that you don't."

"I'm not doing that!"

Eve reached around and took the back of his hand in hers, then placed his palm over his cock. She guided his hand into stroking himself over his boxers. She turned her head and whispered in his ear, "Then do it right here, where I can watch."

His cock twitched under their hands. "Fuck, Evie," he groaned. "Why?"

She licked her lips and guided his hand to the waistband of his boxers. She pushed it in, but didn't follow with her own hand. "Because you need it, and we'll both like it."

She saw his hand moving slowly up and down under his boxers. Her finger hooked around his waistband and tugged it down so she could see him, unobstructed, and she hummed at the sight of his fingers wrapped around his thick cock. She hugged her other arm around his torso, resting her hand at the base of his neck, between his pectorals.

"Tell me what you're thinking about," she whispered.

"No," he grunted.

She slid her hand further up around his neck. "Tell me," she implored. "You know you want to tell me." When he was silent, she touched her lips to his ear. "Are you thinking about me?"

He responded in a strained voice, his fingers tightening around himself. "Yes."

Eve's thighs clenched together, her center revving. "Am I writhing beneath you, begging, 'Fuck me, Daddy'?"

"Fuck," Bo hissed, and she felt his body tense.

"Fuck me harder, Daddy," she whispered.

With a deep groan, he emptied himself all over his hand and the floor. Eve's underwear was soaked with desire all over again.

"So, you *do* like it when I call you Daddy," she mused as Bo hunched forward and rested his elbows on his knees.

"Of course I fucking like it," he spat in embarrassment. "Don't act like you didn't know that."

"Do you feel better now?" she asked. "How's your knee?" She reached for the tissue box on the nightstand and handed it to him.

He moved his knee around a little while he was wiping off his hand. "It's all better. Thanks," he said quietly.

"I'm just glad I didn't poison you."

"I shouldn't have bitten you like that. I'm sorry. I thought I could control it this time. I thought knowing that you were in love with Luc would change things, but…"

"But?"

"…Never mind." He got up and threw away the pile of tissues he'd used to clean up, then returned to bed. He lay down on his back and sighed heavily. "I feel like shit."

"For what?"

He laughed humorlessly. "Are you fucking kidding me? Where should I begin? Fuck."

"Well, maybe now that you've gotten it out of your system, it'll be easier for you to control yourself when I heal you," she offered optimistically.

"It isn't out of my system," he said flatly. "There is no getting it out of my system."

Eve lay down and curled up next to him, pulling the bedcovers up over them both.

"I can't believe you're even willing to come near me after that," he said. He turned his face away from her in shame.

"Everyone masturbates. No shame in that."

He scoffed. "There is shame in what I did. I lost control. Again. It was the hotel bathroom all over again. But worse."

"We didn't cross that line, though," Eve pointed out.

Bo rested his palm on his forehead, pushing his hair back as he looked up at the ceiling. "Maybe not *that* line, but I crossed *a* line. I'm supposed to protect you and make you feel safe. Luc trusts me with you. This was not part of the deal."

Eve touched his jawline and turned his face toward her. "It's ok. We both know this wouldn't have happened without my blood. Let's just chalk it up to the blood healing, and leave it at that." When Bo seemed unsatisfied, she added, "Besides, it isn't like it's something that's totally off the table, anyway. If something happens and I can't trust myself with Zeke and Eoduun, Luc suggested I come to you."

Bo stared at her. "What makes him think it would be any different with me if you couldn't trust yourself with them?"

"I asked him the same thing. He said he knows I wouldn't hurt *you* because I didn't hurt *him*. Whatever that means."

Bo swallowed hard. "Hm."

"Maybe it's our 'domestic synchronicity,'" Eve joked.

"Hm."

"Stop grunting at me. It was a joke. Something Luc said."

"Evie."

"What?"

"Go to sleep."

She made an annoyed sound. "Fine. Goodnight, Daddy."

He sighed. "Goodnight, Evie."

Eve awoke a short while later. She wasn't sure what had awakened her, but she found herself cocooned in powerful arms and legs. Slow, steady breaths rose and fell behind her, and she could feel the stubble of a five o'clock shadow scratch against the back of her neck. Maybe that was what woke her up.

Wait. This wasn't Luc. This was Bo. When she tried to move, he squeezed her tighter, holding her to him.

"Mmm nmm," he grumbled in protest.

Did he do this every time she slept with him? She'd never awakened in the middle of the night with him, and he was always out of bed when she woke up in the morning. This was the same way Luc liked to sleep with her – a tangle of limbs, like a four-legged octopus. She always just assumed that Bo slept on his back and didn't move much through the night, or that he moved away from her once she fell asleep. This isn't what she expected.

She didn't hate it.

She closed her eyes and drifted back to sleep.

In the morning, Eve woke up alone in Bo's bed. She heard him talking on the phone in the other room, and, glancing at her phone clock, knew that the only person he would likely be talking to at 5:30AM was Luc.

She had a 4:45AM text from Luc. *Good morning, love. Text me when you get up. You're going hunting.*

Hunting? She wondered if that was good news or bad news. It had to be good news, right?

She climbed out of bed and padded out to the kitchen. Bo turned to look at her with his mismatched eyes, his mask down around his neck, and Eve smiled at him. She so enjoyed his face. He didn't smile back, but his expression softened.

"Evie's up," he informed Luc on the phone. "I'll let you tell her. I don't want her killing the messenger." He made a few more short responses and grunts, then ended the call.

"Better get your phone," Bo told her. Her phone began to ring from the bedroom. "That'll be Luc," he said.

"With bad news, I take it?" she surmised as she rushed back to the bedroom. She answered it as soon as she reached it.

"Good morning, love," Luc said sweetly.

"Is it, though? It sounds like you have bad news for me," she said as she walked out of the bedroom. She saw Bo lacing up his boots by the door. "Hey, where are you going?" she whispered at Bo.

"Coffee," he said simply. He stood up and pulled his mask over his face. "Are you hanging out?"

"I'll be here," she replied.

"Hello? Eve?" Luc said from the phone.

"Yes! Sorry. I'm here," she replied as she watched Bo walk out the door. "What's up? I'm going hunting?"

"Bo tells me you had an interesting night."

She felt a jolt of dread. "What?"

"He said he had to dispatch a few perverts at the club."

"Oh! Uh, yeah. That wasn't my fault, though. They just came up to us, uninvited."

"I didn't say it was. I know it wasn't. But he also told me you let the damn dream catcher dry up."

Eve laughed nervously. "I didn't mean to. This is why I can't have plants. I forget to water them."

"What did Dagon say about the ichor? Are you sure it was truly him?"

"God, did Bo give you a full report on my night?"

"It's his job."

"To report my activities?" Eve asked defensively.

"No, to report problems. He said you were worried you had toxic blood."

"And what else did he tell you?"

"That it wasn't, and his knee feels better."

Eve felt the blood rush to her cheeks, and she was glad she wasn't FaceTiming him. She told Luc about the dream with Dagon, what he said to her, and about the ichor comment. "I can't be certain it was him, but it sure felt like it. It felt real."

"His seal must be breaking. Fuck."

"So, what do I do about the dream catcher?"

"I'll get another one to you, but it's not going to matter right now anyway. You guys will be camping out in the woods with Team Flannel," Luc said. "Just be careful around Zeke. You'll have to stick close to Bo at night for now."

"But what about extra…*curricular* activities?"

"What about it?"

"Do I need to be worried Dagon is going to try to take over when I'm with Zeke?"

"You always need to be wary, but I'm confident Zeke can control him. He's never overtaken Zeke when you two were fucking before, has he?"

Eve feared Luc was underestimating Dagon, but he was right. Dagon had never done that when she and Zeke were having sex. At least, not yet. But he has proven he can burst through momentarily when Zeke isn't expecting it. Zeke would have to be extra vigilant and keep his walls up when they were together, especially if he wanted to be alone with her.

"How did your meeting go today?" Eve asked, changing the subject.

Luc hedged. "Not the way I wanted it to." He didn't elaborate. A rock dropped in Eve's stomach.

"What does that mean?"

"It means I'm sending you off the grid for a while for a reason."

"I'm going into hiding?"

"A conveniently located and timed hunting trip. I was only going to send Team Flannel, but I thought maybe you could use the experience and some distance from the compound. Best read up on the wendigo before you go, love."

Eve had read a little about the wendigo in her studies in the library. It was a preternaturally tall, emaciated creature with an insatiable hunger for human flesh. It lured its victims into the woods and into its clutches by mimicking human voices and cries. There were even reports of wendigo being able to possess humans, driving them to kill and consume their families. They were mainly a northern creature, found in places with cold, harsh winters.

And they were absolutely terrifying.

"Where exactly are you sending us?" Eve asked.

"Copper country."

"In Michigan, you mean?"

"The northernmost part of Michigan. Hikers have been going missing for years, and there have been a lot of recent reports of bigfoot encounters and strange sounds at night. Last week, a father and son on a weekend fishing trip were staying at a remote cabin deep in the woods, but they never came home. They were found dismembered, scattered all around the cabin, partially consumed."

"And how do we know it isn't a bear? Or a bigfoot?"

"Bigfoot doesn't exist. Most bigfoot reports are bears, but the ones that aren't, are misidentified wendigo or werewolves. And the tracks around the cabin weren't from a bear."

"Luc."

"Yes, love?"

"I don't know if I can do this. This sounds like nightmare fuel."

"It is a monster, after all. They don't usually inspire warm and fuzzies," Luc said. "But you'll have your team and Team Flannel there. I'm not sending you out alone, love. Team Flannel has hunted wendigo before, and with my brother there, too? And Zeke, who could rip the limbs from a wendigo with his bare hands? Fuck, it's a milk run."

"Are you going to come, too?"

Luc sighed. "I'm sorry, love. I'm tied up for the next couple of days." Eve's chest knotted at those words. "I have to bounce to New York later today to take care of some unexpected business-related issues, and then I need to get on a flight back to Rome." He gave a frustrated grunt. "What I wouldn't give for unlimited energy so I could just jump back and forth as much as I wanted, to be able to come home to you every night."

Eve knew he was busy, and she knew he was in Rome *for* her, but she couldn't help but feel upset about his prolonged absence. She chewed the inside of her lip. "Mm-hm."

"I'm not away from you because I want to be, love," he said.

"I know."

"When I get home, I promise you will have my undivided attention. We can do whatever you want to do. Horseback riding. Sky diving. Shopping. Murder. Bank robbery. Ritual sacrifice. You name it, I'm there."

A laugh bubbled from Eve's throat. "Arson?" she suggested.

"Hell yes. I'll bring the gasoline if you bring the matches."

"Chainsaw massacre?"

"Always game for some gratuitous violence."

"Mini golf?"

Luc made a scandalized sound. "Whoa, whoa...settle down, Eve. Let's not get crazy."

Eve laughed again.

"I love the sound of your laugh," Luc said sweetly.

"Oh, thank you. I was going for a unique blend of Ed the hyena and Krusty the Clown."

"Mmm, and somehow you make it work, my sexy little clown-hyena."

"*Sexy* clown-hyena? What the fuck is wrong with you?" she chuckled.

"Oh please. You love everything that's wrong with me," he replied.

It was weirdly true.

21

You're Ours to Protect

As soon as Eve ended the call with Luc, she missed his voice. She wondered if she'd saved that old voicemail he'd left last time he was gone, but she didn't check. She didn't want to be that pathetic and sappy just yet. Instead, she ventured into Bo's room. His dirty manga collection was calling her name. She'd never been into comics, and had never read manga before, but she did enjoy smutty romance novels.

She selected a well-worn manga from his bookshelf and flopped onto his bed. It took a little getting used to reading the pages and panels from right to left instead of left to right, but before long, she barely noticed she was doing it.

The manga she had selected was about a wolf-boy named Kiba who was in love with a promiscuous rabbit-girl named Mei, but he struggled between his sexual desire to love her and his predatory desire to rip her to pieces. The sex scenes were graphic and abundant, and the conflicting and powerful desires portrayed by the wolf-boy felt unexpectedly familiar to Eve.

Kiss or kill.

She was a little surprised at how much she liked it. And for all the wrong reasons.

Did Bo struggle with the same kind of desires?

She felt eyes on her, and she glanced up over the top of the graphic novel.

"What are you doing?" Bo asked darkly, standing in the doorway of the bedroom, two coffee cups stacked in one hand. His eyes flitted over her form sprawled out on his bed, then settled on the manga in her hands. His cheeks reddened above his mask. "Why are you reading that?"

"Are you embarrassed that I'm reading it?"

"Put it back." He turned and went back out to the kitchen.

Eve took the book with her and followed him into the kitchen. She set it on the counter in front of her and sat on the barstool next to him. She picked up the coffee cup he slid toward her, then stared at him.

"What?" he asked, lowering is mask under his chin to drink his coffee.

"You haven't said it yet. I can't start my day until you say it."

He arched a brow. "*Ohayou?*"

She held up her cup, then took a sip. "*Arigatou.*" She opened the manga to the page she left off on and started reading as she drank her coffee.

"I told you to put it back."

"You did," she said dismissively. "How many volumes of this are there?"

"Five. But the story shifts focus after the second one and never really gets back on track."

"Can I borrow it?"

"No."

Eve was taken aback. "Why?"

"Does this look like a library to you?"

Eve shrugged. "I mean, a little, yeah."

Bo eyed her contemplatively. "Why do you even want it?"

"I like it."

"Seriously?" he asked suspiciously.

"What? It's kinda hot." Eve held up the page she was on, and it was filled with scenes of Kiba and Mei in the throes of carnal pleasure. "You know, Kiba kind of reminds me of you, Bo."

Bo's face flushed bright red and he averted his eyes. "Don't say shit like that."

"Because you like it or because you hate it?" she teased.

Bo took a drink of his coffee. "Whatever. You can read it here, but it doesn't leave my apartment."

"That's not fair. We're not even going to be home for a while!" she whined.

"You're not taking it on the road."

She closed the book and looked at the rough condition the cover was in. "It looks like you've read it enough times to be able to recite it to me, scene for scene."

"No."

"Come on. We can snuggle up in our sleeping bags and you can tell me all about Kiba pouring it to Mei until I fall asleep."

"Are you done?"

"What? I'm going to need something to get my mind off the nightmare we'll be hunting."

"Wendigo? Yeah, they're not my favorite, either. Ugly, disgusting fuckers." Bo regarded her for a moment. "Are you scared?"

"You could fucking say that."

"It's ok to be scared. But I won't let anything happen to you," Bo comforted her. "And Luc wouldn't send you out there if he thought we couldn't handle it."

"Does he really think I'm safer out in the woods with a wendigo than at the compound? Did his meeting go that badly?" Eve asked.

"He didn't give me details, but he doesn't trust some of Sister Fiona's associates. And if they did decide to come for you, this is the first place they would look."

"But why me? Dizzy's a shapeshifter. Kai's a skinwalker. Zeke's possessed by an ancient pagan god. You're part werewolf. What's the big deal about *me*?"

"You're no run-of-the-mill monster or god, Evie. You're new. Or, old. Rare, anyway. You're a big question mark. It sounds like there are a lot of speculations about your powers and what kind of dangers you pose as a blood healer who also possesses the Blood of Lilith, but no one really knows for sure what's fact and what's fiction. There's been no one in recent history quite like you."

"Luc said they think I'm evil."

"Well, we know better than that."

"What if they won't listen to Luc and ultimately decide that I need to die?"

"Then we'll go to war," Bo said sternly.

"Fuck that. I'd run. I'm not letting anyone go to war over me. If Ruth can hide from the Vatican, so can I."

"Run, stay, doesn't matter. Do you really think Luc would just let them hunt you? Do you think *I* would? Zeke? Eoduun? Fuck no. You're ours to protect."

"Until I try to kill one of you," Eve said morbidly.

"Eh. As Luc would say, what's a little attempted homicide among friends?"

Eve snickered, then her smile faded. "Too bad he isn't here to say it himself."

"He would be if he could," Bo said.

Eve wondered if maybe Luc preferred it this way. It's hard to get sick of someone when you're never with them.

Eve pushed up from the counter and collected Bo's manga. "I'm putting this away for now, but I *am* going to read it when we get back."

"Whatever you say," Bo said dismissively. "By the way, Team Flannel is in the hallway, headed this way."

"Are they coming *here?*" she asked.

"Probably. Cassie will want to hash out details of the trip before we head out."

Eve paused on her way to the bedroom and looked down at her pajama shorts, tank top, and bare feet. She wondered if anyone was going to say anything. Then she asked, "Have you had a lot of hunting trips with Team Flannel?"

"We do team up pretty often."

"And you and Cassie are both team captains. Has she ever, like, hinted at having an interest in you?"

Bo gave her a quizzical sideways glance. He looked mildly amused. "Why?"

"Just curious."

"That's a weird thing to be curious about." He took a sip of his coffee and lifted his mask over his face. There was a knock at the door.

"Come in," Bo called without ever answering Eve's question.

Team Flannel walked in, and their eyes immediately turned to Eve standing in the middle of the room where she'd paused on her way to the bedroom, manga in hand.

"Oh," Cassie said in surprise. "So this is where you were. I stopped at your apartment earlier, but you didn't answer your door."

Eve laughed uncomfortably. "Uh, yeah. I was just returning a book I borrowed." As she headed back to the bedroom, she heard the conversation continuing in the other room.

"I didn't know you read," Cassie said to Bo.

"Nerd," Ruger teased.

"Like you have room to talk," Remi said to Ruger. "Remember that time I found that *Babysitter's Club* book under your pillow? *Boy-Crazy Stacey*."

"Shut up, I was ten!" Ruger grumbled defensively. "And I was into babysitters. I thought it was going to be hot."

When Eve returned to the kitchen, she found Cassie sitting in her spot next to Bo. Jealousy prickled her insides. She glanced over at Ruger and Remi, but neither appeared to be ill at ease in any way. No signs of jealousy.

She needed to calm the fuck down. Cassie was with Ruger and Remi. She wouldn't *actually* pursue Bo, would she? Was he fair game in their polyamorous relationship? It was possible. But, even if Cass did go for him, Eve had zero say over that. She had no real claim on Bo.

But, as her protector, her guardian, she couldn't have him distracted by the attentions of another woman. He needed to focus on Eve. Eve was his priority. That was his job. So, technically, she did have a right to be uncomfortable.

So there.

"Did you spend the night here or something?" Ruger asked bluntly, eyeing Eve's shorty shorts and bare feet.

Eve's mouth clamped closed and her eyes shot to Bo.

That wasn't a guilty tell. Definitely not. Nothing suspicious about that response.

Thankfully, Bo came in for the save. "Changing the subject isn't going to make us forget about *Boy-Crazy Stacey*, Ruger." He turned to Eve. "Evie, why don't you head back and pack up, and make sure Zeke is up." And then, to Cassie, "What time are you guys heading out?"

The conversation continued around the case ahead as Eve headed out the door.

She was still wondering how much she needed to worry about Cassie and Bo when she knocked on Zeke's door. "Z, you up?" she called. When he didn't respond, she tried the handle, and found it unlocked. She went inside.

Zeke was still in bed, limbs starfished across his mattress, his bedcovers in disarray. She approached his bed and looked down at his peaceful, sleeping face.

"Z."

His eyes shot open. Vermilion.

"Princess." A devious grin curled his lips.

Eve was a split second too late in her retreat. Dagon captured her arm in his vicelike grip and dragged her onto the bed with him, pulling her on top of him and holding her there. She could feel Zeke's morning wood pressing against her leg.

"He's dreaming about you right now," Dagon said.

"It *was* you last night, wasn't it? In my dream."

"Of course. I was a little surprised to get into your dream, though. It's been hard to get into your head lately. But I came to see you after, and your apartment was empty. Whose bed were you in last night, princess? I can sense that Luc isn't around."

"Tell me what you meant about my blood being ichor," she demanded, ignoring his question. She wanted answers of her own, and she wasn't going to let him distract her.

"Ichor is the blood of the gods."

"But what does that mean? Bo said ichor is supposed to be toxic to humans."

Dagon laughed. "Oh, that was a rumor that was started so that the mortals would fear it rather than seek it. The Greek immortals also started the rumor that *all* gods had ichor to keep humans from attempting to spill their blood. 'One drop will kill you!' Rather clever, really."

"Then what is it?"

"Actually, its effects are more akin to what the mortals called ambrosia. It's a more powerful version of Panacea Blood. When I helped you awaken your powers and release your dormant Lilithian traits, it seems to have turned your blood to ichor. Even I couldn't have foreseen that."

"Am...am I immortal? Like you?" Eve whispered, horrified. "Do you have ichor?"

"No. Not all gods have ichor. And ichor doesn't automatically make you immortal. You might be, or you might not be."

"How can you tell I have it?"

"Same way I can tell you are of Lilith's blood. I see things you can't. Just as I can see that you and I belong together, even though you can't."

"We will never be together," Eve hissed.

But caramel brown eyes stared up at her, confused.

"What?" Zeke blinked. "Eve? What is this?" He looked around the room, then back up at her.

"Dagon isn't sealed anymore. He was just talking to me."

"Fuck. I thought something felt off when I went to bed last night." He looked up at her, then down at her body. "Why are you on top of me?"

"You know how handsy he is." Eve moved to climb off of Zeke, but he grasped her waist and pulled her back down so she was straddling his hips. He was still hard.

"I didn't say you had to move," he smiled suggestively. "You could just...stay."

"I can't stay. We're going hunting. We need to pack."

Zeke hadn't yet heard the news, so she filled him in on what she knew about their trip.

"Team Flannel came to Bo's to work out the details, so I came to wake you up. I didn't catch how long we had before we're leaving."

"You were at Bo's?" Zeke inquired.

"What?" Eve tensed, and she knew Zeke had to have felt it.

"You said Team Flannel *came* to Bo's. You were there already?" He looked down at her attire. "In this?"

"What's wrong with this?"

"I'm not sure you should be running around the hallway like this. These shorts can't contain that juicy ass. I don't like the idea of anyone else laying eyes on these sweet cheeks." Zeke squeezed her butt with both hands.

"Luc and Eoduun lay eyes on them."

"They're allowed to. They're part of our little circle. But I don't have to let outsiders look at them."

"Ruger and Remi are outsiders?"

"Were they looking?!" Zeke pouted. "Of course they were. Bo was probably looking, too. He's good at hiding it, but I know he looks."

"Bo's not an outsider," Eve pointed out.

"Why were you there, anyway?" he circled back.

"I can't go to Bo's?"

"I never said that. Why are you being so defensive about it?"

"I'm not. I just don't get why you're being so weird about it."

"You're the one being weird about it."

Shit. She was. But it wasn't his business. "I had some questions for him after I heard about the wendigo case from Luc this morning. Is that satisfactory?"

"You could've just said that from the beginning instead of making it weird, babe," Zeke said.

"You made it weird!"

"I only asked why you were there. How is that weird? If you were at Eoduun's or the Smith's I would've asked the same thing. Why are we arguing about this?"

"We're not!"

"Then why are you yelling at me?"

Eve lowered her voice. "I'm not. Sorry." She really needed to learn the art of playing it cool.

"You know," Zeke said, his voice taking on a low, seductive tone, "if we're going to be cramped together out in the woods with Team Flannel for the next few days, maybe we should take advantage of this time we have alone right now."

"What about Eoduun? We haven't talked to him yet," Eve said.

"If you want me now, you can have me. You don't need his permission. We'll talk to him about it later." Zeke pushed his hips up against her, his engorged cock rubbing between her legs, awakening a heat low in her belly. He reached up and grabbed the back of her head, pulling her down to him. He peppered kisses over her neck and jawline. When his lips touched her ear, he whispered, "Let me have you."

22

Bite Me

Eve leaned up so she could look at his handsome, innocent face. He looked like a college athlete. Her naïve, gentle jock. He gazed up at her tenderly. She ran her thumb along his cheek and smiled down at him. She bent down and kissed his lips, but he clamped them tightly closed.

"What's the matter?" she asked.

He turned his head away. "I just woke up. I probably have morning breath."

"So? I have coffee breath," she chuckled.

"Yeah, but it's cute for you."

"You did not just call my coffee breath cute."

"I sure did."

"You're so fucking lame," she teased.

"We can't all be as cool as you, with your coffee breath."

"Hey. Cute coffee breath," she corrected.

"Fucking right, cute coffee breath." Zeke tangled his fingers in her hair and buried his face in her neck, kissing along her throat. He kissed across the arch of her collarbone, and she felt his fingertips gently slip the straps of her tank top off of her shoulders. He pushed the tight, stretchy garment down below the swell of her breasts.

"And cute, perky tits that fit perfectly in my hands and mouth," he said, then laved his tongue over one nipple while his thumb teased the other.

Eve arched her back and cradled his head in her hands while he sucked at her breasts, the soft swirling of his tongue and light tweaks of his fingers sending hot tingles straight to her core. She bit her lip and whimpered.

Zeke's hand strayed from her breast and slid between their bodies, down her belly, to the thin strip of fabric between her legs.

"There's barely anything covering you," Zeke remarked. "I could fuck you with your shorts on." He slipped one finger under the flimsy barrier and stroked her. "Let me. You're already soaked."

"Let you fuck me with my shorts on?"

"Yes. Please," he begged eagerly.

"Why?" That seemed like such an odd request.

"Because it's fucking hot. Every time I see you wearing these, I'll think about how I fucked you in them."

He tugged his shorts down enough to release his hard cock, and, using his fingers to pull aside the damp fabric of her shorts and underwear, he aligned himself with her opening.

"Fuck me, Eve," he pleaded.

Eve leaned her hips back, slowly impaling herself on him, enjoying the way it felt to have him stretching and filling her. It was strange to have him inside of her while she was still clothed, though. It made this feel dirty and desperate, and she kind of liked it.

She sat atop him and rocked her hips, rolling with his motions. When he closed his eyes and tilted his head back, a delicious moan rising from his lips, Eve's core throbbed at the knowledge that she made him feel that way. She took his hands from her thighs and interlaced her fingers through his, then pressed them down into the mattress on either side of him. She leaned forward over him, her lips ghosting over his neck.

Bite him.

No. Stop. Don't bite him.

Bite him.

Fuck. As she felt that growing ache in her core, the urge to hurt him intensified. She gazed at the thick, muscular column of his neck, admiring all those fine muscles, tendons, and veins, flexing and throbbing, straining as he fucked and pleasured her. She opened her mouth and ran her tongue over the tender flesh, tasting his salty sweat and unique, citrusy Zeke flavor.

She squeezed his hands with her fingers as she moaned against his neck, rocking her hips harder, urging him for more. He thrust up into her harder, deeper, knowing exactly what she wanted him to do.

Choke him.

No.

Just a little.

No! She clung to his hands to keep hers from doing anything nefarious.

"Come with me," Eve urged desperately as she felt the imminent swell of pleasure erupting in her core. She loved the way he moved when he was in the throes of a powerful ejaculation, the way his hips slammed into hers, the way he pulsed and swelled inside of her. It was toe-curling.

And it was more than she could take. He bucked beneath her, their cries of pleasure mingling in the air, and she lost control. Just a little bit.

Just a little bite.

As the waves of her pleasure overtook her, she sank her teeth into the base of his neck and shoulder and sucked at his flesh. She *needed* to do it. She needed him in her mouth, his flesh between her teeth.

He didn't hate it. He made a strange sound, but it wasn't an unpleasant one, and his cock swelled and pulsed again as his hips jerked.

Then a wave of panic crashed over Eve. She bolted upright and looked at Zeke's face. He looked up at her with hooded caramel brown eyes. But...he had closed his eyes earlier. She saw him do it, and she didn't think anything of it. Until now.

"He didn't come out, did he?!" she fretted. She would've noticed the gills, wouldn't she?

Zeke was confused. "What?"

"Dagon!"

"No, it was me. All me. Why?" Zeke was concerned.

"Don't close your eyes during sex. I need to be able to see your eyes at all times."

"He won't interrupt," Zeke assured her. "I can keep him contained."

"I need to be sure. Please." If he could awaken that monstrous power she was trying to learn to control, what else could he do? What else would he awaken?

Zeke pulled her down to him and hugged her against his body. "I promise I'll keep my eyes open. But you have nothing to worry about. I won't let him out."

When he finally freed her from his supernaturally strong arms, she climbed out of his bed and looked down at her shorts. Her apartment was only across the hall, but she didn't trust that she wouldn't run into anyone. "I can't walk out of here like this," she said.

Zeke pulled his shirt off and handed it to her. "Put that on."

Eve saw the mark on his trapezius from her bite. It was obviously a love bite. No one was going to mistake it for anything else.

Zeke watched her attentively as she slipped the shirt over her head, and then he smiled.

"What?" she asked. "I'm swimming in it, I know."

"No, it's not that. I just like seeing my clothes on you." He climbed out of bed and wrapped his arms around her waist, looking down at her with great satisfaction. "It makes it look like you're *mine*."

"Yours? But I thought you told me *you* were *mine*?" she said sarcastically.

"Oh, you want me to wear *your* clothes? Give me your tank top. I don't think it'll fit, but I can give it a try," he teased, sliding his hands up under the shirt he loaned her to get at her skimpy, lacy tank top.

Eve laughed and pushed his hands away. "It's stretchy, but it's not *that* stretchy, you brute," she joked. She wriggled out of his arms and walked to the door. "Now, you got what you wanted, so be a good boy and get ready for the trip."

"Yes, ma'am," he replied as she walked out the door.

When Eve stepped out into the hallway, she realized she should've done a quick peek before exiting.

Eoduun was standing at her door, just raising a knuckle to rap on it, when he turned and saw her standing in Zeke's doorway. In Zeke's shirt.

"You have a knack for this, don't you?" she mumbled to him as she walked past him and opened the door to her apartment. "Always meeting in the hallway at the most awkward moments possible."

He followed her inside and shut the door behind him. She turned and gave him a questioning expression. "Did you need something? Zeke is in his apartment."

"I ascertained that. And Bo is in his, with Team Flannel. I'm not looking for them."

"I need to hop in the shower. Can we make this quick?" Eve said uncomfortably, glad for the oversized shirt hiding the source of her discomfort.

Eoduun crossed his arms and stood in the middle of the room. He eyed Zeke's shirt. "I see I wasn't invited to the party."

"I think we should make allowances for alone time, too, Eoduun. It doesn't always need to be a team effort, right? Not that I don't love it when it is," she added. "Because I absolutely do."

"Is alone time only for you and Zeke?" he asked curtly.

Eve raised a brow. "Well, if you want alone time with Zeke, you'll have to talk to him, not me," she said, only half-joking.

He gave her an irritated look. "You know that's not what I meant."

"I didn't really imagine you would want alone time with me."

"Why the fuck wouldn't I? I can love Zeke and like fucking you. Both things can be true. I don't need Z to be present to have a good time with you."

"But don't you prefer it when he's involved?"

"Not always." Eoduun approached her, and Eve tensed. He stood close to her, looking down at her, but not touching her. "Are you wearing anything under that?"

"Eoduun, I need to go take a shower." She was hyperaware of his proximity as his faint oud noir scent surrounded her.

He touched his knuckle to her chin and tilted her head up so she would look at him. He was taller than Bo and Zeke, but not quite as tall as Luc. He gazed down at her with dark, brooding eyes.

"Because you're fucking dirty?" he asked, his voice deep, his tone loaded. Dominating. Dangerous.

Oh. Dear Jesus.

She averted her eyes, not wanting him to see the embers he'd ignited. "Sure. Whatever," she replied.

She started to turn away, but Eoduun slid his fingers along her jaw and into her hairline, gripping the roots of her locks, holding her fast. He lowered his face to hers, then leaned to whisper in her ear.

"Come on. Tell me how fucking dirty you are," he commanded in the same low voice. "I can smell Zeke on you."

What. The. Fuck. Her body was already frantically running through preparations for round two.

"Eoduun…" She opened her mouth to tell him to stop it, but no words came out. She was breathing heavily, and it had nothing to do with exertion.

"Listen to you panting," he purred. "You want it again, don't you? You're only half satisfied. You need my dick up in that dirty pussy."

Yes.

No.

Yes. Fuck.

Eve clenched her teeth before saying, with a lot less resolve in her tone than she intended, "No. I need a fucking shower."

"Then I'll just fuck you in the shower."

"We shouldn't."

Eoduun laughed darkly and tugged at the hair on the back of her head so she would look up at him as he looked down at her. "If you want it, we should." He pulled her body against his, then brought his lips close to hers. Before he bore his mouth down onto hers, he whispered, "And you fucking want it."

His mouth crushed against her in a bruising, brutal kiss. She wondered if he kissed everyone like that, or if it was just her, like there was something inside of him that resented her. She nipped hard at his lip in retaliation.

He winced, then hummed. "Now you're getting it," he mumbled against her lips. He turned and slammed her back up against the wall. She was grateful for his hand in her hair so that her head didn't bump into the wall. "Fuck the shower," he growled. "Let's fuck right here."

Before she could protest, he reached up under Zeke's shirt and dragged her shorts and underwear down her thighs, and they fell to her ankles. He released her hair, his hand sliding down and wrapping around her neck. He used the pressure of his hand on her neck to keep her pressed against the wall.

In return, she reached her hand up and tangled her fingers in his hair, purposely gripping it too hard.

"Oh, fuck yes," he inhaled sharply as she tugged at his silky black locks. He reached down with his free hand and unzipped his pants, releasing his cock. He came in for a hard kiss again as he hitched her thigh over his hip, but she tugged at his hair and pulled his head back at the last second before their lips made contact. He grunted.

"Be nice," she whispered.

He gave a low laugh. "We both know you don't want me to be nice." He notched the head of his cock against her slick core, and with one deep, powerful thrust, he buried himself inside of her.

Eve cried out, not used to being entered so forcefully, but Eoduun swallowed her cry with a dominating kiss. She pulled his hair and slipped her other hand into the collar of his t-shirt to dig her nails into his shoulder. He plundered her mouth and bit at her tongue, one hand still wrapped around her throat, the other painfully squeezing her thigh. Their hips grinded desperately, violently against each other.

Were they fighting or fucking?

And, holy shit, why was it so goddamn good?

Eve tore her mouth from his, gasping for air. Her breath was ragged and panting, small whimpers squeezing from her throat with every aggressive thrust from Eoduun's hips.

"Say my name," he commanded breathlessly.

"Eoduun...you dirty fucking boy," she gasped.

"Fucking right I am. And you fucking love it, my little whore."

Eve's thighs flexed and she dug her heels into the back of Eoduun's legs as her whole core tightened around his girth.

"Fuck, come all over my cock, little slut," he groaned, his fingers digging harder into her thigh as he slammed into her. "Bite me. Hurt me," he begged.

He didn't have to ask her twice. As her release crashed over her, she clenched her fist in his hair and clamped her teeth down on his pectoral through his shirt, eliciting a pained but pleased grunt from Eoduun. But she wanted his flesh in her mouth, not his shirt. She pulled his neck closer to her and latched onto it, moaning against him as she rode out the remaining waves of her pleasure.

"Mmm, fuuuck..." Eoduun moaned and gasped, then erupted inside of her, his fingers tightening around her throat as he came.

As they came down, Eoduun rested his forehead on the wall next to Eve's head and loosened his grip on her neck. His fingers came up and caressed her jaw.

"You were perfect," he praised. "You're always fucking perfect."

Eve didn't know how to take that coming from Eoduun, so she disregarded it. "Well, now I really do need a shower," she remarked, lowering herself from her perch atop his hips.

Eoduun raised his head from the wall and looked down at her while he zipped his pants back up. He had an incredibly obvious post-sex face. He looked mildly high or drunk, and deeply satisfied. Then his lazy gaze dropped to her neck.

"Oops." He traced his finger over the side of her neck. "Eh, that should fade," he said dismissively.

"Did you leave marks?" she asked, a tinge of annoyance in her tone.

He grinned and held his hand over her neck again, aligning his fingers with the fingerprints on her flesh. "Guilty." Then, with his other hand, he ran a thumb over his lower lip. "But I'm pretty sure you did, too."

He wasn't wrong. She had left a mark on his lip and a bite on his neck.

"Fuck. I'm on a roll this morning," she said with a sigh, eyeing the marks on him. "God, I hope no one says anything. Maybe I should heal you."

Eoduun took a step back and dropped his hand from her neck. "If you try to give me your blood right now, I'll just want to fuck you again, and then we'll end up with new marks, so...just let me keep them."

"Fine. But you better hope the handprint on my neck fades by the time Bo sees me, or you're going to be in trouble."

Eoduun looked at her neck again, and his expression was colored with a hint of disappointment. "It's already starting to fade." Then the disappointment turned to mischief. "I love fucking someone who can take it. Who gives as good as they get. Someone I don't have to worry about breaking. Someone who fucking *gets* it."

"And I get it?"

"You fucking get it."

Eve chuckled as she picked up her shorts and underwear off the floor.

"What?" Eoduun inquired.

"It's just funny, when I first started getting to know you, I thought you were a total bottom. But there's no way that's true." Eve started toward her bedroom.

"Why is that?" Eoduun asked, following her.

Eve leveled a dubious stare at him. "Am I wrong?"

"I've tried it a few times. It's not like I *refuse* to bottom. But it's true; I'd rather top." He stopped in her doorway and watched as she threw her dirty clothes in the hamper.

"Have you and Zeke ever had a go at it?" Eve wondered as she picked out a clean outfit for their trip. She was pretty sure the answer was no, but she couldn't be one hundred percent certain.

"Zeke doesn't see me that way unless you're between us. I'll never have him without you. He won't even talk about the things we've done after the moment is over."

"What do you mean he won't talk about it?"

"He changes the subject or brushes it off with some vague bullshit answer. I tried to ask him how he felt about me kissing him the first time we shared you, and he just shrugged and told me not to worry about it. Then I tried to ask him how far he was comfortable going with me when all three of us were together, and he just said it wasn't about us, it was about you, and then started talking about you."

Eve regarded him with a sympathetic look. "I'm sorry."

"I don't want your pity. And this isn't an invitation for you to try to interfere or try to fix it, either," Eoduun replied curtly. "I don't want you going to him and telling him he needs to talk to me. This is between me and him."

"No, I get it. It's not my place. But I can still empathize with you."

"Empathize? I'm not sure you can even begin to comprehend what it feels like to love somebody you can never have. You can have anyone you want."

"No, I can't."

Eoduun's expression darkened with suspicion. "Oh, really? Who do you want that you can't have?"

Eve sensed that his jealousy had been triggered. "No one. I'm just saying, no one can have *anyone* they want."

Eoduun took a step toward Eve. "Who do you want?" he repeated. "Is it Ramil?" he seethed.

"Calm down. I don't want Ramil."

"Good. Because I'd erase every memory he has of you."

"Eoduun!"

"What? He can't have you."

"Why? I thought you said I could have anyone I wanted," she goaded. She tried to walk past him, but he shot his arm out in front of her and pressed his hand against the wall, blocking her path.

"Are we not enough for you?" he probed.

"Relax, I'm just fucking with you. Besides, I don't get why you're getting all jealous. You only want me because I'm your link to Zeke."

Eoduun's expression faltered. He looked like she'd just punched him in the gut. "Are you fucking kidding me right now?"

"What, you thought I didn't know that? I'm not stupid."

"Are you sure? Because we literally just had this conversation. You know, right before we *fucked? Without* Zeke?"

"Yeah, you like fucking me, but it's not because you like *me*. I just came from Zeke's, still smelling like him, wearing his shirt...I can put two and two together."

"You think I only wanted you this morning because I was using you as a stand-in for Zeke?" Eoduun snarled. When Eve let her silence do the talking, he said, "Eve, that's fucked up. It pisses me off that you think I would use you so selfishly."

"There's no reason to get upset about it. My role in this whole arrangement is about as selfish as it gets, so who am I to judge? We're all just using each other for sex."

"It's more than just that, and you know it."

"I don't know that. I'm supposed to be training with you guys, remember? Feelings have nothing to do with training."

"Were you training with me just now? Is that what that was?"

Eve set her jaw and didn't answer.

23

Drinking, Monsters, and Guns

Eve heard a knock at her apartment door. She looked up expectantly at Eoduun, but he remained in her path for a moment longer, gazing down at her with an inscrutable expression.

"I'll get the door," he said, turning his back to her and sauntering from the room.

Eve stood in her room, clutching her clothes, wondering what the hell had gotten into Eoduun. He loved Zeke, so why was he being so weird about her all of a sudden? It had to be *because* of Zeke. Eoduun was probably afraid of what it would mean if their little arrangement came to an end. If that happened, he would be back to strict platonics with Zeke, and Eve had a feeling Eoduun would do anything to avoid that. At least with Eve between them, Eoduun could pretend that he and Zeke were more than just friends. He needed Eve in order to have Zeke, so he was going to dig his nails in and cling to this relationship with everything he had.

It was never about her, and he was deluding himself if he'd convinced himself otherwise.

Eve heard Bo's voice in the entryway. She walked out of the bedroom and saw him standing in the doorway, talking to Eoduun. Bo's eyes glanced over at her on her way to the bathroom. He paused.

His dark eye flashed yellow, and his brows knitted in concern. "What the fuck? Evie, come here! What is that!?" He pointed at her.

Oh, fuck. Her neck. Eoduun's handprint.

Bo's hand shot out and fisted in Eoduun's shirt. "Was it you?!" Still holding Eoduun, he turned his attention to Eve again. "Is that a handprint? Is that a fucking *handprint*?!"

Apparently it hadn't faded quite enough to escape Bo's sharp eye.

Eoduun held his hands out defensively. "Bo, it's not like that. I didn't hurt her. She's totally fine, aren't you, Eve?" he asked, turning pleading eyes toward Eve.

Bo ignored his placations. "Inexcusable. You'll never touch her again!"

"Bo," Eve interceded, crossing the room quickly. "Eoduun didn't hurt me. It was all in good fun, and it'll fade by the time I'm out of the shower. Chill the fuck out."

"I will not chill the fuck out. He has no right to leave his marks on you, especially in *good fun*."

"I left marks on him," she argued.

"Irrelevant."

Eve placed her hand on Bo's cheek and turned his furious gaze toward her. "Let it go. Please. We were training. I allowed it, so if you want to be angry, be angry with me. You want to punish someone, punish me."

Bo shoved Eoduun away and removed Eve's hand from his cheek. "Don't tempt me," he growled. As much as she wanted to make a Daddy spanking joke, she knew better than to fuck with Bo right now. Bo's eyes dropped to her throat, and, like Eoduun, he reached out and held his fingers over the marks. "Luc will need to know about what he did to you."

"I'll tell Luc myself." She then gave him a meaningful glance. "There may be other things you neglected to tell him this morning, too. I'll make sure I don't miss any details."

Her meaning wasn't lost on him. His hand slid from her neck, and he frowned behind his mask. He turned away from her. "Do whatever you have to do. Now get ready. We're leaving shortly."

Shit. She shouldn't have done that. Watching Bo's back as he walked out filled her with instant regret and guilt.

"Did something happen between you and Bo?" Eoduun asked after the door closed.

"Get out," she grumbled at Eoduun as she turned on her heel and headed toward the shower, disinclined to answer.

Eoduun scoffed. "Whatever. Just don't tell Luc about the mark. I'll fix this with Bo." Then he walked out, slamming the door behind him.

Well, she'd managed to piss off everyone. Awesome.

Instead of taking the cars for this trip, they boarded the jet at the airport. On the way to Michigan, Eve couldn't help but notice that Bo was no longer upset with either her or Eoduun; or, if he was, he was doing a stellar job of hiding it. But he was incapable of hiding something like that, so what had Eoduun said to him to make everything ok?

She was curious, but she wasn't about to bring it up. It was probably best to just let it be for now and be grateful that things had been smoothed over.

When Team Alpha and Team Flannel arrived at the airport in the western end of Michigan's Upper Peninsula, everyone had to leave their phones on the jet to prevent any possible tracking the Vatican might feel inclined to do, and they were given a single satellite phone instead. Upon disembarking the plane, they found two trucks waiting for them, as they still had a two-hour drive to get to the cabin where the wendigo had attacked.

"You should ride with us," Cassie suggested to Eve as the group naturally split into teams to climb into the trucks. She hooked her arm through Eve's. "You look like you could use a break from the dream team."

"Evie needs to stay with me," Bo said, opening the door for her in the big Chevy. He held his hand out, gesturing for her to get in the truck.

Cassie clung tighter to Eve. "We'll all be traveling together," Cassie pointed out. "Come on, Bo, you know she's safe with us."

"You'll see plenty of her when we get to the cabin," Bo replied stubbornly.

"Oh, come on, Daddy, pleeeeease?" Eve pleaded teasingly. "I'll be good, I swear!"

Bo's ears burned red. "Evie," he said in a warning tone.

"Daddy."

"For fuck's sake, *fine*," he huffed in embarrassment, shoving the door closed and disappearing around the front of the truck on his way to the driver's side.

Eve didn't know why she enjoyed getting under his skin so much and making him lose his cool. It must be the satisfaction in knowing that she *could*. But after last night, perhaps the "Daddys" were still too much of a sore spot.

Eve climbed into the back of Team Flannel's pickup truck with Cassie, hoping Bo wasn't too annoyed with her. She also realized that Bo, Zeke, and Eoduun were all going to be alone together for the next two hours, and wondered if they were going to talk about her and what an annoying asshole she was.

As soon as the trucks started off down the road, Cassie began prying. "I want details."

"What are you talking about?"

"You stayed with Bo last night."

"What? No, I was returning a book."

"No one returns books that early in the morning in their pajamas and bedhead."

"Apparently I do," Eve countered.

Cassie gave her a dubious glare. "Liar, liar, pants on fire. Come on, Eve. It's *me*. You can tell me. Was he good? He was fucking gooood, wasn't he?" Cassie bit her lower lip and rolled her body suggestively, and something like jealousy heated Eve's blood.

"Don't talk about him like that," Eve whispered, glancing up at Ruger and Remi in the front seat. Were they ok with her thirsting after another man?

Cassie saw Eve's furtive glance at the guys, and laughed. "What, them? They're worse than I am. You should hear what Ruger says about you."

"Hey!" Ruger protested, embarrassed. He turned his head and smiled apologetically at Eve. "It's not like...I mean, I don't...It's..." he stammered, then just shook his head and shrugged, giving a short, awkward laugh, and turned his attention back to the road without clarifying.

"But I know he loves *me*, so I don't mind it," Cassie smirked.

Eve wished she had that kind of confidence. If Luc said anything about another woman in front of her, she'd be both jealous and suspicious, imagining him with the other woman and no longer loving her. She had a long way to go to finding that kind of confidence in her relationship with Luc. He, on the other hand, seemed to have that kind of confidence in spades. He just *knew* she loved him. It was kind of annoying.

"So?" Cassie nudged Eve's arm with her elbow. "Was he good?" She waggled her eyebrows.

"I didn't fuck him."

Cassie studied Eve's face, then her devious smile faded. "Why not? You want to, don't you?"

"No."

"Really?"

"Really."

Cassie regarded her carefully. "Well, I want to."

Eve's chest cavity erupted in fire. "You can't," she spat.

Cassie raised her eyebrows. "Oh? Why can't I? You don't want him, right?" she challenged knowingly. "Or were you lying?"

"I wasn't lying. I like what I have right now. I'm good. I don't want to mess anything up."

"So, you don't want him, but you don't want anyone else to have him, either?"

"Well, that's not exactly it..."

Cassie rolled her eyes. "Hon, you can't just go around licking all the cupcakes in the box if you aren't going to eat them. Leave some cupcakes for the rest of us."

Ruger turned around and glanced in the back seat. "Cupcakes? Who's got cupcakes?"

"Mindya business," Cassie chastised. "This doesn't concern you."

When Ruger turned to face forward again, Cassie continued prodding at Eve. "So, if you didn't fuck him, why did you stay with Bo? And don't try to feed me that returning a book bullshit."

Eve sighed. "I had a bad dream." It wasn't entirely untrue.

"And?"

"And he keeps the boogeyman away." Also not entirely untrue.

"Does he, now?"

"Yep."

"Do you have to be snuggled up next to him in his bed to reap those benefits?"

"Naturally."

Cassie laughed. "And did you wake up with his morning wood pushing up on you?"

"Oh, he's always up and out of bed before I wake up," Eve replied.

"Probably a reason for—" Cassie paused. "Wait, did you say *always*? As in, you do this on a regular basis?" When Eve didn't answer, Cassie asked, "Does Luc know this?"

"He suggested it," Eve replied, only realizing how weird it sounded after it was out of her mouth.

"Good lord, Eve. You have, and I mean this in the most supportive way possible, *the most* fucked up relationship with Luc."

Eve looked out her window and watched the trees going by. She knew how fucked up it all was. She knew things couldn't continue as they were indefinitely. She felt like she was driving a car with two gas pedals and no brakes, and she knew a big curve was just ahead. Eventually, she was going to crash and burn.

Maybe she should just bail before it all fell apart. She rubbed her finger over the little tattoo on her wrist, and acknowledged that that was no longer an option. Hell, who was she kidding? If she ran away now, it would be like when kids say they're going to run away. Pack a bag with snacks and a blanket, walk to the end of the driveway, cry for five minutes, then come right back and ask what's for dinner.

But something had to give. Sooner or later, the other shoe was going to drop.

"Jesus, Bo, you drive like a little old lady," Ruger complained as he stretched his arms over his head after climbing out of the truck. "If I'd been in the lead, we would've been here half an hour ago."

Bo opened the tailgate of the truck he'd been driving and he, Zeke, and Eoduun began unloading luggage and guns. "And if you got into an accident or pulled over for speeding, you'd still be on your way," Bo replied coolly.

"I didn't see a single cop on our way out here," Ruger pointed out. "We're on fucking dirt roads, man."

"It's the ones you don't see that get you," Bo said.

Ruger scoffed. "Pfft, I just flash a little skin, and I'm on my way." He lifted his pant leg and winked.

"Oh yes, show them a little ankle," Eve joked. "So hot. Do you offer to churn some butter for them or bribe them with handmade quilts?"

"Hey, I happen to have very attractive ankles, thank you very much. No further bribery needed."

"That's what he thinks," Cassie chimed in. "But I hate to tell you, hon, it's my Jedi mind tricks that get us out of tickets, not your ankles. 'These are not the idiots you're looking for.'"

"You just called yourself an idiot," Ruger retorted.

Cassie shook her head dismissively. She looked out at the cabin ahead. "Luc made sure it was ok we were staying here, right? We aren't going to get arrested for a B&E, are we?"

Without missing a beat, Bo said, "We'll be fine. Just have Ruger show the cops a little ankle."

"It's not cops I'm worried about," Eve said apprehensively.

Ruger draped a heavy arm across her shoulder. "You got nothing to worry about, sweetheart. We eat wendigo for breakfast."

Eoduun was suddenly at her side. He casually brushed Ruger's arm off of her shoulders and said, "Unless the wendigo possesses one of us. Then we'll be eating each other for breakfast." With a hand on her back, he guided Eve away from Ruger. "Come on, Eve, let's get our shit unloaded," he suggested.

At the tailgate, as Eve reached for her suitcase, she glanced over at Eoduun. He was standing over her, watching Ruger unloading the other truck.

"Why are you mean-mugging Ruger?" she asked as she dragged her suitcase over the lowered tailgate. "I like Ruger."

"I like when Ruger keeps his hands off of you."

Eve straightened her back and tilted her head at Eoduun. "What the fuck has gotten into you?"

"Nothing." When Eve stared at him, waiting for a better answer, he just gave an annoyed sigh. "Whatever." He grabbed his bag and walked away from her toward the cabin.

Zeke suddenly came bursting from the cabin in a fit. "Jesus fucking Christ! Burn it down! Burn it down!" he shrieked as he ran to the truck.

"What?! What is it?!" Remi shouted, Team Flannel all reaching for the weapons strapped to various places on their bodies.

Eve looked to Bo, surprised to see he seemed entirely unconcerned, carrying the rifle case over one shoulder and his duffle bag over the other, trudging toward the cabin. "Show me where it is and I'll kill it," he said calmly.

"It's fucking *huge!*" Zeke exclaimed, bounding after Bo. "I've never seen a spider so fucking big! Please tell me we packed Raid."

Eve heard Remi sigh behind her. "This is going to be a long trip."

The cabin was small, rustic, and run-down. It was one open room with a moth-eaten couch along one wall and a dusty twin bed shoved in the corner. There was an old woodstove in the middle of the room and a small table with three chairs near the window. There was no plumbing or electricity, and the only water source was an old hand-pump outside. The bloodstains from the recent carnage were still clearly evident on the walls and floor planks.

"Is anyone else a little concerned about the vicinity of the water pump to the outhouse?" Ruger asked as they all walked around the cabin, looking it over.

"I'm more concerned about what kind of bugs are hanging out in that outhouse," Zeke worried.

Eve pointed to the peak in the outhouse roof where a small, grayish black mass was dangling. "Is that a bat hanging there?"

Zeke shuddered. "Fuck, that is a bat." He turned to Bo. "Can I sleep in the truck?"

Eoduun raised his hand. "I second that. This place is disgusting."

"Pussies," Ruger mocked. "You're lucky we *have* an outhouse and a roof over our heads. With wendigo hunts, we're usually out in the middle of nowhere in a flimsy tent, shitting in the woods and huddling around the fire. This is the goddamn Palms."

"Where are we all sleeping, though?" Eve asked. "I only saw one bed in there, and it didn't look fit for human use."

"You can sleep in the truck with us," Zeke offered.

"No one's sleeping in the truck," Bo said, as the group all filed through the door back into the cabin. "We need to stick together. There's plenty of room to sleep on the floor. We have enough sleeping bags for everyone."

"And I have enough Jack and Jameson to make it a party," Ruger added, producing two bottles of Old No.7 and a bottle of Irish whiskey from his bag on the table.

"Just what you need," Cassie said sarcastically.

Ruger twisted the cap off of the Jameson and took a swig. "It is, actually."

"Drinking, monsters, and guns. What could possibly go wrong?" Eoduun said.

"I'm not saying we get shitfaced," Ruger defended. "Just a little fire in your belly. Something to make this place seem a little more palatable for you city boys."

Several hours and two empty bottles later, the cabin was a lot more cozy than it had seemed upon arrival. Everyone seemed to be getting along, laughing, and having a good time. They had a lantern burning on top of the woodstove, casting a soft, warm glow around the room that made this whole adventure feel a lot like camping with friends. Eve had almost forgotten why they were out there.

Almost.

Then came the moment she dreaded most. "Guys," she announced, "I need a bathroom buddy."

Bo immediately pushed off from the counter he was leaned against. "I'll take you."

Cassie untangled her crossed legs and jumped up from her seat on the floor. "No, no, *I'll* take her. Girl code."

Zeke hopped down from the counter where he had been perched next to Bo. "I actually need to go, too."

Ruger raised the last bottle of whiskey and stood up from his chair at the table. He pointed to the door enthusiastically. "The party is moving outside!"

"It isn't a party," Cassie corrected him. "And two bottles were enough. We're done drinking, you slush."

Remi smirked from his seat across from Ruger at the table. "Lush. And I think you're right, two bottles were definitely enough."

Eve stepped out the front door of the cabin, but was promptly pulled back by a rough hand.

"Wait," Bo commanded. He stepped in front of her and shined his flashlight out the door into the woods. "I just scented something."

"That was me. Sorry about that," Ruger joked.

Bo didn't laugh. He hadn't partaken in the Jameson and Jack with everyone else, so he was stone-cold sober. His mismatched eyes scanned the woods carefully. "It's fading, but there was something out here." He turned to the group. "Don't run off. Piss and get back in the cabin, got it?" he ordered.

Ruger saluted him. "Aye aye, captain!"

Bo escorted Eve and Cassie to the outhouse, but he was also keeping a close eye on the boys who had scattered to go piss on trees. Eve used the outhouse first, and when she came out, Cassie went in behind her.

Eve stood next to Bo while they waited for Cassie, and she noticed his head was on a swivel. She looked up at him, surprised to see yellow.

"Bo, your eye," she said.

"It's back," he said ominously, watching the woods. Then he did a head count. "Where's Z?"

"He probably went back to the cabin."

"No one went back to the cabin yet." He called out for Zeke.

And then something called back.

24
The First Rule of Hunting Wendigo

Eve's throat tightened when she heard it. Zeke's voice sounded far away and strange, yelling, "Help! Help me!" She looked to Bo in panic as Ruger, Remi, and Eoduun all forgot their buzzes and went into full alert mode. Before she could say anything, Bo said, "That's not Z. It's a good mimic, but it's not him."

Cassie burst out of the outhouse. "Did you hear it?! Did you hear the wendigo?" she cried excitedly as she unsheathed the machete hanging from her belt.

They all stood in tense silence, listening and watching, weapons drawn. Except for Eve. She'd left Harry, Ron, and Hermoine (her pistol, rifle, and shotgun) in the cabin. She reached down and grabbed the knife from her ankle sheath, but she wasn't sure what good it would do against a wendigo.

Crunch, crunch, crunch.

Something was moving through the underbrush toward them from behind the outhouse.

Eve could barely hear through the blood rushing in her ears. She backed up away from the outhouse, but her back bumped into the immovable brick wall that was Bo. Why wasn't he retreating?

A pair of glowing red eyes appeared around the side of the outhouse, coming toward them, but still, Bo didn't move or back away. Eve stood frozen in panic, her back pressed firmly against Bo.

"What happened?" Bo asked the eyes calmly.

Dagon stepped out into the beam cast by the flashlight, and Eve let out a long, relieved exhale.

Dagon said, "Your wendigo just tried to possess Zeke." His crimson eyes turned to Eve. "Hey there, princess. Do I get a reward for saving your precious fuckboy?"

Zeke came through then, the red eyes switching to brown. "Dude, fucking rude," he chastised Dagon.

"You good?" Bo asked Zeke.

"Yeah, I think so. I was just standing there, pissing at the edge of the woods, and the next thing I know, I got *so* hungry. Hungrier than I've ever been. And then all these dark thoughts and urges started pushing into my mind, but then Dagon jumped in and pushed them right back out."

"What kind of dark thoughts and urges?" Eve asked.

A shadow fell over Zeke's face. "I don't even want to say it out loud."

"You wanted to eat us?" Eoduun supplied.

"It was so much worse than that," he said quietly, his gaze flitting to Eve briefly before looking down at his feet.

"It's not just an urge to eat people," Remi informed them. "It's this insatiable *need* that you just can't fill – wanting to completely consume everything you desire in every way possible. A greedy compulsion to fill the bottomless chasm of emptiness in your soul."

"How did you know that?" Zeke wanted to know.

"I was possessed briefly on one of our wendigo hunts. I still have nightmares about it."

"Everybody inside," Bo commanded. "We need to come up with a game plan."

Once everyone was safely inside the cabin, Bo handed the reins to Cassie. "The first rule of hunting wendigo," she said, "is to make it come to you. Chasing it around the woods is pointless and dangerous. That's their turf, and they have an unbeatable advantage. Now that we know it's here, trying to lure us into the woods, we can start baiting." She looked at Zeke.

"I don't like where this is going," Zeke said.

"Sorry, Zeke, but you're our best option now that we know it can't fully possess you," Cassie reasoned.

"I knew I didn't like where this was going."

"Hell yeah," Ruger cheered. "Finally, I don't have to be the bait. I'm *always* the bait."

"If Ruger's got experience, maybe he should do it," Zeke suggested.

Cassie ignored him. "We'll put Zeke in the tent out behind the cabin, and when it comes in for him, we'll ambush it. Easy peasy."

"And how do you kill a wendigo?" Eve asked.

"Burn its heart," Bo replied.

"That doesn't sound easy peasy."

Ruger rummaged through the big hockey bag full of weapons that was sitting in the middle of the floor and pulled out a large, odd-looking gun with a small propane tank attached to the underside of it. A flamethrower. "This helps," he said with a wide grin.

Cassie went over the particulars of their plan of attack, then asked, "Everyone savvy?"

"I'm not comfortable with using Zeke as bait," Bo said. "I'll be the bait."

Cassie cleared her throat. "With all due respect, Bo, we're the ones with the experience here, and I think Zeke gives us our best chance at success. I'd rather not risk having to fight the wendigo *and* you under possession. You of all people should understand that."

Even behind Bo's mask, Eve saw the clenched jaw Cassie's comment elicited. His voice had an edge to it when he replied, "Noted."

"It's ok, Bo," Zeke said. "If anything goes wrong, Dagon will keep me alive until Eve can heal me."

"I don't like using team members as bait," Bo grumbled.

Ruger looked up from the shotgun he was loading and said, "Ah, it'll be fine, Bo. We're master baiters." He then laughed at his own joke.

"You're an idiot," Remi sighed.

"I'm delightful."

"Let's go with delightful idiot," Cassie compromised, then took the loaded shotgun Ruger handed her and kissed him chastely on the lips.

Bo and Zeke went outside to set up the tent in the middle of the yard behind the cabin while Ruger and Remi set up the tree stand they had packed, overlooking the tent. The perch was secured higher than the typical stand would be, considering how tall a wendigo could be.

Inside the cabin, Eve and Eoduun worked on loading guns and preparing for the hunt while Cassie donned camouflage hunting gear. Not only was Cassie a savant with a sword, she was apparently a deadeye as well.

"I'm going to stay with Zeke in the tent," Eoduun announced when Cassie joined them at the table to select her rifle.

"No, you aren't," Cassie said flatly.

"I wasn't asking your permission. I was just notifying you. He shouldn't have to be out there alone."

"He's a big boy. He can handle it," Cassie replied.

"You don't know Zeke," Eoduun argued. He looked at Eve. "Back me up here, Eve. Tell her."

Cassie looked expectantly at Eve. "Zeke's a grown-ass man. Back me up here, girl. Tell him."

Eve looked between Eoduun and Cassie, then sighed. "Eoduun's right, Cass. Zeke is strong as hell, but he's going to be scared shitless out there by himself."

"Maybe he could just let Dagon take over for a while."

"Dagon can't be trusted," Eve said.

"And what if Eoduun gets possessed?"

"I'm fairly confident I can keep it out of my mind long enough for you to take it down," Eoduun assured her.

"Then maybe we should just put you in the tent and utilize Zeke elsewhere," Cassie considered.

"Zeke won't let me just take his place. I already know that," Eoduun said. Cassie looked to Eve, and Eve nodded in confirmation.

"You Alphas have a real problem with just doing as you're told, don't you?"

"Only Daddy gets to order us around," Eve jested.

"Hm, I'll bet," Cassie said knowingly, winking at Eve.

The gesture didn't escape Eoduun's notice. "What the fuck is that supposed to mean?" he asked in an accusatory tone.

"Don't worry about it," Cassie said nonchalantly. "All right, guys, I'm going to go climb up onto my murder throne. See you on the flip side."

Eoduun leveled a stare at Eve as Cassie left the cabin, but Eve kept her eyes on the magazine in front of her as she loaded bullets into it.

"Are you sleeping with Bo?" Eoduun ventured.

Eve's eyes shot up and met his in surprise. "What?"

"You heard me."

"Why would you ask that?"

"You aren't denying it."

"I'm not fucking Bo. God, why do I keep having to say that?" Eve complained.

"But you sleep with him," Eoduun said matter-of-factly.

Eve narrowed her eyes at him. "Why are you saying that?"

"Because it's true, isn't it?"

"It's not what you think. It's not sexual."

"Isn't it? It looked pretty fucking sexual to me."

Eve was taken aback. "Excuse me? What the fuck are you talking about?"

Eoduun crossed his arms. "You can't let him take it there, Eve. It'll ruin everything. I won't let him ruin everything."

"You need to explain yourself, Eoduun. Where are you getting all of this?"

Eoduun sighed. "I saw it. Straight from the fucking source. How do you think I smoothed the handprint thing over with Bo? I made him forget."

Eve's eyes widened. "Eoduun, you didn't…"

"I did what I had to."

"You fucking *erased* him?!"

"Just that one little thing! I had to, or he was going to fuck everything up!"

"That's forbidden, Eoduun!" Eve hissed in a harsh whisper, looking around to make sure they were still alone.

"I don't give a shit. I had no choice. I didn't hurt anyone by doing it, either. If anything, everyone is better off now."

Eve stared at Eoduun in disbelief and suspicion. Then she quickly averted her gaze. "Wait…have you ever erased *me*?"

"Eve…" Eoduun had an injured tone. "Don't do that, Eve. I wouldn't erase you."

"Until I pose a threat to the *arrangement*? The precious arrangement that keeps you close to Zeke?"

Eoduun slammed his fist down onto the table, startling Eve. "Goddamn it, it's not just Zeke! I like *us*, ok? The three of us. We've barely had time to really explore it, and Bo was going to put an end to it before it even had a chance."

Eve felt like she was entering dangerous territory with Eoduun. "Eoduun…this isn't a relationship. We aren't a throuple. We're just

224

friends with benefits. I worry that you're looking for more than what I can offer you and Zeke." She kept her gaze planted firmly on the gun-laden table in front of her.

"Stop avoiding my eyes, Eve," Eoduun begged. "I'm not going to erase you. I don't think I could even if I wanted to."

"You have to tell Bo what you've done."

"No, I don't, and you don't either. We can keep this between us. It really isn't that big of a deal. You and I had a *consensual* encounter that left marks on both of us, and he was going to blow it out of proportion. And the handprint faded, just as we knew it would. Who are we hurting by keeping this to ourselves?"

"Bo."

"It isn't hurting Bo. He's not missing out on anything just because I took away one little memory. It would hurt us a lot more if I'd allowed him to keep it, and it would hurt us doubly if we told him about it now."

"You're putting me in a tough spot, Eoduun. What the fuck am I supposed to do now? No matter what I do, I betray someone."

"Keeping it quiet is in everyone's best interest. Just think about it, and you'll come to the same conclusion," Eoduun said.

Eve ventured a tentative glance at Eoduun. If he tried to read or erase her, she was ready to push back. "What did you see in Bo's mind?" she wanted to know.

Eoduun lifted an eyebrow. "Really? You're going to try to take the moral high ground on the erasure, but you want the juicy details I got out of it, too? Can't have both, Eve. But I'll tell you what: if you swear to keep this whole thing secret, I'll tell you what I saw."

Eve chewed her lip. It was tempting, but what good was that kind of knowledge going to do her? Still…

She really was a shitty person. "Tell me."

Eoduun's features darkened. "I saw what you did with him. And I fucking hate it."

Guilt sank in Eve's stomach. "And how did he feel about it?" she asked quietly. She wasn't sure she wanted the answer.

"Does it matter?"

"It matters."

Eoduun frowned. "He hated it. He loved it. He hated himself for it. He cares about you more than he should, and he feels like he betrayed both you and Luc."

Eve sat back in her chair. She already suspected those things. Eoduun's revelation lacked the impact she expected.

He saw it on her face. "You're disappointed?"

"No, just…nothing I didn't already know, I guess."

"Well, it was plenty that I didn't fucking know. And I sure didn't fucking love it. And what's the deal with Dagon getting into your dreams? Why haven't you told Zeke about it?"

"Sometimes we have to keep things from Zeke to keep things from Dagon. We have ways to keep him out of my dreams, but we don't want him to know how we're doing it. So, it just seemed best to keep the whole thing quiet."

"Hm." Eoduun looked out the window at everyone finishing up outside. "Don't fuck him," he said suddenly.

"What?"

"Don't fuck Bo."

"I didn't."

"But you almost did. You wanted him, more than you've ever wanted me or Zeke. I could see it in your eyes through his memory."

"It was the blood. You know what it's like."

"Oh, you mean your ichor blood? When were you going to tell us about *that*?"

"When I found out what it actually meant. I still don't know if it's even true."

"You sure have a lot of secrets for someone who is so opposed to keeping one little secret for me," Eoduun said contemptuously. "Whatever. Just…don't do it. Not with him. Not after what I saw between you. It'll fuck up everything."

"Don't worry about Bo. It was a fluke. Besides, you don't get to tell me what to do. And just so you know, if you ever do anything like this again, I *will* tell Bo. Stay out of his head."

"I'll stay out of his head if you stay out of his pants."

"Fuck off, Eoduun."

Eoduun arched a brow. "Good. Keep that anger. Take it out on me next time we're fucking."

Ruger and Remi entered the cabin, ending the conversation between Eve and Eoduun.

"Look alive, people!" Ruger announced, rubbing his hands together gleefully. "It's almost time to hunt."

Eoduun slid Eve's rifle across the table toward her after he finished loading it. "Don't miss." He took up his own firearms and headed for the door.

Bo was walking in just as Eoduun pushed past him. "Whoa, where do you think you're going?" he demanded.

"To be bait," Eoduun replied simply and continued walking.

Bo reached out and caught Eoduun's arm. "But we didn't talk about that."

Eoduun pulled away. "There's a lot we don't talk about," he shot back. "I'll be with Zeke. Let's just get this over with so we can get back home."

Bo watched Eoduun walk away, confusion clouding his face. He looked to Eve.

Ruger said it before anyone else could. "What crawled up his ass?"

"It's Eoduun," Eve reasoned. "Isn't that answer enough?"

Ruger shrugged, seemingly satisfied with her answer. Bo wasn't, though. He came to the table and took his loaded pistol and holstered it at his hip. "Did something happen while I was outside?" he asked, lingering next to Eve.

"He'll get over it. No biggie," she said. She felt Bo's eyes studying her, looking for what she wasn't saying. She looked up at his masked face, knowing that avoiding his gaze would only make him more suspicious. She hoped he couldn't see the betrayal in her eyes. She may not have been the one to carry out the crime, but her complacency made her guilty enough. She stood up in front of him and patted him on the chest. "Let's kill a monster."

25
I Wanted to Eat a God

Ruger and Remi were stationed at the windows, rifles at the ready. Bo sat at the table with Eve, the flamethrower sitting in front of him. He was the one in charge of administering the fiery coup de grâce to the wendigo's heart when the moment presented itself.

Eve could see the unease in his eyes as he anxiously scanned the wood line, back and forth. He hated that Zeke and Eoduun were out there functioning as bait. After several silent minutes of this, he pushed his chair back and stood up.

"I need to be outside. I want to hear and smell this thing coming."

"Cass has got this," Ruger replied. "Let her do her thing. We'll take it down and *then* you can get out there and finish it off. We stick to the plan."

Eve tugged at Bo's sleeve. "The boys can handle themselves. Dagon isn't going to let Z die."

"No, but he couldn't care less if Eoduun does."

"The only thing dying tonight is a wendigo," Ruger said, watching out the window. "Relax, Bo."

Bo suddenly jerked to attention. "I hear it!"

Everyone fell silent, listening. Remi cracked the window open, and faint cries for help drifted in on the cool breeze. It sounded like a child.

"It's keeping its distance," Remi noted. "Dagon must've spooked it earlier."

"Yeah, but it knows there are people here," Ruger said. "It'll come in eventually. Its hunger always outweighs its patience."

The eerie, child-like cries continued for almost an hour, never getting closer or further away, but the direction in which they were coming from shifted as though the wendigo was circling them at a distance.

And then they stopped.

Silence in the woods.

No crickets, owls, frogs, bats, or other nocturnal creatures.

Just dead silence.

"The scent is getting stronger," Bo whispered, standing up from the table. "It's coming in."

Ruger conveyed the message to Cassie through the earpieces they were using to keep in communication. "She says she thinks she can see it through the trees," he relayed to the rest of them.

Eve's fear and anticipation were suddenly drowned out by an inexplicable and overpowering urge to rush to Dagon. Her body yearned for his touch, and her mouth was salivating for his flesh. Her fingers ached to encircle his throat and squeeze while his hips bucked beneath her, his engorged cock deep inside of her, her mouth filled with his blood and flesh. She was starving, and she needed to devour him. Consume him. *Destroy him. Now.*

She pushed past Bo and rushed out the door of the cabin, barely aware of the voices yelling to her as she made a break for the tent where she knew she would find Dagon. She reached down and

230

withdrew the knife from her ankle as she approached the tent, burying it into the flimsy nylon material to get at Dagon. Using the zippered entrance didn't even occur to her.

Hands caught her around the waist and threw her to the ground. She struggled with her opponent, her eyes unregistering as her mind was fully consumed with obsessions over Dagon. The knife was knocked from her grip, so she clawed and bit at the obstacle fighting to keep her from her prey.

And then she looked into the sun. That blazing, golden yellow orb. And…the Moon? *No, the Moon isn't that blue. Is it the sky? It's so blue.*

Wait…it was night, wasn't it? Why is the sun out? Why is the sky blue?

As Eve's vision finally began to focus, she realized she was looking up into Bo's heterochrome eyes.

And she wanted to gouge them out and keep them. And him. Consume him. Tear into his flesh and make him part of her forever.

No…

NO.

These weren't her thoughts. These weren't her desires.

Or were they?

No. NO. This wasn't her. This was *it*.

The wendigo. It was possessing her, pushing its will upon her.

Push back.

The wendigo's will ripped like a thin veil the instant Eve resisted, and the next thing she knew, she was looking out of eyes that were too high. She was on the forest's edge, peeking out at the chaos unfolding around the tent. Zeke and Eoduun had escaped the torn tent and were looking around, bewildered. She could see herself and Bo, her body limply hanging in his arms.

"Now," she heard in her head. Not her head. Its head?

The huge body she was in lunged forward, but she had no sense of it other than what she was passively observing through the eyes.

She couldn't feel the limbs or control any of the movements. She was simply a passenger.

Can I stop this thing? Eve wondered as she watched it rush at inhuman speed toward her and her team. How could she control it? This was nothing like when she had pushed back into Eoduun's mind. Eoduun said that she had pushed him out completely, but that obviously hadn't happened in this case. Was it even possible to push the wendigo out?

Eve didn't have time to strategize. The wendigo was headed straight for her and Bo. She heard a gunshot go off, but the wendigo didn't falter. Cassie must've missed.

Eve needed to do something, so she did the only thing that made sense to her. What do you do when you're playing a fighting game and you don't know the controls? You mash buttons. She began thrashing. Screaming. Kicking and flailing. Well, to be more accurate, she imagined the sensation of doing those things, as though she were trying to make her body do them.

As the wendigo closed in on Bo and Eve's body, Zeke and Eoduun rushed to Bo's side, firing off at the creature. It was then that Eve realized that they weren't missing; the wendigo was just barreling on despite the barrage of bullets. The trio held their ground, standing guard over Eve's body, but Eve could see the fear in Zeke's eyes, the surprise in Eoduun's, and the wrathful determination in Bo's. They had all come to the same realization – somebody wasn't going to make it.

With a pang of guilt, Eve understood that they would all sooner die than let this wendigo get to her.

She couldn't let that happen. She needed to save them.

She thrashed harder, and with every ounce of determination and willpower she possessed, she thrust her own phantom limbs out through the arms and legs of the wendigo like a jack-in-the-box bursting from its confinement. Almost immediately, there was a bright flash of light, and the ground suddenly came up to meet her as the huge body of the wendigo jerked and crumpled to the ground.

Bullets tore through the monster's back, and Eve could faintly feel the impact. The decayed flesh of the beast ripped and flew away, exposing the heart. Then came the roar of the flamethrower, and Eve's vision faded to black.

In a dizzying jolt, Eve snapped back into her own body. Her eyes shot open and she sat up, taking in the scene before her. The enormous wendigo lay in a grotesque heap of charred rot and bone, and Ruger stood atop it with the flame thrower in his hands. Zeke, Eoduun, and Remi stood on either side of the dead thing, breathing heavily, guns lowered. Bo still stood between Eve and the wendigo, holding his hand against his body as though it was injured.

Cassie came running, having just climbed down from her tree stand. "Did I see fucking *lightning*?" she exclaimed as she ran to Eve, who was still sitting on the ground in a daze. "Oh, thank god. You're alive." Cassie's arms flung around Eve in a half hug, half tackle.

"Are you trying to fix that?" Eve choked out as Cassie fell on top of her.

Cassie laughed, her relief clear in the musical sound. She rolled off of Eve and sat up. "What the fuck was that, hey? I've never seen a wendigo derf it like that!"

"Are they usually that hard to kill?" Eve asked, her eyes wandering from Cassie back to the others.

"Sometimes," Cassie said. She stood up and dusted off her camo pants, then held her hand out to help Eve up.

"That was a tough motherfucker," Ruger remarked. "You good?" he asked Eve.

She nodded.

"It got in your head, didn't it?" Remi asked knowingly.

She nodded again, then turned her attention to Bo, who was still clutching his hand. "Bo? What's wrong? Did I cut you?"

"I'm fine."

"Dude, you shot lightning out of your hand," Zeke marveled. "I thought only Luc could do that."

"Let's get moving on the bonfire," Bo deflected. "This thing fucking stinks."

"Weirdest wendigo hunt ever," Ruger mused as he started gathering sticks from the ground.

Everyone helped collect wood, and once they had a good pile of kindling stacked on top of the wendigo's body, Ruger was all too happy to use the flamethrower to start the fire.

"And now, back to drinking!" he shouted, raising his bottle in the air as the flames licked into the sky, and the others cheered along with him.

Eve turned to Bo, who was standing next to her. "You're not cheering."

"Neither are you," he retorted.

She glanced down at his hand. He now had it tucked away in his jacket pocket. "You seem bothered. If I were Luc, I'd probably ask what's eating you."

Bo grunted. "God, don't pick up his terrible humor."

"Seriously, though. What's going on with your hand?"

"Nothing."

"Then let me see it."

"Let's just skip this tonight, ok? You know I'm hurt. You know I don't want to be healed. Let's just leave it at that."

Eve sighed in resigned irritation. "Can I at least ask what happened?"

"It was the lightning. I don't use it because I don't walk away unscathed like Luc does. My hand is fucked."

"Then why use it now?"

"I had to stop that thing somehow, didn't I? Bullets weren't stopping it, but one shot of lightning will stop just about anything."

Realization dawned on Eve. "*That's* what happened. I thought it was me taking control, but it wasn't. It was your lightning that made it collapse."

Bo furrowed his brow at her. "What?"

Eve explained how she pushed back against the possession of the wendigo and found herself hitching a ride inside of it.

Eoduun suddenly spoke behind her. "Reverse possession?"

"Jesus, Eoduun. I'm going to put a bell on you," Eve teased.

Bo interrupted, "Is this the kind of training you're doing with Zephlyn?"

"Not exactly," Eve eluded. "And no, Eoduun, it wasn't a reverse possession, either. I couldn't control it."

"But with practice, you could," Eoduun said.

"Let's not get ahead of ourselves," Eve replied. "I still haven't mastered anything in my skillset."

"We'll just train harder," Eoduun said pointedly. Bo shot him a derisive glare.

Cassie walked up and bumped her hip against Eve's. She handed her the bottle of whiskey she was carrying around. "You look like you need this," Cassie said. "You know, you really threw us for a loop tonight. What did you see when the wendigo possessed you? Why did you go after Zeke and Eoduun in the tent?"

Eve looked out at the burning beast. It smelled like someone left a rotten steak on the grill too long. "I wanted to eat a god," she said cryptically. She wondered what it meant. Why him? Why was Dagon the first one she went after?

"I'm surprised you didn't just come after me, then," Ruger joked.

"If you were showing a little ankle, maybe I would have."

"Don't encourage him," Cassie laughed.

Eve looked around at the group standing around the disgusting bonfire. "Where's Z?"

Remi jutted his thumb behind him. "Throwing up in the woods."

Eoduun added, "I'm not sure if it's the whiskey or the smell of the wendigo. Probably both."

Eve left the group to go check on Zeke. She found him sitting on the edge of the woods on the other side of the cabin, his back against a tree, elbows on his knees, his head hanging.

"You all right, big guy?" she asked as she approached.

He mumbled in reply. It wasn't until she stroked his hair that he looked up at her with bleary eyes.

"How the drink do those Flannel fucks so much?" he slurred.

Eve shook her head. "I see we're already speaking in cursive. Love that for you, but maybe you should go in and lie down for a bit."

Zeke brushed her hand away when she tried to encourage him to stand. "No, I'mma stay here."

"Ok. I'm going to get you a blanket, then."

Zeke reached up and grabbed her arm, stopping her. His grip was too tight for a split second, but he caught himself and loosened it. "Sorry. But stay. Talk to me."

Eve sighed and sat down next to him. "What's up?"

"You wanted to eat me."

"Um...?"

"I wanted to eat you, too."

"Oh. Yeah. That's ok..."

"It's not ok. I didn't just want to eat you. I wanted to do horrible things to you. Disgusting, *horrible* things. Is that...is that what you felt, too?"

"...In a way."

"And not just you. I wanted to eat Eoduun, too."

"Oh."

"Yeah."

After a long silence, Eve ventured, "So, what does that mean?"

Zeke shook his head. "I don't know. Does it have to mean anything? It doesn't, does it? It's just the wendigo making me want weird things, right?"

Eve thought about her urge to consume Dagon. "Yeah, maybe."

Zeke rubbed his forehead, his agitation growing. "I mean, I love Eoduun. He's my best friend. And I'm pretty open-minded 'bout stuff. But...the stuff I was craving when I was possessed crossed a big line that I'm not comfortable crossing. So, what does that mean about me? Does it mean that's something I actually want? Like, way deep down?"

Eve put her arm over his massive shoulders and squeezed him. "I wouldn't fret over what you wanted to do when you were possessed. You don't actually want to eat me, do you?"

Zeke chuckled and glanced sideways at her. "Well...when you put it *that* way..."

"Ok, pukeboy. I don't think any of that will be happening tonight."

"'Pukeboy'?!" Zeke scrunched up his face in offense. "Misten here, lissy. I feel much better now, and I brought a toothbrush. So we are good. To. Go." When Eve narrowed her eyes at him, he gave her a lopsided grin. "I know, I know. I'm just kidding."

Eve chewed her lip. "I feel like you should probably know, full disclosure, that Eoduun and I had sex this morning."

Zeke gave her a puzzled look. "No, you and I had sex this morning."

"And Eoduun was waiting for me at my door when I left your apartment."

"Oh."

"And now he's acting weird."

"Weirder than usual?"

Eve picked at her fingernails. Now was probably not the time to have this conversation. "It's probably nothing. He is always a little weird."

"He's a weird guy."

"Super weird."

"Such a weirdo," Zeke agreed, his eyelids growing increasingly droopy. "But he's a great guy, isn't he? Love that guy."

"Yeah...hey, let's get you inside before you pass out, shall we?"

Zeke grumbled. "I'm good here. Let's just sleep here."

Eve pleaded with Zeke, but he wasn't budging. She called for Bo, knowing he would hear her, and knowing he would come.

And he did. Bo and Eve each grabbed an arm and helped Zeke stumble into the cabin. They made him drink some bottled water and take his shoes off. When Eve realized Zeke's sleeping bag was still outside in the tent, she unrolled hers for him.

"You're so nice, babe," Zeke gushed as she and Bo helped him into it. "I really love you, you know that? I love you too, Bo, but Eve, I love you best."

"Thanks, Z," Eve whispered. She kissed him on the forehead. "Go to bed. And don't sleep on your back, please," she urged.

"We should get to bed soon, too," Bo suggested. "It's going to be daylight before you know it."

Bo went outside to try to get the rest of the crew to come in and settle down, so Eve took the opportunity to quickly change out of her dirty, smoke-laden clothes and into clean sweatpants and a long-sleeved shirt. As she was slipping her shirt on, she felt hands on her bare stomach. She snatched one of the hands and twisted it off of her as she whirled around.

Vermilion eyes.

She should've known.

26

He's a Little Grabby, That One

"You can't break my fingers now, princess. You have to fuck me again if you want the power to do that."

Eve dropped Dagon's hand. "Everyone will be back shortly," she warned him.

"Tell me what you wanted when the wendigo got in your head," Dagon said, twirling a piece of Eve's hair around his finger.

"I wanted to kill you. But that's no different than any other day." She brushed Dagon's hand away and took a step back.

"You thought of me, then?" A low chuckle rumbled in Dagon's throat. "Of course you did."

"No, not 'of course' I did. It means nothing."

"Keep telling yourself that." Dagon ran his finger down the side of Eve's neck. "I know you crave me. You crave my power. And if you'd just let me, I can teach you how to harness your own powers."

"I don't need you."

"You need someone dangerous. You'll never unlock your potential messing around with these fuckboys who make you feel safe."

"I will figure it out."

"Try Ramil."

Eve couldn't hide the surprise that colored her expression. "What?"

"You lost control when Ramil put his hands on you."

Eve raised her eyebrows. "Who told you that?"

"No one had to tell me. It doesn't take a genius to put together what happened in the gym that day." When Eve made no reply, he continued, "Ramil scares you. And he is powerful – a power rivaling Lucius himself. He is an open opportunity. Take him."

"I won't be doing that."

"Then you need me."

"I don't."

Dagon stepped closer to her and looked down at her with smoldering eyes. In a low voice, he murmured, "You want me."

She swallowed hard and met his gaze. "I really don't."

"I see it in your eyes. You want to do it again - subdue me. Bring a god to his knees. You've been chasing that feeling ever since."

"Go to bed."

"Come with me."

Eve crossed her arms and leveled a loathing stare at him. Dagon gave a slow, amused chuckle. "When you can't take it anymore, I'll be waiting. You'll come to me."

Eve watched him return to the sleeping bag, his words repeating in her head. *"Try Ramil."* Absurd. She couldn't go around sleeping with just *anyone*. And she certainly wouldn't ever go back to Dagon. That was Luc's one stipulation. Not Dagon. Not ever again.

Dagon was dangerous.

…Which was why he was so perfect. The devil you know.

No. Stop thinking like that. She didn't even want that power. Right? Maybe it was time to focus on her other latent abilities. Maybe it was time to focus on using her mind instead of her body.

When Bo returned, he had Eoduun and Remi with him, but Cassie and Ruger had insisted on staying out just a little longer to make sure the wendigo bonfire was fully out before heading to bed.

Eve suspected they were putting out a fire, but probably not the wendigo.

"Did anyone bring in a sleeping bag for me?" Eve asked.

Bo dropped his sleeping bag in front of her. "You can have mine."

"But what about you?"

"I'm not tired."

Eve scoffed. "Bullshit."

Eoduun came up to Eve and nudged Bo's sleeping bag away with his foot. "You can share with me, Eve."

"She doesn't need to share. She has mine," Bo asserted.

"Bo, I won't have you sitting at the table all night," Eve insisted. "I can share. It's not a problem."

Bo looked down at his sleeping bag on the floor. "Evie, just take it. I'll go out and get Zeke's from the tent."

Eve relented and climbed into Bo's sleeping bag, and Eoduun laid his sleeping bag out right next to her. As soon as Bo had left the room, Eoduun whispered, "I take it Zeke was ok?"

"Yeah. Drank too much. I think the wendigo possession really bothered him."

"You don't seem any worse for the wear after being possessed."

"I almost derailed the entire hunt," she pointed out.

"True. But you don't seem bothered by it."

"I think I've just reached my disturbing experience threshold. I've kind of gone numb to it."

"Are you going to explore training for possession? Puppeteering? I think you could do it."

"Maybe."

"If you had my powers in addition to your own, you could definitely do it," Eoduun said.

"But I don't have your powers."

"But you could if you took them, like we've been training for. You could take my powers and practice possessing Zeke."

"*You* don't want to be possessed?" Eve mused.

"Not particularly. But with Zeke, Dagon would push you out like he did with the wendigo, so there wouldn't be any risk of you getting stuck in his head or him being pushed out permanently. We could hit multiple training points in one go," Eoduun said.

"That sounds exhausting."

"Training isn't supposed to be all fun and games."

Eoduun might be on to something. Of the three men she was 'training' with, he seemed the most likely to awaken the feelings of threat that gave rise to her power-stealing abilities. He was the one most likely to be willing to take it too far, and that was what she needed.

"Fine. When we get home, we'll train. But we'll need to get Zeke on board, because I think it's going to need to be a lot more intense if we're going to trigger my powers."

"I'm good with intense," Eoduun purred.

"But I don't think he will be."

"Then maybe we'll just have to chain him up and make him watch how it's done."

Heat flooded into Eve's core. The image of Zeke shirtless, chained, and gagged was strangely arousing.

Ruger stumbled noisily into the dark cabin, and Eve sat up. He'd come in alone. "Did you see Bo out there?" she asked. "He went out to get a sleeping bag, and it seems like he should be back by now."

"Cassie saw him and wanted to talk to him," Ruger informed her. He dropped his empty bottle onto the counter, walked a few feet forward, then lay down on the bare floor.

"Ruger!" Eve climbed out of her sleeping bag.

"Leave him," Remi groaned from his sleeping bag across the room. "He's fine."

Eve ignored Remi. She found Ruger's sleeping bag in the corner and laid it out next to where he'd dropped. "Come on, big fella," she grunted as she helped him over to the sleeping bag. Ruger sighed contentedly and reached up and grabbed Eve, pulling her down to him. He rolled onto his side and held her under his arm like a teddy bear.

"Ruger," Eve complained, patting his arm. "Ruger, I'm not Cassie." He must've mistaken her in the darkness.

"You're so little and portable," he mumbled in amusement, obviously on the verge of passing out. He had no idea what he was doing right now.

Eve wriggled out from under his arm and stood up. As she straightened her shirt and brushed the hair from her face, she saw Cassie and Bo standing in the doorway.

"I feel like I've been spending all night getting drunks into sleeping bags," Eve joked. She wondered how much of that they saw, and how much of it Cassie was going to take the wrong way. "He's a little grabby, that one," she laughed nervously.

"Tell me about it," Cassie said lightly. "Maybe he can snore in your ear tonight instead of mine for a change."

Eve wasn't sure how to reply, so she just laughed it off and returned to her sleeping bag. When she was settled in, Eoduun reached over and grabbed her jaw, turning her head toward him.

"Don't even think about it," he whispered harshly in her ear.

She rolled over to look at him. "I didn't!" she whispered back defensively.

Bo dropped his sleeping bag on the other side of Eve and lay on top of it rather than getting into it.

Eve eyed him. "What are you doing?" she whispered.

"Sleeping."

"Aren't you going to be cold?"

"I don't like being confined. Sleeping bags give me claustrophobia."

"But you're going to get cold!"

"Meh."

Eve wormed her way closer to Bo until her sleeping bag was pressed against his side, and then she unzipped the side and snaked her arm and leg out to lay them across Bo's body.

"What the fuck, Evie," Bo complained.

"There, now you won't be cold."

"If I wanted this, I could've slept by Ruger."

"Shut up and accept my heat," Eve commanded.

Eoduun grumbled, "What are you doing over there?"

"Daddy's cold," Eve replied.

"I am not!" Bo argued.

"What if I'm cold?" Eoduun said.

"You want to keep him warm?" Eve suggested.

"I'm not cold!" Bo asserted again.

"Eve, bring your corpse feet over here," Eoduun implored.

"What the fuck is going on over there?" Cassie wondered.

"Nothing," Bo shot back. "Everybody go to sleep."

Eve felt Eoduun's hand grip her sleeping bag and drag her backwards until her sleeping bag was pressed up against his. He threw his arm over her and bunched her sleeping bag into his fist, holding her firmly in place.

Eve awoke sometime later to the sensation of sliding. She opened her eyes and found Bo was pulling her sleeping bag toward him. When she was up against him, he reached into her sleeping bag and grabbed her arm, then draped it over his chest.

"What are you doing?" she whispered.

"I'm cold."

Eve laughed softly and snuggled up next to him.

The morning light came too soon, and Eve squinted her eyes groggily against the sunshine on her face. She rolled onto her back and looked around. Bo was up, sitting at the table, sipping a bottled frappuccino. Everyone else was still asleep. She groaned and sat up.

"*Ohayou*," Bo said quietly.

"Morning." She shuffled to the table and sat at the chair to his left. "You have any more of those?" she asked, nodding toward his drink and brushing her hair back with her fingers.

Bo reached down into the pack by his feet and produced a fresh bottle for her. "I wouldn't leave you hanging," he said as he slid it across the table toward her.

It was only then that Eve noticed his mangled hand. He'd bandaged it up, but from the discoloration of the bandages, it looked to be a nasty injury.

"Oh, Bo," she worried.

"Stop," he said.

"Just a little bit? A tiny little prick on the finger, and I'll promise to slap you if you get frisky."

"You can promise that?"

No. "Yes."

He looked down at his hand, then looked around the room at everyone still asleep. He sighed deeply. "Fine. But only because it looks worse today than it did yesterday, and I don't want it getting infected. We aren't exactly living in luxury here."

"Really?!" Eve asked in surprise.

"It's not a big deal, right? Let's make it quick before I change my mind."

Eve held her hand out to him.

"No, you do it," Bo said. He held his pocketknife out to her.

"You big baby," she complained. She took the knife and twisted the point on the tip of her finger until a bead of blood bloomed from her skin. She then yanked Bo's mask down and thrust her finger into his mouth before he could object.

Oh god. The rush of desire surged through her body like a bolt of lightning. Bo made a soft sound deep in his throat, and he clamped his teeth down over her finger before she could yank it from his mouth.

"Bo, no," she whimpered quietly. *Bo, yes.*

He lifted his mismatched gaze to meet hers, and after an intense moment of eye fucking, Eve felt her core tightening pleasurably. He sucked at her finger, his tongue swirling sensually over the pad of her finger. Fuck, she was going to come.

She chewed her lip and clenched her thighs together as the sweet release washed over her. A small whimper escaped her, and at the sound, Bo released her finger and inhaled sharply.

Eve pressed her fists against her belly as the waves of pleasure ebbed and pulsed to a drawn-out finish. She glanced up at Bo. His wolf eye was still watching her keenly, drinking in every last drop of the visual of her coming unraveled in front of him.

"Why is it always like that with you?" she whispered breathlessly.

"I'm sorry," he apologized. "I knew I shouldn't have."

"No, I'm not complaining," she whispered with a low giggle. "I just meant it's so intense with you. Every time."

"You didn't slap me."

"You didn't do anything to warrant it. And you knew I wouldn't, anyway." She popped open her drink, and raised it to him. "Well, cheers."

Bo gave her an amused grin, then slid his mask back up over his face and began to unwrap the bandages on his hand.

Why *was* it so intense with him? That was a good question. She could only imagine what it would feel like if he drank from her the way Dagon had.

Wait. The blood. When she'd taken Dagon's powers, she'd given him blood first. When she'd taken Varghrir's powers, she'd given him blood first. Was that the catalyst that she was missing in training? Was that the key?

"Shit, I think I figured it out," she mumbled.

Bo stretched and flexed his fingers on his newly healed hand.
"Figured what out?"

"I know how to steal Eoduun's eyes."

27
Play Along

"I'm kind of attached to my eyes, thank you very much," Eoduun muttered from across the room.

"Oh, you're awake!" Eve said, turning in her chair. "How, um, how long have you been awake?"

"Not long enough, apparently. Why are you trying to steal my eyes?" Eoduun crawled out of his sleeping bag and sauntered over to the table, flopping lazily into the other open chair. He then glanced down at Bo's hand. "I see someone had a little blood with their breakfast." There was an edge to his voice.

Bo turned a quizzical eye to him. "Is that a problem?"

"Why are you talking about my eyes?" Eoduun changed the subject.

"I think I know what we need to do to activate my powers, like we were talking about last night," Eve said. "I think it starts with blood."

Bo set his drink down and looked at Team Flannel in their sleeping bags, still asleep. "I think this is a discussion you should be having in private," he said in mild irritation. "This isn't an open-air topic."

"I wasn't going to go into details," Eve defended.

"Good. Because I don't need to know the details," Bo said, pushing his chair back and standing. "Let's get to it. We're going to be here another day or two, so we should probably stick to our training schedule as best we can." He went over to Zeke and nudged him with his foot. "Rise and shine, cupcake."

Zeke groaned and burrowed further into his sleeping bag.

"But we killed the wendigo," Eve said. "We can't go home?"

"Not until Luc calls me on the satellite phone. There's a reason we're up here and off the grid, remember?" Bo nudged Zeke harder.

Me, Eve thought. She wondered if Team Flannel had any idea about what was going on, or how much of her 'condition' was hush hush. Would they have questions about why they couldn't go home today?

Eve stood up from her chair and went over to Bo and Zeke. She crouched down next to Zeke and pulled the sleeping bag away from his face. He squinted one eye open at her.

"I think I'm dying," he whispered.

Bo kicked him lightly, eliciting a grunt from Zeke, and said, "Go throw up and get changed. Time to train."

"Are you fucking joking?" Zeke whined.

"I am not."

Zeke propped himself up on an elbow and rubbed his eyes with his other hand. He looked around the room. "Why do they all get to sleep in?"

"They aren't my responsibility. You are. Get up," Bo said curtly.

"I have some ibuprofen in my bag," Eve comforted Zeke. She took his hands and tried to pull him into a sitting position, but he tugged at her and pulled her down to the floor with him.

Bo reached down and pulled Eve away from Zeke. "No, she's mine today. Come on, Evie. Eoduun, get him up and ready and meet us outside."

When they were outside, Bo led Eve into the woods.

"What are we doing?" she asked.

"Scoping out the area."

"What if we get lost?"

"We won't get lost." After a long pause, Bo inquired, "So, what do you want with Eoduun's eyes, anyway?"

"Hm? Oh. Well, we were just thinking about what happened with the wendigo last night, how I projected into it. If I had Eoduun's eyes, I might be able to do some training to better hone that skill."

"But isn't the power temporary?"

"Yeah, but I would get several hours, maybe a day out of it before I needed a recharge. That's plenty of time to work on training with his eyes."

"Hm."

Eve knew that tone. "What's bothering you?"

"Eoduun's getting possessive. I can't be the only one noticing it. Don't you worry that making him the focal point of your training is only going to make it worse? Maybe you should focus on Zeke instead."

"No, it has to be Eoduun. At least to start."

"Why?"

"Because…it just does."

"Enlightening."

Bo's pace suddenly slowed, and he stopped. He reached out and caught Eve's hand in his own. Eve looked over at him questioningly. He inhaled deeply, his eyes searching the forest. "Let's head back and see if everyone is awake yet," he said quietly. Calmly. Too calmly. With a firm grip on her hand, he led her back the way they had come.

Something was wrong, but he was trying to play it cool. What had he scented? Was it another wendigo? Some other monster? She glanced at him again as they walked at a steady, unrushed pace. He was on high alert.

Eve's heart began to race. She fought the urge to look behind her, and she tried to control her trembling legs that wanted to run.

"Luc should be arriving any time now," Bo said conversationally. "He's probably already at the cabin."

What? What was he talking about?

"In fact, I wouldn't be surprised if he comes looking for us," Bo added.

Eve looked up at him again, and he gave her a meaningful sideways glance.

Play along.

"Good, I've missed him," Eve replied. "But don't ever tell him I said that. It'll go right to his head."

"I'm just glad we were able to clean up that wendigo mess so quickly. It really helped to have the other teams here, especially Ramil. It was a good team-building exercise," Bo went on.

He continued chatting about nonsense until they returned to the cabin. Once he'd ushered her through the door, he locked it behind him and looked out the window.

"She's here," he said ominously. "And she's not alone."

Zeke and Eoduun jumped to their feet. "She? You mean Ruth?"

"How the fuck did she find us?" Bo hissed, drawing the dusty curtains.

Cassie and Remi were awake now, and they roused Ruger.

"We spent most of our ammo on the wendigo last night," Remi informed Bo. "We're not equipped for a showdown with Ruth!"

"Did you see her?" Cassie asked.

"I caught her scent in the woods. It was faint, but it was definitely her. She's either here and keeping her distance, or she *was* here."

"Let's hope it's the latter," Ruger muttered.

"Even if that is the case, she'll be back. She wouldn't have tracked us down like this and left empty-handed."

"But how did she know we were here?" Eve revisited Bo's original question.

"Either some kind of location spell or someone who knew where we would be told her. We already suspect there's a mole in Knighco."

Everyone turned to look at Zeke.

"What?" he asked innocently. Then Zeke's eyes flashed red, and Dagon's voice erupted from his lips. "I'm not a damn mole, you insolent peasants! I have no interest in playing messenger boy to that silver-haired slut!"

"I'd say it's more platinum blonde than silver," Eve remarked.

"Not the time," Bo reprimanded her.

"I was just sayin'…" Eve mumbled.

Zeke pushed Dagon back down and his eyes returned to brown. "I really don't think it's Dagon, for real," he insisted.

"You were off on your own for a long time last night, Zeke," Remi pointed out suspiciously.

"I was puking my guts out over there in the woods! You can go check, if you really want to!" Zeke shouted, pointing. "And then Eve put me to bed! I was in control the whole time! And what about Ruger and Cassie, huh? You two went off on your own for a while last night too!"

"Yeah, to fuck!" Ruger argued. "I think that was pretty obvious!"

"Hey! Enough!" Bo bellowed. "We need to be a united front right now, not tearing at each other's throats!" When everyone was silenced, he continued, "We need to get the fuck out of Dodge. This isn't a safe place for us to be right now. Hopefully, she'll think Luc and Ramil are with us, and won't make a move on us. She's always avoided tangling directly with them."

So that explained the name-dropping in the woods. He was hoping that Ruth would overhear him.

As everyone began to quickly pack up, Eve asked, "When you said Ruth wasn't alone, what did you mean? Did she have another Titan with her?"

"I don't know about a Titan, but she had several *somethings* with her. I think she's been cooking up more monsters."

While the rest of the crew hurriedly loaded up the trucks, Bo made a call on the satellite phone to Luc and apprised him of the situation. Eve couldn't overhear what was being said, but Bo was agitated by the time he hung up.

"He doesn't have the juice for a jump," Bo growled.

"What are we going to do?" Eve fretted.

"Asses in seats, everybody!" Ruger shouted, slapping the top of Team Flannel's truck.

"Eve, you're with me. No argument," Bo commanded. She climbed into the back behind him without complaint.

They took off down the two-track at a dangerous speed, following Ruger's lead.

"Is Luc going to get on a plane home?" Eve asked, clinging to the back of Bo's seat as the truck bumped roughly along the path.

"It wouldn't do us any good. It'll take too long, and we'll either be caught or clear before he could get to us. He said he'll come to us as soon as he's charged up." Then Bo swore under his breath. "How the fuck did she find us?" he wondered aloud again.

"She has Eve's blood," Eoduun spoke up. "I don't think it's too far-fetched to think she could've used it to cook up a spell to locate Eve."

"Plausible," Bo granted.

Eve felt the truck suddenly lurch and jerk, sputtering and faltering, before coming to a shuddering halt in the middle of the road.

"Hex bags!" Bo shouted. "Look for hex bags! Fuck, we should've checked before we left!"

Eve glanced out the windshield at Team Flannel's truck speeding away ahead of them, wondering how long it would be before they noticed Team Alpha was stranded. To her horror, she watched as several of the enormous trees that were lining the road suddenly came crashing down, landing squarely on top of Team Flannel's truck.

Eve shrieked.

"Holy shit!" Zeke cried from the passenger seat, clutching the dashboard as he gawked out the windshield at the wreckage. Under all the branches and foliage, Eve couldn't even see the truck anymore. She had no idea how bad the damage was, and could only imagine the worst.

Cassie. Ruger. Remi. Were they all dead?

A giant wall of flame erupted around Team Alpha's vehicle in a wide, symmetrical circle.

"She's got us trapped," Bo said defeatedly. Eve looked over at him, and he was speaking into the satellite phone.

"What the fuck are we going to do now?" Zeke panicked.

Bo's face grew grim. "Understood," he said into the phone, then dropped it to his side. With reluctance, he told Zeke, "Luc wants you to let Dagon out."

Eve saw gill slits appear suddenly behind Zeke's ears. Dagon's ears.

"Oh, hell yes," Dagon said mischievously. As he reached for the door handle, Bo grabbed his arm. Dagon looked indignantly down at his hand. "Unhand me, monkey!"

"Step out of line, you will pay for it later. Protect Evie. That's your *only* role in this," Bo snarled.

Dagon scoffed. "That's exactly what I *am* doing." He then flung the door open with such force that it ripped off of the truck and fell to the ground. "I'm going to extinguish this threat once and for all."

28
You Think He'd Do It?

The wall of flames parted in several places, and Ruth and an entire entourage stepped into the circle and surrounded the truck and Dagon. Her posse looked like regular people to Eve, but she knew they must be monsters.

"Get out of the truck," Ruth commanded the rest of Team Alpha, brushing her long hair over her shoulder. She regarded Dagon with a flirtatious smile. "Hello, Dagon. I've missed you."

As Dagon took a purposeful step toward Ruth, one of Ruth's flunkies grabbed Eve by the hair and dragged her from the back scat of the truck. No sooner had she been pulled out, however, the creature released her and collapsed, a knife handle sticking from the side of his head.

"Evie!" Bo cried, stepping over the monster he'd killed and lunging for Eve. Another minion came after him while a replacement for the fallen creature stepped in to grab Eve. Bo landed a devastating assault of strikes, slashes, and kicks on the minion that attacked him, sending it falling backward, bloodied.

The creature holding Eve suddenly released her, a confused expression on its face. Eve glanced over at Eoduun, who was rushing around the other side of the truck to get to her, and saw that his eyes were purple. But he didn't make it past the tailgate before two more minions tackled him to the ground.

An all-out brawl was on the verge of erupting.

"Stop! Everyone!" Ruth shouted.

Eve looked toward Ruth and found her holding Dagon at bay with and extended hand, like an invisible wall was protecting her.

Bo and Eoduun shook off the minions that grabbed at them, and the fighting came to a tentative halt.

"You need to just die, bitch," Dagon seethed, his sides heaving with rageful exhalations.

"I have a better idea, Dagon," she replied coolly. "How about I live, and you get your own body back?" When Dagon paused, and Ruth was sure she had his attention, she continued, "I can do it. I can free you from that boy, free you from your contract with Lucius, and restore you to your original, glorious flesh. All I need you to do is turn over the blood healer. And to sweeten the deal, you can keep her as your own little pet. I would only need her occasionally to replenish my Panacea Blood supply." Ruth smirked at Dagon. "It's everything you want, isn't it? You have no loyalty to these hunters. They've done nothing but chain you and repress you and treat you like a prisoner. Don't you want to be free, finally?"

The satellite phone in Bo's vest pocket started ringing.

"Did we forget to turn our phones to silent before the start of class, Bo?" Ruth mocked.

Bo reached into his pocket and withdrew the phone, then put it to his ear.

"Are you seriously taking a call in the middle of this? Have you been taking lessons on douchebaggery from Luc?" Ruth said in exasperation.

Bo held the phone out. "It's for you."

Ruth furrowed her brow. "Who is it?"

"Luc."

With an annoyed roll of her emerald eyes, she waved Bo over to her, making all the bracelets on her wrist jingle chaotically. "Bring it here, for fuck's sake."

Bo walked the phone to her, warily eyeing the minions he passed on his way to her. When he reached her, he regarded Dagon with the same wariness. He handed her the phone.

She shook her hair away from her bejeweled ear and raised the phone to it. "Hello, dear brother. You're interrupting a very important meeting, you know."

The smug expression on her face slowly faded, and her eyes widened, her lips parted, and her breath suddenly came in gasps. Her trembling hand dropped the phone.

"Run!" she shrieked in terror. "Everyone, run! Now! That's an order!" The wall of flames instantly extinguished, and without explanation, Ruth turned tail and fled on foot, all of her monsters scattering like cockroaches.

In mere moments, Team Alpha was alone again.

Eve wasted no time wondering what had happened. She had a job to do. "Cassie!" she cried, running as quickly as her legs could carry her toward the crushed truck up the road. She hoped she wasn't too late. She remembered that, up until now, Ruger and Remi had a knack for not staying dead, but Cassie didn't have a power like that. She needed to save Cassie.

Bo popped up at the truck before Eve reached it. It startled her for a moment, as she wasn't used to seeing him teleport like Luc. Eoduun and Dagon were close on her heels, but when she reached the truck, she realized that it was Zeke who lifted the giant trees off of the truck, not Dagon.

They pulled Cassie, Ruger, and Remi from the crushed pickup. The scene was grim. None of them looked like they could possibly be alive, but Eve didn't even wait for Bo to check Cassie for a pulse. She sliced a gash across her arm and let her blood trickle into Cassie's mouth.

"Please don't die. Please don't die," Eve begged, tears streaming down her face. Her eyes searched frantically for signs of healing on Cassie's wounds, but nothing changed.

Then Ruger coughed and groaned, and Bo summoned her to Ruger's side. Eve shook her head.

"No, not yet. I need to save Cassie. Just a little more. She's going to wake up any minute now," she asserted in a tremulous voice.

"Evie…"

"Babe," Zeke said softly, resting his hand on her shoulder. "That's enough. It's out of our hands now."

"No! She just needs more!" Eve cried.

Bo came to her side and lifted her shaking arm away from Cassie's mouth. "More won't make a difference at this point," he said calmly. "Let's give Cass some air, ok? Ruger and Remi are suffering severely, and you can fix that. Let's fix what we can, ok?"

"I can fix Cassie!" Eve insisted feebly as Bo hooked his arms under hers and lifted her to her feet.

"It'll be ok, Evie," Bo comforted her as he led her to Ruger.

But it wasn't ok. Eve stared at Cassie's lifeless, battered body as Bo held her arm to Ruger's mouth, then Remi's. What did it matter if she healed the two who couldn't die? She couldn't save her friend. When it really mattered, when it came down to life and death, she'd failed, and she'd let her friend die.

As she stared at the bruised and bloody face of her fallen comrade, Cassie's eyelids fluttered.

Eve's heart leapt, and she yanked her arm free from Bo's grasp. She scurried to Cassie, sliding across the dirt to her side like she was stealing home. Cassie looked up at her with bleary eyes, and Eve choked on a relieved sob. The wounds on Cassie's face were visibly beginning to heal.

"Holy shit," Eoduun marveled, joining Eve at Cassie's side. "I was sure she was dead."

"Eoduun!" Eve reprimanded. "Don't say shit like that!"

"What? I thought she was." When Eve continued to glare at him, he added, "But I'm glad she *wasn't*, all right?!"

Bo and Zeke came to see the miraculous turn of events, and they were both just as shocked as Eoduun had been.

"I've never seen a recovery like that," Bo said in astonishment as Cassie sat up. He turned and looked at Ruger and Remi, who were similarly rallying. He turned back to Eve, and if she wasn't mistaken, he looked at her with pride. "Amazing, Evie."

Zeke suddenly pulled her up into a bear hug. "That's our girl," he gushed, then planted a kiss on her cheek.

Bo surveyed their surroundings. "Guys, not to be insensitive, but we really need to get out of here. I have no idea what Veris said to Ruth to make her and her monsters run, so I don't know how long we have before the manipulation wears off. Ideally, I'd like to be far away before it does."

Bo and Eoduun searched Team Alpha's truck and found the hex bag tucked up underneath the vehicle. Once it was removed and burned, the truck started right up. Zeke and Eve salvaged what luggage and supplies they could from Team Flannel's truck and got it moved over into the other vehicle. Then Zeke pushed the truck off of the road to clear the path for the other truck to pass through.

By the time they were ready to go, Cassie, Ruger, and Remi were all back on their feet, almost as good as new. Bo found the satellite phone that Ruth had dropped and called Luc to let him know that the trick with Veris had worked, and for now, they were in the clear, and Luc was no longer needed.

The phone died before the conversation was finished.

The seven of them crammed into the six-seater pickup, and Eve and Cassie had to squish together in the middle of the back seat, sharing a seat belt.

"So, Luc's not coming?" Eve said, her voice dripping with disappointment.

"We don't need him now," Bo responded from the driver's seat.

"Speak for yourself. I didn't even get to talk to him," Eve pouted.

"He did his part. He's the one who called Veris and had him save our asses. But, by all means, should I call him back and tell him you've requested his presence?" Bo teased.

"No!" she blurted. "God, I'd never hear the end of it."

"Speaking of which, Z, plug that phone into the charger," Bo said, passing the phone to him.

"Can you drive *any* slower?" Ruger asked sarcastically from the passenger seat, leaning away from the branches slapping into the truck through the gaping opening left by the missing passenger door. "You should've let me drive."

"You just *died*," Bo countered.

"Yeah, but I got better."

Zeke twisted around in his seat between Bo and Ruger so he could look at Eve behind him. "Luc will be home before you know it. And in the meantime, I'll be happy to distract you."

"You're distracting *me*," Bo said. "Turn around."

Eve felt Eoduun's warm hand on her thigh, and he slid his fingers under the hand she had resting on her leg. He intertwined his fingers with hers and clasped her hand in his. She looked over at him, but he had his head turned, looking out the window, ignoring her.

"Z," Bo said, "any insights on where Dagon stands with Ruth's proposal? How worried should we be?"

"He wouldn't fall for that," Zeke said nonchalantly. Then, as an afterthought, "Though he did go weirdly quiet after she brought it up. And he didn't even fight me when I took control after she and her monsters ran."

"He's got nothing to say about it?" Bo pressed.

After a short pause, Zeke said, "Nope. He's ignoring me."

"Don't love that," Eve commented.

Zeke twisted around in his seat again. "You think he'd do it?"

"If it were a real offer? If she really could give him his body back? Yeah, I think he would betray us in a heartbeat. He's probably just sitting in there," Eve tapped Zeke's forehead, "contemplating whether she can really do it or not."

Zeke's hand shot up and caught Eve's wrist aggressively, and Dagon's eyes blazed red. "I thought you wanted me out of your little boytoy," Dagon taunted.

"Not if it kills him!" she hissed as Eoduun released his grip on her hand to throw his arm protectively across her body while his other hand grabbed Dagon's arm.

But Zeke had pushed Dagon back down before Eve had finished her sentence, and Eoduun let go of his arm. "Sorry! I thought he was powered down," Zeke apologized.

"Sounds like he's considering joining Team Ruth," Ruger said.

"Or he's just picking on Eve. He does that," Zeke reasoned.

Remi said, "Well, it seems to be clear that Dagon *wasn't* the mole all along...but now he can't be trusted for all new reasons."

"Agreed," Bo said. "But I felt a lot more comfortable believing it was him over one of our hunters."

"No kidding," Cassie sighed. "Who could it be? Who else would have anything to gain from joining Ruth?"

"I don't know, but for the time being, maybe we should refrain from discussing sensitive matters in front of Dagon," Remi suggested.

"Sorry, Z, but he's not wrong," Bo agreed.

"No, I get it," Zeke said solemnly. "It's not the first time I've been left out of the loop because of him. I understand the stakes."

Eve wanted to rub Zeke's shoulder comfortingly, but as soon as she began to lift her hand toward him, Eoduun intercepted it. When she glanced at him questioningly, he gave her a discouraging shake of his head and slipped his fingers through hers again, resting their clasped hands in his lap.

What was this going to mean for Zeke? Eve stared at the back of his head, wishing she had a window into his mind. There was no way he was as calm about all of this as he seemed outwardly.

Dagon was eclipsing Zeke's sunshine.

29

Welcome to the Zoo, Padre

Bo delivered the two teams to the airport safely, despite Ruger's constant driving "tips." They all climbed out of the truck to stretch their limbs after being crammed together for so long. They could see the Knighco jet waiting for them, but now that the satellite phone was charged, Bo wanted to call Luc to see if he wanted them to return to the compound yet or if they needed to remain off-grid. He dialed Luc's number and raised the phone to his ear.

Eve heard a familiar, jaunty ringtone behind her, and her chest burst with butterflies before her brain registered the reason for the reaction.

"Hello?" a low, mischievous male voice answered the phone.

Eve's head whipped around, her eyes anxious to take in the man walking up behind them.

Luc.

"What the hell?" Bo said, hanging up the satellite phone. "I thought you weren't coming."

"No," Luc said smoothly. "*You* said you didn't need me anymore, so I shouldn't waste my time coming. But I like to be the one to decide how to waste my time. And my frequent flyer miles."

Eve's feet were moving. Like a magnet, he drew her in. She couldn't resist his inescapable pull. Luc bumped his sunglasses down his nose and gave her a dashing smile, his shockingly blue eyes sparkling with delight as he watched her approach him.

"My love," he crooned, extending his arms to her. She fell into them, allowing him to scoop her up off her feet as she threw her arms around his neck, and he hugged her small frame to his giant one. "Oh, how I've missed you," he confessed, his voice muffled in her hair.

As Eve clung to Luc like a love-stricken koala, she glanced over his shoulder and saw a man standing behind him. He wore a black, button-up shirt with a white clerical collar, and black slacks. Eve could see two knives holstered on his belt beneath his black jacket. He was standing with his rough, large-knuckled hand casually resting on the handle of one of the knives, his dark brown eyes watching her disinterestedly from beneath bored, sleepy eyelids. He appeared to be in his thirties, but it also looked like they had been a rough thirty.

"Who's he?" she asked Luc.

"Hm?" Luc lowered her to her feet and turned around. "Oh! So quiet, I almost forgot he was there." Luc swept his hand toward the apathetic clergyman. "Eve, meet your (hopefully) temporary probation officer. He is the Vatican's answer to their uneasiness regarding your...condition."

The priest scratched his dark, crew-cut hair and said nothing.

"Hey, I'm Zeke," Zeke introduced himself as he walked up, giving a little wave.

When the priest laid eyes on Zeke, the bored expression vanished, replaced in a flash by a fiery wrathfulness. His hand white-knuckled the knife in his belt and he softened his knees, prepared to spring into an attack.

Luc made gestures with his hands as he said, "At ease, padre. You're not here to fight with Dagon."

The priest relaxed a little, but kept a wary eye on Zeke.

"This is Father Isaac D'Angelo," Luc introduced the priest. "He's an exorcist, and he can see the monsters behind human faces, kind of like Dagon does."

"Were you just signing to him?" Eve asked Luc. "You know sign language?"

Before Luc answered, the priest signed something to her. She shook her head, not understanding, and looked back to Luc.

"He doesn't think I'm very good at it," Luc relayed, amused.

"He's deaf?"

"Yep. But don't let your guard down around him. If he can see your mouth, he can read your lips. But he also likes to pretend he can't understand you whenever it suits him."

"How's a guy with ears like that wind up being deaf?" Ruger mocked.

Isaac's ears did protrude slightly, but Eve didn't think they were outlandishly large.

Isaac gestured crudely to Ruger, but it didn't require any kind of interpretation.

"Ok, so he *can* read lips," Bo mused. "I'm not sure if that's a good thing or a bad thing for me," he said, touching the mask over his lower face.

"Oh, fuck, I didn't even consider that," Luc admitted. "Guess you'd better brush up on your ASL."

"Shit," Remi spoke up from the back of the group. "Father Isaac D'Angelo...*the* Isaac D'Angelo? The Vatican's Angel of Death?!"

Luc waved his hand dismissively. "Just a silly nickname."

"Angel of Death? What is his role here, exactly?" Bo asked suspiciously. He and Isaac measured each other up with mild contempt and distrust.

"He's here to observe Eve. He may not be the Vatican's favorite priest, but he's the one they turn to when they have a monster problem they don't know how to deal with."

"Wait," Eve said. "Is he here to *observe* me, or *kill* me?"

"You won't give him a reason to kill you," Luc assured her.

"How could you agree to this?!" Bo growled, stepping up to Luc.

Luc turned his back to Isaac, and his calm façade broke. His face twisted with rage. "I had no choice! It was this, or turn her over to *them*, and I refuse to do that!"

"I'll kill him if he lays a finger on her," Bo pledged.

"That's what I'm counting on," Luc imparted pointedly. He straightened his tie and ran a hand through his hair, the easy smile returning to his face as he turned back to Eve. "He'll see that you're no threat, and the Vatican will honor his opinion. You have nothing to worry about, love. You aren't a monster."

Isaac signed something, and Luc glanced at him with pinched brows.

"What did he say?" Eve asked.

"He's hungry. Let's get back to the compound."

On the jet ride home, Eve sat between Bo and Luc, and Isaac sat across from them, watching Eve. *The Angel of Death.* That revelation had sent chills down Eve's spine. What did he do to earn a name like that? He was visually unassuming, and he couldn't have been more than 5'10" and 160lbs. He moved gracefully and silently, and hadn't uttered a sound, but those bored, apathetic eyes that he turned to Eve were hiding something sinister.

He scared her.

When they disembarked from the plane, Luc made the short jump back to the compound to make quick preparations for Isaac's arrival, leaving Eve in Bo's hands for the car ride home.

Cassie took up Eve's arm on their way to the cars. "I don't think I've ever been into a priest before, but Isaac is kind of cute, isn't he?" Cassie whispered.

Eve glanced over her shoulder, and sure enough, he was there. His eyes may have been focused on the cars up ahead, but she knew he was watching her, waiting for a wrong move. Waiting for an excuse.

"Remi told me some stuff about him on the way here," Cassie continued. "I guess he's killed more monsters than any other hunter on the Vatican payroll, by, like, a *wide* margin. He's never failed a mission. But the higher ups hate him because he doesn't listen."

Eve gave Cassie a flat look.

"Oh, you know what I mean. He's a bit of a loose cannon. Remi said he's even been known to take out other members of the clergy if he thinks they're corrupt." As an afterthought, she added, "Oh, and he doesn't feel pain. I wonder if he can feel pleasure." She waggled her eyebrows.

"Cass, just because he can't hear you, it doesn't mean the rest of us can't," Bo said from behind Eve. While Isaac was following and watching Eve, Bo was following and watching Isaac.

"What? I'm only making conversation," she defended.

"Make different conversation."

"Why?" Eve interjected. "I should probably know all I can about the Angel of Death shadowing me."

"You don't need to know if he feels pleasure."

Cassie shrugged. "You don't know that, Bo. Knowledge like that can come in handy in a pinch." Cassie whispered conspiratorially to Eve, "He's obviously never had to flirt his way out of a sticky situation."

A laugh escaped Eve. She couldn't even picture Bo trying to flirt. "I don't think he knows how."

"Different conversation," Bo pleaded in exasperation.

Eve turned her head and winked at Bo. "Ok, Daddy."

Isaac's disinterested expression was briefly replaced by a curious glance between Eve and Bo.

When they started loading into the cars, Eve noticed Isaac was standing next to her, waiting to climb into the back seat with her. Bo also noticed.

"Maybe you can ride with them," Bo suggested to Isaac, pointing to Ruger's car.

Isaac looked over at Team Flannel, then back to Bo. He didn't go.

"He doesn't know what you're saying," Eve said, pointing to her mouth, indicating Bo's mask.

"He knows what I'm saying," Bo assured her.

Eoduun sidled up between Isaac and Eve, then gently pushed Eve toward the passenger seat. "Take shotgun. I'll keep Ears company in the back."

Isaac saw Eoduun's remark, and gave him an unamused expression.

"Come on, man," Zeke reprimanded from the other side of the car. "No need to be an ableist prick."

"I'm not being ableist. Dude's got big ears."

Eve puckered her lips and surveyed Isaac. "I don't see what the big deal is. He has perfectly nice ears."

Isaac eyed her warily.

"Just get in the fucking car," Bo commanded impatiently.

When they arrived at the compound, Luc was waiting for them, and he escorted them all back to Eve's apartment. Zeke and Eoduun went straight to the fridge, and Bo took up his perch at his spot at the kitchen island. Isaac walked in behind Luc and Eve, looking around at the apartment. Luc guided Eve to the couch.

"I know this isn't ideal, love," he said, watching Isaac walk by. Luc sat down next to her and stretched his arm across the back of the couch behind her shoulders and crossed his ankle over his knee. "But I have full confidence that you'll have Isaac on our side in no time."

Isaac approached them and signed something to Luc.

Luc signed back as he said, "You can bunk with me."

Isaac snapped his first two fingers and thumbs together, shaking his head. He pointed down.

"No, you can't stay here," Luc replied. "This is Eve's apartment."

Isaac pointed to his chest, pressed two Y-handshapes downward, and pointed down more firmly.

"You're not rooming with her," Luc argued.

Isaac signed at Luc with an annoyed expression on his face, and Luc sighed and rubbed his thumb and forefinger on his forehead. "Fuck."

"He's staying *here*?" Eve fretted.

"Don't worry, we won't leave you alone with him."

"So, when you say he's here to observe me, you meant 24/7? Is he going to be up my ass every minute of every day?!"

Isaac nodded in response to Eve's question, and Luc gave her a tight-lipped look of resignation. "I'm sorry, love. But if we want the Vatican to be satisfied and leave you be, we need to meet their demands."

"You mean meet *Father D'Angelo's* demands," Eve muttered, looking contemptuously at Isaac. Isaac shrugged his shoulders, then signed something.

"He says he's not unreasonable," Luc shared.

"Right. I'm sure the Angel of Death is the very definition of reason," Eve replied.

Isaac exhaled deeply, then wandered off to the kitchen.

Ruger burst into the apartment, singing, *"Don't ask me, Ruger, whyyyy do you drink? Ruger, whyyyy do you roll smoke?"*

"You don't roll smoke," Cassie said as she strolled in behind him.

"And it certainly isn't a family tradition," Remi added.

"Guys, that just makes me sound like a regular old alcoholic," Ruger complained.

Eve twisted around and held out an imaginary object over the back of the couch to Ruger. "I think that's your shoe. Put it on and lace that bitch up."

"Ouch, Eve," Ruger feigned injury, holding his hand over his heart. "I thought you were supposed to be a healer, you fucking savage."

Cassie plopped down next to Eve. "How was Rome?" she asked Luc.

"Not as exciting as Michigan. Bo tells me you almost died today."

"I'm not entirely sure I didn't. But somehow, Eve brought me back. Our own, personal Jesus over here," Cassie beamed, hugging her arm around Eve.

"*Someone to hear your prayers, someone who cares*," Ruger sang. Badly.

Cassie threw her head back. "Oh my god, stop with the honky-tonk karaoke."

"What?" Ruger protested. Then he pointed at Isaac. "This guy gets it." Isaac stared at him with a vaguely annoyed expression. Ruger nodded and grinned. "Yeah, he gets it."

"Fucking idiot," Cassie chuckled.

Isaac signed to Luc.

"Yeah, welcome to the zoo, padre," Luc smiled.

"*And hungry eyes are passing by, on streets we call the zoo!*"

30
I Expected Him to Be Bigger

After a while, Luc ushered everyone from Eve's apartment. Everyone save for Isaac, that is. Luc brought her to the kitchen while Isaac sat out in the living room, browsing Netflix.

Eve sat down at the kitchen island while Luc began pulling out pans. "What on earth is he watching?" Eve wondered. She leaned over the counter and looked out at the television. "He's watching a French show without any subtitles. What the fuck?"

"Just be glad he's watching something other than you for five minutes," Luc said, leaning down and stealing a kiss from Eve.

Mmm. She'd missed those lips. She wanted to thrust her fingers into his hair and pull him closer, to drag this out into something more.

Then she glanced at Isaac over Luc's shoulder, and she pulled back and sat in her seat. "He's still watching me. He just wants us to think he isn't."

"I know. It's adorable," Luc said, returning to his dinner prep.

"It's creepy."

"You used to think I was creepy."

"You are creepy. You just get away with it because you're really, really, ridiculously good-looking."

Luc looked over his shoulder at her. "Aw, aren't you just the sweetest."

"I'm pretty sure you don't like me because I'm sweet."

"True. You'd never be anything so boring."

Eve sat with her chin in her hands, staring at Luc's broad back and tight ass as he cooked at the stove. What a delicious chunk of man. Her eyes shifted over to Isaac, sitting out in the living room, and was startled when their eyes met. He signed to her with his eyebrows raised questioningly, but she didn't understand.

"Luc, what does this mean?" She mimicked Isaac, rather badly, by pointing off to the side, flipping one hand over top the other, and touching her hand to her chin and arcing it downward before repeating the sideways point.

"I think he was asking you if I was a good cook. I know he wasn't telling you I was, because he wouldn't know."

"How do I say yes or no?"

Luc looked over his shoulder, eyeing her over top of his sunglasses. "Which is it?"

"Tell me both."

"You could just nod or shake your head."

"I know, but I want to know the signs."

Luc held his fist up, thumb over his fingers, and "nodded" his hand. "Yes." He then opened his first two fingers and thumb, then snapped them closed. "No."

Eve looked eagerly back over to Isaac, but he wasn't looking at her anymore. She waved her hand wildly.

"Pick me, pick me," Luc teased.

"Shut up, you ass."

"Loveable ass."

"That's a stretch," Eve mocked.

"That's what she said."

But Eve's gestures caught Isaac's attention, and he looked over. Eve held up her fist and bobbed it up and down.

He nodded once and turned back to the TV.

"What am I supposed to do when you're not here? No one else knows ASL," Eve pointed out.

"Start learning? Never a bad time to learn it. But no, you're right. I should probably find someone who can translate for him when I'm not here, even though I'm ninety-nine percent sure he *can* talk." Luc pulled his phone from his pocket and started texting while he stirred the pot on the stove.

"Why does he sign in ASL? Isn't he from the Vatican? Don't Italians have their own sign language?"

"He's from Chicago."

"But he speaks French? Or, rather, reads French lips?"

"How should I know? We aren't besties. I barely know the guy." Luc's phone chimed, and he glanced down. "Excellent. Ramil knows ASL. He can be my stand-in."

Try Ramil.

God, why was she thinking about that now? But thinking about Ramil made her think about Veris, and his trick with Ruth. "Hey, since Isaac can't hear, would Veris' specialty work on him?"

"Nope," Luc answered.

"Does it work on Dagon?"

"Eh…not really. Why?"

"I don't know. I thought maybe Veris could tell him to turn down Ruth's offer. Or tell him to forget he ever heard it. I know Eoduun can't erase him."

"Yeah, Bo briefed me on what went down. He also told me you possessed a wendigo."

"Sort of. Not really. More like I hitched a ride, like a parasitic little eyeworm."

"Mm, sexy."

"Mm, quite."

"We'll have to explore that skill further. And you need to master the specialties they already suspect you have so you can prove that you have a handle on them. They're most afraid of having a Dizzy situation. A loaded gun is arguably more terrifying in the hands of a child than that of a skilled marksman. At least you know the marksman is only going to kill their intended target."

"What specialties do they suspect I have?" Eve asked as Luc slid a plate over the counter toward her.

"The limited literature they have on the Abomination indicate a propensity for seducing men and stealing their souls. As we know, though, it isn't their soul – it's their power. In the lore, it seems like a permanent arrangement, but we know it isn't, which looks better for you. Point in our favor. An Abomination is also supposedly able to read minds to find what her victim desires most, and can manipulate her victim into thinking they can get it from her. The main reason they chose 'Abomination' for the name is from the bible – Abomination of Desolation. They believe an Abomination is so powerful that one could rise as a false idol and become the Antichrist."

"Are you fucking serious? I'm not the fucking Antichrist! I might be able to learn how to read minds, but I can't trick people into thinking I'm their new god!"

"I wouldn't freak out just yet, love. I don't think anyone *truly* believes you're the Antichrist, but they want to be sure."

"So what exactly do I have to do to prove I'm not a danger to the world?"

Isaac walked into the kitchen, and it startled Eve. For a moment, she'd forgotten he was there. He signed to her, and she looked to Luc to translate.

Luc handed Isaac the food he'd plated for him. "He says you need to show him good character, good judgement, and full command of your specialties."

Well, I'm fucked. "And if I don't accomplish that?"

Isaac pointed at her, then held his hands out with one palm up and one palm down, then flipped them both over.

Eve looked at Luc, and he gave her an appeasing smile, though she could see his jaw flexing as his teeth clenched behind his lips. Instead of translating, he simply said, "That won't happen. Now, eat."

Isaac took his plate and started to move back to the living room.

Eve raised her hand, "Hey, sit down and eat," she said when he looked at her, then she indicated the seat next to her.

"Offering him *Bo's spot?*" Luc asked in feigned shock. "Wow, you're really going all out to get on Isaac's good side." He signed to Isaac and said, "That's a seat of honor in this kitchen."

Eve shook her head. As everyone began to eat, Eve pulled out her phone and downloaded an ASL learning app. She then googled a description of Isaac's flipped hands sign.

As she suspected. *Death/dead.*

Maybe she should've let him eat alone.

Isaac ate quickly and left the kitchen before Luc and Eve were halfway through their meal, returning to the living room to stretch out on the couch.

"Oh, I almost forgot to tell you," Luc said to Eve as she was finishing up her dinner. "We know who your father is."

Eve choked and sputtered on the food she was swallowing. "What?!"

"We traced the genetics three times – we could hardly believe it. But it seems dear old dad is *really* old. Biblically old."

"Who is it?!" Eve pressed impatiently.

"If we're right, it could be Enoch, son of Cain."

Eve dropped her fork.

"As for your mother, she didn't seem to be anyone special. Just a regular Jane. We believe all of your special abilities come from Enoch."

"Then how did I get the Blood of Lilith? Cain was a child of Eve."

"Though it's not canon, it's been rumored that Enoch's mother was a lilim born of Lilith and Asmodeus. The blood was mixed before you."

"What does that mean?"

"It means that Enoch was, in a way, the first Abomination. But since he was born male, he didn't have the Panacea Blood or the unique specialties of a true Abomination. In essence, he's just a carrier."

"How is he still alive?"

"The Vatican doesn't think he's been alive this whole time. He may have been raised with spells and witchcraft, perhaps from Lilith's grimoire. Or, perhaps he inherited the Mark of Cain and is cursed to roam the earth for eternity, unable to be killed. That's still unclear."

"But why?"

"That is the big question, isn't it? And were you the intended outcome, or an unexpected complication they decided to unload onto an unsuspecting family? Did they even know what you were? What I wouldn't give to be able to ask your mother what she knew, but you can't raise a normie from the grave."

Eve's stomach dropped. "My mom's dead?"

Luc raised his eyebrows. "Oh, not your Mom mom. Sylvia is still kicking. I meant your biological mom."

"You know who she is? …Was?"

"Of course. But she wasn't anyone special."

"She was the woman who gave birth to me. That makes her a little special," Eve said quietly.

"Oh. I've made a misstep. I only meant she had no specialties. It wasn't an assessment of her qualities as a person."

"What was her name?"

"Stacey Rose." Luc studied Eve as she sat silently, then said, "I can gather more information about her, if that's something you would like."

"I would like that."

They heard a voice in the hallway. "Oh, hello." It was Ramil. Eve leaned over so she could see the door. Isaac was standing with Ramil in the doorway.

Ramil saw Eve. "I heard you were back. This must be your Vatican Anubis, here to weigh your sins," he mused with a tilt of his head toward Isaac. Isaac signed something to Luc as he and Eve went out to the living room, but Ramil understood what he was saying and spoke up first. "Yes, I was in the hall a moment ago, composing a text. Last I checked, I live in this building and am free to walk the halls, too."

Isaac gave Ramil a measured look, then walked away to the kitchen and leaned against the counter, watching them from afar.

"A little intense, isn't he?" Ramil said.

"Did you expect anything less from the Angel of Death?" Eve replied.

"Is that who he is? I've only heard the rumors," Ramil remarked. He looked past Eve at Isaac. "I expected him to be bigger."

"Nope. Compact and quiet as a church mouse. I guess I could've been less lucky in terms of a flatmate," Eve commented.

"He's staying *here*, then, in this apartment?"

"For now," Luc said. "Where's Veris? He's usually with you."

"He headed down to the war room ahead of me. We are still having a meeting today, aren't we?"

Luc looked down at his expensive watch. "Oh, shit. The time got away from me. Yes, we'll be down shortly."

Ramil excused himself, and Luc and Eve got ready to go. Isaac stayed in the kitchen, leaned against the counter with his arms crossed.

"Come on, Isaac, we have a meeting," Luc signed.

Isaac shook his head.

"What do you mean 'no'?" Eve asked. "I'm not leaving you alone in my apartment."

Isaac signed.

"What could you possibly have to do? Unpack? You brought one duffle bag," Luc quizzed.

Isaac crossed his arms again and stood there obstinately.

Eve turned to Luc so Isaac couldn't see her mouth, and asked, "He's a man of the cloth, so he wouldn't do anything weird, like get in my underwear drawer, would he?"

Luc threw his head back and laughed uproariously. "Oh, love, you have no idea. The Catholic church is full of weirdos. And even those weirdos look down on him. What's that tell you?"

Eve looked back at Isaac suspiciously. "Stay out of my room when I'm gone!" she ordered accusingly, pointing to her bedroom door. "I'll know if you go in there!"

Isaac raised a quizzical eyebrow at her, then waved them off.

As Eve closed the apartment door behind her, Luc teased, "Do you suppose he's already trying on your favorite thong?"

"I'm buying new underwear."

They stopped to pick up Bo and Eoduun from their apartments so they could all walk together. They stopped at Zeke's place last, because Luc had to tell him that he needed to stay behind and keep an eye on Eve's apartment.

"Isaac insisted on staying," Luc explained, "and I'm curious as to what he's doing. So, if you could pop in and check on him, I'd appreciate it. You won't be missing much at the meeting. It's all stuff you already know."

"Really?" Zeke seemed skeptical. "He refuses to leave her alone for five minutes, and suddenly he's cool with sending her off to another building without him there to monitor her? What's the deal?"

"That's what I'd like to know. Maybe you can find out for me," Luc said, patting Zeke on the shoulder.

"Maybe he just wanted to take a shit in peace," Zeke suggested.

"More likely, he wants to snoop," Bo said. "If I were in his shoes, it's exactly what I would do."

"He's not going to find anything incriminating," Eve said. "I just hope he stays out of my underwear."

Luc shot her a scandalized look. "Don't you dare let him get into your underwear!"

"I'll kill him," Eoduun added.

"I second that," Zeke chimed in.

"Over my dead body," Bo asserted.

"Shut up, you guys know what I mean!"

Zeke hugged Eve to his side warmly. "Aw, we know. I'll make sure he stays out of your *unmentionables*."

31

He Can't Do Anything Without Fanfare and Pageantry

On the way to the war room for the meeting, Luc advised everyone that there was an ulterior motive for keeping Zeke behind. "Dagon can't be trusted at all right now. I don't want him to know our plan to take down Ruth, and that's what this whole meeting is about. So, Zeke needs to be kept in the dark for now."

"You have a plan?" Bo asked. "Why is this the first I'm hearing of it?"

"It's the first anyone's hearing of it. Myself included," Luc replied.

"What?"

"It's a work in progress. I'm hoping it's fully formed by the time we get to the war room."

"This is not the time to be flying by the seat of your pants," Bo argued.

"Let's just see where it goes," Luc replied casually. "I think best on my feet." He then turned to Eve. "Just a heads up, I think this plan is going to rely heavily on you mastering some skills *real* quick. No pressure."

"Wow. Yeah, no pressure, for sure," Eve shot back sarcastically.

"I don't want her on the frontlines," Bo said firmly.

"You underestimate her, Bo."

"No. I value her."

"Don't fucking insinuate that I don't," Luc said in a measured tone. "I see how powerful she is. How resourceful. She is an asset to this organization, and to your team. She's going to surpass us all, but to do that, we need to help her grow, not clip her wings."

"Not to undermine your grand speech about me, Luc, but I can't help but feel that your faith in me is misplaced."

"Luc's not wrong," Eoduun said to her. "I've felt it when you were in my head. You're on a different level. You just need to hone your skills."

Luc stopped in his tracks and turned to gape at Eoduun. "Holy shit, did I just hear Eoduun fucking Kwon *compliment* someone?" He looked at Eve. "What did you do to him?"

"I bribed him with pickles. You caught me."

Luc turned to Bo. "See? I'm not the only one who sees it. She's a peacock, Bo. You gotta let her fly."

"I don't think peacocks really fly that well…" Eve pointed out.

Luc held up his finger to Eve's lips. "Shhhh. Not the point."

"I'm not trying to hold her back, and I know she is powerful and capable. I just want to keep her safe," Bo reasoned. "I don't want her taking unnecessary risks or being put in danger so she can try to live up to whatever unachievable standards you're inevitably going to set for her, whether wittingly or unwittingly."

Luc raised his eyebrows. "Well fuck, Bo. We'll need eight sessions on a couch in a safe space to unpack all of *that* baggage, but unfortunately, I don't have that kind of time or emotional availability right now." He turned his back and started walking toward the bunker again. "I would never put her in a position I didn't think she could handle. You fucking know that. Now let's go. We're fucking late."

"Well, this is fun," Eve said flatly.

When they walked into the war room, everyone was already present, except for Ramil and Mira, who strolled in behind them.

After a moment of talking with Eoduun, Luc started the meeting and addressed the room. "I've already spoken to some of you, but for those of you who are unaware, we have a visitor here at Knighco. He's only here to observe and clear our newest hunter, Eve, with the Vatican. You know how cautious they can be. I was going to introduce him today, but he's back at the apartment, resting. You'll meet Isaac eventually. He is deaf, so be aware that if you are trying to hail to him and he doesn't respond, there's only a fifty-percent chance he's just being rude and ignoring you.

"In other news, we've had another run-in with Ruth. She's now trying to appeal to Dagon, offering to give him bodily autonomy and Eve in exchange for access to Eve's blood. Obviously, we were worried –"

"Wait, she offered Dagon Eve?" Ramil interrupted.

"You're surprised?" Luc responded.

"Are you sure that's correct?"

Luc turned to Team Alpha, and Bo answered, "We heard it straight from her mouth. Why?"

Ramil wore an expression of confusion. "No reason. It just seems like an odd bargaining chip."

"Well, it's one we were afraid he would be tempted by, but thankfully, he's not. We're confident he wants Ruth dead even more than we do. He's not falling for her tricks."

What the hell was he talking about? Eve had to consciously unfurrow her brows. He was up to something.

"And what if it isn't a trick? What if she really can do it?" Mira asked.

"Doesn't matter. Dagon doesn't want to be in league with her."

"Where is he, anyway? Why isn't Zeke here?" Zephlyn asked.

"I have him working on something," Luc explained. "We have a plan of action, but everyone needs to trust me and do their part to keep quiet about it outside of this room."

"What's the plan?" Mira wanted to know, leaning back in her chair, crossing her arms.

"Dagon is going to pretend to go along with her plan. As soon as Ruth is within his grasp, he's going to destroy her and get the grimoire."

"Just him, by himself?" Cassie inquired, concerned.

"I want to keep this operation as small as possible. I don't want to bring an army and risk alerting Ruth that anything is amiss. She needs to believe that Dagon is on her side."

"Are we even sure Dagon *can* kill Ruth?" Roy wondered. "He's gone toe-to-toe with her before, and she's managed to weasel her way out of it every time."

"He can kill her. I'm confident of that," Luc assured him.

"What if Dagon really *does* betray us in the end, and doesn't go through with this shit plan?" Bo demanded.

"It's a risk, I know. But it's our best option right now."

"I don't like it," Eoduun said.

"I fucking hate it," Bo agreed.

"I'm all for it," Mendal said. "I'm so sick of Ruth. Let's just finish it once and for all and move on."

"If you're sure it will work, I'll second it," Levi said. "You've never led us astray before."

"It'll work. If I know one thing, I know Dagon hates and mistrusts Ruth. He wouldn't work with her."

"Maybe someone should go as back up," Ramil suggested, "just to make sure everything goes smoothly. I could do it. And if he does betray us, I'll kill him myself."

"If you kill Dagon, Zeke dies too," Eve said.

"If Dagon betrays us, Zeke dies anyway," Ramil pointed out.

"No, Dagon goes alone," Luc said. "He'll get it done."

"Sounds like a terrible plan," Mira said in an annoyed tone. "But if Dagon is the only one being put at risk, then I won't stand in your way."

"Zeke is being put at risk, too," Eve mentioned. She hated this plan. It wouldn't work. Luc was deluding himself if he thought that Dagon would throw away his only chance at freedom over his hatred for Ruth. He was capricious and opportunistic, and Ruth was just a tool to him.

"Not a dealbreaker," Mira said coldly. "And evidently, Luc agrees."

"Everything will go as planned. Zeke will be fine," Luc said confidently.

When the meeting adjourned, Eve stormed out of the war room without waiting for Luc. Bo and Eoduun caught up with her.

"He's a fucking idiot," Eve snapped.

"There has to be more. There's no way this is his plan," Bo said. "It's too simple for his taste. He can't do anything without fanfare and pageantry."

Eve slowed her angry pace. "Then why would he tell everyone that that was the plan?"

"Because we have a mole. He must want that plan to get back to Ruth," Eoduun surmised. "He asked me to covertly read everyone at the table at the meeting to see if I could discern any obvious signs of erasure or firewalls, so he must have something else up his sleeve."

"I only worry that I'm going to like his real plan even less," Bo sighed.

Luc suddenly appeared next to them. "Thanks for playing along, guys," he said in a low voice. "Obviously, I have a much better plan."

"A little warning would have been nice," Eve complained.

"I did it on a whim. But I think it'll work better to have Ruth thinking she has the upper hand on us. Whoever our mole is, they'll feed her this plan, and her ego will do half of our work for us."

"So what's the real plan?" Bo asked.

"Before that, I need to know who I can trust. Eoduun?"

"I know you're not going to like this, but it seems like Mira's memories have been tampered with. And Zephlyn and Ramil are notoriously hard to read, so I couldn't make a determination on either of them."

Luc adjusted his sunglasses. "My mother used a spell to block Mira's memories and knowledge regarding Fagerberg Enterprises from prying eyes, so that could be what you detected."

"Then again, it might not be," Bo stated.

"We'll just have to put all three of them on the no-fly list for now. Nothing on Dizzy, Veris, Kai, or Levi?"

"No hint of tampering that I could detect," Eoduun confirmed.

"Excellent. They're the ones I need, anyway. We'll use Dizzy as our Dagon. We will contact Ruth, and Dizzy and Veris will persuade her to meet with Dagon. I'll have Levi survey the meeting place and, using the earpieces, direct Kai, Bo, and Eoduun in taking out key lookouts and guards in her entourage. Eve, you'll accompany Dizzy to meet with Ruth."

"What?" Bo blurted. "Absolutely not!"

Luc ignored him. "You, my love, are going to incapacitate Ruth while I bind her. I'd rather not kill her just yet if I don't have to, because I may have use for her."

"How the hell am I supposed to do that?"

"You'll temporarily possess her."

Eve laughed cynically. "Yeah. And Santa Claus is going to fly out of my ass with all eight reindeer."

"We'll train. You can do it."

"On Dasher, on Dancer, on Prancer and Vixen…" Eve's mocking continued.

"She's not even close to being ready for something like that," Bo said.

"I'll be the judge of that," Eoduun piped up. He smirked. "Let me have her for a while. I'll give her the boost she needs."

Tendrils of heat tingled between Eve's legs.

Luc saw the blush in Eve's cheeks and the burning gaze Eoduun leveled at her, and he raised a brow at Eve.

She cleared her throat and crossed her arms. "After the wendigo situation, Eoduun and I were working on a plan to help improve my chances of performing a possession by using the power of his eyes..."

"And you have to steal his power first," Luc said knowingly.

"Yeah," Eve nodded self-consciously.

Bo offered, "I'll distract and restrain Ruth. Leave Evie out of it."

"No. I think things will go more smoothly if she's quietly and quickly incapacitated. We know she'll likely bring an army, so if Eve possesses her, no one will be any the wiser that anything is amiss."

"What about a tranq?" Bo suggested.

"Back-up option. But again, hard to administer something like that without anyone noticing. We want it to be over before it begins, ideally, so she needs to go down first. Cut off the head, so to speak."

"And where is Isaac going to be for all of this?" Eve asked.

Surprise lit upon Luc's face. "Oh, right! Isaac. I forgot about him. Again. Why is he so forgettable?"

"Maybe it's part of his personality," Eve said. "He seems like he prefers to fade into the background and just watch people."

"You're suggesting he likes to watch?" Luc teased. Then he caught himself. "Shit, how are we supposed to have any alone time?" He leaned down, his voice low in Eve's ear, as he said, "Maybe we should sneak off to my place for a little bit before we head back to your apartment."

"I thought she was going with me," Eoduun interrupted.

Luc shot Eoduun a dangerous look over his sunglasses and draped a long, heavy arm possessively over Eve's shoulders. "She's mine first. Always."

Eoduun was unfazed. "Don't you have some coordinating to do? I imagine you're going to be rather busy working out the details of your plan with the others for a while."

Luc narrowed his eyes at him, then adjusted his sunglasses. "I don't like how much you're enjoying this, Eoduun," Luc said darkly. "You may want to reconsider that smug look on your face."

"Whatever. Eve, come find me when you're ready," Eoduun said, then walked on ahead into the apartment complex.

Luc looked after him. "Not a fan of that," he disclosed. He glanced down at Eve. "I'm not saying you should kill him when you go for his powers, but you have my full blessings to put him in the infirmary."

32

No Interruptions

When they walked through the door of the complex, they found Isaac sitting on the steps, waiting patiently for them. His hair was damp.

"Oh, I see," Luc signed and spoke. "You wanted the place to yourself so we wouldn't hear you singing in the shower."

Eve laughed, and Isaac's unamused eyes shifted to her. He stood up, turned around, and climbed the stairs.

"Tough crowd," Luc pouted. "Listen, love. Unfortunately, Eoduun was right. I do need to make the rounds. I'll catch up with you tonight. And then...I'm going to make up for being away." He winked at her over his sunglasses, then lifted her hand and bowed down to kiss it softly. "I'll make you forget everyone else."

Eve returned to her apartment with Bo, and Isaac was waiting outside the door. He pushed a Y-handshape toward the door, then grasped one open hand into a fist while twisting it around and touched the back of his fists together.

"What?" Eve said aloud, then reached for the doorknob. It was locked. She gave Isaac an exasperated look. "You locked yourself out."

He shrugged at her.

"Angel of Death, my ass."

He shook his head. He pressed his hand to his chest, then tapped two H-handshapes perpendicularly. Then, finally, something she recognized. Letters. I, S, A, A, C.

"Your name is Isaac," she surmised. He nodded. "I know," she said.

"I don't think he likes it when you call him Angel of Death," Bo guessed.

"You don't like 'Angel of Death'?" Eve repeated, knowing Isaac couldn't read Bo's lips through his mask.

He shook his head distastefully and held both hands out and flicked his middle fingers away from him aggressively, like he was flicking a cigarette.

"Oh." She grabbed her phone from her pocket and looked it up. "You hate it." He nodded again. She did another quick search, then held her fist in an A-handshape and circled it over her chest. "Sorry."

Isaac just stared at her while Bo walked through Eve's door so he could unlock it from the inside.

"I probably look like an absolute moron when I try to sign," she said, discouraged, then walked into the apartment when Bo opened the door for her.

She felt a hand on her shoulder, but in a flash, Bo had snatched it off of her, and the next thing she knew, Bo and Isaac were holding knives to each other.

"Whoa, fuck! Stop that!" Eve cried, then bodily pushed them apart.

Isaac's nostrils flared and he signed quickly and angrily as he walked past Eve and Bo. Then he grunted in annoyance and dropped down into a chair in the living room.

"Not cool, Bo," Eve chided.

"He grabbed you. What was I supposed to do?"

"He didn't *grab* me. He was probably just trying to tell me something, and you attacked him. Look at him, I think you hurt his feelings."

Isaac was flipping through the Netflix lineup and doing his best to ignore them, a stern expression on his face.

"I don't care about his feelings. I care about you."

"Aww," Eve gushed, then hugged Bo's arm. "I love you too, Daddy," she said cloyingly.

"I didn't say I love you."

"I can read between the lines."

She felt Isaac's eyes on her, and she glanced over. He was watching her and Bo with that quizzical expression again. She reflexively dropped Bo's arm.

"Oh, *now* you're embarrassed," Bo remarked.

"He's probably trying to figure out just what the fuck is going on around here," she said with her face turned away from Isaac. "What's the sign for 'slut'?"

"Is that it?" Bo asked, pointing behind Eve. She turned around, and Isaac had both index fingers hooked in X-handshapes. He touched them together vertically, then arced them out to the sides.

"But…how did he see me?" Then Eve noticed his reflection in the side of the fridge, which meant he could see *her* reflection in the side of the fridge. She turned to face him. "Pretty sneaky, sis," she said with narrowed eyes.

He pointed two fingers at his eyes, then turned the fingers to point at her. That one was a universal sign. *I'm watching you.*

Eve sarcastically blew him a kiss and went to the cupboard to get a snack.

"You shouldn't taunt the Vatican assassin sent here to kill you if you misbehave," Bo warned.

"You started it. You're the reason he's in a bad mood. Maybe you shouldn't attack the Vatican assassin sent here to kill me."

"Eve," Eoduun called from the doorway. "I thought you were coming to my place. What's the fucking hold up?"

He and Zeke walked into Eve's apartment.

"How'd the meeting go?" Zeke asked.

"Boring. Nothing new. Did you make sure no one was rifling through my panty drawer while I was gone?"

"He locked the door and wouldn't let me in."

"To be fair, he probably didn't hear you knock," Eve said.

"And then I saw him wandering down by Ramil's door a little while later."

Eve tapped her chin. "Speaking of Ramil, isn't he supposed to be Isaac's translator when Luc isn't here? We can trust him enough to do that, can't we?"

Zeke frowned. "What do you mean trust him enough?"

Eoduun shot Eve a pointed glance.

Shit. Zeke's supposed to be in the dark about what's going on. "Hm? I just mean he's capable enough to do it, I hope."

Zeke seemed satisfied. "I can go get Ramil. I saw him go back to his apartment a few minutes ago."

Isaac stood up and coughed, and everyone turned to look at him. He held up two fingers and his thumb and snapped them together. *No*. He placed his hand on his chest, then pulled it away as he flicked his middle finger, and began spelling Ramil's name. The gesture was similar to when he signed that he hated the Angel of Death nickname.

"I don't think he likes Ramil."

Isaac pointed at her and nodded in confirmation.

"What's not to like?" Zeke asked in surprise. "He's a good dude."

Isaac shook his head again.

"Well, I know he looks kind of scary, but once you get to know him, you'll like him," Zeke assured Isaac.

Isaac turned his eyes to Eve, then shook his head again. He touched his chest, swiped his thumb under his chin and outward, then squeezed both hands and stacked them together like he was grabbing a rope. He ended by pointing in the direction of the hallway. Eve opened her ASL app again.

I don't trust him.

"What's he saying?" Zeke asked.

"He just doesn't like him. Maybe we'll go get him later, but for now, I think we should go do some training."

"Right now?" Zeke raised his eyebrows, then a mischievous grin spread across his face.

"Bo, can you stick around and keep an eye on Isaac?" Eve implored as she ushered the boys to the door. She felt a presence behind her, and found Isaac intending to follow her out the door. She held her hand out to stop him. "No, you stay here," she said, pointing down, like she'd seen him do.

He shook his head, gestured between the two of them, then put the knuckles of two A-handshapes together, thumbs facing upward, and arced them away from himself.

"I'm only going down the hall, and I'll be back before you know it. I have private training to do. I'm not going to run away."

Isaac stared at her flatly for a moment, and she stared back. He reached past her and grabbed his black jacket from the hook by the door, slipping in on. He reached in the pocket and pulled out a pack of cigarettes, tapped one out, and stuck it between his lips. He arrogantly waved Eve and the boys aside, then headed down the hall to go smoke outside.

Eve, Zeke, and Eoduun all headed in the other direction, toward Eoduun's place. As Eve walked through the door, she glanced up and saw Isaac had stopped in the hallway and was watching her enter Eoduun's apartment. Once they were all in, Eve turned the lock.

No interruptions.

Eoduun snaked his hand around to the small of Eve's back and pulled her up against his body. "Sorry, Z, but you're going to have to take a more passive role this time." He glanced over at Zeke. "I think this is going to be a little more aggressive than you're comfortable with. I just need you to make sure she doesn't kill me. Can you do that?"

Disappointment colored Zeke's features. "You mean I don't get to join? I'm just supposed to watch?"

"Eve needs to focus. She's trying to take my eyes, and then she's going to try to use them to possess you."

"Like the wendigo? Dagon will just push her right back out again."

"That's what we're counting on," Eve said. "I just want to know if I can do it. It's a skill I could potentially learn to use on my own, but I think I need a boost from Eoduun to get started."

Eoduun grabbed Eve's hand, then Zeke's, and began to lead them both back to the bedroom. "First things first," he said mischievously, "we need to make sure you're going to behave and keep your hands to yourself."

Eve had never been in Eoduun's room before. The walls and bedding were both dark gray. There were a few articles of clothing on the floor, but for the most part, it was clean. The setup was the same as Eve's room, but Eoduun had a desk with an office chair along the wall.

Eoduun directed Zeke to the office chair.

"What are you doing?" Zeke asked as Eoduun grabbed two belts.

A wicked grin curled Eoduun's lips as he began to strap one belt around Zeke's arm and the armrest. "Just a reminder to stay put." He strapped the other belt over the other arm.

"You know I can break through these if I wanted to," Zeke said.

Eoduun rolled his eyes. "For fuck's sake, just play along. You never know – you might like it. But if she does try to kill me, by all means, break my chair and belts. Otherwise," Eoduun turned his hungry gaze to Eve as he warned, "don't interfere."

Eve looked up into Eoduun's smoldering dark eyes as he stalked toward her, a belt in his hand. "If you want to dominate me, you're going to have to fight for it," he purred dangerously. He fisted his fingers painfully into her long hair and brought his lips to her ear. In a low, threatening tone, he said, "If you want my power, you're going to have to *take* it from me, little girl." He lashed the belt suddenly across her ass, eliciting a sharp yelp from her throat. His teeth nipped her earlobe, and his hard cock pressed against her belly through his jeans.

A stirring awakened in Eve's core. She reached into his pants and wrapped her fingers around his hot shaft, stroking his length. "Shut up and fuck me, *boy*."

Eoduun tightened his grip in her hair and pulled her mouth to his, his kiss aggressive, forcing her head back against his fist, his teeth clashing against hers. She felt cool leather slide up over her neck, and Eoduun untangled his fingers from her hair just long enough to strap the belt around her neck.

A moment of unease gripped Eve's chest as he tightened the belt. Was he going to strangle her? Her hand shot up to his throat as he fastened the buckle, ready to choke him right back, and she felt his lips smile against hers.

"Are you scared?" he taunted.

Eve spun him around and shoved him down onto the bed. She saw his gaze shift past her to Zeke.

Eve straddled his hips and grabbed his jaw, forcefully turning his attention back to her. The loose end of the belt dangled down over her chest. "Eyes on me, asshole."

Eoduun smirked. He caught her wrist in his hand and pulled her fingers from his jaw. With his other hand, he tugged the belt, yanking her down so her face was inches from his.

"Shut your filthy mouth. I'll look wherever the fuck I want," he growled. He thrust his hip and rolled her onto her back, pinning her arms to the bed over her head. His hips pressed between her legs, and he looked down at her, his black hair falling in disarray around his handsome face, accentuating his darkly desirous expression.

294

"Where should I drink from you?" His eyes burned over her skin, moving slowly down her body.

Eve heard the chair creak, and she glanced over at Zeke. His cheeks were flushed, his brown eyes fixed on her, the bulge in his pants proclaiming his arousal at the performance before him. Heat simmered in Eve's belly to see him like that – wanting her, but unable to have her.

Her view was suddenly blocked as Eoduun lifted her shirt over her head. He cast it aside, and it fell at Zeke's feet. Eoduun brought his lips to the tender flesh below her ear.

"Focus on me, or I'll punish him for distracting you," he whispered, then licked and sucked at her neck. Now that Eve's hands were free, she stripped his shirt off of him. He sat up, dragging his hands down her bare torso to her thighs spread on either side of his hips. "Then again, maybe this is punishment enough," he sneered. He hooked his fingers into Eve's pants and underwear and tugged them off. She lay naked beneath his gaze. "What torture it must be to have to watch and not be able to touch."

"Don't make me break these restraints, Eoduun," Zeke warned.

"He wants to touch himself," Eoduun teased, not looking at Zeke. "He wants to relieve that throbbing need in his pants."

"No, he wants to touch *me*." Eve took Eoduun's hand and ran it up the inside of her thigh until his fingers grazed her folds. "He wants to touch me here."

Zeke shifted uncomfortably in his chair.

Eoduun lowered his lips to Eve's inner thigh while his fingers stroked between her legs. He gave her a light bite, eliciting a sharp inhale from Eve, then trailed kisses up her leg. "He wants to taste you here," Eoduun said, then dipped his tongue into her heat.

Eve's back arched, and she let out a soft moan. She looked over at Zeke again, pleased to see the wild desire in his eyes. His fists were clenched, his breath heavy. He shifted again in the chair, trying to find any kind of relief against the swollen rod straining against his zipper.

Eoduun raised his head, licking his lips. He twisted his hips and hooked his leg under her knee, and with a sudden jerk, he flipped her forcibly over onto her belly and snatched up the loose end of the belt around her neck. He pulled it taut, causing Eve to arch her back, her ass pressing against his hips. He leaned over her back and kissed her shoulder, then gave her a sharp nip of his teeth.

His breath ghosted over her skin as he tugged a little harder on the belt and whispered, "You're completely at my mercy, my little slut. I can do anything I want to you." He thrust his hips against her bare ass, grinding his bulge against her. He smacked his hand smartly on her round glute.

Eve only growled at him, unable to form words with the pressure on her throat. The heat in her belly was spreading tendrils of need through her body, awakening more than just her desire.

Hurt him.

Eve fought to tamp down on the urge, but the belt squeezing at her neck was drawing it out like a goddamn snake charmer.

When Eoduun leaned forward again, Eve twisted to the side, throwing her arm back and hooking her elbow around his neck. She threw all of her weight into torquing her body and flipping Eoduun over onto the bed on his back.

But he was still gripping the belt. He pulled her down over top of him and wasted no time rolling on top of her. He gazed down at Eve with exhilaration as she yanked the belt from his hand. She quickly unfastened it from her neck and threw it aside.

"You're way too much fun," he purred. He leaned back and reached into his pocket, producing a small knife. He flipped the blade open, his eyes fixed on a place between Eve's legs. He touched the blade of the knife to the crease between Eve's hamstring and the swell of her glute.

The blade drew across her flesh in a burning arc, and Eve cried out. The cry of anguish quickly melted into one of ecstasy when Eoduun's mouth covered the wound. Sparks ignited the tinder already smoldering in Eve's core.

Zeke groaned helplessly from his chair.

Eve thrust her hands into Eoduun's dark locks as he licked and sucked at her blood. Every lave of his tongue brought her higher and higher, the ache between her legs growing to an unbearable need.

Fingers gripping his hair, Eve forced his mouth from the cut in her flesh to her center. His fingers dug into her muscular thighs, the knife cast away, as he eagerly pleasured her from back to front with his tongue. Her breath quickened when he moved his focus to the apex of her sex, sucking expertly at her clit. She gripped his hair and mewled shamelessly as the orgasm surged through her.

But she needed more. *More.*

Eoduun unfastened his jeans and pushed them down his thighs, his throbbing erection springing free from its restraints. He was already dripping with pent-up arousal. He hooked his hands under Eve's knees and pressed her legs open against the mattress as he aligned himself with her slick opening.

Eve fought to control the pace, but Eoduun was holding her down. She reached around and grabbed his firm ass, pulling him deeper, but he grabbed her wrists and slammed them down into the mattress next to her ears.

He leaned down and growled, "You want it? *Take* it from me." His hips hammered into her, hard, making her yelp.

Zeke protested from his chair, but Eoduun and Eve ignored him. It was on now. The battle for dominance.

Eve snaked her hands around Eoduun's wrists, breaking the hold he had on hers, and took control of his wrists with a vice-like grip. She wrapped her legs around his waist and squeezed, drawing him into her as deep as he could go. She pressed her shoulders into the mattress and lifted her hips, rolling herself over on top of him. He tried to keep the momentum so he could roll back on top, but Eve swung one leg out to stop them. She squeezed Eoduun's wrists and looked down at him.

Bite him.

Instead of suppressing the urge, she gave in. She rolled her hips, reveling in the way he felt so deeply inside of her, then leaned forward. She grazed her lips over his, then bit his lower lip.

He moaned appreciatively. "Yes. More," he begged.

She dragged her tongue over his throat, skimming her teeth over his Adam's apple. *Kill him.*

No.

She sank her teeth into the side of his neck, and he moaned again. Something sweet and metallic graced her tongue, and her excitement revved.

She'd drawn blood.

She dipped her head lower, kissing and biting at his chest, before settling her lips over his nipple. She licked it lightly, and Eoduun thrust his hips up into her in response. She took the bud between her teeth, and he inhaled sharply.

"Oh, fuck," he groaned.

She licked, bit, and teased, drawing delicious moans from the man beneath her.

She sat up and released his wrists. One hand went to his throat, and the other to his nipple. She squeezed them both.

Ruin him.

Eoduun cried out, and she squeezed his nipple harder. His strangled keens of agony and bliss stirred her insides, awakening the slumbering beast inside of her. Her teeth tingled with rage. Her belly filled with fire. Her body zinged with electricity.

DESTROY HIM.

He gripped at the wrist of the hand around his throat, but his other hand went to her hip, his fingers digging into her flesh as he fucked her harder. Eve clenched her thighs around him and gyrated her hips, looking down at his enthralled, yet slightly terrified expression with deep satisfaction. He was ready to accept whatever fate she dealt him. He was hers to break.

His power was hers for the taking.

The fire between her legs had reached a state of inferno, and she was about to explode.

"More," Eoduun pleaded breathlessly.

She twisted the pebbled nub between her fingers, and Eoduun threw his head back and cried out in anguish as his cock throbbed inside of her.

Power and pleasure lanced through Eve like a bolt of lightning, and her cries mingled with Eoduun's as they found their violent release together.

The next thing Eve knew, she was off the bed, trapped by two impossibly powerful arms, watching Eoduun cough and recoil. Her body still shuddered and clenched with the aftereffects of her pleasure, but the raw rage and compulsion to kill had passed. She glanced over to the chair where Zeke had been, and the armrests were ripped off. She looked down at the tattooed arms around her, noticing the belts and armrests were still attached to them.

"Are you ok?" Zeke asked Eoduun fretfully.

Eoduun sat up and coughed again, rubbing his chest. "I'm fucking perfect." His eyes met Eve's. "Did it work? Please tell me it worked."

33

Shawshank Redemption

Zeke lowered Eve to her feet. Both he and Eoduun stared expectantly at her, as though they were anxiously waiting for her to transform into a monster in front of them.

"I don't know. I think so," Eve replied hesitantly. She began to gather up her clothes. "Should I try possessing you right now?" she asked Zeke as she slipped her shirt on.

"As long as you're not feeling murdery anymore, I guess now's as good a time as any," he said. "You're not going to make me do anything weird, right?"

Eve raised a brow and looked at Eoduun, who was also getting dressed. "What do you think, Eoduun? Should I make him do something weird?"

"If you can stick around long enough before Dagon pushes you out, you should make him say he's thirsty for Bo. I'll have my phone ready to capture the moment."

"If that's the best you can come up with," Zeke said, "I'm not worried. And maybe I am thirsty for Bo. You don't know."

"Good point. You embarrass yourself all on your own," Eve teased. She sat down on the bed, and Zeke wheeled the armless office chair up and sat in front of her.

"Ok. I'm ready," Zeke said.

Eoduun instructed, "Ok, Eve, to get in, just look into his eyes and imagine casting yourself *into* his mind. *Will* yourself into his head. Beyond that, I can't help you with a possession. You'll have to figure that part out on your own."

Eve inhaled a shaky breath. Her heart was racing. "Well, here goes nothing."

She stared into Zeke's caramel brown orbs, and tried to imagine pouring her own essence into his body and mind. She felt a strange tugging sensation inside her brain, and a tunnel opened up in her mind's eye.

She dived into it with gusto, and when she reached the other side, it felt like she came crashing through a brick wall.

Dagon, in his true form, was standing before her. He raised his dark eyebrows, his vermilion eyes shining inquisitively. "How the fuck did you get in *here*?"

Eve looked around at the blank, black walls. "This isn't how I imagined Z's head," she frowned, confused.

"You're in *my* mind, inside *Zeke's* head. How the fuck did you do that?"

"What?! How is that even possible?"

"I was going to go looking for you in Zeke's mind, but you jumped straight into mine." Dagon smirked down at her. "Almost like I was the one you were seeking in the first place."

Eve scowled up at him. Way up. Fuck, he was tall. "I'm not here for you, and I'm not here to chat. I need to get out of here. This isn't how this was supposed to go."

"I'll tell you what: if you stay and listen for a few minutes, I'll show you back to Zeke's mind," Dagon offered. "I have something I need to discuss with you. A proposition, if you will."

Eve sighed. She didn't have much of a choice. "Make it quick," she relented.

Dagon grinned. A chair suddenly appeared behind his tall, muscular form, and he sat down, running his hand through his thick, black hair. He was handsome, even if he was an evil creep.

A chair bumped Eve behind the knees, and she fell clumsily into it.

Dagon leaned forward, his elbows on his knees, his hands clasped loosely between them. "What if I told you that Zeke doesn't have to die if I am extracted?"

"I would say you're full of shit."

"And you'd be right. He does have to die. But he doesn't have to *stay* dead."

"I don't make deals with the devil...anymore," she added.

"I'm hardly the devil. And it has nothing to do with making a deal. You can revive him. You've done it already, with your friend Cassie."

"She wasn't dead."

"She was."

Eve's eyes widened, but she shook her head. "No, you're mistaken. She was just close to death."

"No, she was expired. They were all dead, actually. The Smith brothers would have revived on their own, as they do, but Cassie would have remained very deceased. Your ichor blood is so potent, it restored life to her veins." Dagon raised a brow to Eve. "If Ruth pulls me from Zeke, you could do the same for him. Everyone lives. Everyone wins. There is no downside."

Eve was speechless. This had to be trick, right? He just wants out, and he doesn't care who he must kill to obtain his freedom. "No," she said simply.

Dagon laughed cynically. "That's it? Just 'no'?"

"Exactly. Just no."

"You don't want to finally have your bumbleheaded jock all to yourself? You don't want him to finally be free of my curse? Think of how much better his life would be if he didn't have me trapped inside of him."

"And just unleash *you* out into the world? That sounds like a positively terrible idea."

"You make me sound unhinged. I'm not a bad god. And if you're so worried about me, I'll stick around so you can keep tabs on me. Maybe I'll join Knighco. Go Team Alpha, and all that," Dagon said, pumping his fist in the air mockingly.

Was he serious? Did he really think *anyone* would want that? "If you get out, you'll be uncontrollable. You're barely controllable now. I'm not stupid."

"You must be if you don't see what a beautiful opportunity this is. I'm giving you a chance to save Zeke, because I care about you, and you care about him."

"I don't have to save Zeke if I don't agree to free you."

"I'm not asking for your permission. I will be freed one way or another. I'm just trying to be considerate - for you. If it weren't for you, I would've run off with Ruth back in Michigan. I stayed for you, and only for you."

"Much obliged," Eve replied cynically.

Dagon pushed up angrily from his chair, and two huge, black wings sprang up from behind him, spreading into a truly menacing display. Fear gripped its claws around her heart as Dagon's crimson eyes glinted. "You really don't appreciate the lengths to which I go for you. The sacrifices I make. The restraint I show. You call me evil, but you don't know evil. If I were evil, I would just keep you here, forever, trapped in my mind with me. Just you and me and all the time in the world."

Eve's blood ran cold. She'd poked the tiger while in his cage, without even thinking.

"Please don't do that," she said quietly.

"Oh, what happened to all that righteous bravado?" he mocked.

Eve started looking around, wondering how she was going to escape Dagon's mind. If she forced her way in here, she must be able to force her way back out. She just needed to find a crack.

...Or make one.

And there it was.

Dagon glanced over to the Raquel Welch poster that suddenly appeared on his wall. "What the fuck is that?"

"*Shawshank Redemption*," Eve said, a sly grin spreading. "Well, Dagon, that's my cue. I really must be going."

Eve bolted for the poster and threw herself into it.

She was staring at two frantically pacing and panicking boys.

"I swear, she isn't in here anywhere! I don't know where she is!" Zeke whispered harshly.

"She has to be in your head! Where else would she go?! Find her!" Eoduun whispered angrily back.

"I don't know how! You couldn't find her either!"

Eve stood up, and Zeke and Eoduun both startled. Relief washed over their faces. Zeke fell to his knees and threw his massive arms around her waist, burying the side of his face in her stomach. "Oh, thank god!"

"What happened?!" Eoduun demanded, his anger surging back.

"I went too far." She told them about ending up in Dagon's mind, and the proposal he offered.

Zeke and Eoduun blinked at her in disbelief.

"You think he was telling the truth?" Zeke asked. "He hasn't said a thing to me since Ruth attacked."

"I don't know. But we need to talk to Bo and Luc, either way. Dagon is not on our side," Eve deduced.

Eve opened Eoduun's apartment door, and there was Isaac, leaned against the wall in the hallway, waiting. His arms were crossed, a bored expression on his face. When he saw Eve, he pushed off from the wall and stood there, waiting to follow her back to her apartment.

"Jesus, were you out here the entire time?" she blurted.

He shook his head and stared at her.

Eve narrowed her eyes. "Did you lock yourself out again?!"

He shook his head, then pointed at himself, held his hands up, palms facing himself, and wiggled his fingers, then touched his temple and pointed at her.

Eve pulled out her phone.

"He says he was waiting for you," Ramil said from behind her.

Eve turned and saw him standing by his apartment door, having just exited. "Oh, thanks," she said. She looked at Isaac, and he looked back at her. His eyes were trying to say something. *Don't trust him.*

"Perhaps it's a good thing he can't hear, hm?" Ramil suggested knowingly, with a low chuckle.

Eve's face burned in a deep blush.

"Training was rough today," Zeke explained nonchalantly.

"I know I'm spent," Eoduun added.

Isaac pointed at Eoduun's neck, then held one hand in front of his own chest, palm toward himself, while he moved the other hand up and down in front of it with four fingers splayed.

"You're bleeding," Ramil supplied as he approached the group.

"Shit, I didn't heal you," Eve whispered. She'd also left red finger marks on his neck that were likely to bruise later. She glanced furtively at Isaac. Was this going to count against her?

"I'm fine. It's nothing," Eoduun reassured her.

"Shall I accompany you back to your apartment? Or are you going out?" Ramil asked Eve. "Luc asked me to translate for our guest when he is otherwise occupied, and I see he is not with you."

Isaac signed.

"Oh, he'll be back soon? That's fine, I can fill in for now, even if it's only for a few minutes," Ramil offered.

Isaac signed again, shaking his head.

"Are you sure? I see. Well, if I'm not needed, I suppose I'll be on my way." Ramil patted Zeke on the shoulder and added, "So good of Dagon to offer to take out Ruth for us. I have full faith that he's powerful enough to do it."

Zeke's eyebrows snapped together. "What? What are you talking about?"

"The plan to kill the witch? I'm just relieved he wasn't tempted by Ruth's offer. That really could've spelled trouble for us if he'd decided to take her up on it." Ramil crossed his hands behind his back. "But I've taken up enough of your time. Good day." He nodded his head to Eve on the way by. "Eve."

"What the fuck was that about?" Zeke asked Eve and Eoduun. "Did I miss something at the meeting?"

Eve tried to look as perplexed as him. "I have no idea. I think he might be confused."

While Zeke stood and looked puzzled, Isaac reached out and grabbed Eve's hand, then aligned it with the marks on Eoduun's neck. When he saw they matched perfectly, he cocked an eyebrow at her.

"It was only training, and it was consensual," Eve explained. "And in case you wondered, I was successful. I stole his eyes."

Isaac looked at Eoduun's eyes, confusion contorting his face.

"No, not his *eyes* eyes, but his mind-reading powers," she corrected.

Isaac pointed at his chest, circled his index finger around his temple, then held both hands out, palms up, in a questioning manner.

"What was I thinking?" Eve guessed.

He shook his head, then pointed at himself again.

"What are *you* thinking?" she tried again.

He nodded, then crossed his arms and tilted his head skeptically. He was issuing a challenge.

"Not in the fucking hallway," Eoduun said. "Let's get back to Eve's apartment."

When they walked in, they found Bo napping on the couch with a pillow over his face. Zeke tiptoed over to him and teased, "I could just push down a little…" and mimed pushing the pillow over Bo's face to suffocate him.

"I'd rather you didn't try to kill me in my sleep," Bo muttered. He groaned and sat up. "How'd the training go? It sounded…rather intense." His ears tinged red just from saying it.

"We fucking did it," Eve announced proudly. "I have the eyes! But I kind of whiffed on the possession." She sat on the couch next to Bo and relayed to him what happened in Dagon's mind.

Bo eyed Zeke warily. "So, Dagon's planning to betray us. Less than ideal, but not unexpected." He turned to Eve. "And he said your blood can cure death?"

Eve nodded. "I don't know if I believe him, though. I don't know how he could know that. Not definitively."

Bo raised his eyebrows and shrugged. "I honestly thought Cassie was dead when I pulled her from that truck. I didn't think you'd be able to revive her. But you did. I don't think we can rule it out."

Then Eve realized Isaac was standing there, watching every word they were saying. Was it safe to let him in on all of this?

"We'll need to inform Luc as soon as he gets back," Bo continued. "In the meantime, have you tried to possess anyone else? What about Eoduun?"

"Fuck no, I'm not letting her in my head again," Eoduun protested, taking a step back with his hands up defensively. "I'll give her my power, but I don't want her using it on me."

Isaac stepped forward and pointed to himself.

"Oh yeah, Isaac wanted me to read his mind," Eve remembered.

He shook his head and held his hands out, palms down. He touched the thumb and index finger together on both hands, splaying out his other fingers, and moved his hands up and down, alternately, like he was playing with marionettes. Then he pointed to himself.

Puppet? He wanted her to try to possess him?

Eve scoffed. "You're an exorcist. Isn't it your job to *not* get possessed?"

He rolled his eyes, then sat down in the adjacent chair and faced Eve. He motioned for her to get on with it.

"I don't think this is a good idea," Bo said, concerned.

"Don't get stuck," Eoduun warned.

"*Shawshank Redemption*," Eve mumbled.

34
Don't Pity Me

Isaac stared steadily at Eve, waiting. This was a terrible idea. He was the last person she should be experimenting on. Luc had warned her that incompetence could seal her fate, and this little sideshow act might just end up being proof that she was, indeed, a child with a loaded gun.

Or it might prove that she's capable of handling her powers, and Isaac can go tell the Vatican to fuck off and leave her alone.

Eve stared into Isaac's apathetic, ebony eyes, and imagined pouring herself out of her own eyes and into his. The tunnel appeared, spinning and swirling like the Doctor Who opening scene, which was different from what it looked like with Zeke. She hesitated. Why was it different? Would it be different every time, or was *she* doing something different?

She jumped through.

Her world went silent, and she was staring at herself. But something was odd – as she looked across at herself, she observed a swirling cloud of alternating darkness and light surrounding and emanating off of her, like storm clouds with sunlight shining through. It was unlike anything she'd ever seen before.

She tried to move Isaac's body, but found herself only in stillness. Was she just hitching a ride again?

Memories that weren't hers began to trickle into her mind's eye, and she was suddenly slammed with Isaac's haunting flashbacks. Sneering children's faces looking down at him while he bled and cowered, their kicks landing all over his head and body. He could feel the impact, but there was no pain. He could see the mouths of his foster brothers and sisters forming nasty words of hatred, but he heard nothing. They all had faint swirls of color around them, but the colors were barely discernable. His foster siblings wouldn't get punished for this. They would say the kids at the Catholic school did this to him, and his foster parents would believe them, because the kids at school often did this to him, too. He was everyone's punching bag. He was miserable, but there were strangely no tears. There were never tears. Wordless thoughts permeated his consciousness. *What did I ever do to them? Why do they hate me? Why can't I be normal, like them? I wish they'd die. I wish everyone normal would die.*

She slipped seamlessly into another nightmare. An old man with a loose double chin was smiling at him as he closed and locked the door behind his back. It wasn't a kind smile, and an ominous black haze surrounded the man. He was still wearing his vestments, as mass had just ended. They were in a small room with a desk and a couch. An office in the church. This priest's office.

Looking at the couch made his stomach turn. It was a bad couch. Bad things happened on that couch. Wrong things. He felt that man's hands on him, in places they shouldn't be. He closed his eyes and tried to imagine being somewhere else. Things were happening to him, things that should've been excruciating, but pain didn't exist for him. The only pain he ever seemed to remember feeling was the pain in his chest – that dull ache that never went away.

More memories of the man in the vestments sprang up, one after another after another. The malicious smile. The black miasma. The evil couch. The roving, disgusting hands. The unspeakable violations. The sense that he was a shameful plaything, and nothing more. A disgusting toy to keep hidden behind closed doors. Dirty and disposable. Not a person.

Eve was then cast into a new scene. A funeral. There was the man, but he was in a box, and the black cloud had dispersed. Isaac had put him there. It was one thing to treat *him* like a plaything, but when Isaac had grown too old for his tastes, the priest had moved on to another. That was unacceptable. He couldn't let the man make another monster like him.

He had to die. All monsters had to die. Killing was a sin, but Isaac was already damned. All he could do was embrace his damnation and rid this world of monsters like the man in the box.

Memories of slaughter and death flooded her mind. Hideous, monstrous faces lurking beneath human masks, as well as monstrous humans surrounded by a murky black haze. One, two, three, twenty, fifty…his body count piled up, but the ache in his chest remained. Someday it would be enough. Someday he would kill enough monsters to make that pain go away. Someday he would earn his redemption in the eyes of God by destroying the evil that pervaded the church, that pervaded His world.

The devil wasn't a creature in a pit.

The devil was Man, in all his monstrous forms.

Eve was drawn away from these memories by something wet running down her face. She reached up and touched her face, then looked down at her hand. But it wasn't her hand. It was Isaac's thick, heavy-knuckled hand, and his callused fingertips were wet.

Tears.

I don't cry, she thought. No, *he* thought. *It's time to get out.*

Eve looked at herself sitting across from Isaac. It was strange to see herself like this, staring vacantly, surrounded intermittently by churning black clouds and radiant sunshine.

What the hell did that mean?

She imagined a tunnel leading back to her own body, and the Doctor Who wormhole appeared. She jumped through.

The sensation of sound filled her ears again, and she was now staring at Isaac. Tears wetted his cheeks, and he wiped them away in annoyance. He signed with a scowl on his face, but it was too fast for Eve to follow any individual sign. He was angry with her. He stood up and stormed off, grabbing his jacket from the hook and slamming the door behind him.

"What did you do?" Bo wanted to know.

"I think I saw things I wasn't supposed to see," Eve replied.

"Like what?" Eoduun wondered.

"Not my place to share." Eve leaned back on the couch, her stomach in knots. "I need to go talk to him," she said. She stood up, and Bo rose next to her with the intent to join her. She held her hand up. "No, you guys stay here. I'll only be a few minutes."

"He seemed pissed," Bo observed. "Maybe you should give him some time."

"I don't want him stewing in it. I need to clear the air."

Eve found Isaac standing outside the apartment complex, leaned against the wall under the glowing sodium light, smoking a cigarette. He ignored her.

She stood in front of him and said, "I didn't mean to intrude on your memories. They just kind of came at me."

He scowled and continued to ignore her.

"I'm sorry about what happened to you," she continued, circling her fist over her chest.

His scowl deepened and he signed at her. He brushed his thumb under his chin, held one hand up and circled it with his middle finger bent, then pointed at himself.

She stared blankly at him, and he huffed in annoyance. Eve leaned her back against the wall next to him, and her arm brushed his. He jerked his arm away and moved away from her so they weren't touching.

"Don't pity me," he said suddenly, and her eyes widened in surprise. His voice was much deeper than she had expected and had a mildly slurred quality, a bit like Sly Stallone, and it took her a moment to decipher what he had said. Mostly because she wasn't expecting him to speak.

"So you can talk, but just choose not to," Eve said, frowning.

"You can learn to sign, but just choose not to," Isaac retorted.

"I can't *learn* to sign just like that," Eve said, snapping her fingers.

"And I didn't learn to speak just like that," he said, snapping his fingers in response. "It was hard."

"Hey, I'm making an effort. You have to give me that. And I know the alphabet, at least," Eve said, and began signing through the letters to demonstrate.

He took a drag from his cigarette as he watched her fumble with a few letters, but ultimately make it from A to Z. He just nodded when she was done.

"Well?"

He held his hand out horizontally and wobbled it side to side, the universal sign for "so-so."

"Oh, fuck off. And I don't *pity* you, by the way. I'm trying to empathize with you. Everyone can use a little empathy."

Isaac said nothing.

"What do the colors around people mean?" she asked.

He tapped the ash from his cigarette. "Character."

"Black is bad," Eve deduced.

Isaac nodded.

"And bright is good?"

He nodded again.

"Why do I have both?"

Isaac looked at her contemplatively, taking another drag from his cigarette. He touched his forehead and twisted his palm away, shrugging and shaking his head. He must be done speaking.

Eve got her phone out and looked up his gesture, even though she was pretty sure she knew already.

I don't know.

She had a guess. Blood of Lilith, Blood of Eve. Darkness and light, fighting for dominance. She was a healer, but she had the potential to go dark side.

"I see why they call you the Angel of Death," Eve commented after a long silence. "You've killed more monsters than I even knew existed."

Isaac signed and shook his head.

"Why do you hate that name?"

He brushed his thumb under his chin, then touched both shoulders with his fingertips, flipping them both outward. Eve checked her phone.

Not an angel.

"Well, maybe you're not an angel. But still, it's kind of cool. I wish I had a cool nickname."

Isaac signed again, spelling this time.

Abomination.

Eve was unamused. "Fine. I get your point."

He touched the fingertips of two V-handshapes together and pulled them wide apart, then he hooked his finger and twisted it near the corner of his mouth. His expression dripped with sarcasm. Eve looked at her phone.

Very cool.

"Shut up. I'm going in," Eve said.

As she turned to leave, she could've sworn she saw Isaac crack a smile around the cigarette hanging from his lips, just for a second.

When Eve returned to the apartment, the boys were all in the kitchen, eating.

"Eoduun, you better not have your fingers in the pickle jar again," Eve called out.

"He did!" Zeke tattled.

"I'm the only one who eats them!" Eoduun countered.

"Then why are they in *my* fridge?" Eve wondered.

"Is it your fridge?" Eoduun pondered. "Or is it the community fridge?"

Zeke moved off the barstool so Eve could take up her spot next to Bo. She rested her elbows on the counter, her chin in her hands. "I wonder how I would go about learning ASL," she posed.

"Why?" Eoduun asked. "Isaac isn't going to be here for long."

"No, but he's not the only deaf person in the world," Eve said. "It wouldn't hurt to know it. It could come in...*handy*." Eve was laughing hysterically at her own terrible pun before she'd even finished her sentence.

"Good lord, Luc *is* rubbing off on you," Bo complained, staring down at the manga on his phone.

"That's what she said," Zeke snorted.

Bo looked up at him. "Oh god. It's spreading."

"I wish there was a specialty that could make me instantly learn something," Eve said, "like Nero in *The Matrix*. Just plug me into a knowledgeable person, and poof! 'I know kung fu.'"

"You mean plug you into Luc, and poof! You know ASL?" Bo interpreted.

"Yes. That."

"Well, technically, you could," Eoduun offered.

Eve perked up. "Really?!"

"But you'd have to erase it from him if you wanted to keep it," he added.

Her face dropped. "Oh."

"He'd probably let you have it," Zeke said around a mouthful of cheese puffs.

"I'm pretty sure he needs it," Bo countered.

"Maybe Ramil doesn't need it," Zeke suggested.

"And I'm sure he'll just give it to me," Eve said sarcastically.

"That's what she said," Eoduun muttered, a pickle hanging out of his mouth.

"*Et tu*, Eoduun?" Bo sighed.

Isaac walked through the door and hung his coat on the hook. He walked to the kitchen and looked at everyone, then signed to Eve.

Had she somehow become his designated handler when Luc wasn't there? She looked down at her phone, then held her arm out and dragged her other hand slowly up it. "Slow down. I can't keep up with you," she said.

Isaac pointed at the boys and Bo, then held both hands out flat, palms down, and lifted them diagonally while closing his fingers. Finally, he held his index finger up and swirled his other index finger around it until his fingertips touched, his brows furrowed.

Something about the boys. She looked on her phone. *Leaving. When.*

When are they leaving?

Eve looked at the clock on the stove. It was almost 10PM already. She looked down at her phone while everyone else watched her. She looked at Isaac, held her hands out flat with her palms up and see-sawed them, then made a 90-degree chop with her hand.

Maybe never.

Isaac gave her a skeptical look.

"No, I don't like this," Bo said, only half kidding, narrowing his eyes at Eve and Isaac.

Ruger, Remi, and Cassie strolled into Eve's apartment.

"Are we celebrating tonight or what?" Ruger asked as they all made their way to the kitchen where everyone else was gathered. He spied Zeke with the snacks. "Ooh, cheese puffs. Hit me," Ruger called to him, then pointed at his face. Zeke started throwing cheese puffs across the kitchen into Ruger's mouth.

"Oh boy, dinner *and* a show," Remi said sarcastically.

Cassie climbed up on the counter so she could reach what was left of the bottle of Johnnie Walker on top of the fridge. "I think a little pregame is in order," she announced.

After consulting her phone, Eve looked at an overstimulated Isaac. She held her cupped hand out and drew it toward her chest, then finger spelled a Z and two Os.

Welcome to the zoo.

"I don't think I like it, either," Eoduun agreed with Bo, pointing at Eve's signing.

"I think it's neat!" Zeke said cheerfully as he tossed another cheese puff. "It's like they have a secret language!"

"That's why I don't like it," Bo said.

35
I Think I'm Adorable

Luc walked into the chaos with his usual impeccable timing. "Are there more of them? Are they multiplying?" he said with mild displeasure as he spied the congregation in the kitchen.

"Don't look at me, you brought the newest addition," Eve replied, gesturing toward Isaac.

"Ramil isn't here to translate for him?" Luc asked.

"No, Isaac didn't want him. But we're doing fine without him," Eve said. She took Luc aside. "He keeps telling me not to trust Ramil. He doesn't like him. Maybe the static Eoduun was running into when trying to read him wasn't just because it's Ramil. Maybe there is more to it. And then Ramil told Zeke that he was glad Dagon was going to take out Ruth. Basically blurted the fake plan to him."

Luc frowned. "Well, as far as anyone else knows, Zeke already knows the plan. What did Zeke say?"

"We just tried to get him to brush it off as Ramil being confused or mistaken, but I wouldn't be surprised if he asks you about it."

"I'll think of something. But even if Zeke was happy to accept it as a mistake, Dagon won't be. He's probably already worked it out that we're planning a ruse." Luc sighed. "I should probably have a chat with him, see where he stands these days."

"About that…" Eve told Luc about what happened when she tried to possess Zeke, and everything Dagon said.

"Well, fuck. Fuck!" Luc spat. "Ugh, he's going to be a big fucking problem." His irritated expression quickly abated, however. "But hey, lots of good news!" he said, holding his hands wide, a pleased grin on his face. "Your blood healing is getting stronger, *and* you were able to complete a specialty transfer! You'll master the possession, too. You can try it on me later."

"Actually, I was able to *kind of* possess Isaac."

Luc's pale eyebrows leapt into his hairline. "You practiced possession on the exorcist?"

"I felt like a passenger again at first, but after a while, I was able to move his hand and eyes. I didn't stay long because he wanted me out."

"I'm impressed, love! Huge strides today!" He pulled her close and hugged her to his chest. "My little peacock," he said adoringly.

"I think you need to let the peacock thing go," Eve mumbled with her face pressed against his chest.

"I'll never let my little peacock go."

"Are you coming out with us, Luc?" Cassie called across the kitchen.

Bo interjected, "Do you guys really need to go out? Didn't you have enough of that last night?"

"I think Eve and I will be staying in tonight, Cass," Luc said. "And, ideally, the whole team could use some rest."

"I'll rest when I'm dead," Ruger said, lifting the bottle of Johnnie Walker to his lips.

"You make that evidently clear on a daily basis," Cassie said. She turned her attention to Isaac. "What about you, handsome? I see the white collar, but that doesn't mean you can't have a little fun, does it?"

"I don't know about *handsome*," Ruger muttered jealously. "Maybe, if you can get past those ears, I guess."

"There's nothing wrong with his ears!" Eve disputed, stepping to Isaac's side to defend him against the insult.

"Well, obviously there's *something* wrong with them. I mean…" Ruger shrugged and grimaced.

"Ok, let's leave Isaac alone now," Eve said, moving herself between Isaac and the group, agitation in her tone.

"I apologize for the asshat," Cassie said to Isaac. "He's an idiot. Ignore him."

Isaac's expression remained unchanged as he looked from Ruger to Cassie to Eve as they each spoke. Now he turned to Eve and signed. He indicated Team Flannel, then held his hands out flat, palms down, and lifted them diagonally while closing his fingers, then swirled one index finger around the other.

Eve recognized it. *When are they leaving?*

She consulted her phone, then tapped an F-handshape to her chin.

Soon. Then, as an afterthought, she scrunched her face, pointed to herself, then to her temple. *I think.*

"What's this now?" Luc asked, wearing a wide grin. He gave Isaac a sly look and signed while saying, "I see why you didn't want Ramil. You got yourself a much prettier translator."

Isaac shrugged, pointed at Eve, then stuck his fists side by side, the thumb of one hand tucked into the other fist. Like he was revving a motorcycle, he twisted one fist and splayed the fingers of that hand. He then held up his index fingers and made alternating vertical circles toward his chest.

She'd seen him do that before. It was the first thing he'd signed when she met him. What was it again?

"Hey!" she protested when she recalled Luc's translation: *He doesn't think I'm very good at it.* "I'm learning!"

Luc laughed then signed and said to Isaac, "I'd rather watch her sign badly than watch anyone else sign perfectly. It's adorable."

Eve saw him sign "adorable" by holding his thumb out and raising his first two fingers to his chin, like a finger pistol. He then curled those fingers like he was stroking his chin. In annoyance, she mimicked his sign for "adorable," but instead of raising both her index and middle fingers, she only raised her middle finger. "Is it *adorable*?" she asked, copying the stroking motion with her middle finger.

Luc bit back an amused grin. "Exceedingly."

No mistaking it this time. Isaac smirked. Only briefly, but it definitely happened.

When Team Flannel finally accepted that they were going out alone, they headed out to the bar. At Luc's urging, Zeke and Eoduun left shortly after, but to their apartments rather than the bar.

"I'm off, too," Bo said after the boys had left.

"Isaac, are you sure you don't want to go bunk with Bo?" Luc asked hopefully, signing.

Isaac looked at Luc flatly and shook his head.

"Then maybe Eve can come stay with me tonight, and you can have the apartment to yourself," Luc suggested.

Again, he shook his head.

"Things might get a little uncomfortable for you in this apartment tonight, Isaac," Luc warned good-naturedly.

Isaac pinched his fingers together, touched his nose with his finger tips, then flung his hand away while opening his fingers.

"You might care later," Luc replied in a singsong tone while signing.

Isaac strung together a series of signs that Eve couldn't follow, and it was a reminder to Eve that she had a long way to go to be able to keep up with Isaac in casual conversation. Luc laughed at whatever he had said, and Eve looked to Luc questioningly.

"He said it's not like he's going to hear anything," Luc explained.

"Well, I will, so be considerate," Bo reminded them. "I've had to listen to more than enough of that today," he added as he opened the door to leave.

"'Night, Bo. Happy stroking," Luc taunted.

Bo flipped him off as he closed the door behind him.

"And then there were three," Eve said.

Luc pointed a finger at her. "No funny ideas, young lady."

"Wouldn't dream of it." She got up and headed to the bathroom, then added teasingly, "Not until I've had a shower, first."

When Eve exited the bathroom some time later, her pink hair in a knot at the top of her head and a soft towel wrapped around her nude form, she padded across to the kitchen to get a drink from the fridge.

As she opened the fridge door, Luc announced from the living room, "You know he's deaf, not blind, Eve."

She glanced up over the fridge door and saw Luc and Isaac staring at her from the couch and chair, respectively.

Eve touched her fingertips to her nose and flung her hand away like she was throwing away a tissue, like she'd seen Isaac do. *I don't care.*

Then she grabbed a flavored water and sauntered as slow as possible back toward her room.

"You think you're funny, don't you?" Luc said.

She pointed at herself, at her temple, herself again, and then did the "adorable" sign with only a middle finger. *I think I'm adorable.* Then she disappeared into her bedroom.

Eve sat on the bed with her towel cinched in her hand and waited with the lights turned down. Luc appeared in the doorway, his hands casually resting in the pockets of his perfectly tailored suit. He leaned a shoulder against the door frame and gazed at Eve from behind his round sunglasses.

They heard the rustling of Isaac's jacket out in the other room, followed by the apartment door opening and closing. Luc raised an eyebrow. "Should I lock him out?"

"No, that's mean," Eve objected. "Don't be mean. Nothing's more unattractive than cruelty."

Luc took off his sunglasses and stuck them in his jacket pocket. "Is that right?" He closed the door behind him and swaggered across the room toward Eve, slipping off his suit jacket and tossing it onto her dresser as he passed. He stood in front of her, looking down at her with those mesmerizing aquamarine eyes. They almost glowed in the low light. "I noticed what you did to Eoduun's neck. That looked pretty cruel."

Eve opened her legs around Luc's knees and leaned back slightly, resting on one hand while the other continued to hold the towel together around her. She looked up at him. "It's not cruelty if he likes it."

Luc started unbuttoning his shirt, and Eve's greedy eyes dropped to his long, nimble fingers. *Take it off. Take it all off.* God, he was sexy, and he fucking knew it.

"Why didn't you heal him? Did you want me to see it? Did you want me to be jealous, making me imagine what you were doing with him when you made those marks?" he asked in a low, taunting tone as he slowly freed one button after another, revealing the flesh of his chest to her, inch by inch.

She peeled her gaze from his chest to look him in the eye. "Not my intention. But if it was – did it work?"

He unbuttoned his sleeve cuffs, then let his shirt fall off onto the floor. He towered over her, and her eyes roved the bare skin of his torso, so firm and taut over his lean, well-defined muscles. Her fingers were drawn to him of their own accord, abandoning their task of holding her towel closed as they traced either side of his obliques.

"Oh, it worked. And then you go prancing around in front of Isaac in nothing but that thin little towel, practically inviting him to look." He began to unclasp his belt.

"Or maybe I was just thirsty," Eve whispered, running her fingers over his hipbones.

"I fucking bet you were," Luc said in a sultry tone. "You get off on making me sweat, don't you?" He unbuttoned his slacks.

Eve pouted up at him. "I'm sorry. What can I do to make it up to you?" She asked as he unzipped his fly.

"Reassure me that I'm your favorite," he implored in a husky tone, bringing his large hand to her cheek. "Stroke my...ego."

Luc's pants fell to his ankles, and he stepped out of them. Eve hooked her fingers into the waistband of his boxers and lowered them down his hips, releasing his thick cock. She wrapped her palm around his girth, loving the way he felt in her hand. Hard as a rock, yet soft like velvet. She flicked her tongue out and licked the underside of his length, reveling in the way his eyes darkened with need.

"Stroke *this* ego?" she said seductively, her lips brushing the crown of his cock.

Luc hummed and bit his lower lip between those beautiful white teeth. The way he looked at her, like she was the only thing in the entire world that he cared about, made her chest flutter. Desire. Adoration. Pride. Obsession. All tied in a glittering aquamarine bow.

She took him into her mouth, wriggling her tongue in tight circles as she bobbed her head back and forth. He moaned, sliding his fingers into her hair. She cupped his testicles in her other hand, letting her fingers stroke him underneath, slowly moving her finger a little further back with each gentle stroke, testing the waters. He made no sign of protest or discomfort, only heavy breathing and appreciative hums as she sucked and fondled him.

When her fingertip made contact with his tight hole, though, his hand reached down and caught her wrist, stopping her exploring finger, and she felt him swell in her mouth.

"Sorry," she apologized quickly, backing off. "I should've asked if that was ok."

Luc laughed breathily. "Oh, it's quite alright. I just don't want to come yet," he explained, his cock twitching and weeping in Eve's other hand. "I've missed you madly, and I already feel like I'm about to explode."

He pushed her back onto the bed and knelt in front of her, bringing her bare foot to his lips. He kissed her toes lightly, then the inside of the arch of her foot. He moved his way up the inside of her calf, behind her knee, and up her inner thigh. Her anticipation grew, slickening her core as his soft kisses and hot breath inched closer to her center.

When his lips skimmed the petals of her sex, he paused. "Tell me what you want," he whispered.

"Don't stop," Eve replied.

"You can do better than that," he urged, squeezing her thighs in his huge hands.

"Make me come with your tongue," she ordered.

"Mmm, I can do that. If you say please." He gave her one tiny stroke with his tongue, making her core pulse.

"Please, Luc," she begged, trying to pull him closer with her feet on his back.

He resisted briefly, just to playfully spite her, but when she huffed in annoyance, he chuckled and gave in. His tongue danced skillfully over her sensitive nub, drawing a breathy moan from her lips.

The ache in her core tightened with every circle and flick of his hot, wet tongue, but something was missing. It wasn't that he was doing something wrong – he was absolutely worshipping the heat between her legs – but rather she needed something else. She needed connection with him. Her heart longed for his. Her arms wanted to be around him, holding his body flush against hers. She wanted him to surround her. She wanted him inside of her.

She needed his love.

"Luc," she whispered. "I need you. Get up here and fuck me." It wasn't exactly what she meant, but "make love to me" just sounded corny. Lame. Sappy. Not her brand.

"Is something wrong?" he asked as he climbed up over top of her on his hands and knees. "Was I giving an unsatisfactory tongue lashing?"

"No, you're wonderful." She looked up at the monument of a man looking down at her. She couldn't understand what she'd done to inspire such adoration from a man like Lucius Fagerberg. She reached up and cupped his perfect, chiseled face in her hands. "You're quite possibly the most beautiful thing I've ever seen," she whispered.

Luc smiled softly. "That's quite possibly the nicest thing you've ever said to me." He leaned down and kissed her, brushing her hair back tenderly.

Eve flung her arms around his ribs and pulled his big, lean body down onto hers, wrapping her legs around him to keep him there. She could feel his heart beating next to hers, and it filled her with the warmth that his tongue couldn't.

"I love you, Eve," Luc whispered. "I've wanted a lot of things in my life, but you're the only thing I've ever *needed*. You're the only thing I know I can't live without."

What she wouldn't give for those words to be true. He probably believed them himself, in the moment. But things change. Feelings change. Love turns sour. Relationships fall apart.

And when it inevitably happened, she would be the one left holding the bag. She'd hoped maintaining her connection with Zeke and Eoduun would save her, but she still loved Luc too much. She couldn't stop herself.

"Make me believe it," she susurrated.

She felt his lips curl into a smile against her ear. "Gladly. Every day for the rest of my life."

36

Luceve

Luc peppered kisses from Eve's forehead, over her eyelids, down her nose, across her lips, to her chin. His fingers raked through her hair as his lips skimmed over her throat, pausing to swirl his tongue over her pulse point.

He pressed himself against her awaiting opening, and she impatiently coaxed him on with her calves against his ass. She was desperate for him. She needed him inside her *now*. He filled her in a way no one else did, and she whimpered contentedly as she stretched around him.

Eve slowly rocked her hips against him as he drove into her deeply. His breath was hot against her neck as he held her to him, his muscles bunching and flexing against her body, his deep, sensual moans elevating her arousal. She thrust her fingers into his wild, platinum hair and pushed it back from his face so she could admire those gorgeous aqua eyes. So fucking handsome. A goddamn masterpiece.

And he was hers. For today, for this moment, he was hers. Maybe tomorrow he would change his mind, but right now, this impossibly beautiful psychopath belonged only to her.

The urge bubbled up from her belly. *Bite him. Own him. Devour him.*

She swallowed it back down. Now was not the time for that. She didn't want to steal his powers or dominate him.

She just wanted his love.

And he gave it, freely and unreservedly, until Eve was a panting, writhing mess of pure ecstasy beneath him.

As she lay there in the afterglow, still clinging to him, she whispered those dangerous words. "I love you. So fucking much. Goddamn it."

Luc chuckled, the sound vibrating through his chest and into hers. "You make it sound like an insult."

"Say it back or I'll never say it again," Eve demanded.

Luc raised himself up on his elbow and looked down at her with an arched brow. "I do love you, and I believe I told you that *before* we made love."

He did. She knew that. Still…

"Sorry," she apologized. "I don't mean to be like that."

He wrapped his arms around her and squeezed her tightly to his chest. "You're like a cute, spikey little naval mine," he said adoringly.

Eve snorted. "I make compliments sound like insults, and you make insults sound like compliments."

The fridge door closed noisily in the kitchen. Then the cups in the cupboard rattled, and a cup clunked loudly on the counter.

Eve and Luc looked at each other. "Is that Isaac?" Eve whispered.

"Why are you whispering?" Luc whispered back. "Are you afraid he's going to hear you?"

Eve smacked his arm playfully. There were more noisy clunks and rattles out in the living room, and then in the bathroom.

"He wasn't that loud the entire day," Eve said. "Is he doing it on purpose?"

"Maybe he's trying to remind us that he's here so no one makes an embarrassingly naked trek to the bathroom. Joke's on him if he thinks that'll deter me."

"I wonder how long he's been here. I never heard him come back in."

Luc shrugged and sat up. "I'm pretty sure we weren't bothering him." He then looked down at Eve with interest. "Speaking of Isaac, what was it like to possess him?"

Eve sat up next to him. "Silent and horrifying. Although there was a kind of ringing sound in some of the memories that came through, like tinnitus, so I guess it wasn't always silent."

"Horrifying?"

"Just...so many monsters."

"Oh. So, you have access to *everything* when you're possessing someone?"

"I didn't mean to dig into Isaac's memories. They came at me on their own. And when I jumped into Dagon's mind, I didn't get any memories, just him in the present."

"Like when I speak with him in Zeke's mind," Luc remarked. He surveyed Eve momentarily, then said, "I want you to try to possess me."

Eve looked away. She was terrified to possess Luc. What if she saw things she didn't want to see? What if she felt things she didn't want to feel? What if she learned something that changed how she felt about him? Everyone has secrets. Everyone has done something they hope no one ever finds out about. She had a closet full of skeletons like that. She was afraid to stumble across whatever dark secrets he had hidden away.

"I don't want your memories," she blurted.

"You want me to try to block them? I can block Eoduun."

329

"But I still need to get in somehow."

"Let's try it. If you get into memories that you don't want, just stop digging."

"That's just it, though. I wasn't digging when Isaac's memories attacked me."

Luc gave her a look of realization. "Trauma," he stated.

Eve nodded.

"From what I understand, traumatic memories don't behave like normal memories. They're unrelenting and unpredictable, and, unfortunately, almost always unavoidable." Luc's face brightened. "Luckily, I don't have anything in my head that'll come at you like that." When Eve continued to hesitate, Luc added, "Love, you need to practice this. We'll be facing off with Ruth soon. A matter of days, likely. So, let's roleplay. I'll be my sister."

Eve raised her eyebrows and grimaced. "Those are two sentences I hope to never hear together again."

"Fair. We'll never speak of it again." Luc climbed out of bed and stood up. He was still naked. "But I still want you to possess me. You can pretend I'm, I don't know, an extremely handsome and naked mugger."

"Put some boxers on at least."

"Make me."

Eve reached over and grabbed an oversized and marginally dirty pajama shirt from her floor and slipped it on. She stood in front of Luc.

"Stick 'em up!" Luc said, pointing his finger at Eve like a pistol. "I'm going to steal your shirt because, as you can see, I have no clothes!"

Eve stifled a giggle. "I can't do this if you're making me laugh."

"How dare you laugh at my nakedness! Give me your shirt, or I'll finger you to death!" Luc threatened, poking his finger pistol against Eve's chest a few times.

She bit back a smirk and shook her head. "When I possess you, I'm going to make you walk naked to the fridge," she warned.

"Then grab me a snack while you're out there. I'm starving. My metabolism has to work twice as hard to keep me warm on these cold, lonely streets…on account of my nakedness."

"Just going to keep it going, huh?" Eve asked flatly.

Luc tapped her sternum with his finger again. "Just get inside me already, you tease."

Eve took a deep breath and looked into Luc's eyes. She opened the gate between them, but it took a little more effort this time. She had to focus harder. When the tunnel finally appeared, it didn't look like a tunnel. It looked more like a slowly spinning black hole, and it made her nervous about jumping into it.

She did it anyway.

She felt crowded, like she was trying to enter a room that was already packed to the brim. Pressure pushed on her from all sides, threatening to crush her if she didn't move back. What was it? And why was everything still black? Why couldn't she see out of Luc's eyes?

Then it dawned on her. She hadn't broken through yet. She was still trying to push her way in, and his mind was resisting. She pushed harder, and felt the wall give slightly. Oh yeah, she could do this. She gathered all of her strength and, in a burst of energy, blasted through, like an Armored Titan.

Only the body, not the memories. Only the body, she repeated mentally, making it her mantra, as her sense of sight was restored.

Holy Jesus, she was way too tall. She looked down…way down…at herself, staring vacantly, just standing in a stupor.

I am an Oompa Loompa, she thought in disgust.

She tried to move Luc's enormous body, but she couldn't feel his limbs. It was like she wasn't properly 'wearing' him. She imagined stretching herself out, sliding her arms and legs into his like a giant jumpsuit.

Oh yes, fill me up, baby, Eve heard Luc's voice in her mind. His mind.

"Gross," Eve said…through Luc's mouth, in Luc's voice. She gasped.

"Uh oh," Luc's voice said, but this time it wasn't Eve saying it. "I still have control, too." His right hand raised up on its own.

"What the fuck," Eve said in Luc's voice. She raised his other arm, then slapped the arm he was controlling.

"Hey!" Luc protested, then smacked the arm she was controlling. "Behave!" He then moved both arms, wresting control from Eve. *You're slipping,* Luc thought to her. *Take control. This won't work with Ruth if she can still talk and move. You need to push me out of the way.*

How the hell was she supposed to do that? Luc was a mountain, and not just physically. Trying to push his will aside was going to require gargantuan force.

He sensed her thoughts. *Not force. Manipulation,* he advised.

How do you manipulate someone in their own head? She thought about Isaac. She gained control over him after she'd been in his traumatic memories. Was that the key? Lure the will into emotion-laden memories and trap it there?

But she didn't want to be in Luc's memories.

Just do it, Luc urged.

"Ugh, fine," Eve said aloud from Luc's lips. With a bit of effort, she was able to push into Luc's memories. Floating images and scattered feelings and sensations surrounded her. She caught a glimpse of herself through her old apartment window, in her days before Knighco, viewed from a distance, and she was overwhelmed with a feeling of obsessed longing. As badly as she wanted to investigate *that* memory further, because what the fuck, she pushed it aside. She wanted something she could trap him in, so she focused on the feelings that stem from trauma.

Fear jumped out at her. Absolute horror.

Perfect.

She latched on.

The memory cracked open and spilled out, like the water in a coconut. She was standing in her kitchen, as Luc. He was looking down at Bo when Bo's eyes suddenly shot wide. He raised his head and inhaled.

Something was wrong.

"I just caught a hint of Ruth's scent. And someone else. No, *on* someone else," Bo clarified. Then he took off out the door at a sprint.

Luc teleported to the front of the building just as Bo was bursting out the doors, Zeke and Eoduun hot on his heels. "Where's Eve?!" Luc demanded from Bo. Panic was beginning to rise in his chest.

Bo sniffed, and the color drained from his face. "I don't know."

A boulder dropped in Luc's gut. "What do you mean?!"

"She's...she's not here. She's just...gone," Bo revealed in confusion and dread, looking around, desperately trying to catch a scent.

Bo's revelation brought Luc's world crashing down around him. *Not Eve. Anyone but Eve.* Horror and desperation rent his heart in two. If anything happened to her, it would kill him. Hot tears burned his eyes, but he forced them back with a surge of rage - a powerful rage that split the air with a cacophony of thunder and lighting.

He would chase her down, to the ends of the Earth. No one was taking Eve from him. Ever.

Because he couldn't bear the alternative.

Eve's own feelings overwhelmed her and pulled her from Luc's memory, grounding her in the present. She'd had no idea the true depth of Luc's emotions toward her. It both warmed and terrified her.

Love of that intensity could make a normal person do crazy things. What could it drive a psychopath like Luc to do?

Eve pushed the thoughts from her mind and focused on the task at hand. She moved Luc's arms and wiggled his fingers, unimpeded. Was she fully in control now? She seemed to be.

She looked for Luc's boxers on the floor, which seemed impossibly far away. It was dizzying up here. When she found them, she bent down to pick them up, and she half-expected her ears to pop from the elevation change. She sat on the bed to put them on, not trusting herself to balance on one foot in Luc's enormous body.

Then she walked out the bedroom door, surprised at the length of her strides with Luc's long legs. She was on stilts. Only a few steps were necessary to carry her to the fridge.

There was an urgent pounding on her apartment door. "Luc! Eve! We have a problem." It was Bo.

Isaac bolted upright on the couch, and Eve realized he must have been able to feel the vibration. He looked over at Eve – Luc – standing in the dark kitchen, illuminated by the fridge light. He signed.

Eve didn't even have to look it up. Luc's memories of ASL supplied her with a translation: *What was that?*

She pulled from that same memory bank and signed back, *Bo is at the door.*

She strode to the door and opened it. Bo and Zeke looked up at her. It was weird to see them looking *up* at her.

"Dagon was up to something," Bo said. "You need to get him under control."

"I'm not Luc," Eve blurted.

"...Are you Patricia?" Zeke ventured jokingly.

Bo looked her up and down. "Eve?" Bo guessed.

She put her hand on her hip. "In the flesh," she said ironically.

"He let you possess him?" Bo asked in mild awe.

"Oh, he made me work for it. But I got it figured out," she said proudly, holding out Luc's hands and wriggling his fingers. Was it just her imagination, or was she getting tired?

"That's amazing!" Zeke marveled. "What's it like?"

"Really high," Eve replied with a chuckle.

"That's so weird, you still laugh like *you*, but you're laughing in *his* voice," Zeke said.

Bo interjected, straight to the point. "I need Luc, Eve. Is he in there?"

Eve called to Luc in his head, and when he finally responded, he seemed lost.

"What the fuck happened?" he asked aloud from his own mouth.

"I trapped you in your memories, I think," Eve replied, also from Luc's mouth.

"Oh, that's fucking trippy," Zeke remarked, staring. "What do I even call you? Luceve?"

Isaac joined them in the doorway. He furrowed his brow and flipped two horizontal D-handshapes from palms up to palms down, then held flat palms up questioningly. *What's happening?*

"This is so much better than having to look it up," Eve said, enjoying the access to Luc's mental ASL dictionary. But she was exhausted. She felt like she needed to lie down and take a nap.

Luc spoke and signed, overriding Eve's control. "Eve and I are sharing a body. But I think she's running out of juice."

Oh, that makes sense, she thought, no longer able to control Luc's mouth. She felt an increasing pull as her hold on Luc slipped through her grasp.

37
He's Not Your Friend

Eve was thrust back into her own body like the snap of a rubber band. And it fucking stung. An icepick was lodged in her skull, like she had brain freeze, but it passed quickly. Her limbs tingled and ached like they had fallen asleep, so she shook them out and wiggled her fingers and toes. She threw on some shorts and joined the boys back in the living room.

"Should I get Eoduun?" Eve asked.

"No, it'll be like trying to wake the dead right now," Bo replied.

"What did Dagon do?" Luc asked Bo and Zeke.

"I woke up because I sensed something was off," Bo recounted. "Z wasn't in the building. So, I tracked him down and found him standing in the field next to the training grounds, not far from where we found the portal Ruthie had left when she took Eve."

"I have no idea how I got there," Zeke said. "I think Dagon took me for a walk while I was sleeping."

"I wonder if he was trying to contact Ruth," Eve said.

"It's possible he already made contact and was on his way to meet her," Luc said. "We should do a sweep."

Isaac pointed to himself, then pointed both index fingers away from himself.

Eve wished she still had Luc's ASL knowledge.

"Fine, you go, Isaac," Luc said. "Bo, you go with him. I'm going to see what I can do with Dagon."

Eve saw Isaac and Bo off. "You boys be careful," she told them. She wished she had her phone on her so she could look it up and sign it to Isaac.

Isaac just nodded at her.

Bo patted her cheek. "Always."

She caught his hand in hers. "And if you happen to get yourself hurt, you *will* let me heal you." She pointed at him threateningly.

"Yes, dear," he said dismissively, then left with Isaac.

Luc sat down with Zeke. He put two fingers against Zeke's forehead and closed his eyes.

Eve wondered if he could do that if she was in his head still, or if it would've been too much of a strain on Luc. She still had so many questions about what was possible.

After a few minutes, Luc sighed irritably, and Zeke's eyes flashed blue.

"Ow! Fuck!" Zeke yelped.

"That fucker," Luc grumbled.

"What happened?" Eve asked, leaning forward in her chair.

"He gave me the same choice he gave you: get on board with extracting him, or he's going to take matters into his own hands."

"And?"

"I sealed him, like I should've done earlier," Luc said. "We don't have much time. We need to take Ruth down before Dagon gets to her. That would be catastrophic." Luc turned to Zeke. "If you feel so much as a scratch from Dagon, let me know immediately."

Zeke nodded.

"So," Eve ventured cautiously, "what happens if we find out that I *can* cure death? What if we *could* extract Dagon *and* save Zeke? Is there a way we could seal Dagon away again like he had been before Ruth awakened him?"

Luc reclined against the back of the couch and sucked his teeth. "Well, love, that's going to be a huge decision to make, if it's even possible, and one that we can't make on our own. This is why we need to take Ruth alive – we may need her. Otherwise, I'd just kill her."

"Even though she's your little sister?"

"She's a threat. She's killing people and turning others into monsters. That's not my sister anymore. She's a monster, and nothing more," Luc said impassively. Not a shred of compassion or empathy.

"You don't think she can come back from this? Redeem herself?" Eve asked.

Luc turned ice-cold eyes to Eve. "I don't give second chances. She took you from me, and she would've never given you back. She's beyond my forgiveness."

Eve softened her voice. "And what if I asked you to show her mercy?"

Luc frowned at her. "You would put me in a very tough position. Please don't do that." His tone was dangerous.

"You're a good person, babe," Zeke said, smiling at Eve.

Eve scoffed. "Hardly." Zeke was just naïve. He always saw the good in people, even when it wasn't there.

"He's not wrong, love," Luc said, his hard gaze softening. "You are a good person. But you're not a fool. I know you understand that not everyone can be forgiven for their misdeeds. Don't let Bo's bleeding heart cloud your judgement. He's always been soft when it comes to Ruth."

338

Eve sensed that this wasn't a persuasion she was going to accomplish tonight, so she dropped the issue.

Bo and Isaac returned, and they both seemed annoyed.

"We are completely incompatible as a team," Bo complained, indicating Isaac. "He can't read my lips, and I can't understand his signs. It's fucking frustrating."

"Then take your fucking mask off, Bo," Luc reasoned simply.

"That's not going to make *me* understand *him* any better."

Luc turned to Isaac and signed. "Don't you have a phone you can text on or something?"

Isaac just shrugged indifferently.

Luc said, "You *can* talk, can't you? That's the word at the Vatican."

Isaac signed back, holding his palms up, fingers curved, then flipped them over and pushed his palms away. He then held four splayed fingers vertically, his palm facing sideways, and touched his index finger to his chin, then moved his hand away again.

Luc translated, "Oh, you don't *want* to talk. Helpful."

Isaac signed again with agitation, pointing to Bo.

"I know he won't take his mask off. It annoys me sometimes, too," Luc said. Then, with an amused smirk and a southern accent, he added, "'What we've got here is failure to communicate. Some men, you just can't reach.'"

Eve sashayed to Bo and bumped his shoulder with hers. "We can learn ASL together. Maybe we'll learn it faster that way."

Bo grunted noncommittally.

"So, I trust you found nothing on the grounds?" Luc asked.

"Nothing. Did Dagon tell you anything?" Bo inquired.

"He didn't say where he was going or what he was doing," Luc replied, "but he's got designs to take Ruth up on her offer. I've sealed him for now."

Luc dismissed Zeke back to his own apartment, but before Bo left, Luc took a moment to speak to them without Zeke's presence. "Even if Dagon was able to contact Ruth tonight, I'm hoping she's already been fed the fake plan, so it's unlikely she'll believe he comes in peace, anyway. But we need to act now. Tomorrow morning, we'll meet here with the others to finalize our plan and move into Phase One."

The next morning, Eve awoke to Luc uncurling his huge body from around hers and climbing out of bed. "Why do you and Bo always get up so early?" she grumbled, looking over to the bedside clock.

"Somebody has to fetch you coffee," Luc teased as he pulled on his slacks from yesterday. He shrugged into his oxford shirt, but didn't bother to button it.

"Aren't you going to teleport to your room and get some clean clothes?"

"Nope. I'm saving my energy. I have no idea what the day is going to bring. Speaking of which," Luc looked over at Eve, "how are your stolen powers today? Do you still have them, or did we exhaust them yesterday?"

"I have no idea. Do they run out faster if I use them more?"

Luc shrugged. "I have no idea, either. I thought maybe you did."

Eve got out of bed and followed Luc out into the kitchen. He opened the fridge, then turned to look at her as she walked to the kitchen island. His eyes darted toward the living room, then back to Eve.

"Eve!" he reprimanded.

"What?"

He pointed at Isaac doing crossfit in the living room. He'd paused in his workout and was looking at them impassively.

"Deaf, not blind, remember?" Luc reminded her.

She looked down at her underwear and realized she'd forgotten she took off her shorts when she went to bed last night.

"Oh." She looked over at Isaac, who dropped down and started doing pushups. "He doesn't seem to care."

"I care. Go put some clothes on. Please."

"My t-shirt covers most of my underwear anyway," Eve argued, fingering the edges of her shirt.

Luc closed the fridge and stalked toward her with purpose. She leapt back with a startled laugh. "Ok, prude!" She walked back to her room. "But it's not like I'm naked," she called back.

When she stepped out of her room, wearing the shortest shorts she owned, just for spite, she caught Luc signing at Isaac. Perhaps a little threateningly. But as soon as they saw Eve, they both stopped and Luc feigned innocence.

"Hungry?" Luc asked.

"Not yet," Eve replied, frowning at him and Isaac. "Should I go get Bo and Eoduun?"

"Bo is already out and about. He'll gather everyone."

Eve went out to the living room and sat across from Isaac. He was taking a break from his exercise. "So this is why you're an exorcist. You *exercise*," she said, biting her lips in an impish grin.

Isaac just stared at her flatly. Not a hint of amusement.

"What *possessed* you to make a joke like that?" Luc called from the kitchen.

Eve's grin widened, but she didn't comment. To Isaac, she asked, "Want to see if I still have my powers today?"

He pointed at himself questioningly.

She nodded.

He shook his head and snapped his fingers together. Not a chance.

Luc called from the kitchen, "You can try it on me when I finish breakfast."

Eve got out her phone, then faced Isaac. She pointed at him. *You.* She held one hand out, palm up, and acted like she was grabbing something from her palm and touching it to her forehead. *Learn.* She then made a gesture she'd seen him do by holding four splayed fingers and touching the index finger to her chin. *Speak.* Finally, she tapped her fingers to her temple, and as she pulled her hand away, she made it into a Y-handshape. *Why?*

Why did you learn to speak?

He looked thoughtful for a moment, then tapped an I-handshape to his cheek and shook an E-handshape side to side. *If emergency.* He hooked his finger in an X-handshape and bent his wrist to arc it down. *Need.* He tapped his splayed fingers to his chin. *Speak.*

He was signing much more slowly and carefully than usual. She wondered if he was purposely simplifying for her so she could look up his signs.

"If you only learned it for emergencies, then why are you so good at it?" she asked, signing *if, learn, emergency,* and *why* because she didn't even know where to begin with that question.

He shrugged.

She said, "Since I'm learning to sign more," as she pointed to herself and signed the words *learning* and *sign*, "then maybe you can talk more." She pointed at him and signed the words for *maybe* and *speak.*

He narrowed his eyes at her. "Fine," he said aloud, tapping his thumb to his chest with his fingers vertically splayed, his deep voice startling her.

The spatula clattered to the floor in the kitchen and Luc popped his fair head around the fridge. "Holy shit, did you just get him to talk?"

Bo walked in the door, two coffees in his hand. He spied Eve on the couch, and handed her a cup. "*Ohayou*," he greeted, his eyes crinkling in the corners from a smile hidden behind his mask.

"Good morning," she replied. "*Arigatou.*"

He continued on to the kitchen and slid onto his barstool, and as he pulled his phone out of his pocket, Luc asked him, "Where is everyone?"

"They'll be here. I told Dizzy to shift before he arrived, but to make sure no one saw him on his way here. I know how the shifting process makes you gag."

"I appreciate that. Hungry?" Luc asked Bo.

"No thanks." Bo looked over at Eve sitting with Isaac. "He's not your friend, Evie. Do you forget why he's here?"

"I haven't forgotten," she said, rising from the couch to join Bo at the kitchen island. "I believe what you mean is he's not my friend *yet*. I will win him over."

"It's only going to make you more upset if he tries to kill you and we have to kill him," Bo replied with a contemptuous glance at Isaac, knowing he couldn't see what he was saying behind his mask.

"She got him to talk," Luc remarked as he flipped the eggs in the pan in front of him. "I think that's a good sign."

"Aren't you going to get properly dressed before our meeting?" Bo asked Luc, changing the subject.

"Good idea. Go fetch me some clothes from my apartment," Luc requested.

"Not going to happen."

"Pretty please?"

"Come on, Bo," Eve said, hopping off of her barstool. "I'll go with you."

Bo pulled his mask down to take a sip of coffee, then pulled it back up. "Fine," he grumbled. "But only because I know you'll go do it yourself if I refuse."

As Bo and Eve walked to the door, Isaac got up to join them. Bo held his hand up to stop him.

"You don't need to supervise this," Bo said.

Isaac pointed at himself, then held his fist up near his temple, shaking his head as he pointed his index finger upward. He then cupped his hands over his face and curved them around to the sides of his face. He looked around Bo at Eve.

"He can't understand you through your mask, Bo," Luc said casually from the kitchen.

Eve pointed at Isaac, held her hands up and wriggled her fingers, then pointed down. *You wait here.* "We're just going up the hallway," she added without signing.

Isaac looked at Bo and gestured toward Eve, raising his eyebrows, then held his hands out to the side in a motion that wasn't

ASL, but rather a general statement. *That wasn't so hard, was it?* He then waved them off dismissively.

"I hate that guy," Bo growled as he and Eve left the apartment.

"I don't think he's particularly fond of you, either," Eve replied, mildly amused. "Think about how frustrating it must be for him to not be able to see what you're saying."

"How frustrating it is for him? What about me? I can't understand what he's saying, either!"

"That's why I keep my phone on me, so I can look it up."

"I don't have time for that."

"You always have your phone in front of you," Eve pointed out. Bo huffed. "I think a little effort goes a long way with him," she added. "And you've made none."

"I won't make an effort to befriend the exorcist assassin sent here by the Vatican to kill you if you step out of line."

Eve sighed and slipped her arm around Bo's as they made their way to Luc's apartment. "He's not just an assassin. He's a person. And, just *maybe*, befriending the person will discourage the assassin."

"Or it'll just make it easier for him to kill you because you've let your guard down around him. Don't be so naïve, Evie. The Angel of Death doesn't get a name like that by making friends."

Bo's reasoning gave her pause.

Perhaps she *was* mischaracterizing Isaac, painting him in a color she liked better than the one he truly wore.

Isaac didn't like her. He wasn't interested in being her friend. He was just letting her believe whatever delusion she was creating for herself. He didn't even have to do anything – she was tricking herself. God, she was so gullible. What happened to her mistrusting nature? She'd grown too comfortable inside the circle of love and safety that Luc and her team had created for her. It was making her soft. Weak.

Trusting.

Ew.

38

Everyone On Board?

When Eve and Bo returned with Luc's change of clothing, she followed Luc into her bedroom. She needed to get properly dressed before their meeting, too.

As she pulled on her jeans, she asked Luc, "Do you think Isaac can be trusted with all the information he's been picking up?"

Luc worked on buttoning his shirt. "If we aren't forthright with him and he senses we're hiding things from him, it'll only count against us. It's not that I *trust* him, but we need him to trust *us* if he's going to give you a pass with the Vatican."

"I shouldn't be so friendly with him," Eve said.

Luc's fingers hovered over a button as his aquamarine eyes rose from his task to meet hers. "What makes you say that? I thought you were doing a beautiful job of winning him over."

"He's putting on an act," she replied simply. "He's letting me think I'm winning him over. I'm an idiot."

"You're not an idiot. And if it's an act, it's a damn good one. You ever think he may be wondering the same thing about you? That you're just being nice to him so he won't decide to kill you? If anyone has reason to be suspicious, it's him."

"Bo thinks –"

"And, there it is. 'Bo thinks,'" Luc interrupted. He walked up to Eve as he buttoned his cuffs. He lowered his voice. "Bo doesn't like him because they're too much alike. No one hates Bo more than Bo, so he's going to hate anyone that reminds him of himself."

Eve was conflicted. She knew Luc's assessment to be the truth, but she couldn't shake the mistrust Bo had instilled in her earlier. What he had said about Isaac wasn't insensible, and going forward, a little more reserve and distance between Isaac and herself was probably for the best.

He wasn't her friend.

He was her judge and potential executioner.

Eve heard voices in the other room. The Knighco members Luc had invited to their secret meeting were beginning to arrive.

Luc took her face in his large hands and kissed the top of her head. "Don't worry about Isaac. We have other things to focus on today, love."

When she exited the bedroom behind Luc, she felt like she was in someone else's apartment. The strange mix of characters in her space felt foreign. Levi, the viewer; Veris, the persuader; Kai, the skinwalker; and Dizzy, the shifter – but he looked like Dagon in Zeke's body. Eve couldn't peel her eyes from him until he turned those familiar red eyes in her direction. Then she quickly averted her gaze.

Her team, sans Zeke, had assembled as well, so she moved to the comfort of their proximity. Eoduun sat cross-legged on the floor in front of an empty chair, while Bo stood next to it with his elbow leaned casually on the back of it. Bo gestured for Eve to take a seat, so she gladly plopped into it. She noticed Isaac was leaned against the wall by the door by himself, his arms crossed, his typical bored expression on his face. He rubbed the back of his neck and yawned.

Levi and Kai from Team Gamma sat uncomfortably next to Dizzy on the couch. Kai pointed to Dizzy's neck. "You got a little, uh, leftover gunk there, pal."

"Huh?" Dizzy reached up and picked a shifter flake from his neck. "Oh. Whoops. 'You missed a spot!' Heh heh," Dizzy laughed awkwardly. His voice sounded like Dagon, but the cadence and inflection were all wrong. All Dizzy. Was he really going to be able to fool Ruth into a meeting?

Luc went over the plan again, then handed Dizzy a burner phone. "You and Veris need to convince her to meet you at the old paper mill up the road, tonight at midnight."

Dizzy opened the phone and dialed the number Luc read off to him. When it started to ring, Veris reached over and put it on speaker phone.

A man answered. "Hello?"

"Put Ruth on," Dizzy said, suddenly sounding exactly like Dagon.

"Who?"

"Don't play fucking games. Put Ruth on the goddamn phone." Was that really Dizzy?

"Excuse me sir, but that kind of language is unnecessary. I think you have the wrong number," the man on the other end replied firmly.

Luc snatched up the phone and looked down at it, comparing it to the number on the sheet in his hand. He rolled his head back in exasperation. "So very sorry, sir, my apologies," Luc said, hanging up the phone. He gave Dizzy a scathing glare. "I'll dial it this time, you chucklehead."

"Sorry. I get numbers mixed up all the time. Can't do math for the life of me!" Dizzy said, his Dagon mimicry lost again.

Luc dialed and handed Dizzy the phone. "Don't fuck this up or it's *your* ass."

It went to voicemail, so Dizzy left a message that sounded just like Dagon again. "You know who this is. Call me back at this number before this idiot wakes up."

The phone rang almost immediately. Veris reached over and put the call on speakerphone. "Using a phone this time?" Ruth asked.

Dizzy looked up at Luc with Dagon's red eyes, confused. Luc shook his head and shrugged.

"Do you want to do this or not?" Dizzy asked Ruth impatiently. He even made the same arrogant face Eve had seen Dagon make so many times.

"You tell me. You're the one who didn't show," she snapped back.

"I was interrupted. But I won't be tonight."

"Same time and place?" she asked.

Veris took the phone and quietly said, "Meet Dagon at the paper mill tonight at midnight. You want to come alone, and you want to show him Lilith's Grimoire."

"How about we meet at the paper mill? Midnight. I have something to show you," Ruth said. "Are you bringing me the blood healer?"

"Of course," Dizzy replied, taking the phone back from Veris. "But don't fucking disappoint me. If you're lying about anything, you die." He flipped the phone closed, and all of the Dagon-esque qualities he'd displayed so masterfully for the phone call instantly vanished. "Sorry for all of that foul language, guys," Dizzy said.

"It's fucking fine," Kai said.

"Good job, Dizzy," Luc praised. "Nice work, Veris."

"It would appear Dagon did make contact with the witch," Levi said in his oddly monotone voice. "So, the question now is, what exactly does she believe? Is she playing us, or are we playing her?"

Luc replied, "As long as everyone plays their part and keeps this little operation a secret, we'll have the upper hand. If our mole told her about our fake plan, then she won't be expecting the ambush. Only Dagon and Eve. She'll be overconfident and, thanks to Veris, hopefully alone."

"Are Kai and I still required now that we know she'll be alone?" Levi asked.

"Yes, I still need you to do a remote sweep, and I still want Kai on site. We need to be prepared in the event that she isn't."

"Should I just stay like this for the day?" Dizzy asked. "I kind of like it. I'm muscley and handsome. I got rizz."

Luc said, "No, Dizzy, you need to shift back. I can't have you running around as Dagon all day, raising all kinds of questions and concerns."

"Why did he have to shift for this? He can't just change his voice?" Eve asked.

"Oh, if only!" Dizzy said, widening his eyes and slapping his knee awkwardly. "No, ma'am, it's all or nothing."

"What do you need in order to shift to another person?" Eve asked. "Do you just have to see them, or do you need something from them?"

Delight danced in Dizzy's red, Dagon eyes. He wasn't used to anyone engaging him in conversation or being genuinely interested in anything about himself. "Well, not to brag, but I'm pretty dang good at making a copy just by sight and the sound of their voice. But if I have DNA…" Dizzy shook his head enthusiastically. "Woowee! Even their mama wouldn't know the difference! No cap!" Dizzy's smile broadened. "For example, if I were to shake your hand…" He suddenly lunged forward and thrust his hand out toward Eve.

Bo was between them before Eve even felt him move away from her side. He must've teleported, like Luc. His scarred, yellow eye flashed dangerously, and Dizzy fell backward on his ass, in surprise. Everyone tensed.

"Don't touch her!" Bo snarled.

Isaac pushed off from the wall by the door, his hand lingering near the blade he'd holstered at his hip before the meeting started. He studied the situation closely, ready to act.

Luc stepped in and held his hand out to Dizzy to help him to his feet. "At ease, Bo," Luc chastised, shooting him a scathing glance. Then, to Dizzy, Luc said, "I think your current form has him a little on edge. Pay it no mind."

Once Dizzy had returned to his seat, everyone relaxed again. Everyone but Bo. He stepped back, but remained standing slightly in front of Eve, his leg touching hers. Isaac observed Bo, his eyes dropping to where his leg was in contact with Eve's. He looked at Luc, then Eoduun, scanning their faces and body language.

Eve wondered if he was puzzling over their unusual relationship dynamics.

Luc continued the meeting, going over tonight's plan. "We'll arrive an hour early and wait by the wastewater treatment area on the other side of the mill. Levi, you'll be keeping an eye on everything from above. Kai, you can take the form of whatever discreet animal you wish and do a ground sweep. When Ruth arrives, Levi and Kai will watch for any reinforcements she may bring along, and either Kai, Bo, Isaac, or myself will take them out *quietly*. Meanwhile, Dizzy and Eve will be waiting for Ruth in the front parking lot. Eve, you will possess and incapacitate Ruth until we get her bound. It may be a few minutes, depending on whether there are monsters we have to take out first. Do not release her until I tell you to. Everyone on board?"

"What about me?" Eoduun asked.

"You will be here, keeping an eye on the compound and our fellow hunters, and making sure to keep Zeke occupied – and far away from Ruth."

"Where will you be taking Ruth once we've captured her?" Eve wondered.

"Somewhere far away from here, secret and secure," Luc answered.

Eve's heart sank. "Which means you'll be far away from here again."

Luc gave her an apologetic look. "Only for a short while."

Everyone was dismissed to attend to their usual training for the day, and Bo went across the hall to fetch Zeke, acting as though Team Alpha was just now gathering at Eve's apartment. Luc implored Eve to attempt to possess him again, but as soon as she settled in to try, she knew it wasn't happening.

She was out of juice.

Eoduun still bore the marks of their last encounter, having chosen to keep them as some twisted memento rather than allowing Eve to heal him. He now smiled sinisterly. "I'd be more than happy to pump her full of my powers again." He then glanced over at Zeke, who had just joined them. "As long you can keep her from killing me again."

Isaac signed, but Eve was looking at Eoduun and missed half of it. She looked up at Luc. Luc frowned at Isaac, then turned to Eoduun. He lowered his sunglasses and stared at him meaningfully as he said, "She didn't *actually* try to kill you, though. You're exaggerating, yes?"

Eoduun glanced over at Isaac, and Zeke answered for him, "Of course he's exaggerating. He wasn't in any real danger."

Eve wondered if there was any truth to that statement. She felt pretty murdery when Zeke pulled her off of Eoduun. She still wouldn't trust herself to do this training without a third wheel.

Isaac shook his head and swiped his thumb under his chin, then pointed at Zeke. Eve recognized that. *Not him.* She didn't recognize the rest of the signs that followed.

"That's not going to happen," Luc said firmly.

"What?" Eve asked.

"He says he should supervise your training, not Zeke."

The whole team protested in unison.

Isaac signed again, too quickly for Eve to keep up.

"You're here to make sure she's not a danger to the church and society. You're not here to get your jollies," Luc replied, his irritation growing.

Isaac frowned and signed with emphasis.

Luc toed up with Isaac, drawing attention to their vast height difference. The top of Isaac's head came only roughly to Luc's chin, but he stood his ground and stared defiantly up at Luc.

Luc was clearly used to using his height as an intimidation factor, and he leaned over Isaac slightly. "Find another way to verify her level of control."

Isaac drove the angled fingertips of one hand perpendicularly into the palm of his other, then circled the wiggling fingers of one hand near his temple. He pointed to himself, then jerked an X-handshape downward and slapped the back of one hand into the palm of the other, rather forcefully.

"I'm not going to reconsider. Find your proof another way," Luc repeated in a measured tone.

Isaac signed again, and Luc glanced briefly over at Eve, unease written in his features. But when he turned his face back to Isaac, he smirked confidently. "Fine. She doesn't need a chaperone. When Eoduun comes out alive, you'll know she can be trusted to control her power, right?"

Isaac considered the proposal, then shrugged and nodded.

They both looked to Eve expectantly.

Shit.

39

Today, You Play

She didn't trust herself. Not yet. And she wasn't prepared to risk Eoduun just to get rid of Isaac sooner.

"No. I want Zeke to be there," she said simply. "I'll prove myself another time. I don't want any distractions or extra pressure right now."

"I second that," Eoduun said, raising his hand.

"As do I," Bo agreed. "Now, let's hit the training grounds." He looked at Eve. "You can wrestle with Eoduun later."

Eoduun gave Eve a scorching look. "You and I can spar. Consider it foreplay."

Luc held his hands out to the sides, palms out. "I'm *right* here, asshole," he said in jealous irritation. He turned to Eve and pointed at Eoduun. "Permission to harm?"

"Permission denied," she replied.

Eoduun smirked as he stood up and walked past Luc, so Luc informed him, "Enjoy your temporary protection, boy."

"Whatever," Eoduun said dismissively.

"Don't worry," Bo said, clapping his hand on Luc's shoulder, "I'll kick his ass for you. I don't need permission to harm."

Zeke got up and joined Eoduun, walking out the door. "Dude," Eve heard him warning Eoduun in the hallway, "you better watch yourself or Luc's going to take Eve from us."

"He can't. It isn't his choice. It's hers." Eoduun replied smugly before their voices faded.

Eve pushed up onto her tiptoes and tugged at Luc's lapels as he scowled at the door, listening to Eoduun and Zeke. He turned his eyes down to her, looking at her through his round sunglasses, and his face brightened as he graced her with a smile.

Her heart summersaulted in her chest.

He folded his hands behind her back and bent down to kiss her eager lips. "You're mine, in every way that matters," Luc declared, smiling against her mouth. "And I'm yours." He released her and straightened his collar. "I know you hold some affection for Eoduun, but please understand, the moment he ceases to amuse you, I want to be the one to deliver the devastating news to him."

"You assume that you'll still be in my good graces if and when that ever happens?" Eve teased.

"Of course. You love me, unequivocally." Not an ounce of doubt. He kissed her on the top of the head. "Have fun training. Don't be afraid to give Isaac a black eye. He looks like he could use one."

Isaac just crossed his arms and ignored Luc.

Luc left to work on company business that he couldn't put off any longer, while Bo, Eve, and Isaac headed out to meet Zeke and Eoduun at the training grounds.

As promised, Bo partnered up with Eoduun and went after him without restraint, so Zeke sprang to Eoduun's aid to help keep the ass whooping in check.

Eve saw movement out of the corner of her eye, her hand reflexively reacting to catch the Escrima stick Isaac had tossed at her. She raised a brow at him.

"Show me something," he said aloud, tossing her the other stick. He held a pair of his own Escrima sticks, and he took a defensive stance.

"I've only trained with these once before," she informed him. "I'll disappoint you."

"I'll go easy," he said, but the small grin lifting the corner of his mouth said otherwise. "The only one you can disappoint is you."

And then he came at her, without warning or telegraphing. She barely got her sticks up in time to block the strike intended for her shoulder. He followed up with a strike to her thigh, which she didn't block.

It fucking hurt. She hissed through her teeth, her eyes meeting his in frustration. His little grin only widened.

She swung her stick at that mocking smile, but he easily deflected it and went for her ribs. She sprang back, and he followed, flowing into every space she opened, like a wave crashing after her.

"What the fuck!" she snarled as he somehow ended up in the blind spot behind her, his stick whacking into her ribs. She whirled around, throwing the full centrifugal force of her spin into the stick, and it cracked loudly off of Isaac's hip.

He didn't even flinch. He took that split second that Eve hesitated, when she was expecting his reaction to her strike, and he used it to hit her back, ramming his stick into her gut.

Eve fell backward, the wind temporarily knocked out of her. She coughed and sputtered, looking up furiously at Isaac. He put both sticks in one hand and held his free hand out to her to help her up. She refused it, leaping to her feet. This anger and frustration boiling inside of her felt strangely consuming.

"Losing your temper will make you sloppy," Isaac said, readying his sticks for her attack.

"I fucking know that!" she spat, gnashing her teeth. But fuck, she wanted to get her hands on the little fucker. She couldn't swallow this rage. She whipped the training sticks at his face to try to catch him off-guard, then threw herself into him, tackling him to the ground.

Destroy him. Own him. Make him surrender.

They struggled on the ground briefly as she tried to get an arm around his neck and her thighs around his ribs, but she soon found herself on her back, a stick across her throat, Isaac's knee pressing into her heaving chest.

"Your mist is black," he said, no longer amused. "You want to kill me."

But she didn't. Not *really*. Not *yet*. She wanted to play with him first. She wanted him on his knees. She wanted him helpless. She wanted to slake the thirst twisting her insides, aching between her thighs.

Bo's appearance behind Isaac brought Eve to her senses. What the fuck had she been thinking? Bo's knife tapped the side of Isaac's throat, but Isaac didn't seem even remotely surprised, and he didn't shy from it. He took no notice of Bo.

"What *is* that behind your eyes?" Isaac asked Eve, leaning closer to her face, his ebony eyes searching hers. "Even when the light comes back, I still see it. Your monster wants to eat me. Can you control it, Eve?"

"I am controlling it," she said.

"No, *I* am *subduing* it because you weren't controlling it," Isaac corrected. He stood up and held his hand out again to help Eve up, and Bo sheathed his knife. "Rage is a powerful tool, but you're letting rage control you. Subdue it. Bend it to your will," Isaac advised as he pulled Eve to her feet.

"Well, he's a real chatterbox all of a sudden," Bo said humorlessly, inspecting Eve for injury. Isaac saw him looking Eve over carefully, and signed at him. Bo looked at him with displeasure. "Seriously?" he mumbled. "*Now* he stops talking."

"I'm fine," Eve said, wincing as Bo pressed his probing fingers into the contusion forming on her thigh.

"He really came after you," Bo growled. "Look at these fucking welts."

"Does Daddy want to kiss my booboos and make it all better?" Eve teased, pouting her lips. When Bo rolled his eyes at her, she said, "I'll heal by the time we get to the gym."

"We're not going to the gym today. Only tactical training."

Eve grabbed Bo's hands to halt their worrying over her injuries. "Well, I have a little bit of other training to do today, too. And, if you don't mind, I might borrow the boys and go do that. I'm suddenly feeling...inspired."

Anger flashed over Bo's face, his charcoal eye blazing yellow. "Because of *Isaac*?"

His response made Eve smile like a cheshire cat. "Is Daddy jealous?" she poked.

"He's out of bounds, Evie. Don't even think about being...inspired...by him."

Eve narrowed her eyes and ran her finger down the vertical scar over Bo's eye, forcing him to close that golden orb. "Oh, you can't stop me from thinking about it," she whispered.

"He's not part of this team. I'll kill him if he touches you," he whispered back threateningly. His tone sent splendid shivers down Eve's spine. His jealousy was positively decadent.

She shimmied her shoulders. "Mmm, I get all tingly when you talk like that." She was still holding one of his hands in hers, so she raised it to her lips and kissed his palm. His cheeks and ears blazed.

He pulled his hand away and stepped back, clearing his throat. "You'll have to heal Eoduun," he returned to the original subject at hand. "I didn't hold back today."

"Don't worry, blood is part of the ritual," Eve said. "He'll get healed before I hurt him again. I don't hold back, either."

"Just don't go too far, hey?" Bo said, giving Isaac a wary side-eye. "I don't want any more trouble today."

"If I'm not giving you trouble, what the hell am I even good for?" Eve teased.

Back at the apartment complex, Eve, Zeke, and Eoduun met in Eoduun's apartment again. Eve's body was already thrumming with sexual energy from the morning's training shenanigans, and she knew exactly what she wanted to do with these boys.

Her boys.

She strutted up to Eoduun. He was bloody and battered. "Bo sure did a number on you, didn't he?" she asked, reaching up to stroke his cheek. "What a brute." She slid her hand behind his neck and gripped his nape, pulling him down to her. She ran her tongue along his bloody lip. "But you deserved it, you naughty boy, and you know it."

Eoduun smiled against her lips. "I'm not one to mince words. I won't apologize for claiming you in front of Luc."

"Well, your punishment isn't over yet." Eve pulled Eoduun's shirt off over his head, then pushed him down onto the bed and turned to Zeke. She looked up at him from beneath her dark eyelashes. "You don't have to sit back and watch today." She cupped his sweetly innocent face and kissed him voraciously. "Today, you play. Tie his wrists to the headboard," she instructed Zeke, handing him two neckties.

Eve undressed as she watched Zeke's bulky arm muscles flex and work as he wrapped the neckties around Eoduun's wrists. She noticed Eoduun's eyes greedily roving those same muscles as Zeke made sure the restraints weren't cutting off circulation, but also making sure the knots were tight. Eoduun was enjoying this just as much as she was.

"I'm trusting you, Z," Eoduun said.

"You're safe," Zeke assured him. "I got your back."

Eve climbed onto the bed and straddled Eoduun's hips. He was already hard beneath his joggers. "Unless I decide to devour you both," she said, grinding herself against his hard length while checking his restraints. She leaned forward and kissed Eoduun's bruised lips, and he winced and moaned, his arms flexing against the ties, his hands wanting to touch her bare flesh.

"Now, be a good boy and quietly wait your turn," she said, putting a silencing finger to his lips. She turned around and straddled his abs, facing away from him. "Zeke, take your clothes off and come here," she implored, holding her hand out to him. He did as he was told and climbed onto the bed, and Eve guided him into position straddling Eoduun's hips. His bare cock was mere centimeters from Eoduun's clothed bulge, and when Eve reached down and stroked his length, the back of her fingers grazed along the ridge in Eoduun's pants. Eoduun's hips flexed beneath Zeke and Eve.

Eve thrust her other hand into Zeke's hair and pressed her body flush against his as she continued to stroke him. She crushed her lips against his and devoured his tongue, undulating her body against him in tandem with the undulations of her tongue against his. He moaned into her mouth, one hand tangled in her pink mane, the other gripping her firm, round bottom.

"Fuck me, babe," Zeke pleaded. "It's been too long."

"Fuck him, Eve," Eoduun begged, thrusting his hips up into her and Zeke again.

Eve turned her head and gave Eoduun a smoldering look over her shoulder. "You will speak only when spoken to, and not a moment before," she reprimanded. He smiled deviously at her.

She returned her attention to Zeke, her lips touching the underside of his chin, the tip of her tongue tracing his jawline. She straddled his hips and trailed kisses down his thick, corded neck, then lowered herself slowly onto his rigid cock. He groaned and pressed his hips up into her, a deep groan rumbling in his throat.

"Oh, god," Zeke breathed as she sheathed him fully, and Eve heard Eoduun hum behind her. She leaned back onto Eoduun's chest while Zeke was deep inside of her, her legs splayed over Zeke's thighs. She turned her head and kissed Eoduun as Zeke fucked her on top of him. Eoduun fought against his restraints, his breath heavy in Eve's ear.

"I'm going to lose it," Eoduun lamented. "Please…"

Eve rolled her hips against Zeke. "Fuck me harder, Z," she moaned. She reached up and curved her fingers around the back of his neck and pulled his body down against hers, sandwiching her body between his and Eoduun's.

Oh, fuck yes. Zeke's hot breath in one ear, Eoduun's in the other. Two hard bodies against hers. Glorious.

But not what she was truly here for. She turned to Eoduun. "Make me bleed," she demanded, her lips brushing his.

Without hesitation, he took her lower lip between his teeth and bit her. She cried out and clenched her thighs around Zeke, and Zeke moaned and throbbed inside of her in response. Eoduun drank from her lip as he kissed her, sending thrills of pleasure straight into Eve's core, tightening her walls around Zeke's manhood. She threw her arms around Zeke, her fingernails clawing into the thick muscles on his back, and she used her powerful legs to control his pace, rocking her pelvis up off of Eoduun.

She tore her mouth away from Eoduun so she could take Zeke's, overtaken by an irresistible urge to consume him. When the blood from her lip touched his tongue, his hips jerked and he spasmed inside of her, a desperate moan escaping his throat. She keened, her back arching off of Eoduun's chest.

Bite him.

Hurt him.

Drain him.

She reared up and sank her teeth into his massive shoulder, blood filling her mouth as a searing fury surged through her, her core pulsing as rage and euphoria spun her into blissful oblivion.

She faintly heard someone calling her name. She knew that voice. Hints of reason trickled back into Eve's brain, and she recognized Eoduun calling for her.

And she wanted him. She wanted to claim him. She *needed* to take him. She was still hungry. She pushed away from Zeke and flipped over, quickly undoing Eoduun's pants and pulling them down to his thighs.

She licked Zeke's blood from her lips as she sank her greedy sheath down onto Eoduun's twitching, weeping erection. He thrust up into her, his hands fisting against the headboard as he pulled at the neckties around his wrists. His head tilted back as a delectable moan poured from his parted lips.

She clamped her mouth over those lips, swallowing that moan as she clenched her core around him, feeling every twitch and swell as he thrust up into her. He kissed her, licking the blood from her lips and tongue. She slid her fingers into his hair, then gripped it, holding his head in place as she hovered her lips over his. "You're mine," she hissed. She moved her lips to his ear. Squeezing her core around him, she whispered, "And *this* is mine."

"All yours," he panted.

She gyrated her hips, her pleasure mounting yet again. Her teeth began to tingle, and the urge to gnash into his flesh swept over her. She wanted to taste his blood. She wondered how it would taste when it mixed with the lingering flavors of Zeke on her tongue.

Bite him.

Crush him.

Ruin him.

She used the hand fisted in his hair to yank his head to the side, baring his vulnerable neck to her. She bit into the tender flesh behind his ear, near the nape of his neck.

"Fuuuuuck!" Eoduun cried out in blissful anguish, his headboard banging against the wall as he jerked his arms against their restraints. He bucked as he burst inside of her, but she held him down, her fist squeezing even tighter into his hair as she sat up and threw her head back, another wave of rageful pleasure washing over her, unleashing a primal desire for violence.

Kill him.

The next thing she knew, she was pushing Zeke away from her, and he flew across the room, slamming into the wall with force.

"Oh my god! Z! Are you ok?!" she cried, running to him.

He threw his arm up defensively over his face, wincing. She grabbed his arm and helped him to his feet.

He studied her warily for a moment, then took her up in his arms. "Oh, thank god. You're you again."

"Of course I'm me. Why, what happened?"

"You tried to fucking kill us," Eoduun replied, still tied to the bed.

40
A Storm Is Coming

Eve healed Zeke and Eoduun with a pinprick on her finger, afraid to offer them any more than that. As they dressed, Eve accidentally ripped her pants when trying to pull them on.

Panic surged through her. "Uh oh."

"You can borrow a pair of my gym shorts," Eoduun offered, tossing her a clean pair of athletic shorts.

"No, you don't understand. I think I have superstrength."

Eoduun and Zeke both gaped at her as she stepped into the baggy shorts.

"Shit, so does that mean…" Zeke began.

"…You took Z's power instead of mine?" Eoduun finished.

The real question was, did she just completely fuck up tonight's mission?

She reached down with one hand and lifted the end of the bed with Zeke and Eoduun still sitting on it. It was no more difficult than lifting a book.

"Fuck," she hissed, dropping the bed, making the floor tremble. "Fuck!"

"Sorry," Zeke apologized. "I know you wanted Eoduun's power to train with."

"It wasn't your fault," Eve replied. "It was my mistake. I did this. I didn't mean to give you any blood, only Eoduun."

"Maybe if you try again, just with Eoduun?" Zeke suggested.

"I don't think I can handle another round right now," Eoduun said. "She almost killed me the first time."

"I'm sorry about that," Eve apologized. "I think two at once just pushed me too far. I lost control."

"Wait." Eoduun narrowed his eyes and stepped in front of Eve. "What if...what if you took *both*?"

Was it possible? She looked into Eoduun's eyes, and she focused on entering through them.

A swirling, psychedelic purple tunnel opened up in her mind's eye. She heard Eoduun exclaim, "Oh, shit, not me! Stop, Eve!" She backed off, allowing the portal to dissipate.

Zeke and Eoduun both looked at her with raised eyebrows. "Damn, babe," Zeke said simply. "Looks like you opted for a bit of both."

"Greedy little bitch, aren't you?" Eoduun hummed, skimming his finger along her jaw.

"Hey, don't call her that," Zeke scowled.

"It's ok, Z," Eve smirked. "Just a compliment from one bitch to another."

Eoduun gave a short chuckle. "Let's go get debriefed," he said, heading toward the door.

"I thought we just did that," Zeke joked, slipping his hand into Eve's, following along behind Eoduun.

Isaac was outside the door to greet them, yet again.

"Boy am I glad that dude can't hear us," Zeke whispered loudly when he saw him standing there, leaning against the wall directly across the hallway.

Bo came out of his apartment. "But I can. And I did." He gave the three of them a stern glare. "And I don't like what I heard."

"Stacked powers? How can you not like that?" Zeke asked.

"I don't like what it almost cost. But we'll discuss this another time." Bo dipped his head toward Isaac as he spoke. "He can't see what I'm saying, but you three are an open book to him."

Zeke put his hand up over mouth and said, "Not if I do this."

"Stop that," Eve said as she slapped Zeke's hand down, but she forgot about her stolen strength and accidentally yanked him off balance. She quickly caught him. "Sorry!"

"Back to the training grounds," Bo ordered. "Evie needs to get a handle on Z's superstrength, and I don't want anyone going through a wall in the training room."

"Come on Isaac," Eve said, knowing Isaac couldn't see what Bo had suggested. "Let's go to the training grounds and see if I can throw you like a frisbee."

On the way back outside, Eve noticed that Isaac was walking at the back of the group, alone. Eve dropped back so she could walk with him.

"Can I see your phone?" she asked.

He frowned at her, and shook his head.

She held her hand out. "Come on. Give me it. I won't snoop, and I'll give it right back."

He touched his temple, then drew away a Y-handshape. She recognized that one. *Why?*

"I want your number so I can text with you," she said.

He shook his head again.

"What do you mean, no?"

He looked at her pointedly, then held his fist up, snapping his first two fingers and his thumb closed. *No.*

She signed back at him. *"Why?"*

He curled his fingers, palms up, then turned his palms down, like he was throwing away trash. She recognized that from last night when Luc was asking him about talking. *Don't want to.*

She got her phone out and consulted the ASL dictionary she downloaded. She then looked at Isaac with puppy dog eyes and held her palm on her chest, rubbing it in circles. *Please?*

He ignored her.

Well. Fine then. She didn't really want to text him anyway.

At the training grounds, it was immediately apparent that Zeke and Eoduun were helpless against Eve. She felt like every move they made, she was two steps ahead of them. She could read them like she knew what they were going to do before they did, like they were telegraphing on a psychic level. And when they did manage to land a strike, she easily deflected and overpowered them. It was like fighting children.

But the moment Bo stepped in, he proved that, despite her new colossal strength, Eve was still beatable, putting her on her back after only a few minutes of sparring. And when he took on Zeke and Eoduun, they didn't put up any less of a fight than they did this morning.

The difference was only between Eve and the boys. She hadn't just stolen their powers. She'd seized power *over* them. To them, she had become untouchable.

Isaac watched all of this unfolding with great interest.

"I'm your queen," Eve gloated to the boys. "I wonder if that means you have to do what I say?" She tapped her chin. "Zeke, ruffle Bo's hair."

Zeke just stood there. "I don't think you have Veris powers. I mean, I don't feel like I *have* to, but…I totally *would.*"

"I've never seen anything like this," Bo said, still amazed at her physical command over Zeke and Eoduun. "It's like they're incapable of intentionally harming you," he said to Eve.

Eve eyed him mischievously. "Even with Zeke's ridiculous strength, I still can't win against you. Maybe I need to take *your* power so I can finally beat *you* in a fight," she said, grinning impishly.

"I'm not sure I'd survive the process," he replied. "And it sounds like Zeke and Eoduun almost didn't survive it this time, either."

Eve scoffed. "I bit off a little more than I could chew this time, I'll admit. But I'd never try to kill *you*."

"You try to kill me all the time," he replied. When she gave him a confused look, he just smiled at her with his mismatched eyes.

Eve hugged his arm and leaned her head on his shoulder. She looked out at Eoduun and Zeke sparring with Isaac. "Wasn't it you who said 'What's a little attempted homicide among friends?'"

Bo chuckled. "Yes, but I was saying it as something *Luc* would say."

After a moment of internal reflection, Eve asked, "I wonder if I would get your werewolf powers, too."

"Hm?"

"If I stole your powers, would I only get the powers that come from your eyes, or would I get the werewolf powers, too?"

"Huh. Probably both, I would guess. Not sure what good the werewolf powers would do you, though, and my specialty powers aren't nearly as great as my brother's. You'd be better off taking Luc's power."

"Luc's power wouldn't make you automatically lose in a fight against me. I want power over *you*," Eve teased.

Bo gave a cynical laugh. "I don't think you need any more power over me. You have enough as it is."

"I do not," she disputed. "You're always telling me what to do. And what not to do."

"Well, I am still your captain."

"'Don't even think about being *inspired* by him,'" she said in an exaggeratedly deep voice, echoing his warning words from earlier. "That was my captain speaking?"

"I'm sure I don't know what you're talking about."

"Fucking liar," Eve laughed.

A few moments later, Bo added, "But I would kill him."

That night, Eoduun convinced Zeke to stay over at his apartment to play video games and have a guys' night, since Eve was supposedly going to be with Luc. Bo, Eve, and Isaac met Luc in his apartment before they planned to rendezvous with the others.

Eve told him about her newly discovered ability to combine her stolen powers, which made Luc raise his eyebrows, then grin widely. Bo told him about how Zeke and Eoduun were completely useless in a fight against her afterward. Luc laughed gleefully. "Wow. We're just scratching the surface of what you can do, aren't we?" he praised proudly. Then his smile faded. "I wish I had something half as thrilling to contribute to this discourse, but unfortunately, all I have for you is troubling news.

"Zephlyn told me he had his vision again today. Remember, the one with Dagon running with the grimoire, Ruth and that evil entity, and their army of monsters? But he said this time he got the distinct feeling that Dagon was stealing the grimoire and fleeing, and there was thunder and lightning crashing all around."

"Was the evil entity the Egyptian god Celeste had suggested?" Bo asked.

"Zephlyn didn't know. Whatever it was, it was cast in shadow, which might mean it isn't a done deal." Luc chewed his lip. "Or, if he's the mole, he could be trying to mislead us. Scare us."

"So, what does that mean for us?" Eve inquired.

A low rumble of thunder shook the apartment, and Isaac startled from the sudden vibration. His eyes darted to the window. Black clouds were gathering in the night sky, enshrouding the bright moon in darkness.

"A storm is coming," Luc warned, his eyes also turning to the window. "We need to be prepared."

A creeping sense of impending doom crawled through Eve's veins.

It's all going to go wrong. Someone's going to die.

Eve clenched her eyes closed and took a long, deep inhale, held her breath for a beat, then exhaled slowly. *NO. Don't think it, don't say it. Don't think it, don't say it. Do. Not. Think. It. Or you'll make it happen.*

"Evie?" Bo's hand touched her knee. She opened her eyes and realized everyone was looking at her.

"Everything all right, love?" Luc asked, concern creasing his brow.

"Yep, just nerves. Let's make sure to be extra careful tonight, though, ok?"

"Of course," Luc said, satisfied.

But Bo still surveyed her. Walking lie detector.

"Is there something you're not thinking, not saying?" he asked softly.

"Intrusive thoughts. Perfectly normal," she rationalized. "Nothing psychic about that."

"Hm." He wasn't buying it. "Anything that would be helpful to know if it *were* psychic?"

"No. No one will die, and everything is going to go according to plan."

Bo touched her jaw and turned her face toward his. He looked at her meaningfully. "Everything will go smoothly, and everyone will be fine. Believe it. Count on it."

Isaac signed, and Bo and Eve looked to Luc to translate.

"'Nothing goes as planned.' Thanks, Isaac. Those were exactly the words we needed right now," Luc said sarcastically.

But Isaac wasn't wrong.

And now that Eve had brought attention to that stupid voice in her head, now that she'd thought it, she'd said it...now it was real. It would come to pass.

She'd opened Schrodinger's box, and the cat was dead.

41

Alone

Eve stood with Dizzy under the overhang in front of the main doors of the abandoned paper mill, trying to shelter from the storm, but the wind swept the rain into their faces relentlessly. She twisted the handcuffs on her wrists, annoyed by the way they were collecting rain and making her shirt cuffs wet. Luc hadn't said anything about handcuffs earlier, so it came as a surprise when Dizzy pulled them out and slapped them on her after everyone had gone to their positions. He wanted to be sure that Ruth was going to believe them, because Eve would never willingly go with Dagon.

Well, that much was true.

She kept stealing glances at Dizzy, unsure how to feel about the visage before her. That face brought about such conflicting feelings, drawing out memories of fear, loathing, ecstasy, intrigue, mistrust, and power. She never knew where to put Dagon. Friend, lover, nemesis, evil, opportunist. He couldn't be yoked with an easy label. He'd helped her. He'd hurt her. He'd manipulated her. He'd obsessed over her. He'd saved her.

He'd awakened her.

So what was he planning to do once he shed Zeke's vessel?

Eve had to remind herself that the man she was looking at wasn't actually Dagon. Dizzy was doing a phenomenal job of pretending to be him now. So much so, that it was making her incredibly uncomfortable. It was the phone call to Ruth all over again. One minute he'd been a weird guy who looked like Dagon, and now he *was* Dagon. It was unsettling.

Eve looked across the mill yard, knowing she couldn't see Bo and Luc, but looking for them anyway, taking comfort in *knowing* they were out there. Levi had been monitoring remotely, right up until Eve and Dizzy went to the front doors to wait for Ruth, and he'd seen no signs of treachery, no hidden traps, no ambush. Kai had shifted into a raccoon and done a sweep on the ground, and he didn't find anything, either.

It was strangely quiet.

So why did she still feel so uneasy? Why was she still so sure that something was going to go wrong?

A crow flew up and landed on a nearby building. Was it Kai? It had to be. Why else would a crow be out flying around in this storm?

"She's here," Dizzy said in Dagon's voice.

A figure approached in a long, hooded poncho. Eve's adrenaline surged, and her heart began hammering loudly against her ribcage. Her whole body trembled with each beat.

She was up. The whole game rested on her shoulders now. If she fumbled...shit would be royally fucked.

Failure was not an option.

"I brought her, as promised. I even handcuffed her for you," Dizzy-Dagon said. He then pushed her roughly out into the rain toward the hooded figure.

Eve squinted against the driving rain, but as the figure came closer to the sodium light they were standing under, she recognized Ruth's comely face beneath the hood.

"Such a good boy, Dizzy," Ruth said.

Wait.

WAIT.

What the fuck?!

"They didn't suspect anything," Dizzy said, a dorky giddiness in his Dagon-esque tone. "They didn't find the portals I buried, so they think you're alone." He looked around just as the crow flew away. "But you might want to summon them soon. Our skinwalker just went to warn the guys."

Fuck! Fuck! Eve realized she'd just been standing here watching everything unfold like a fucking idiot. She easily snapped the handcuffs with Zeke's stolen strength, and with frantic energy, she reached out and grabbed Ruth's arms, forcing her to face her. She stared into Ruth's wide, startled eyes and ripped open a portal into her head. It wasn't a spinning tunnel or a black hole or anything like that this time. It was a fractured split, like she'd taken a sledgehammer to stone. She slipped in.

What?! How the fuck did you get in?! Ruth's voice rang out. *I warded against you!*

She'd known Eve would do this. Dizzy had warned her. Eve had to get to work. Ruth was still moving and in control, and right now, she was chanting an incantation. Without having to search her memories, the knowledge came straight to Eve's mind. Ruth was summoning an army of monsters through portals that Dizzy had buried all over the paper mill yard today when he was supposed to be out training.

And something else was coming through those portals, too. Something diabolical. Something that even Ruth was a little afraid of.

Eve dived into Ruth's memories. She needed to trap her before she could finish the spell. She reached out for feelings. Something irrepressible and overpowering.

And it was everywhere. Crushing disappointment. Heartbreak. Desperation. Loneliness.

They all flooded in at once, shoving and jostling and crowding, all demanding to be seen. Empty chairs at the dinner table. A cold, distant nanny serving her a plate, which she eats alone, in silence. A young Bo strolls in, and Eve almost doesn't recognize him. He's unscarred and his eyes are both blue, but the mask is already in place. How long has he been wearing it? How long has he been hiding those teeth, the only outward evidence of the monster that lives within? Bo ruffles Ruth's hair affectionately, steals a breadstick off of her plate, and leaves the room.

So many meals like this. Sometimes Bo is there, but more often than not, she's alone. The nanny isn't allowed to eat at the dinner table, so she eats in the kitchen. Only family and guests eat at the table, and her family is rarely there to join her.

Alone.

Ruth is surrounded by spell books, confused. Bo had tried to get her started, since her mother had informed her that she just didn't have time to help her today, as usual. But he didn't know much more than she did, and he left to work with the martial arts trainer. She was going to have to figure this out on her own.

Alone.

Pride filled her heart as she watched the vase on the stand levitate two inches. "Mother! Mother, look!" she shouted.

She heard her mother's footsteps on the landing above, but she couldn't hold the levitation. By the time her mother came down the steps and rounded the corner, it was only in time to watch the vase drop back down, then teeter, then crash to the floor, shattering.

"Ruthlys!" her mother shrieked. "What have you done?! Do you know how expensive that vase was?!"

"But I made it levitate! Did you see? I did it!"

"Do you expect me to be impressed with simple parlor tricks?" she snapped. She started an incantation, and the pieces began to swirl and reassemble. But before they had finished, she paused, then let them all fall back to the floor. "No, I'm not fixing your mess. You do it." She then stormed off back to her office.

Ruth worked diligently for days trying to master the spell to repair the vase.

Alone.

When she finally succeeded, she brought it to her mother. Now she would be impressed.

"What's this?" she asked.

"I fixed it!"

Her mother looked at her and the vase blankly. "That's lovely, dear. On your way out, can you tell Barney to bring me a scone and a cup of tea? That's a dear." She then returned her attention to her computer.

Her sense of accomplishment drowned with her sinking heart.

A beautifully decorated birthday cake sits on the counter. Finally, her family is here. There is a mountain of presents on the table, and she's filled to the brim with excitement. The butler brings everyone a slice of cake with a scoop of ice cream, but when Ruth looks down, she sees that the cake is strawberry.

She hates strawberry cake. She wanted chocolate.

"Mother, I asked for chocolate cake," she complains.

"Don't complain dear. It's unbecoming of a young lady," her mother replies coldly.

"But it's my birthday. I wanted chocolate cake. I hate strawberry cake."

"Well, what do you want me to do about it? I didn't make it. If you don't want it, don't eat it."

A dashing young Luc sits across from Ruth. His eyes sparkle like they're made of diamonds. "I'll eat it if you don't want it," he says hopefully. Ruth jumps at the chance to make him happy, and she smiles as she slides her cake to him. He winks and grins. "Thanks, Ru."

Ru. He was the only one who called her that, and she loved it. It made her feel special. Bo always called her Ruthie, and it made her sound like a baby. But Ru was cool. Luc was so damn cool.

"Ruthlys, dear, I apologize, but we really must be going," her father says, wiping his mouth and placing his napkin over his half-eaten slice of cake. "I need to get Lucius to cello practice, and your mother and I have dinner with important clients, and we simply cannot be late. Are you all right to open your presents without us?"

Everyone looks at her.

"I can wait until you get back," she suggests, even though she really wants to open those presents.

"Oh, no, wouldn't dream of it," her father says, waving his hand. "You must be excited to tear into them. There's a gorgeous dress in there that I know you'll want to try on, and of course that sweater you asked for. You'll have all evening to yourself to enjoy your gifts."

Her mother, father, and Luc all rise from their seats. Luc points at a small box on the table of gifts as he walks past and says, "This one is from me. Open it first, ok?" he implores as he follows their parents out of the dining room.

Only she and Bo remain. She looks down at the empty placemat in front of her.

"Did you want some ice cream, at least?" Bo asks.

"No, thank you."

"Do you want to open your presents?"

She looks at the stack of presents, then the empty chairs around her. "Just one."

Bo knows. Bo always knows. He reaches over and grabs the small box Luc had pointed out, and he hands it to her. She tears into it, and her eyes light up when she sees the gorgeous little white gold necklace. It has a delicate chain with a diamond-encrusted R pendant hanging from it.

She loves it.

It's special.

Bo carefully takes it from her hands and helps her put it on. She places her hand over the little R, holding it to her chest.

"It's perfect," she says. And it was. But it did little to chase away the disappointment squeezing her heart and the tears welling in her eyes. She wished Luc would've stayed just a few moments to watch her open the gift.

"Do you want to open mine?" Bo asks, reaching for another box on the table.

"No, I'll open the rest later," she says, pushing back from the table. She turns her back on him and walks quickly to her room. Bo knocks on her door a few minutes later to make sure she's ok, but she sends him away. She just needs some time to think and wallow.

Alone.

Happy birthday.

But it was one of her happier ones. At least they were all together for part of it.

But graduation would be different, right? She remembered when Luc graduated. Her parents invited all of their distant family, and they all wore specially made shirts with lettering on them, and when Luc walked up to get his diploma, they all stood up and cheered for him, and their shirts spelled out, "We're proud of you, Luc!"

She wondered what kind of surprise they had for her. If she was being honest, she'd lain awake the past two nights, excited about finally having her moment in the spotlight, when they would all be looking at her. Proud of her. Cheering her on.

The presenter called her name, and her heart burst with joy and excitement. This was her moment. She smiled broadly as she raised her head high and strutted across that stage.

One voice cheered, and there was a smattering of applause.

She took the diploma and looked out at the crowd. She found the one cheering voice among all those faces, but she already knew who it was. Bo. With three empty seats next to him.

That was the moment something broke inside of her. The monster that had been incubating all these years had finally hatched.

Get out! Get the fuck out!

Eve felt herself being shoved out, so she reached out and grabbed on for dear life. She couldn't let Ruth push her out just yet. She needed to stop her from summoning the monsters. She needed to stop her from summoning *him*.

But she was too late. The spell had been cast. She saw monsters erupting from the ground all around her. Shit. Shit!

She saw her own vacant body standing across from Ruth. She needed to possess Ruth so she could protect herself, but Ruth was pushing *so hard*. Eve dug in even deeper, like she was throwing Lovecraftian tentacles out into everything she could grasp. Memories, feelings, thoughts – anything to anchor her in Ruth's mind.

But she was sliding. She could feel her foothold slipping. In one last-ditch effort, she spread herself wide, clinging desperately, trying to gather in everything she could to make herself too big to fit through the crack she'd come in through.

The extraction was excruciating. She was being pulled apart and crushed at the same time, like being stretched and compressed to fit through the eye of a needle. And she felt heavy. Too heavy. She was carrying too much.

When she slammed back into her own mind, the pressure in her head was immense. It was too…full.

"What…what's going on?" Ruth said, looking around blankly. Confused. "Where am I?"

42

Save Her

Mayhem had been unleashed around them. Monsters swarmed the grounds, and Luc, Bo, Kai, Levi, and Isaac were doing all they could to cut them down as more climbed out of the opened portals buried all over the mill yard.

One man, however, stood out from the rest. He was tall and lean, like Luc, wearing a rain-soaked black suit. Even from a distance, Eve saw his bronze eyes glowing maleficently. Dark power radiated from him, like an oppressive, heavy pressure, and as he drew closer, Eve's throat tightened with terror. She was frozen in place as he sauntered up to her, his demeanor completely at ease in the chaos unfolding around him.

Luc suddenly appeared at her side, holding an arm protectively across her body. Rain and blood dripped from his sleeve. Eve doubted any of that blood was his.

"Are you ok?" he asked her, his eyes focused on the evil presence in front of them.

"I'm fine, but I fucked it up."

"Where's Dizzy?" Luc asked.

Eve looked around. He was gone. In all the pandemonium, he'd slipped away. "He betrayed us. He must've run."

Luc looked up at the well-dressed man in front of them. "You stay back," he warned.

The man took no notice of Luc, and kept his cold, bronze eyes only on Eve. "The Abomination," he said in a low, whispery voice. Lightning flashed, and Eve thought she saw the faint indication of reptilian scales on his face beneath the rivulets of water running from the ends of his unnaturally burgundy hair.

Apep. The Egyptian god of chaos, the spirit of evil, the ruler of darkness and destruction. Ruth had unsealed and raised him, and had bound him to her as she had bound Varghrir, and as she'd intended to bind Dagon. But the contract she had forged with Apep was now null and void, because Ruth was no longer Ruth. Ruth was empty.

Eve's mind told her all of this, but it wasn't information from her own mind. It was Ruth's memories and knowledge.

In the struggle in Ruth's head, Eve had tried to dig in and cling to everything as she was being pushed out, so when she was ejected, everything she was holding on to came with her.

She'd erased Ruth.

All that Ruth was, was now in Eve.

Apep glanced at Ruth and saw her state of confusion.

"Who are you?" Ruth asked, terrified.

Apep laughed evilly, then snapped his fingers. Ruth's neck snapped, and she collapsed in a heap on the muddy ground.

"It appears I'm bound to *you* now," Apep said to Eve, intrigued. "But...not entirely. What an unexpected turn of events. So deliciously chaotic." He licked the raindrops off of his lips and took a step closer to Eve.

"Stay away from her," Luc snarled, stepping in front of Eve.

"You're an annoyance," Apep said impassively. He raised his hand, and all of the monsters in the mill yard turned and began stalking toward Eve and Luc. "Die."

"Bo, clear the field for demolition," Luc called.

Eve couldn't clearly see what was going on through the rain and darkness and mass of bodies moving around, but she caught sight of Bo. He grabbed Kai and pointed, and they both disappeared again in the mayhem.

The creatures Ruth had summoned were still rising from the ground, but Eve realized she knew how to close the portals. She began to chant the spell, and Luc whipped his head around, gaping at her in confusion.

She recited the spell, but nothing happened. Monsters continued to pour from the portals.

"What was that?" Luc queried.

"I know the spell to close the portals from Ruth's memories, but it's not working. I don't have Ruth's witch powers."

"Say it again. Loud and clear."

Eve called out the spell again, but this time Luc repeated her words as she said them. As he echoed the last word, they looked around as all of the portals closed at once, some of them severing monsters in half as they were coming through. He grinned.

"Let there be light," he said, then raised his hands over his head. He swept them down forcefully, and as his arms dropped, lightning rained down from the sky all around them. Eve clenched her eyes against the blinding flashes and clapped her hands over her ears against the cacophony of thunderous explosions.

This is where I make my exit. Apep's voice whispered into Eve's mind. *We will meet again.*

When the dark returned and the world went quiet, Eve opened her eyes. The smell was horrendous, and the sight even more so. Exploded carcasses and charred chunks of flesh littered the ground. A hazy smoke or mist permeated the air, and the rain hissed as it fell upon hot embers.

Eve looked up at Luc. Rain dripped from his hair and the end of his nose. A deranged smile twisted his face as he admired his work. He looked down at Eve with wild eyes. His enormous body shuddered. "God, that was good," he said, breathlessly elated. He looked back out at the grounds. "Beautiful," he whispered, his eyes drinking in the destruction once more.

Fucking psychopath.

Eve looked down at Ruth's lifeless body. It had fallen close enough to her and Luc that it had been untouched by the lightning assault. She knelt by Ruth and touched her neck as Bo and the rest of the crew ran to them from outside the range of destruction. There was no pulse.

Bo dropped to his knees next to Eve. "Save her," he beseeched.

"She's not her anymore, Bo," she whispered apologetically. "I accidentally erased her."

"I don't care. Save her." He raised his eyes to Eve's and gave her a pleading expression. "Please."

Eve used Zeke's superstrength to crush and break the handcuffs from her wrists. She then took a knife from her hip and sliced it across her palm and dripped the blood between Ruth's pale lips. Everyone stood around and watched, silently. Waiting. While she allowed the blood to flow, she glanced around at the hunters circling her. They were all battered and bleeding, and they all needed to be healed. She shouldn't blow her load in one go.

Before he had time to protest or fight back, Eve tugged down Bo's mask and lifted her hand from Ruth's lips, shoving the bloody side of her palm to his mouth. His eyes widened, his wolf eye activating. His nostrils flared, and his teeth sank into her flesh. She came unraveled in an instant. She bit it back, though, giving only a small gasp as the orgasm tore through her, turning her legs to useless noodles.

Why was it always like that with him?

Luc pulled Bo away and took Eve's hand to his own mouth, lapping up the blood that ran from Bo's bite marks and the knife cut.

The pleasure surged again, but not quite to the point of cresting this time. Then Luc handed her off to Kai, and then Levi, and the response was dulled for both of them. At least, it was on her end. They both looked at her like she'd just rocked their fucking world.

When Eve held her hand out to Isaac, he looked disgusted. He shook his head and snapped his fingers together. *No.*

She was too tired to fight over it. She held her bloody hand splayed open, vertically, and touched her thumb to her chest twice. Then she fisted her hand and touched her thumb to her chin, twisting it side to side as she moved it down her chin. "Fine. Suffer," she said aloud.

Isaac gave her a quizzical look, but didn't respond.

Ruth stirred, drawing everyone's attention. Bo reached down and cradled her head into his lap.

"Ruthie?" he said softly.

She blinked her eyes open, and sat up. Bo hugged her tightly, and she looked at everyone over Bo's shoulder, confusion and fear in her eyes. She pushed away from Bo. "What's going on? Why don't I know who I am? Or where I am?" She stood up and backed away from them. "Who are you people?"

Eve held her hand out to Ruth. "It's going to be hard to explain, but I'll do my best. Why don't you come talk with me, and we'll let these boys clean up their mess."

"Bo, can you scent Dizzy?" Luc asked, leaving Eve to deal with Ruth.

As Ruth hesitantly took Eve's hand, Bo answered, "Nothing. He's not here. He must've taken one of those portals back through to the other side, wherever that was."

Eve paused before leading Ruth away. "They led to a ranch in Montana. That's where she and Apep were building the monster army with my blood."

Luc scowled. "How do you know that?"

"Because everything from her head is in my head."

Luc's brow jumped to his hairline. "Holy fuck."

"And I know for a fact that she came here with the grimoire. And she obviously doesn't have it now. I think Dizzy took it before he ran."

"So, it wasn't *Dagon* who was fleeing with the grimoire in Zeph's premonition," Bo realized. "It was Dizzy, wearing Dagon's visage. Why the fuck didn't we even consider that?"

"Because it didn't even occur to me that Dizzy would be our mole. Eoduun had cleared him," Luc said.

"The grimoire had a spell for an undetectable wall to block memories and thoughts. It was what she used on Dizzy," Eve supplied. "She used it on herself, too, but I broke through."

"So, that guy was Apep?" Luc remarked, crossing his arms. "She really did raise him, then. And, what, he's bound to you now because you've essentially absorbed Ruth?" he asked Eve.

"I guess. To some extent, anyway."

"I know I didn't kill him with that lightning assault. He's out there, somewhere." Luc dragged his hands down his wet face. "We came here to end this, but we've only sunk deeper into it. How did we even do that?"

"It's a rare skill I have," Eve replied.

"You tried to warn us," he pointed out.

"No, I tried not to think or say it, but Bo made me. Blame Bo. It's all Bo's fault." Eve gave Bo a falsely sour face.

"Blame Bo. Goddamn it, Bo," Luc chastised teasingly.

Isaac signed and gestured to the mess around them. Something about *clean* and *hurry*. Why did she know that?

"Yeah, yeah, let's get to work," Luc said with a heavy sigh. "Let's throw all the monster bits in the wastewater pond."

"Who the hell *are* you people?" Ruth asked.

Eve and Ruth sat under the overhang where she and Dizzy had been waiting earlier that night, and they watched the rest of the crew schlepping creature corpse chunks to the stagnant pond nearby. Eve tried to explain everything to Ruth about who she is, why she's here, and what happened to her. "I am so sorry," Eve apologized. "I didn't mean for this to happen. But we'll find a way to fix it. There must be a way to fix it."

Ruth laughed mirthlessly. "It sounds like I may have brought it upon myself. But why? Why did I do any of this? Why would I want an army of monsters and ancient gods? There had to be some kind of reason, right? Was I misguided?" She paused and looked at Eve thoughtfully. "Or are you guys the misguided ones?"

"You had your reasons, Ruth, but I don't think they're going to make sense to you right now."

"Do they make sense to you?"

Eve chewed the inside of her lip. With Ruth's life in her head, yeah, her reasons made emotional sense. She understood, to an extent. But it didn't make any of it *right*. "We've all done things that seemed to make sense at the time, but regretted after gaining a little perspective." She looked at Ruth, then poked her forehead. "Did I leave any memories in there? Glimpses, fleeting feelings, tidbits?"

Ruth looked out at the boys. "My brothers. I still feel something for them. I can't remember them, but their faces *feel* familiar. The one who hugged me – Bo? He felt safe, but I don't know why he feels safe. And the tall one – Luc. There are lingering feelings of adoration for him." She turned back to Eve. "But I kind of hate him, too. Not a clue why. Did he do something to me?"

Eve rested her chin in her hands, propping her elbows on her knees. "That's complicated. The short answer is, Luc wasn't there for you when you needed him, and you resent him for it. Bo was there instead, but Bo wasn't the one you wanted. And you resent *him* for *that*."

"For being there for me?" Ruth asked, perplexed.

"For not being Luc."

"Why was I so obsessed with Luc?"

Eve watched Luc throw a severed arm at Bo, then laugh boisterously when Bo got angry and threw it back. He then turned to Eve and Ruth, saw Eve looking at him, and blew her a kiss – using the hand from the severed arm Bo had thrown back at him.

"Why, indeed," she said ambiguously, smirking at Luc.

43
Don't Be Such a Prude

The plan to bring Ruth to a remote location away from the compound was abandoned since she posed no real threat to anyone in her current condition. She was of no use to Dagon, either, since she had no idea how to extract him from Zeke anymore.

Eve held that knowledge now. But it was knowledge that wasn't useful to her without Lilith's grimoire, and either Dizzy or Apep had disappeared with that. Her money was on Dizzy.

When they returned to the compound, soaking wet, filthy, and stinking, they convened briefly in the parking garage before dispersing for the night.

"Levi, Kai," Luc addressed them, "good work tonight. Go get some rest, and I'll call a meeting in the morning. No more secrets, now that we know Dizzy was our mole."

Levi and Kai nodded and started to leave, but Kai stopped. "Maybe I should get one more dose of Eve's blood, just to be sure my shoulder is fully healed."

"Fuck out of here," Luc said.

Simultaneously, Bo gave a sharp, "No."

Kai shrugged, "Ok, fine. Jeez." He saluted Eve with two fingers to his forehead and gave her a cocky grin. "Goodnight, Eve."

When Kai and Levi left, Bo crossed his arms. "Great. Another admirer."

"You guys are going to have to get me a stick," she joked. When they looked at her blankly, she added, "'Beat the boys off with a stick'?"

"Absolutely not. You will not be beating boys off." Luc retorted.

Eve laughed. "I should've known your mind would go there."

"My mind is always there."

Bo interrupted, "Where are we putting Ruthie up? She's welcome to stay at my apartment."

Luc looked to Ruth, waiting for her to reply.

She hesitated uncomfortably. It was such a stark difference in demeanor than what they were used to seeing from her. "Um, if it's all right, I think I would rather stay with Eve." She looked to Eve. "If that's all right?"

"Oh! With me?" Eve glanced over at Isaac. "I'm already hosting a houseguest right now. I'm not sure where I would put you."

"Maybe Isaac can stay with Bo instead," Luc suggested.

Bo shot daggers at Luc, and Isaac shook his head. Isaac pointed to himself, held out two Y-handshapes, palms down, and pressed them down once. He held his fists together, palms together, then raised his middle finger to his chin and imitated the vulgar variation of "adorable" that Eve had used.

Eve again realized that she understood, and now it dawned on her. Ruth knew sign language. She wasn't as quite as fluent as Luc, but she had learned it in college.

But this one was confusing. "You'll stay with adorable?" she repeated, signing back at him with a questioning expression. "What do you mean?" she asked, furrowing her brow while twisting a horizontal V-handshape with her fingers against her other palm.

Isaac shook his head and swiped his thumb under his chin and made the true *adorable* sign. *Not adorable.* He held his first two fingers out on each hand and tapped the sides them together in a cross shape and pointed at her. Then he did the middle finger *adorable* sign again, and fingerspelled E-V-E.

Your name. Eve.

She'd been given a signed name. Her very own sign. She'd looked into it online, and discovered that it was poor etiquette for a hearing person to assign themselves a unique sign for their name. Only someone from the Deaf community could do that. But she had found a regular sign for *Eve*, and just assumed that Isaac would use that.

But he'd given her her own name. Sure, it was a sign *she'd* butchered to add taunting sarcasm to the word, intending it to be offensive. And now Isaac had chosen that sign to signify her. To label her. But rather than being insulted by it, she loved it.

It was fucking perfect.

She fingerspelled *joke* because the sign wasn't in Ruth's mental bank. She then stacked the fingers of one flat hand on the other and pointed at Isaac. Then she kissed the back of her fist and moved her fist away from her face.

Joke's on you. I love it.

"Care to share with the rest of the class?" Bo said in mild irritation.

"He says he's staying with Eve," Luc answered, shoving his hands in his pockets. "And he gave her her own name sign, and she loves it. It is rather fitting, I must agree."

"I guess I can stay with Bo," Ruth spoke up.

Luc said, "I'll get you set up in your own temporary apartment as soon as I can get one furnished. It'll only be a few days." He ruffled

Ruth's hair, and Eve was reminded of the way he'd done that when Ruth was younger. "Welcome to your second chance, Ru. Don't fuck it up."

That night, Luc went to his own apartment to change and shower, and Bo took Ruth to his place, leaving Eve and Isaac on their own for a while.

As soon as they were inside the apartment, Eve began peeling off her wet, filthy clothes in the entryway. When Isaac tried to go around her, she grabbed his arm to stop him.

He tried to jerk away from her violently, reflexively, but she still had Zeke's strength, so the action was futile. He stumbled when his motion caused him to jerk toward her instead of freeing himself, and he shot her a startled expression. She quickly released him, stepping back and holding her hands up defensively, palms out. She put her fist to her chest and circled it. *Sorry.*

His eyes dropped to her shirtless form, watching her hand circle her chest over her bra. He looked up at her face and gestured to her, clearly asking why she was half naked.

Eve ran her hands down either side of her chest, then hitched her thumb up and off to the side, repeating the gesture with the other hand. *Take off your clothes.* She pointed to the washing machine to her right, then walked over to it and threw her nasty shirt into it. She signed, *I'll wash them.*

Isaac cocked his head. He pointed to her and signed, *How do you suddenly know sign language?*

"It's Ruth's memories in my head. Turns out she took classes in college, and she remembers most of it," Eve explained aloud. Then she pointed to his shirt. "Now, take off your clothes."

He shook his head.

"Don't be such a prude. I've been in your head, remember? I know how 'priestly' you really are," she said. She'd seen glimpses of women here and there when she was looking through his career kill highlights. He definitely wore the white collar more as a means than a moral code.

"I don't need to be naked with *you*," he replied, pointing at her. His voice always startled her when he spoke.

"It's not like that, Isaac," she argued, resting her hands on her hips. "I don't want mud all over my apartment. Just take it off," she said, signing the thumbs to the side again. "You can keep your underwear or boxers on. Trust me, I won't be overcome with desire and attack you. I can handle your naked little body."

"Little?" he scoffed, offended. "I'm not little. I'm *normal*. You're just used to those fucking ogres," he said, holding his hand up high to indicate their height.

"Ooh, sore spot, hey?" Eve teased. "Do I detect a little insecurity?" She then stripped out of her pants and threw them in the wash while he watched her with an annoyed expression, his jaw clenched. She stood there in her underwear. "If you don't want trouble, you'll do as I ask. And then get in the shower. You're way dirtier than I am."

Isaac made two fists and pressed them down, then tapped his index finger against the flat palm on his other hand, moving them backward and forward.

That one wasn't in Ruth's memory bank. Eve walked past Isaac to go find her phone to consult it, and he reluctantly began to strip down.

While Eve was in her room getting her phone, she threw on some shorts and a t-shirt. Then she looked up the sign.

Debatable.

"Hey!" she complained as she walked out of her room, ready to tell Isaac to fuck off for that comment.

Then she saw him inspecting the wounds on his bare torso. He looked like he'd just hit the top score from the inside of a pinball machine.

"Holy shit," she gasped, rushing to him. "Why didn't you tell me it was this bad?!"

He signed, *I didn't know.*

"How the fuck could you not know?!" Eve fretted, grabbing his hips and turning him to the side to get a better look at a particularly nasty contusion that ran from the center of his chest all the way down to the back of his ilium.

"I don't feel pain," he said aloud.

"Fuck, Isaac," she spat, irrationally angry at him. She huffed, "Let me get a knife. I'll fix this."

"No!"

"What do you mean, no?"

He scowled at her. "I don't want to feel that way." When she stared at him, confused, he elaborated, "I saw what it did to the others. And you. I don't want that."

"It passes. It's only for a moment," she reasoned.

"I saw you heal Bo. A moment was all it took."

Eve's cheeks and ears burned in embarrassment.

"I don't want that," he repeated, signing for emphasis.

Eve ran her hand along his ribcage, and before he angled away from her and pushed her hand away, she could feel the damage to his body. He definitely had broken ribs. She was surprised he wasn't coughing up blood. Yet. If he wouldn't let her heal him, he was going to need a hospital, or trip to the infirmary, at the very least.

Even Bo would've taken healing from her, without a fight, if he was in this state. It had to be something else stopping him, and she had her suspicions.

"What's the real reason?" she asked, her face becoming somber. "You're not afraid of a little pleasure. You're afraid of something else." She looked up at him. "You're afraid of the *unclean* portion of my blood, aren't you?"

He stared at her, his face completely inscrutable.

"I'm not going to contaminate you or make you a monster," she said, crossing her arms and taking a step back. She set her jaw, then pointed at herself, brushed her thumb under her chin, and touched her thumb to her temple, curling her first two fingers like air quotes. *I'm not evil.*

When he still didn't reply, she threw her hands in the air in frustration. "Fine," she said. "I'm going to have to text Luc or Bo and have someone bring you to the hospital, then."

Isaac's eyes widened and he shook his head quickly.

Eve frowned at him. She made the Y hand shape and tapped her chin with it. *What's wrong?*

He snapped his fingers together, then made a cross shape on his opposite arm with the letter H. *No hospital.*

Why? Eve signed.

He only repeated, *No hospital.*

But she could see it on his face, clear as day. He was terrified of the hospital.

Eve exhaled deeply. "Well, we need to do something with you. Look at yourself, buddy," she said, gesturing to his condition.

They stood and looked at each other in silence. Then he asked, aloud, "Is that how you take power over them?"

"What, from healing them?!" He nodded. "No. God no." She laughed, "No, that requires the *whole* wild, sweaty process. Just drinking my blood to heal won't give me any power over you." She drew her hands to her hips and took a step toward him. "Is *that* why you don't want to take it?! You're afraid of giving me *power* over you?"

He didn't answer. Instead, he looked away from her. He splayed his hand vertically and touched his thumb to his chest, then extended it away from him. He touched his shoulders and drew his hands away, closing them into fists, and pointed at himself. *Fine. Heal me.*

"I see how it is," Eve chided. She went to the kitchen to grab a paring knife. "Can't possibly let the little girl save your bacon if it means temporarily sacrificing a little bit of power to her," she said as she turned to him. He'd followed her into the kitchen. "No, I totally get that, you little bugger. Makes sense. Very manly."

He scowled and chopped one vertical flat hand onto the palm of the other hand. He pointed to himself, brushed his thumb under his chin, then held his hands out like he was measuring something, moving his palms closer together. *Stop! I'm not little.*

"No, of course not. Big man. Very strong," she said sarcastically, flexing her arms for added effect. She took the paring knife and made a small slice on the fleshy side of her palm.

"I'm bigger than you," he spoke grouchily.

"Well, to be fair, I'm an Oompa Loompa, so…" She held her bleeding hand up to his mouth.

Her knees buckled, and she caught the counter with her free hand. A vulgar whimper slipped past her lips before she clamped them shut. She stared at Isaac with startled, wide eyes, and he stared back with dark, lustful confusion as he sucked at her hand.

44
So, Still Deaf?

Shit. She thought it would be no different than it had been with Team Flannel, or Levi and Kai. No one outside of her teammates and Luc drew this kind of reaction from her.

She was completely unprepared for it.

She forced herself to yank her hand from his mouth as her core began to throb, aching for him. "Good enough," she panted. "You'll heal." She dropped her eyes from his, but made the mistake of glancing down at his black boxer briefs.

He was hard.

And he was *not* little.

The darkness inside her stirred. *Touch him.*

No! No. She needed to keep her greedy hands to herself. But her eyes...they skimmed back up his healing torso, noticing just how fucking fit he was. She unconsciously licked her lips. He wasn't a large man, bodily, but he was strong, and he had a *presence*.

Her monster was hungry.

But Isaac is out of bounds. Don't even think about it.

The salivating beast inside of her wasn't listening. *I want to taste him.* Her hand reached out and touched his tight abdominals, then slid around to his obliques, and Isaac just stood there. He didn't jerk away or dodge or push her hand away. He just let her touch him. She ran her fingers up into the dusting of curly dark hair on his chest, and she felt his racing heartbeat under her palm.

He wants it, too.

She inhaled sharply and took a decisive step back, averting her gaze to the counter. "Yep, you seem to be healing nicely," she rasped, then cleared her throat. She rounded the kitchen island and sat at her barstool, putting an obstacle between them before she allowed her eyes to return to him. He just stood there, still staring straight ahead.

It had caught him unprepared, too. Perhaps she'd downplayed it too much when she was trying to sell him on it.

"You seem shocked. What's the matter, did I restore your hearing, too?" she asked jokingly. Then, "Wait, *did* I restore your hearing?!"

He didn't react. She waved her hand, and he glanced over at her as though she'd just roused him from deep thought.

"So, still deaf?" she said and signed, her eyebrows raised as she touched her index finger from her ear to her chin.

He signed back. *Still deaf.*

"Huh. So, I guess my blood doesn't heal *everything* after all," she said.

He pointed to his ear. "This is genetic. Not an injury," he replied.

"Oh. Well, how about everything else? All healed?"

He looked down at his healed torso. He nodded and tapped his chin with his fingers, then drew his hand away from himself toward her. *Thank you.* Then he walked away and shut himself in the bathroom.

No one needed to know about this. Totally didn't happen. With everything going on right now, this would only be a distraction from the much bigger fish to fry. Box it and shelve it and let it collect dust.

She needed to focus on Ruth. She had to find a way to give her all of these memories back. Eoduun had said memories couldn't be returned, but there had to be a way, didn't there? They were all inside of her head, intact. She pulled them out, she had to be able to put them back. In the meantime, she was trying her best to keep them apart from her own. Could they become tangled together? She didn't know, so for now, she was avoiding triggering or accessing anything that she didn't have to.

Then there was Apep. The power emanating off of that monster was stifling. Crushing. What did it mean to have him bound to her...sort of? Did it mean he couldn't harm her? Did it mean she could take command of him? He could obviously speak telepathically to her, but was it only when he was in proximity to her? Or could he just pop up and say something at any moment, like Dagon did when she called to him? She wasn't about to call to Apep to find out.

And Dagon. What was he going to do now? He tried to betray them. And even though Ruth could no longer perform the extraction, Eve potentially could, if she had the grimoire. Could they use that to elicit Dagon's help in acquiring it?

Even if they got the grimoire, and Eve could extract Dagon from Zeke, would she? She'd brought Ruth back to life, so she now had undeniable proof that her blood could raise the dead. But after an extraction, would Zeke's body still be viable? Would it be in such a state that she *could* restore it? If he turned to ash after the extraction, then that was it. He was gone. There was no coming back from that. Would she be willing to risk that?

Eve flexed her hands as she sat in the kitchen. She could feel Zeke's strength fading. Eoduun's must be fading, too. She wondered how many powers she could hold at once. How many could she stack before she lost control and killed someone? She'd almost killed Zeke and Eoduun last time. She was afraid to try it again. They might not be so lucky next time. She needed to put a goddamn muzzle on this monster inside of her. She needed to control the rage. Tame it. Bend it to her will, as Isaac said.

Isaac. Had she convinced him yet that she wasn't evil? That she wasn't the fucking Antichrist? She doubted it. She still hadn't fully convinced herself of that, as much as she liked to declare it to him. He was still wary of her. He still had reservations about her and her monstrous desires, and rightfully so. She'd just proven to him a moment ago how powerful her temptation can be. If she'd wanted to seduce him, she could have, and then she could've killed him. For a few moments, she'd held his free will in her hands, but instead of crushing it, she'd released it. She'd let him go. That had to count for something, right?

She wasn't a monster. She *had* a monster, a curse, one she never asked for, and she was learning how to deal with it. She had an entire team around her that supported her, that she relied upon to help her tame it. She *would* master it and bring it to heel. It would work for her. It would work for *good*, not evil.

She would prove to Isaac, and the Vatican, that she was more than the Abomination.

After Eve showered that evening, she heard Luc humming out in the other room. She picked up her phone as she prepared to exit the bathroom, and saw she had a text from an unknown number.

"Fine. You can text me."

She texted back, grinning. *"Who dis?"*

No reply. That was answer enough. She saved the contact information under "Padre."

She walked out of the bathroom, and she caught Isaac's eyes. She held her phone up and raised a brow. He shrugged dismissively and returned his attention to the knife he was sharpening.

Luc suddenly swooped in behind her and scooped her up, making her squeal like an idiot. God, she hated girls who squealed.

He nuzzled his face into her neck as she wrapped her legs around his hips and draped her arms over his shoulders. "Mmm, you smell good enough to eat," he crooned.

"I'll bet," she replied, "but first we should probably have a talk about what happened at the paper mill tonight. And what to do about Ruth."

Luc chuffed. "All of that can wait until tomorrow morning." He turned and glanced at the clock on the wall. "Which is approaching rather quickly." He turned his brilliant blue gaze back to her, capturing her attention fully. "Me, on the other hand, I can't wait until tomorrow. I need you now, love."

As Luc carried her off to the bedroom, he turned his head and bid Isaac, "Goodnight. Don't be alarmed if you feel the walls shaking."

"Ew, Luc, stop." Eve scrunched her face.

"Oh, there's no stopping me tonight," he snarled playfully, carrying her through her bedroom doorway.

Before Luc swung the door shut behind them, Eve glanced up over Luc's shoulder at Isaac. Isaac was watching her with a bored, impassive expression. But he touched his chin, and as he drew his hand away, he twisted his palm down and rested it over the back of his other hand. Then Isaac signed her name, using the unique sign he'd bequeathed her.

Goodnight, Eve.

TO BE CONTINUED

If you enjoyed *Eve's Curse*, look for the next book in the Abomination series:

Eve's Sins

Read on for a preview of the first chapter of *Eve's Sins*.

1
Old Habits Die Hard

At the morning meeting after the paper mill incident, there was a lot more chatter than usual. Rumors had already started flying about what went down the night before, and everyone was up in arms about being left out of the loop.

Except for Levi and Kai, of course. They were just exhausted. Kai had his chair tipped back on two legs, his head lolled back with his long, black hair draped like a curtain behind him. He had his eyes closed and his bare foot on the edge of the conference table. Levi had his chin in his hand, his eyes bloodshot and droopy. They'd had a long night.

Eve felt the same. Luc had kept her up well into the early hours of the morning because he was all jazzed up from the fight. Everyone else was exhausted from it, but it had invigorated him. He slept an hour or two, and then he was up again, banging around in the kitchen.

Eve felt like she hadn't had a full-night's sleep in forever. How long had it been? It was catching up with her. She needed a break.

"You look tired," Eoduun said, looking over at her from his seat next to her. He'd beat Zeke to the only open chair next to her, so Zeke was on his other side. Bo was back at his apartment, watching over Ruth.

"Hm, so sweet," Eve replied sarcastically. She leaned over to look at Zeke. "You promise you aren't mad about us not telling you about last night?" They'd filled him in at Eve's apartment that morning before the meeting.

"Of course not," he replied good-naturedly. "I mean, obviously I wish I could've helped out, but I understand why you had to leave me out."

Luc walked into the room, and, even behind his sunglasses, Eve saw his gaze gravitate straight to her. He smiled.

"So, is this going to be a regular thing now?" Mendal asked when Luc walked past him. "Are we all about morning meetings and riding the pine exclusively?"

Luc pulled on Kai's reclined chair as he walked past him, and Kai jumped, thinking he was falling over, and just about did. Luc pushed his chair back down and continued to the head of the table, next to Eve. "I made a strategic choice using the information available to me. And this will be our last meeting for a while, I hope. I'm just as tired of seeing all of your faces as you are of seeing mine."

Everyone was briefed on the events concerning the secret plan and Dizzy's betrayal. Luc told them about Apep's appearance, and, finally, about what happened with Ruth.

"She's *here*?" Celeste choked. "Dude, I don't care if she's been erased. That bitch is fucking certifiable. She shouldn't be here."

"Bo's keeping her under surveillance, so don't panic," Luc said dismissively. "And, like I said, she doesn't even know who the fuck she is. She's not hatching any master plans while she can't remember how to work a spell. She doesn't even remember why she hated us in the first place."

"Hold on, let's back up a minute," Mira said. "Eve brought Ruth *back to life*? As in, Ruth was, for certain, *dead*, and Eve revived her? How the hell is that even possible?"

"Because she's awesome," Luc replied simply, like it was obvious. "And I'm sure she'll continue to push the boundaries of what we thought was possible."

"Is that necessarily a good thing? Isn't that why she requires a Vatican watchdog?" Mira muttered.

"Aw, are you jealous because you've never been powerful enough to earn the attention of the Vatican?" Eve asked sardonically.

"I'd never want *that* kind of attention from them," she snipped, shooting a disdainful look at the wall behind Eve where Isaac was leaning with his arms crossed.

"Leave him out of this," Eve scowled.

Mira leaned in, arching a beautifully sculpted dark brow. "Oh? So, what, has the watchdog become your new pet, now that your silver wolf has his beloved sister to take care of? You just aren't happy if you don't have your own little doting shadow, are you?"

Eve scoffed and looked back at Isaac. He returned her gaze with that usual bored, impassive expression on his face. Eve turned back to Mira. "Does he look *doting* to you?"

"Don't worry," Mira replied, leaning back in her seat. "I'm sure you'll have him doing tricks in no time, just like the others. It seems to be the one thing you're good at."

Luc's hands slammed down hard on the conference table, startling everyone. "Mira," he said, his tone deceptively calm, "I'm trying to run a meeting. Do I need to send you out to the hall so you can sit and reflect on your behavior?"

Eve's eyes roved Luc's splayed hands and flexed forearms under his rolled-up sleeves, and she suddenly wanted to be on the receiving end of his wrath. *Punish me, sir. I was misbehaving, too.* She squirmed in her chair.

"No, sir. My apologies," Mira said quietly.

"Good," Luc said, suddenly cheerful. He stood up straight and fixed his sleeve cuff, and the room seemed to brighten. "Now, Roy's still looking into how to kill Apep, and I'm sure he'd appreciate any help he can get with that. Dizzy's in the wind, possibly with Apep, and Lilith's grimoire has slipped through our fingers. But, hey, we still got a big, fat W on Ruth. I'll fucking take it."

Zephlyn spoke up. "If I had only realized that the 'Dagon' in the vision was just Dizzy shifted into Dagon, that could've changed the game. I should've seen it. Sensed it. I don't know how I could've missed his deception right under my nose. But...I never would've suspected Dizzy."

"Don't blame yourself, bro," Mendal said. "I didn't see it either. And I'm fucking pissed. If I ever get my hands on that bastard, I'll tear him limb from fucking limb before I chop his ugly gourd off his shoulders."

"Dizzy will be dealt with when we find him," Luc assured them. "And we *will* find him." Luc opened a folder on the table in front of him and consulted the papers inside of it. "In the meantime, Celeste, I'm going to need to move you to Team Delta, and you three will be headed to Montana. There's a case up there, but I also want you to make a detour to check out a property there that Ruth may have been using as some kind of monster army base. Dizzy might be there. But do not engage. Apep might also be there. Recon only." He passed down a packet of papers for the team to peruse. "Team Gamma, you'll be headed to Florida. Something's lurking in the swamps of Polk County." He handed Roy a packet. "And Team Beta, you're off to Washington state. Go kill some sparklers." He slid a packet to Mira.

"Sparklers?" Eve asked.

"*Twilight*. Vampires," Eoduun clarified.

"Pacific Northwest vampires," Zeke elaborated.

"That's all. Dismissed," Luc said.

"Nothing for Flannel?" Ruger asked, disappointed, as everyone else stood up and started filing out the door.

"Not this time."

Cassie leaned over the table toward Eve. "Girl, we're getting together tonight. I'm taking you shopping for an outfit, and then we're going dancing. You've earned a night out."

Eve's immediate response was to look up at Luc to read his face before answering, but Cassie slapped the table. "Hey, don't look at him. Look at me. You don't need his permission," she said sternly.

Old habits die hard.

"I would love to, but I'm exhausted, Cassie," Eve confessed as she pushed up from her seat. "I'm running on fumes. Maybe we could just hang out at the apartment tonight?"

"Sure, of course. But no boys allowed! I need some girl time. And maybe we can hang out with Ruth, too," Cassie suggested as she and her team also rose from the table.

"Eve, I need to talk to you for a moment," Luc said as she started to walk toward the door. She didn't like his tone. He had bad news.

"I'll bring some takeout later today," Cassie said as she left with Remi and Ruger. "I'll text you."

"We'll wait for you in the hall," Zeke said to Eve. He and Eoduun walked toward the door. Isaac surveyed the situation, then decided to follow Zeke and Eoduun to the hall.

"You're leaving," Eve guessed once she and Luc were alone.

"Sorry, love. Duty calls." He folded his arms loosely around her and pulled her to him.

"When?"

Luc looked at the expensive watch on his wrist. "Soon. An hour or two."

"Where are you off to this time?" she asked with a mildly annoyed sigh.

"My father needs me in Paris."

"Ew, Paris. How unfortunate for you," Eve deadpanned.

"I know. Disgusting. Such an ugly city," Luc replied in kind. "But thankfully I only have to be there for two days."

"And then you can come home?"

Luc hesitated. "For a day. And then I'm off to Michigan for a couple of days."

Eve groaned.

"I know, love. I'm sorry." He smiled sadly at her, then pressed a light kiss to her lips. "Keep the guys in line for me, will you? I've asked Bo to be around as much as he can so you don't have to be alone with Isaac for too long. I've also reactivated the dreamcatcher spell under your bed to keep Dagon out of your head at night. Can you *please* remember to replenish the water in it this time?" he implored.

"I may need to be reminded," Eve admitted. "But I'll try."

"I'm not going to tell you to be good, but I would ask that you don't kill anyone when Isaac is looking. Agreeable?"

"Agreeable."

"Have fun tonight with Cass and Ruth." Luc kissed Eve's forehead, then slapped her ass. "I'll catch up with you before I go."

Eve started toward the door, then paused. "Luc?"

"Hm?"

"Why weren't you at Ruth's graduation?"

Luc's face went blank. "Huh? Wasn't I? Uh...hm." He scratched the back of his head. "God, that was so long ago. I honestly can't remember. Why do you ask?"

"Because she remembered your empty seat."

"Oh. Well, I'm sure I must've had something going on that day. I wouldn't have just skipped it," Luc reasoned.

"Your parents weren't there either. Bo was the only one there when she walked across that stage."

"Yeah, he was usually around. He didn't have a whole lot going on."

He was missing the whole point, Eve realized. "Were they at your graduation?" Eve asked.

"I'm not sure. I don't really remember."

"You don't remember your graduation?"

Luc shook his head. "Not really. Like I said, I had a lot going on, and it was a long time ago. Things kind of blur together." He stuck his hands in his pockets. "What's with the sudden interest in graduation?"

"Nothing. I was just curious. I've been trying to stay out of Ruth's memories, but that one keeps popping up on me randomly. Bo, and three empty chairs. She was heartbroken, you know."

Luc looked genuinely shocked. "Why? It was just graduation. It wasn't like she was getting married or anything."

Clueless. "Never mind. I just thought you should know."

Luc stood there, perplexed, as Eve left to join the boys in the hallway. She hoped he would take some time to reflect, but with everything he had going on, she wondered if he would even have time, or if he would forget about it as soon as he left the war room.

She tried to ignore the creeping fear that she was going to end up like Ruth – vying for his love and attention when he had already moved his focus on to other things.

Old habits die hard.

www.ingramcontent.com/pod-product-compliance
Lightning Source LLC
Chambersburg PA
CBHW021126260626
47169CB00005B/1476